D1221835

DEB KASTNER
A Perfect Match

The Christmas Groom

Love Inspired

Recycling programs
for this product may
not exist in your area.

 LOVE INSPIRED BOOKS

ISBN-13: 978-0-373-65150-4

A PERFECT MATCH AND THE CHRISTMAS GROOM

A PERFECT MATCH
Copyright © 2002 by Debra Kastner

THE CHRISTMAS GROOM
Copyright © 2002 by Debra Kastner

www.LoveInspiredBooks.com

Printed in U.S.A.

CONTENTS

Books by Deb Kastner

Love Inspired

A Holiday Prayer
Daddy's Home
Black Hills Bride
The Forgiving Heart
A Daddy at Heart
A Perfect Match
The Christmas Groom
Hart's Harbor
Undercover Blessings
The Heart of a Man
A Wedding in Wyoming
His Texas Bride
The Marine's Baby
A Colorado Match
*Phoebe's Groom
*The Doctor's Secret Son

*Email Order Brides

DEB KASTNER

lives and writes in colorful Colorado with the Front Range of the Rocky Mountains for inspiration. She loves writing for Love Inspired Books, where she can write about her two favorite things—faith and love. Her characters range from upbeat and humorous to (her favorite) dark and broody heroes. Her plots fall anywhere in between, from a playful romp to the deeply emotional. Deb's books have been twice nominated for the *RT Book Reviews* Reviewer's Choice Award for Best Book of the Year for Love Inspired. Deb and her husband share their home with their two youngest daughters. Deb is thrilled about the newest member of the family—her first granddaughter, Isabella. What fun to be a granny! Deb loves to hear from her readers. You can contact her by email at debwrtr@aol.com, or on her MySpace or Facebook pages.

A PERFECT MATCH

For by grace you have been saved through faith,
and that not of yourselves, it is the gift of God,
not of works, lest anyone should boast.
—*Ephesians* 2:8–9

A big thank-you to Pam Hopkins for all she's done for my career. You're my own "perfect match" for a literary agent. What can I say? You're the best!

To Melissa, editor extraordinaire.
Thanks for all your hard work and enthusiasm.
You encourage me with your kindness.

To the Love Inspired Ladies. Your love, integrity and work ethic inspire me to new heights.

Love always and forever to Joe, Annie, Kimmie and Katie.

Chapter One

"You marry a man, not an occupation." Lakeisha Wilson made her point, loud and clear.

But it wasn't as if Julia Evans hadn't already considered every angle of her Great Scheme. It was simply a matter of helping her dear friend grasp the concept.

"He is a man," Julia reasoned aloud, though softly. She didn't want Thomas and Evy Martin, sitting across the round table from them, to overhear the private conversation. Goodness knows she didn't want her exceptional ideas exposed to the eyes of the whole waiting world.

It was enough that Lakeisha was going to give her a hard time about it. And if her dear friend of twenty-four years didn't understand, no one would. It was a wretched way to begin.

Smothering a half smile, she coolly shifted her

gaze to the subject in question—the Object of her Affection.

Well, not *affection*, precisely, but be that as it may...

Father Bryan Cummings.

Tall, dark and handsome.

More to the point, *ordained* to the ministry and headed for a great career in evangelism, maybe even internationally.

He didn't know it yet, but she'd chosen him for a very special project.

Marriage.

Sunshine glistened off his straight, dark hair, and his smile was perfect and white. Practiced, even.

He'd told her once that image was everything. If he smiled to himself in the mirror to get it just right, no one was the wiser. And Julia would never tell.

Father Bryan was surrounded by a raucous group of young men dressed in everything from khakis and polo shirts to little more than patchy fluorescent swimming trunks and bare feet.

Though he stood on the opposite side of the swimming pool from where Julia sat sipping her iced tea, she could tell he was in the middle of a heated theological discussion with his friends.

In Julia's experience with him, Bryan didn't speak about much else besides the tenants of the faith. His idea of polite conversation was debating the merits and nuances of each of the five points of Calvinism. *With* Scriptural proofs.

That, Julia supposed, was part of the allure. She glanced back to Lakeisha and chuckled at the stunned look on her childhood friend's face. Lakeisha had obviously followed the direction of Julia's gaze, and followed her thoughts, as well.

"I take it you don't approve of my Great Scheme."

Lakeisha snorted. "That's the understatement of the year."

Even as she shook her head disparagingly at Julia, Lakeisha smiled pleasantly at a couple of working associates who'd stopped to say hello. Julia recognized the women as being from the accounting office at HeartBeat, and cheerfully pointed them in the direction of the iced tea and cookies.

As she looked around, she realized nearly every employee of the HeartBeat Crisis Pregnancy Center was here for this Labor Day gathering at the Martins' home. The sun shone brightly, which, with the fickle Colorado weather, was a blessing in itself.

People crowded around the pool, though no one was swimming. Julia had never quite become accustomed to the city version of a pool party. In the eastern Colorado country town where she was from, a pool party meant everyone went swimming. People brought along their inner tubes and blow-up balls. Old and young alike played water volleyball and Marco Polo.

Here, people came to a pool party to schmooze, not swim. They brought their business cards, not their beach towels. It was a different world.

She leaned back in her chair and smiled. She'd dreamed of this world all her life. A challenging ministry in a fast-paced atmosphere. Those around her were her colleagues in ministry.

Ministry.

The word alone made her shiver in delight. She didn't know many names of people here, having only been with HeartBeat for a few months, but a lot of the faces were familiar. Many volunteered their time to the center. Others, like Julia, worked full-time for the crisis center.

There was Mr. Movie in his fancy sunglasses, who worked on the camera side of the video department where they developed audiovisual materials for and about the center; Merry Maid, the administrative assistant who always picked up after everyone else in the office. In the far corner was her boss, Sarah Straight-Arrow, the artistic perfectionist, speaking to Little Miss Muffet, a counselor ever on a persistent insect-killing mission at the center. Julia's toes curled at the very thought of spiders.

Lakeisha probably knew all the names and backgrounds that went with all these faces, instead of the safe but not very effective stereotypes Julia tended to slap on people.

"I'm not finished with you, girlfriend," Lakeisha

said, interrupting her thoughts. "Because I'm not getting the point of your little *plan* at all." She waved one hand and slammed the other down on the glass tabletop. "You've gone completely out of your mind, girl, and I'm *not* following."

"Who's gone crazy around here?" Thomas Martin asked with a laugh as he turned around to face them.

"Me," Evy Martin groaned, rubbing a gentle hand over her burgeoning pregnancy. "Or at least I will be crazy, if this kid doesn't stop using my ribs as monkey bars."

Julia laughed. "Do you feel him move a lot?"

Evy pointed to one spot on her rib. "This bump right here is his heel. He likes to kick the same spot over and over."

Julia ran her hand over her own trim abdomen. She couldn't even imagine how it felt to be kicked from the inside, to have the blessing of a little life inside her.

"It's a boy?"

Evy shook her head and laughed. "Oh, no. We don't know yet. We want it to be a surprise. But we decided early on that *it* or *he or she* wasn't working for us. We settled on the generic form of *he* when we speak about our baby."

She smiled softly at Evy. Someday, maybe, she'd be ready for a baby of her own. At the moment, she was still working on the *marriage* part of the equa-

tion. And that required the *un*gender-neutral form
of a *he*.

"Let's walk," Thomas suggested, holding out his
hand to Evy.

Evy flashed her husband a grateful look, then
turned to explain to Julia and Lakeisha. "Sometimes
it helps to walk out my cramps. And the rocking
motion of walking puts this little fellow to sleep."
She patted her stomach once again.

Thomas hovered over her, leaning into her ear to
whisper something that made Evy laugh.

Thomas took such good care of Evy, and there
was no doubt she and their baby were the center of
his world. Deep down, Julia had to admit to being a
little jealous of such a close, loving relationship.

"You'll never have that kind of commitment if
you keep pushing this Great Scheme of yours,"
Lakeisha commented wryly, as if reading Julia's
mind.

Julia bristled. "It's not like I'm picking a name
out of a telephone book, or putting my face on a bill-
board to advertise my dilemma."

"Oh, no, of course not. Your system is sooo much
better. *Excuse me, sir. May I see your résumé?
You've had how much education? Years of experience in ministry?*" Lakeisha's high, squeaky tone
suggested her cynicism.

Julia laughed. "It isn't as coldhearted as all that. I
simply feel that I'm ready to move to the next level,

you know? I'm twenty-eight years old, and I don't even feel like a grown-up."

Lakeisha laughed. "And that's bad?"

"Depends on your perspective, I guess. Right now, marrying a decent, godly, *professional* man is a critical part of my impending equation. What in the world is wrong with that?"

As soon as the question was out, Julia regretted asking. It was like inviting a politician to share her views on the economy.

"Impending equation?" Right on cue, her friend grinned like the Cheshire cat and raised her eyebrows so high they were lost underneath her wiry black bangs. "Okay, first of all, what is *wrong* with this little scenario of yours is that you can't just choose a man at random—by whatever means—and then expect him to agree to meet you at the altar."

Lakeisha had a point, Julia acknowledged. But that wasn't an insurmountable difficulty. She'd simply get to know Bryan a little better. He'd notice her, and…problem solved.

Okay, a *lot* better. But it could be done. She could show what a great partner in ministry she would be. She'd just do something to get him to notice her, and that would be that. Wouldn't it?

"You think just because *you* made a unilateral decision that Bryan meets your marital requirements, that he is going to ask you to marry him?"

"Not right away, of course, but—"

"What about sparks and fireworks, Julia? Don't you want to fall in love?"

Julia shrugged. Sparks and fireworks were highly overrated commodities, in her mind. She could live without them, and good riddance.

"Look around you, girlfriend. Right here in this backyard. This place is swarming with young, eligible, handsome Christian men. Bulging biceps and bulging portfolios, my dear."

She gestured toward the jostling group of men surrounding Bryan. "So why settle for Father Bryan? You've been working with the man on a regular basis for months, and I've never heard you say a single word about being attracted to him, or that something was developing between the two of you."

"That's just it, Lakeisha," Julia argued, wishing she could easily explain what she held deep in her heart. It was crystal clear in her mind, but she knew how shallow and stupid it sounded when she talked about it out loud. "The thing is, I'm *not* attracted to Father Bryan. At least not in the way you mean."

"Then why in the world would you…?"

"Marry him? Because he's a man with a future. Bryan knows exactly where he's going and how he's going to get there."

Lakeisha took a deep swig of her iced tea before answering. "Charisma? Under normal circumstances, I would expect you to be telling me how handsome he is. How kind and generous. How he makes your heart flip over when he looks at you."

"What, and major on the trivial?"

"Trivial?" Lakeisha gave her a long, pointed look, then shook her head as if conceding. Or more accurately, giving up on her hopeless roommate.

"I'm not like you, Lakeisha," Julia said softly, a catch in her voice. "I'm not a romantic. I just want stability, security and ministry."

"Hogwash!" Lakeisha exclaimed. "Not a romantic? What if there's someone special out there you've yet to meet, someone God made just for you? What if you're too busy with your own plans to see God's plan?"

Julia raised an eyebrow. "Oh, right. Mr. Perfect, stamped Made for Julia Marie Evans. Bring him on, Lakeisha."

"Well..." Lakeisha paused just as a large shadow passed over them. Seeing the source of the shadow, she grinned impishly. "How about Zeke Taylor?"

"Paul Bunyan?" Julia spouted a laugh that she quickly covered with her palm. "I always picture that man in the company of a big, snorting blue ox."

"Julia!"

"Well, I do."

Zeke Taylor was a local carpenter who volunteered his time to the shelter. Well over six feet tall, he was blond, bearded and always wore flannel shirts and steel-toed boots. A lumberjack wasn't such a big stretch.

"Zeke!" Lakeisha called, to Julia's immediate distress.

The big man turned and strode back to where they sat, then crouched beside them with a smile. Julia had to admit he had the biggest, bluest eyes she'd ever seen.

His kind, friendly gaze looked directly at her, and she felt as if he were really *seeing* her, not merely giving her a polite perusal. She swallowed dryly and struggled to erase the imprint of his smile in her mind.

"What can I do for you ladies?" His voice was the low, rich bass she expected it to be. Julia had the uncomfortable notion the question was directed at her. He was looking at her, even though Lakeisha had been the one to call him over.

"Julia and I have just been discussing true love," Lakeisha began, despite Julia's stricken look in her direction. "We were wondering your opinion on the topic."

Zeke laughed, and she was struck again by how genuinely friendly he appeared. "That's an awfully big topic."

Julia just barely restrained herself from saying that he was an *awfully big man.* But Lakeisha clearly captured her train of thought, and they shared an amused, meaning-filled glance.

"Let me narrow it down for you," Julia said, deciding it was better to take the bull by the horns, so to speak, than to sit there and let Lakeisha dictate the conversation. "Do you believe there is a Mr. Right?"

Zeke slapped his palm against his broad chest. "For me, I'd have to say *no.*"

Lakeisha roared with laughter, and didn't stop even when Julia pinned her with a glare.

"That's not what I meant and you know it."

Zeke nodded, his amused glance sliding over Lakeisha and landing squarely on Julia. "I didn't believe it was. I was just joshing you."

Her eyes widened. "Oh."

He cleared his throat. "I know I sometimes come off gruff, because of my size…." He ground to a halt, and then continued tentatively. "People often mistake my meaning. My humor is a little cockeyed at times."

"You didn't answer the question," reminded Lakeisha, who was obviously having difficulty composing her features. "Do you believe God has one special someone out there for you?"

"One special woman," Zeke said slowly, catching Julia's gaze with his own. "'This is now bone of my bones, and flesh of my flesh….' She's out there, Lord willing." His voice got lower and richer with every word he spoke.

"Waiting for you?" Julia queried softly.

Zeke shook his head. "No. Not waiting for me."

He ran a hand over his beard and smiled. "Working. Serving the Lord wherever she's at."

Julia tried to swallow and couldn't. Why did that sound so romantic?

"You'll excuse me," she said, her words tumbling one over another. "I need to go ask Father Bryan about something."

It was true—she did need to speak to Bryan about the upcoming ad campaign at HeartBeat. So why did her words feel so much like a lie?

She hurried away from Zeke and Lakeisha as fast as she could without looking rude, glancing back only once to see Zeke following her progress with his gaze.

Flustered, she spoke to everyone she passed, trying to make up for what felt like rudeness by being extra kind to everyone she met.

When she reached Father Bryan, she laid an arm on his shoulder to get his attention, and then waited quietly while he finished his conversation with his seminary buddies.

She didn't understand half the words they were saying, and wondered if, as a pastor's wife, she'd have to get a seminary education herself, just to communicate with her husband.

Husband.

She glanced up at Bryan, picturing them together in her mind. Helping others, like the desperate, pregnant mothers who came into HeartBeat. Like the people in his congregation, wherever God led. Who knew what else they could accomplish?

She waited, but there was nothing. Not a single emotion.

But marriage wasn't about emotion. Weddings might be, but she'd seen firsthand how quickly those feelings faded. Wasn't her way better?

"Julia?" Bryan looked a little put out, and she wondered if he'd tried more than once to get a hold of her wandering attention.

"I'm sorry. I was woolgathering."

"Not a problem. I should be the one apologizing for making you wait." He flashed her a toothy grin.

Julia wondered if that was what his true smile looked like.

"I just wanted to chat with you about the new ad campaign," Julia began, though Bryan's attention, or at least his gaze, was wandering elsewhere. "If now is a bad time…"

"Not at all." His gaze returned to her, and he smiled squarely. "I've assembled some Scripture passages we can use on the brochures, but I'm still working up something for the full-page magazine ad."

"That's fine, but we need a mock-up of the ad by Thursday noon at the latest."

His gaze shifted to somewhere over her left shoulder. "I've got class Wednesday, but I'll try to fit it in on Tues— What *is* that?"

"What is what?" Disheartened by her failure to attain Bryan's attention, never mind his interest, Julia spun around to see where he was looking.

It didn't take long to find the source of his surprise. A dirty brown-and-white Jack Russell terrier had somehow gotten through the high fence surrounding the backyard. She knew the Martins didn't own any animals because of their traveling, ministry lifestyle.

At first it was amusing, watching the guests' varied reactions to the filthy animal, but it was another thing entirely to discover the poor thing was limping, favoring its left back foot. Julia wondered uneasily if a car might have hit him.

With a spontaneous spurt of sympathy, she decided she should take care of the dog herself, especially since no one else appeared to be moving.

She turned to let Bryan know she was leaving, but his attention was elsewhere. He burst into laughter.

"Well, I'll be doggoned," he said, shaking his head. "*Literally.* What a crazy mutt."

She whirled around. To her surprise, the Jack Russell somehow launched himself into the middle of the swimming pool.

"What a joke," Bryan said from behind her.

A joke?

Maybe, under normal circumstances. But within seconds, it was clear the dog could not swim, perhaps because of his broken leg.

He flipped over once in the middle of the pool, not making as much of a splash as Julia would have expected. And then, in a single, heart-wrenching moment, the dog's head popped under the waves and disappeared. He sank as if he were a rock.

Panic freezing her to the spot, she croaked Bryan's name.

But it wasn't Bryan who came running to the poor little dog's rescue.

It was big, burly Zeke Taylor.

In a second, he was in the pool, pulling the dog to the surface and into his arms. He hadn't waited even to remove his steel-toed boots. He'd simply reacted.

And saved the irascible puppy, who was wagging his tail in Zeke's arms despite being wet and wounded.

Bryan was still laughing at the sight, which raised Julia's hackles. She guessed it was funny, from one perspective, but she could have no reaction except one—blatant and sheerly feminine admiration for Zeke Taylor.

A true hero at work.

Chapter Two

Glancing at the sky, Zeke stopped pounding nails into a two-by-four wood frame and slipped his hammer into his belt. He swiped in a deep breath of sawdust-filled air, pulled a crumpled red bandanna from the back pocket of his faded blue jeans and mopped the sweat off his forehead and the back of his neck.

It was a brisk morning, typical of Colorado in the early fall, but the cool breeze didn't do much for Zeke. He was pushing himself harder than usual, and every muscle in his body was groaning in protest.

He'd been working extra time at HeartBeat lately, and consequently was behind on this project. He was quietly determined to catch up, maybe get ahead, to make up for the time he spent in volunteer work.

There was so much need in the world, and so little hours in the day. He was compelled to do as much as he could for the pregnant women who came to

HeartBeat for care and assistance. He only hoped it was enough.

It could never be enough.

Zeke blew out a frustrated breath and picked up his hammer, hoping to find solace in pounding nails. The familiar sound and feel of working with wood had often given him an odd sort of comfort in the past.

Lately, though, it seemed he was more inclined to concentrate on something far more pleasant than building with his hands. The silver-toned laugh of a certain blond-haired, green-eyed angel.

Julia Evans.

No matter how hard he tried, she was never far from his mind. He mulled over her every word, reconsidered every look and smile.

It wasn't just that he was attracted to her beauty, though he certainly was. But Julia was different from the other women he knew. She seemed to know just what to do to make a hurting soul smile. She stood up to fight when everyone else was sitting down. She had strength of heart that surprised him, yet a quiet sense of vulnerability that made him long to protect her.

Which was ridiculous. He hardly knew her.

No. that wasn't right. He knew her.

She didn't know *him*.

He pounded five nails out quickly, slamming them neatly into a perfect row. The pressure of finishing the project on time only helped his strength, without marring his accuracy.

Even without this unusual, intense emotional current rushing through him, Zeke could pound nails with his hammer faster than a man with a nail gun.

More accurately, too, he thought, though he'd never tested his theory.

A grin tugged at his lips as, once again, Julia's face drifted into his thoughts. He ought to ask her out and get it over with, he thought. Once she'd turned him down, maybe he could get on with life.

And she would turn him down. Ironically, that was one of the many things he admired most about her—her devotion to the center at whatever cost to her personal life. She must have men clamoring to take her out, yet she worked days and many evenings, not to mention weekends, helping shelter women personally, in addition to being in charge of the center's advertising.

But even if her evenings were free, Zeke doubted Julia would take an interest in him. He was Beast to her Beauty.

Still, stranger things had happened.

At least he got to see her almost every evening at the center. Not that Julia was the reason he volunteered there, he thought, a surge of electricity running through him. He put his time in to serve God and the people of the HeartBeat Center, helping people like his sister, who'd found themselves at a rough crossing.

He prayed that was the truth.

But now he wondered if his motivation for helping out at the clinic had become *because Julia Evans was there.*

Was it true?

She'd only just spoken to him for the first time yesterday at the pool party, and even then it was because of her friend Lakeisha. And yet he had to admit that the desire to see her again tonight ranked right up there with the desire to do good works.

His thoughts tearing him up, he worked frantically, until suddenly he heard *her* voice.

"Zeke? Zeke Taylor?"

Now he was hallucinating. Next he'd be put in a straitjacket. He whistled a birdsong and imagined stars floating over his head.

"Hello! May I come down there?"

Zeke turned around to see none other than the true-to-the-flesh Julia Evans slip-sliding her way down a steep, gravel-covered driveway and onto the job site. Her arms flapped wildly as she struggled to maintain her precarious balance.

She wasn't dressed for visiting a construction job site. For one thing, she was wearing a dress. A pretty, soft, flowery-looking thing that Zeke thought might disintegrate underneath the touch of his rough fingertips. It was a dress that could easily be torn to shreds in a work area full of protruding nails and rough lumber.

And then there were her shoes. High heels from the looks of them, and they were sinking into the gravel with every step she took.

Feeling like a bumbling giant, he lumbered to her side and offered his arm for assistance.

Her eyes widened to enormous proportions as she laid her hand upon his forearm and allowed his other arm to encircle her tiny waist, and Zeke wished for the millionth time that he wasn't so big.

Sure, men admired his strength, but to a delicate young woman like Julia, he knew he must come off looking and moving like a big, dumb ox.

For Julia's part, her lungs had simply refused to work from the moment Zeke jogged to her side to the time she stood safely at the bottom of the hill. He was so athletic, his muscles and ligaments working in perfect harmony. His autumn-blond hair shone like a gold halo over his expressive blue eyes.

She wished she could enjoy the picture, but she had other problems, like being about to plunge head-down on the gravel driveway. Her shoes were the worst possible choice.

Warmth flooded to her cheeks. She was mortified. She hadn't given her attire a single thought when she came here, to this dirty, rocky job site.

What must Zeke think of her? He was all kindness. But honestly, what kind of an idiot wore patent leather pumps to a construction site?

Even Zeke had a hard hat on.

As if seeing the direction of her gaze, Zeke moved to a trunk and picked up an extra hard hat. "I'm afraid I'm going to have to—" he cleared his throat "—to ask you to wear one of these guys for the length of your visit. It's for your own safety, as well as our regulations."

He tacked the last part on so swiftly Julia barely understood the words.

She thought she saw Zeke cringe slightly, as if anticipating her answer. No doubt he thought, based on the little he knew of her, that she'd criticize or whine at having to meet with safety requirements that were nothing less than good, common sense.

Well, she'd do neither, she thought, reaching for the hat with her best smile.

Even though she knew she'd look ridiculous. Even though the hat was two sizes too big.

Zeke jammed his hands into his front jeans pockets and raised his eyebrows. His huge blue eyes were gleaming with mischief, and she was certain she detected the corner of his mouth twitching under his beard.

Her dander rose quickly, and just as quickly departed. What could she say, when he was right? "Feel free to laugh out loud," she said wryly, and with a smile.

A bubble of deep, hearty laughter burst from his lips, though he looked like he was struggling desperately to restrain it.

"Sorry," he apologized when he could speak. He wiped his eyes with his thumb. "It's just that you're by far the cutest carpenter I've ever seen on a job site, this or any other."

"Thank you very much." She curtsied slightly, turning her head to conceal the blush she knew clouded her cheeks. "I'll take that as a compliment."

"It was meant that way." His voice was deep and husky, and Julia looked away.

There was an extended silence while Zeke collected his mirth and Julia collected her thoughts.

"Did you come here about HeartBeat?" he asked quietly, leaning a shoulder against the wood framework he'd earlier been pounding upon.

"No. Not directly, anyway." Julia's chest tightened around her breath as she quickly gathered her thoughts and gained her courage.

Yesterday, at the pool party, Zeke had left as soon as he'd pulled the dog from the pool. She'd never had the chance to thank him, or to help take care of that poor little dog.

"Actually, I'd like to find out what happened to that little Jack Russell terrier you rescued. Is he okay?"

"Tip? Yeah, *she's* fine." He cocked his head and

stood silently for a moment, taking in her mettle. "You really care?"

"I think I've proved my worth with my pumps, don't you?"

He looked puzzled, and she explained with a laugh. "My high heels."

He grinned. "You have a point."

"How do you know her name is Tip?" she asked, self-consciously fiddling with her hard hat.

"Because I named her. Would you like to see her for yourself?"

"The puppy is here?" Julia asked in astonishment. "At the construction site?"

He nodded. "I didn't want to leave her home alone all day. Especially while she's healing from her wounds."

Julia's heart fell. "Oh, my. She's badly hurt, then? Is there anything I can do?"

Zeke smiled gently and shook his head. Offering his hand, he led her toward a gentler incline than the one she'd come down. "Tip will be okay, give or take a few weeks. No permanent damage."

He grinned down at her, and her racing heart stopped still. "Her leg is broken. And I think there's a screw loose in that brain of hers, jumping into the pool the way she did."

"Oh, no," Julia objected, wondering at the squeak in her voice, and hoping Zeke could not hear it. "I'm sure she must have thought she knew how to swim."

Zeke chuckled loudly. "Yeah. *Thought* being the key word."

She met his gleaming eyes, and they laughed.

"Seriously, though," Zeke continued, swinging Julia's hand as they walked, "Tip is going to be just fine. Nothing a little good, old-fashioned R and R can't fix."

One step at a time, he led her back up the gravel to where his full-size blue truck was parked. In the bed of his truck, tucked securely into a torn box and curled up on an old scrap of blanket, was Tip.

Zeke picked her up, and she immediately wagged her tail and began licking his chin enthusiastically.

"You can sure tell who Tip likes," Julia teased. "It didn't take long for the two of you to form an attachment."

Color crept up Zeke's cheek above his beard, and Julia smiled in delight. There was nothing made up about Zeke Taylor. He was all man, the genuine article.

"I made a report to the Humane Society, but if no one claims her, she's mine," Zeke explained tenderly. As he spoke, he stroked the dog's fur, almost mechanically. Julia marveled at how gentle Zeke's big hands appeared against the small dog.

"So she'll recover completely?" Julia reached forward to stroke the dog's wiry coat. Tip had had a recent bath, she noticed. No more dirt spots were clinging to her, and the white part of her coat was fresh and sparkling in the sunshine.

"Completely," Zeke agreed. "And she has a home. I figure she can keep me company, and I can keep her away from large bodies of water."

Julia smothered a laugh. "I'm glad she has a good home, now," she said softly. "I hope I'm not over-stepping my boundaries, but if it's okay with you, I'd like to buy a few things for Tip." She paused and caught his gaze. "Sort of a homecoming present for her."

"Things?"

"Bowls for food and water. A collar and leash. A couple of squeaky toys. Dog bones. And a big bag of puppy kibble, of course. Things," she concluded, feeling suddenly foolish for coming out to the site at all.

Zeke had things well in hand, and he clearly didn't need her interference. Of course, he'd made her feel more than welcome, but it was obvious she wasn't needed here.

She hadn't even been sure she could find Tip again, thinking Zeke would most likely drop her off at the Humane Society.

She was thrilled to know Zeke would be keeping her. Tip was a lucky puppy. And buying things for Zeke's new housemate would not only be fun, but a kind of catharsis, a way of doing something now for Tip, when Julia's own inertia had kept her from helping yesterday at the pool.

The longer Julia's list had grown the wider Zeke's gaze grew, and now he was staring at her outright.

"What?" Julia asked, wondering if he was going to call her an idiot. *She* would call herself an idiot. What a dumb thing to suggest. At the least, she probably should have called first and asked if he needed anything for Tip, and if he didn't mind her stopping by the site.

But there she was, the typical Julia, always going off half-cocked, trying to help when she was really just getting in the way, even if everyone was too polite to say so.

Perhaps she'd learn her lesson this time.

"You are a godsend," Zeke said, carefully replacing Tip in her box with one last gentle rub.

Julia felt like someone had brushed a finger down her spine. Adrenaline coursed through her. "What?"

He turned to her, leaning his muscular arm against the side of his truck. His eyes gleamed with a combination of appreciation and genuine male admiration that made Julia's stomach swirl with unusual and unnamable emotions.

Zeke continued, his voice low and resolute. "Unfortunately, I barely made it to the vet's last afternoon, and then Tip needed looking after. I haven't purchased anything for her. I've been feeding her from one of my cereal bowls with the sample food the vet gave me."

"You don't have anything for her?" she repeated numbly.

"Anything. Or is that nothing?" He smiled wide and belted a strong laugh. "So you see, Julia, you're an answer to prayer today. For Tip. And for me. You're a blessing disguised as an angel."

This time, it was Julia's turn to blush.

Chapter Three

As the Colorado Indian summer faded crisply into late fall, Julia found her mind often on Zeke. His unconventional good looks were part of it, to be sure, but that didn't explain why she now anticipated his presence at HeartBeat, or why their frequent conversations lingered in her mind long after the lights were turned out and the doors safely locked.

On this overcast Tuesday evening she was hauling charitable baby gifts she'd volunteered to pick up at various community bins, located inside grocery stores and department stores.

During her commute from store to store, her mind often shifted to her budding friendship with Zeke. She was surprised to find they had a lot in common, not so much in hobbies or background as in values, interests and viewpoints.

She realized with a start that she *should* be thinking about Bryan Cummings, about her future. About stability and security.

It was just as well, pushing Zeke from her conscious thoughts. At least thinking about Bryan didn't confuse her, or make her feel all these new, foolish sensations Zeke aroused in her.

Happy and sad.

Threatened and safe.

Give her a stronghold of security any day of the week. Father Bryan Cummings was safety. She would do well to remember that, she reminded herself severely as she got in her car. She had a plan to carry out.

She pulled her car into the Grace Church parking lot. Grace Church had opened its doors to the struggling ministry, given the small, dedicated staff of HeartBeat a place to assemble, and main offices where they could conduct the nonprofit business of benevolence without having to pay a high rent for the space.

The pregnant women who came for help often needed shelter. HeartBeat owned and maintained three houses in the neighborhood, where women in need were encouraged to stay and prepare for their little blessings to arrive.

After their babies were born, they often stayed around until they'd arranged, with HeartBeat's help, new lives of their own.

Julia's heart welled when she thought of the brave women who sought help here. It took courage to admit they needed help, and wisdom to fight their way through to new lives.

Julia opened the trunk and surveyed with pleasure the hodgepodge of gifts—pink, blue, green and yellow baby blankets; fuzzy-footed sleepers; bottles and big cans of formula. The back seat of her car was full to overflowing with diapers, which was a good thing. If there was one thing HeartBeat could never have enough of, it was diapers.

It was a remarkable baby shower, there in her trunk, and that's exactly what it was meant to be.

"Hey, girl, what took you so long?" Lakeisha's sudden speech nearly jolted Julia out of her shoes.

Placing a palm over her chest to still her racing heart, Julia whirled on her friend. "Do you mind not sneaking up on me that way? You nearly scared the wits out of me."

Lakeisha laughed and waved her hand as if brushing away the comment. "You don't have any wits to scare out of you."

"Thanks for the compliment," growled Julia affectionately. "Did you come out here to give me a hard time, or to help me with these packages?"

Lakeisha's black eyes grew wide. "Well, I'm not carrying all this stuff inside, if that's what you mean."

"That's exactly what I mean, and you know it. Come on, hon, it's not any worse than carrying groceries up to our apartment."

Lakeisha grinned, her eyes gleaming. "True. But at our apartment, we don't have a smorgasbord of handsome men to choose from. Men willing and able to carry these meager boxes in for us poor damsels in distress."

Julia hoisted a box from the trunk. "Lakeisha, you are too much."

"Put the box down," Lakeisha suggested. "I'll run and get that mighty conqueror of baby boxes, just to prove it to you."

"Make it Father Bryan," Julia suggested, giving in to the inevitable. She might as well get something out of this charade.

Lakeisha snorted. "Like Father Bryan would condescend to carrying boxes."

Julia shrugged. She was probably right. "I wish you weren't so dead set against Father Bryan."

"It's not that I don't approve of Bryan, exactly," Lakeisha explained. "I just don't think he's the right man for you."

"He is," Julia muttered, folding her arms tightly across her chest. "He just doesn't know it yet."

"Don't worry," Lakeisha assured after an extended silence. Her voice was unusually bright and cheerful. Clearly feigned. It was an open disagreement between them. "I'll bring back the best man for the job," she assured. "And if he's good looking, so much the better, huh? It'll only take a minute."

Julia sighed and slumped against the back bumper. It would take more than a minute to find the *best man for the job.* Such a man as Lakeisha painted with her words didn't exist. Not in this world, anyway.

It was a busy night in the HeartBeat office as groups of volunteers worked on mailings. The church's new janitor was even mopping his way around the compound. And Zeke was right in the middle of it, making wood frames for signs, his hammer swinging as fast as his thoughts.

But his busy hands couldn't take away the excruciating stillness of his heart. He'd seen everyone but Julia, and he was dismayed to find how very much it mattered to him that she wasn't there.

Fortunately, at that moment, Lakeisha came bursting in the door, her brown cheeks flushed pink from the crisp air, and breathing as if she'd been running.

Her gaze made a quick sweep around the room before settling solidly on Zeke. She lifted one eyebrow, as if asking a question.

He didn't know the answer, so he shrugged.

Apparently, that was the answer she was looking for, because she grinned like a cat and beelined for him as if he were the proverbial mouse. With the gleam in her eye, he thought he just might be. He slung his hammer into his belt and accepted her friendly hug.

"I'm glad you're here," Lakeisha burst out excitedly. "You're just the right man."

Zeke frowned, furrowing his eyebrows low over his eyes. "Thank you." He paused and grinned thoughtfully. "I think."

"It's a compliment," Lakeisha assured him. "Where's your coat?"

"Are we going somewhere?"

"Just outside. Julia needs your help."

His heart jump-started with a vengeance, and his scowl deepened. He was elated, but he didn't want Lakeisha to pick up on that.

"At your service, ma'am," he said, shrugging into his lined jean jacket. With a grim half smile, he gestured Lakeisha out the door ahead of him.

Zeke spotted Julia's car immediately, parked just out the door, pulled in backward with the trunk open. Julia leaned negligently against the rear bumper, her arms crossed in front of her. Her black jeans and pink sweatshirt only served to make her cheeks look flushed and beautiful, even in the muted light of the parking lot.

Her eyes widened noticeably when she saw him. He grinned, wondering if that was good or bad.

"See, I told you," Lakeisha crowed from behind him.

Julia glared at her over his shoulder. Lakeisha just laughed.

"Told her what?" he asked, wondering if he really wanted to know. Clearly, whatever they'd been discussing involved him, either directly or indirectly.

"It was nothing," Julia muttered immediately.

Again, Lakeisha chuckled.

"What can I do for you ladies?" he asked, changing the subject, hoping to quell the internal power struggle going on between the roommates. It was friendly tension, but tension none the less.

He swiftly decided he really didn't want to know the cause.

"I was going to haul these boxes of baby things into the church so I can wrap them up for distribution," Julia explained, gesturing toward her trunk. "Lakeisha, however, thought we needed a man's help. Scarlett O'Hara and all that."

Comprehension unfolded around him in waves, and he smothered a grin. "If we all go in together, I'll bet we can get this stuff in one trip," he suggested quietly, careful not to look at Julia, lest she see the gleam of amusement in his eye.

Julia didn't let him off the hook that easily. She took his arm and pulled him around to meet her gaze. She studied him carefully, and Zeke put all his energies into counseling his features and swallowing the huge lump in his throat that formed when he stared into her beautiful eyes.

He was about to break away when suddenly she smiled. Zeke's heart stopped cold.

"Where'd you get this stuff?" he asked, ignoring his scratchy throat.

Taking refuge in activity, he loaded Lakeisha's arms with boxes, then turned to do the same with Julia. He was careful not to overload them—he could easily get the bulk of the boxes himself.

He didn't want to insult Julia in the process, so he made sure he gave her a decent armful.

"These are all from local community bins," Julia said over her shoulder as she moved toward the door.

Zeke was impressed by the quality and quantity of items the community gave.

He followed the women into the church and down a long hallway, into a vacant Sunday school room. From the look of the pictures on the wall, he thought it might be a younger grade. Lots of bright colors, depicting major Bible characters with round, smiling faces and rosy pink cheeks.

"What are you going to do with this stuff now?" he asked, dumping the load in his arms into one corner.

"We're going to wrap all these gifts up in pretty baby-shower paper," Lakeisha said brightly, a cunning gleam in her friendly black eyes. "I don't suppose you transport *and* gift wrap?"

Zeke chuckled loudly, as much at the way Julia cringed as by the question itself. "I think I may surprise you."

Lakeisha took him up on his boast. "This I've got to see." She immediately began digging around in the Sunday school cubby for scissors and tape.

With an audible sigh, Julia moved to one of the boxes and pulled out the gift wrap. "You did this to yourself," she reminded him, handing him a tube of baby-blue paper covered with big, fluffy white clouds and brown cows jumping over orange crescent moons.

Lakeisha placed the scissors and tape on the table, then retrieved a baby monitor in a rectangular box and set it before him.

"You're not even going to challenge me?" he asked, with a wink at Julia. "How can I prove real men gift wrap if all you give me is a box?"

Julia laughed, the high, bell-toned chime like the ones that filled Zeke's dreams. "Here. Try this one." She shoved a stuffed monkey into his arms. It was brown and tan and held a half-peeled banana in one hand. "No more straight edges and square corners for you to deal with. But don't squeeze the banana."

Zeke, of course, squeezed the banana.

The monkey let out a screech worthy of its real-life jungle counterpart, and Zeke laughed. "That's more like it. Now watch, ladies, and learn at the hands of a master."

Lakeisha and Julia burst into laughter, and he waggled his eyebrows.

Without another word, he measured, cut, folded and taped with the accuracy of years of carpentry and the dedication of his loving mother's early training.

The women watched, wide-eyed and slack-jawed. He struggled not to grin. It served them right. And he had to admit he liked this, being the center of female attention, most particularly Julia's.

"I beg your pardon, Zeke," Lakeisha said as he finished. "I have misjudged your talent and ability with gift wrap."

He held up his big hands. "It's an easy mistake to make."

"I wasn't talking about your hands," Lakeisha admitted.

"The hands of an artist," Julia acknowledged softly, and Zeke stood a good two inches taller.

"You know," Julia continued, "you're just the sort of person I need for my planning committee. The special dinner is coming up, you know. Would you consider it?"

Zeke swallowed hard. He tried to force clumsy words through his dry throat, but nothing would come.

"You really should," Lakeisha encouraged. "I certainly underestimated your..."

"Artistic skills?" he provided hoarsely.

"Gender," Julia said with a laugh. "Don't ask."

"My gender," Zeke repeated dumbly.

"You're a guy," Julia explained, rolling her eyes at her roommate and friend. "You know—all bulk, no brains."

Zeke backed up a step and put a dramatic hand to his chest. "I'm wounded. Mortally wounded."

Julia laughed. "Well, don't take it too hard. Maybe Lakeisha has learned her lesson. Women can tote boxes. Men can wrap presents. There is no happily ever after."

Julia's words shocked Zeke far more than Lakeisha's insinuations ever had. "What's this? No happily ever after?"

"Julia insists that Prince Charming lives only in storybooks," Lakeisha explained lightly, though the look she gave Julia was anything but light. "No white steeds, no shiny armor. Nothing."

"She's wrong," Zeke responded without thinking. His angel didn't believe in love? What kind of nonsense was this?

He whirled to her. Her golden hair swirled about her like a halo, and his breath caught before he could speak. He forced words through his tight throat. "You're wrong."

"Am I?" she asked, sounding genuinely surprised. Or confused.

He wanted to take her into his arms and prove it,

but he could hardly act on those feelings. Nor could he leave it quite alone.

He reached out and gently swiped a thumb down her cheek. "You are wrong about love. And if it takes me forever, I'm going to prove it to you."

Chapter Four

"What do you think, girl?" Zeke asked the dog wryly as he scrubbed a hand over her soft muzzle. "Am I a fool for hoping?"

Tip merely nuzzled into his hand, bumping his palm with her nose to indicate that, in her opinion, he wasn't done scratching yet.

Zeke laughed and continued petting her with one hand, and squeezing the steering wheel with his other as he maneuvered his truck down the highway.

He was feeling introspective today. He had more free time on Saturday. Without work to keep his mind occupied, it was easy to get caught up wrestling with his thoughts. Having Tip with him helped him to not get bogged down thinking.

The more time he spent with Julia, the more he lost his focus. When she was around, there wasn't room for anything else in his mind and heart.

If he was completely honest, he'd admit he was

terrified out of his wits at what he was feeling. She made him feel such a hodgepodge of emotions he wanted to run away when he saw her, yet he was drawn to her with all his heart, every fiber of his being.

Was God in this?

That was the question that beleaguered him now. That, and the fact he just couldn't shake the feeling Julia needed him somehow.

For one thing, she didn't believe in happy endings.

He desperately wanted to know why, what had jaded her. He knew beyond a doubt she was a Christian, and had a personal relationship with Christ. *That* story ended well, didn't it? And if it worked for the Creator, why not for His creations?

He flipped his blinker and moved his truck off the highway. He didn't know what he could do for Julia, or what God would have him do for her. He cared for her, but he was hardly in a position to offer her any type of assistance or comfort.

He was determined. She'd done something for him no one else had ever done.

She'd looked past the carpenter and saw a man beneath. Hey—maybe that was the answer.

She'd asked him to sit on the planning committee for the quarterly special dinner the staff and volunteers at HeartBeat put on for the women currently in their care.

No one had ever asked him to sit on any kind of committee before.

He was the man people called to get the job done, not design the plan. He'd served a year's worth of dinners for HeartBeat, filling in whenever he was needed and doing whatever needed doing.

He hadn't been sure what to do with Julia's invitation. He'd been surprised, and honored. He turned his truck back onto the highway, in the direction of Julia's apartment. He knew where she lived. He'd made it his business to know, even if it was none of his business, technically speaking.

God help and bless him. His decision was made.

"Come on, Tip. Let's go see Julia."

"There are bound to be some dry times in a Christian's life," Julia muttered to herself, closing her Bible with an audible thump.

Maybe it was just that she was reading through the minor prophets.

Maybe it was just that she was distracted.

Zeke the Carpenter and Tip the Wonder Dog. Lakeisha pushing her to drop her Great Scheme and concentrate on true love, whatever that was.

And in the meantime, God felt far away, as if an invisible barrier had been erected between heaven and earth, leaving her all alone.

Julia remembered with longing the times when she just couldn't read enough of the Bible. Now it seemed she had to struggle through each paragraph, fight to understand each word.

"Lord, what am I doing wrong?" she whispered in misery.

Julia walked outside onto the small balcony and leaned as far as she could into the redwood railing to see around the corner of the building and get a glimpse of the rising sun. The wood under her hands had eroded from the elements and she had to be careful for splinters, but it was worth the discomfort to feel the heat of the sun on her face.

Besides, it had been her habit since childhood to watch the sun rise. She breathed deeply, letting all her stress go for that one moment. The warmth on her face was like an instant connection with the Son, a reminder that in His arms was true warmth.

It was her favorite time of the morning, where the world was still fresh and clean, not marred by the contents of the day. As always, she wondered what this day would bring. Only God knew.

Lakeisha was a late sleeper, so early morning was Julia's special time with the Lord. It was a good thing she had this time alone, because she sometimes talked aloud when she prayed.

Like this morning.

"I'm not doing enough, am I?" she asked, looking up at the cloudy sky as if waiting for an audible answer, though of course she knew better than that. Oh, that life was so easy.

As she looked back down at her worn burgundy leather Bible, she traced the gold lettering that graced the front. As much as she'd like her answers face-to-face, she settled for knowing she could take Bible 101 when she got to heaven and have all her questions answered to her satisfaction.

The telephone rang, and she raced to the kitchen to grab the phone off the wall. She juggled and then dropped the receiver in her haste to answer before the ring disturbed Lakeisha.

Swiping up the receiver from where it dangled near her feet, she cleared her throat and muttered a greeting.

"Julia."

Once again, the receiver hit the floor, this time sliding right out of her limp hands.

She stared down at the swinging handset, praying desperately this situation would simply go away, for on the other end of the line was the one man's voice she *never* wanted to hear again. Not ever.

So help her God.

"Julia, it's Daddy."

Julia cringed, inwardly and outwardly, as her stomach flipped over and hurled itself around like a carnival ride.

He still had the nerve to call himself *Daddy,* after all this time. Shaking, she pulled the receiver close, pressing it hard against her ear. She could hear the sound of her father's rapid breathing on the other end of the line and knew it matched her own.

He cleared his throat. "I'm in Denver."

Silence crackled on the line, and Julia knew he was waiting for a response.

She had none to give. Her father was in Denver? It was too much to fathom.

"Why?" Her question was low and guttural.

"I've been thinking about you. How have you been?"

Julia opened her mouth, but nothing came out. Her mind swam with thick gray rage until she thought her head might burst. She couldn't talk to him. There were no words to express what she felt.

"Like you care." That was a start.

"You know I do," her father replied, his voice hoarse and cracking with emotion.

Julia shuddered. She didn't want to hear this. Not a word of it. This man had no right to call himself her father. She swallowed hard as she bit back tears.

"Can we meet somewhere for coffee? Please? I just need to see you again. See with my own eyes that you're doing okay."

"No." No way. Knowing bitterness had crept into her tone, she gripped her fingernails into her fist until the sting of her pinched flesh replaced the sting of her heart.

"No? Just no? That's it?"

"That's it."

"I can't accept that, Julia. I came to Denver so we could—"

"*We* aren't going to do anything. Do you understand that?"

"I understand," her father said quietly. "But I can't accept it."

"That's my final answer. You're going to have to accept it. I'm too old to need a father watching over me. Don't try to come into my life now. It's too late for that. Just go on your merry way and stay out of my life."

Quietly, shakily, she replaced the receiver on the phone, finding comfort in its audible click. Taking deep breaths, she consciously shoved the painful memories back into a dark pocket in the recesses of her mind.

She had a life of her own now. She didn't need, or want, her father in her life. Closing her eyes and slumping against the kitchen counter, she ferociously ignored the painful tug of her heart.

"I've got to get on with my life, Lord," she said aloud, but the words just floated away on empty space.

A knock sounded on the front door. Julia glanced at the clock. It was still early for visitors, just past eight-thirty. Still, she was glad for the excuse to push her own dilemma aside for the moment, and she rushed to answer the door.

Zeke Taylor stood on the other side, shifting from

foot to foot and jamming his fingers through his thick blond hair. Tip wandered around his legs, sniffing at the concrete landing.

Not quite sure what to do with the man, Julia crouched and welcomed the dog. Tip immediately came to her, barking in delight and rubbing her head against Julia's hands. The dog didn't even seem to notice the splint on her leg. It hardly hampered her movements at all.

"She's looking great," Julia commented, looking up at Zeke.

The big man stuffed his hands in his pockets and grinned. "I wish I could take the credit for it, but it's all Tip's doing. She's a real trooper."

Julia stood and gestured for Zeke to come in. "You're just being modest."

Zeke chuckled. It was a deep, affectionate sound that warmed Julia's heart. "If you say so."

"I do." Julia settled on the sofa, and Zeke sat in the easy chair catty-corner to her.

He leaned his elbows on his knees and caught her gaze. For a moment he said nothing, just stared at her as if he could read her mind.

"What's wrong, Julia?" His question was such a low murmur Julia wondered if she'd even heard him correctly.

"I beg your pardon?"

"Maybe I should be begging *your* pardon," he said softly, a smile tugging at the corner of his mouth.

"But I can't shake the feeling that something is wrong."

She laughed shakily, a little unsettled by Zeke's discernment. Maybe he could read her mind through her eyes. Or maybe she was wearing her heart on her sleeve for all to see.

She straightened her spine and tipped her chin a notch or two. It wasn't Zeke's business why she was feeling this way, and he had no right to pry. She didn't have to tell him anything.

But as she looked into his kind gaze, she quickly realized it wasn't Zeke she was angry with. And Zeke wasn't pressuring her—he was sitting patiently, looking concerned and a little out of place.

She opened her mouth to tell him she was okay, but that's not what came out. "My father just called."

His eyes narrowed, and he stroked his beard with one hand. "I see," he said, though he clearly didn't.

"We're not exactly on speaking terms."

Zeke didn't ask why, but he looked ready to listen. And for some strange reason, she felt like talking. To Zeke Taylor, the carpenter. She didn't have time to figure out the swirl of emotions running through her. She was simply glad he was there.

"I haven't seen him since the day I graduated high school and walked out that door," she explained fiercely. "He tries to call once in a while, but I've always managed to avoid him. Until this morning."

"Did he abuse you?" Zeke's question was almost

a growl, and his hands were back in his lap, clenched tightly together. He looked as if he were ready to punch someone, and Julia wondered if he would do her a favor and punch her dad.

Not that punching Dad that would solve anything, other than give her a sense of revenge. But she wasn't looking for revenge. She was simply looking to be left alone.

"No. Yes," she said in answer to his question. She took a deep breath. "Sometimes I wished he'd hit me. At least then he would have noticed me."

"Absentee father, huh?"

"Deadbeat Dad. In the worst sense of the word. I don't remember a time when he treated me like his daughter. He never even remembered to buy me a present for my birthday. He didn't care if I had decent clothes for school or not. I don't even think he cared if I got enough to eat."

She paused. "I don't think he wanted a daughter. I don't think he wanted *me*."

Zeke reached out to her. His hand engulfed hers, and the feeling was oddly reassuring. He stroked the back of her hand with his thumb. "That's tough for a little girl," he said, his voice husky.

Julia pinched her lips together. "Yes it was. But it's over now."

He squeezed her hand. "Are you sure about that? Why's the man calling, anyway?"

She appreciated the fact that Zeke didn't call Greg

Evans her father. "I couldn't tell you. Maybe he suddenly found his conscience or something. Too little too late, in my book."

"Could he be stalking you?" His tone was deadly serious, and a chill went down Julia's spine.

But she wasn't afraid of her father. He'd never hurt her, at least not physically. The emotional scars he left were big enough, but she didn't worry that Greg was going to do something rash. "No. I don't think so. Hopefully he hasn't resorted to following me around."

"If he does, Julia, you tell me, okay?" His gaze pulled at hers, willing her to agree with him. He really cared.

And it felt good. Julia chuckled. "If my dad starts in with any cat-and-mouse stuff, I'll be sure to let you know."

Zeke leaned in to her, until their gazes were mere inches apart, and she could feel the warmth of his breath fanning her cheek, coming in quick, short bursts.

"This is serious, Julia. I want you to promise me."

Julia wasn't sure her mouth would work. Her heart had suddenly taken to calisthenics, and she wasn't sure she'd be able to speak over the noise. "I—I promise."

He leaned back as fast as he'd moved in on her. "Great. Then we have a deal."

"A deal," Julia echoed, placing a hand over her

racing heart. Why did Zeke's nearness affect her even more than her father's phone call? Maybe she was just confused, given the way the day was going.

"You never asked me why I'm here," Zeke reminded her with a grin bright enough to let her know he was intentionally changing the subject.

"Why are you here?" He was going to think she was a parrot if she kept this up.

"I've been thinking about that committee you wanted me to join."

"For the service supper."

He nodded briskly. "That's the one."

"And?"

"I'm happy to help."

"You didn't have to come all this way just to tell me that." Julia chuckled. "You could have phoned."

"No—I wanted to thank you personally for asking. It means a lot to me. I…wanted you to know."

"Well, I'm glad I asked," she said, realizing just how true that was. She was growing to regard Zeke as a dear friend. "I have a suspicion you're going to be a great ally to have in my corner."

In more ways than one.

Chapter Five

Before the evening was through, he was going to choke to death in this monkey suit with its fancy ruffles and wickedly snug-fitting bow tie, Zeke thought as he pulled his car into the lot at Grace Church and shut down the engine with a groan.

He wouldn't be caught dead in a tuxedo for anyone, but he couldn't turn this engagement down. The pregnant, often heartbroken women at Heart-Beat, many of whom were facing one of the biggest crises of their lives, were expecting a formal dinner, the service supper Zeke had had a part in planning.

For them, he'd wear a suit. Even a tuxedo with a baby-blue cummerbund and a bow tie.

Naturally, he'd tried to talk Julia out of it, thinking they could do something a little less—*constricting*—but she just laughed and told him baby blue matched his eyes, and that he better get used to the idea. As if that were going to happen.

Sighing aloud, he got out of the truck and wrapped the fancy black jacket around his thick shoulders, then reached for the white orchid corsage he'd picked up on a whim.

A really stupid whim.

He was always doing goofy things where Julia was concerned. He couldn't seem to help himself. Thinking of her made him think of flowers and sunshine.

It was his propensity to *act* on his crazy ideas that disturbed him. Think of flowers, buy flowers. Next thing you know, she'd have him buying her the sun.

Chuckling under his breath, he clutched the corsage box in his hand and whisked it behind his back. He was an idiot, but at least he was a happy idiot.

He had no idea how Julia would react. Hopefully she'd take pity on the Happy Idiot, and let him get out of this getup and back into blue jeans.

"What do you think?" Lakeisha asked loudly, if cheerfully, as Zeke walked in. "I look ridiculous, don't I?"

"You look great," Zeke assured her, meeting Julia's amused gaze with his own, and thinking that if anyone looked out of place here, it was him. The women looked surprisingly feminine in their black coats and soft pink bow ties.

Lakeisha wasn't finished. She pulled on his jacket arm to get his attention.

"I look like a penguin. Observe." She demonstrated with the side-to-side rocking motion of the black-and-white bird. "Why do the women have to wear tuxedos?"

"Because," Julia answered as she demonstrated with a waiter's suave bow, "we're offering white glove service tonight. And we're the white gloves." She donned the elegant accessories as she spoke.

Despite Lakeisha's complaint, Zeke thought Julia looked stunning in her outfit. She'd swept her hair up so it surrounded her face like a halo. Her cheeks were attractively flushed, and her eyes were beaming with excitement.

He fingered the corsage in his hand. He'd definitely dived clear off the dock. Maybe he should just leave well enough alone. But when he saw her expectant gaze on him, his hand pulled the corsage out from behind his back on its own accord.

He meant to present the corsage and say something sophisticated and classy, but all that came out of his mouth was, "For you."

Julia's color heightened as Lakeisha let out a hoot. "I...Zeke..." she stammered, but when she looked up and met his gaze, she simply said, "Thank you."

Slowly, carefully, he unwrapped the orchid and placed it on her left wrist. "I, know this dinner is for the pregnant ladies, but I, uh, just wanted tonight's formal to be special for you, too."

Julia's eyes flooded with tears, though she tried to stop them. Zeke couldn't possibly have known.

Looking down at the corsage on her wrist, she almost felt as if she hadn't missed her senior prom because her father had walked out with all their money all those years ago.

Julia's heart slammed into her chest, and she was certain everyone could see the way she labored to breathe. Who had taken all the oxygen from the room and not told her about it?

And she didn't even want to think about the way her face must be flushing as red as a rose.

Her eyes sought Zeke's, but her mortification only increased as he smiled back at her, his gaze taking in the blush on her cheeks and, she suspected, the thoughts of her heart.

Feelings coursed through her—happiness, wistfulness, and most of all, joy. Because of her upbringing, she wasn't a hugging kind of person by nature, but she had her arms around Zeke faster than a person could say *senior prom.*

For a moment, Zeke stood stiff and still in her embrace, and she was concerned she'd overplayed the moment. But before she could step back and apologize, he wrapped her in his arms and squeezed her tight, swinging her gently around in a circle and lifting her completely off her feet. She realized belatedly that he was laughing.

"Thank you," she said again as he set her down. "You've made my night."

He winked and then spun away, bellowing something about getting the tables set and ready. Julia's heart was still beating double time in her chest, but she valiantly attempted to school her thoughts, placing an open palm over her heart and breathing deeply.

Lakeisha, coming up behind her, gave a low whistle. "Have you got an admirer, or what?"

"The corsage is lovely," Julia agreed.

"No, girl, I was talking about the *man*. Mmm, baby."

"Lakeisha!" Julia cracked up. "I can't believe you sometimes."

"Don't you go saying you weren't thinking the same thing, because I won't believe you."

She knew what Lakeisha was trying to do—make light of the situation so Julia wouldn't obsess over it all night. Which is exactly what she was prone to do, she realized.

Some things were better off left as they were, and Zeke's wonderful gift was one of them.

Thank heaven for understanding roommates, Julia thought, charging into gear. Within the hour, she'd put up decorations, laid elegant white tablecloths on the tables, folded cloth napkins around the silverware, and polished the glasses until they sparkled.

As she worked, she made a concerted effort not to look at Zeke. Even an eyeful of him would be too much, sending her heart to fluttering again.

Father Bryan arrived, immediately taking center

stage as he began ordering the others around, telling them what to do without consulting anyone about anything.

And he wasn't even in a tuxedo.

Apparently, he hadn't seen fit to dress like the rest of them. He was in his usual pastoral attire, khaki slacks and a blue pinstriped clerical shirt and white collar. He was wearing a black sport coat, but Julia was still annoyed.

Her gaze slid to Zeke, who was seating the pregnant ladies one by one, showering each with attention until they beamed with delight. What a contrast.

She wasn't the least attracted to Bryan, she realized. But that was the point, wasn't it? That her head was making the decision and not her heart?

"The Lord be with you," announced Father Bryan loudly. Everyone immediately stopped talking and all eyes were on him.

"And also with you," came the immediate response from the people.

"Let us pray."

Bryan certainly had a take-charge attitude, Julia thought. He was so firm and sure of himself. And he was always the first to assume the lead. That was something to admire, wasn't it?

Maybe, but it had no effect on Julia, she realized as the prayer ended and they began serving.

"Come on, Julia. These gals are hungry, and I understand why!" Evy Martin laid a hand on her shoulder. Julia stifled a laugh. Evy really did look like a penguin dressed in black and white, with her eight-months-pregnant stomach and waddling gait a dead ringer for the bird.

Julia twisted her lips into a half smile, knowing her gleaming eyes gave her away. She and Evy shared a laugh and a hug before heading for the kitchen.

It wasn't often Julia had the opportunity to spend direct time with the center's pregnant women. Advertising was a background occupation. She'd been looking forward to this dinner for weeks, in order to meet and mingle with the women she served in Christ's name, and to give them a special time of their own.

Zeke lumbered past with a comic grin on his face, and bearing a plate of appetizers like a master waiter. Julia's heart skipped, and she sighed inwardly. She couldn't figure it out. And it was time to put an end to it.

Her future was with a man who served the Lord full-time, someone she could join in ministry, helping others, so their children could see what was truly important in life.

She wanted someone able to support his children—not rich, necessarily, but what could Zeke give his children on a carpenter's salary? Julia wanted—*needed*—to give her children all the many things she never had as a child.

Father Bryan was going to be a famous evangelist. Her future, and her children's, would be sealed. But it was becoming increasingly difficult to convince even herself of the merits of her Great Scheme anymore.

She was pondering her dilemma as she slipped into the kitchen, preparing to take the first course out to the women.

Someone picked up a platter and handed it to her. She looked up, vaguely, hazily seeing the stained white apron and puffy white chef's hat as if she were in a dream.

She tried to drag in a breath and couldn't, and thought she might gag with the struggle. The world began turning and spinning at an alarming rate.

The tray clattered to the floor, chips and dip splattering on the tile around her feet.

She had to breathe, had to speak.

She closed her eyes and labored with the effort to inhale. Finally, gradually, she found her voice, albeit a shaky one.

"Who let *him* in here?"

Zeke saw Julia's face go white, saw her point shakily at the white-bedecked chef behind the counter, and rushed to her side. Something was clearly wrong, but though he continued to take in clues to this strange scene—Julia's hyperventilation and shaky grasp—he was at a loss.

Even more baffling was the chef's odd reaction.

He narrowed his eyes and pinched his lips in a cold, hard line, almost as if he were *expecting* the reaction he'd so surprisingly provoked.

A moment later he proved Zeke's theory, unwrapping his apron in a series of irritated yanks and hurling it down on the countertop with a disgusted grunt. Without a word of explanation, he whirled and stalked out of the kitchen, obviously troubled.

The explanation to all this was probably a doozy. And he had the most peculiar notion this was somehow his fault.

He wrapped Julia in his arms to shield her from the sight of the chef leaving. The poor woman looked as if she'd seen a ghost.

But why?

The "chef" wasn't really a chef, of course any more than Zeke was a Tuxedo-clad waiter. He was simply Greg, the new janitor at Grace Church. Everybody helped out on these dinner nights. Seeing an unfamiliar face—or even the new janitor at Grace Church shouldn't have bothered her.

Unless she knew him.

"Julia," Zeke said softly, crouching next to her. "What happened, sweetheart? What's wrong?"

Julia propped her elbows on her knees and buried her face in her hands. "I'm so embarrassed."

At least, that's what Zeke thought she said. Her voice was muffled from her palms.

Lakeisha rubbed Julia's back soothingly. "It's

okay, hon. No one even noticed except Zeke and me. Just catch your breath, okay?"

No one noticed, Zeke thought gravely.

No one except that new janitor.

The more he thought about it, the more he thought there was something fishy going on. And though he wanted to protect Julia from hurt and pain at all costs, he had to get to the bottom of this mystery.

"Who was he?" he asked earnestly, his voice clouded with emotion.

Lakeisha glared at him. *Not now,* she mouthed before turning her attention back to Julia.

Zeke wanted to turn and walk away. But something, perhaps Someone, compelled him to stay and see the end of this.

Especially because this was *his fault.*

He'd been the one to invite the janitor to participate in the evening's festivities. *He'd* been the one to insist he play the part of a chef, giving him the opportunity to mingle with the staff at HeartBeat and maybe get to know them better. He thought he'd been doing a favor to a lonely old man.

He didn't know much about the fellow, but he knew Grace Church and the HeartBeat Center did background checks on everyone before hiring them. So Greg, whose last name he didn't know, wasn't a convicted felon, anyway.

It was a small comfort.

And then the realization of his error hit him,

slammed him like a two-by-four to the head so hard he could almost hear the sharp crack.

He was seeing stars.

He was seeing the truth.

Greg the janitor was…

"He's your father, isn't he?"

Chapter Six

Julia nodded miserably.

Zeke knelt before her, taking her hands in his. It was an earnest gesture, as he struggled to find words and none came.

"I'm sorry. I didn't know." His voice, low and husky, cracked with the effort of speaking.

Julia's gaze snapped to his, probing into his heart. Surprise and anger gleamed in her green eyes, but not the condemnation he expected and thought he deserved.

"Didn't know what?" Lakeisha demanded, planting her hands on her hips and giving her hair a saucy flick. "What's going on, here? Start talking, brother, 'cause I want answers."

Zeke cringed. "This is all my fault."

Julia swept in an audible breath. "Don't say that." Her voice was harsh and grinding.

Zeke scowled. "Why not? It's the truth. I was the one who invited him here tonight."

"Ha!" Julia looked as appalled as she sounded. "That's what *he* would want you to think. He manipulated you into this."

Zeke shook his head, adamantly refusing to believe he'd been duped. "No, this was *my* fault. I was the one who asked him to come here tonight, and I take full responsibility for that. I should have at least asked him for his full name."

"He's a coldhearted con artist," Julia insisted.

She looked better now, Zeke noticed. Color had returned to her face, an attractive pink shade of angry. And she wasn't shaking anymore.

"Oh, girl, he sure is bad," Lakeisha agreed. "What do you think he was trying to pull, showing up here tonight like this?"

Julia made an unladylike snort. "To do exactly what he did. Shake me up. Let me know he's here and waiting for me."

Zeke frowned. Julia had insisted her father was no threat to her, but he'd certainly shaken her up, if that was his intention. Again he wondered at the relationship between janitor Greg Evans and his daughter.

Julia, however, was moving beyond those thoughts and into action. Her father was not going to get the best of her. Not tonight, and not ever.

With a breath for courage, she stood on shaky legs

and moved back to the counter, taking a fresh tray of garden salads into her hands.

Zeke stopped her with an arm on her shoulder. "Why don't you take the night off, Julia. Go home, put your feet up, and relax. Everything will be all right here without you."

Julia jerked away from his touch. "Why don't you mind your own business?"

She knew she sounded harsh, but at the moment, she couldn't deal with her feelings about her father and Zeke, too; especially when he wanted to play the part of the scoundrel. Which he was not, of course, but she didn't feel like arguing over it with him right now.

Zeke looked hurt for a moment, but not offended. Only as if he expected that was the best he was going to get. He took his hand away and backed off, and that was what she wanted, wasn't it? She'd apologize and straighten things out in the morning.

In the meantime, she was desperate to find something to take her mind off her father. She was determined to persevere with the evening, no matter how she felt inside.

Avoiding Zeke's eyes, she began serving salads, stopping to chat with each of the women she served. It quickly helped her remember her problems weren't monumental in the big scheme of things.

Pouring herself into helping others worked for a

while, but ultimately it was Father Bryan who rescued her from Zeke's dogged shadow.

Father Bryan didn't serve, but had settled himself at a table with his Bible, ostensibly so he could mingle with the women. Indeed, many of the women whom he counseled spent a moment or two speaking with him, but when Julia approached, he was all alone.

He offered her a seat with a casual wave of his hand. His other hand rested softly on his Bible, his fingers lightly tapping the worn leather.

Gratefully, she accepted the chance to get off her feet for a moment. She tossed a glance over her shoulder to where Zeke stood, a dessert tray in his muscular arms. His mouth shifted to a frown as their eyes met.

He quickly looked away, sculpting his frown into a kind smile as he engaged a woman in conversation, and Julia breathed a sigh of relief.

She found it surprisingly easy to talk to Bryan, for a change. He immediately turned the conversation to spiritual things, as she knew he would, but this time it didn't vex her. At least not much.

Right now, she needed someone to listen, and Julia immediately plunged in, sharing her hopes and dreams—her ideals—with Bryan. He was a good listener, making eye contact and nodding his head at appropriate intervals. The passionate gleam of his own goals glittered in his brown eyes, mirroring Julia's green ones.

This was, she realized with a backward sort of pleasure, the well-rehearsed conversation of her Great Scheme, the one where Father Bryan would not only notice her, but realize her immense capacity to serve as a pastor's wife.

This was the conversation that would set the ball rolling so that she and her children would absolutely never end up with a man like her deadbeat, lowlife of a father.

"It's nice to talk to a woman who knows her theology," said Bryan, his fine black hair flopping over his eyes as he leaned toward her. "I didn't know you were so interested in the Lord's work."

Deciding not to take offense in his choice of words about the female gender, she nodded, her fervency burning in her eyes. "I can't think of anything I want more."

"Yes," he said slowly, drawing out the word. "I can see that." A half smile hovered on his lips.

Again, Julia refused to acknowledge the slightly flippant tone to his voice, preferring to think it was unintentional on Bryan's part. "Ministering to other people is my passion, Bryan. I know an advertising executive isn't exactly on the front lines, but I'm trying to use what God gave me to help others."

A thoughtful look clouded his eyes. "You know, Julia, you're really quite a remarkable woman."

Julia buzzed with excitement. Father Bryan's intense look created no rise of emotion, but his words about the ministry did.

Busy, boisterous chatter accompanied the comfortable, satisfied guests, and the HeartBeat staff who had now, for the most part, joined the women at the tables.

Zeke, Julia immediately noticed, was not in the room at all. Neither was Lakeisha, for that matter. Probably chasing after her father, if she knew the two of them well.

Julia refused to acknowledge that it bothered her. It didn't. She simply wouldn't think about it. She was here now, accomplishing her goals, just as she'd dreamed, and no one could stop her. It was just as well Zeke Taylor had fled the scene. And good riddance.

Forcing her thoughts away from the strong, annoying man, she turned back to Bryan with the brightest smile she could muster. There was an ear-splitting bark of laughter from one of the tables, but for Julia, the cacophony of voices was nothing more than background mist.

This was her moment, she reminded herself, her adrenaline surging until her ears thundered with it. *The moment.*

Wordlessly, Julia reached for Bryan with her gaze, trying to communicate the depth of her commitment to the Lord's work. Working by his side, they could accomplish so much. Surely he could see it.

But his eyes didn't flicker in response as she'd hoped they would. She focused hopefully on his significant smile.

Bryan cleared his throat, as he often did when preparing to make a speech. He flipped his hair out of his eyes and gripped the pliable leather of his Bible, his knuckles whitening under the pressure. "Julia, I—"

The room broke out in laughter, utterly destroying the delicate, fragile bond she'd forged with Bryan. His hand snapped off the Bible and back into his lap, where he threaded his long, finely boned fingers together tightly.

It was not a nervous action. The crease in his dark brow as he looked toward the center of the room indicated his exasperation more powerfully than words could have done.

Julia turned to see what everyone was laughing at. Zeke had Tip in the middle of the room. She was out of her cast, and dressed in a dog-size tuxedo, complete with a top hat.

While the others watched, Zeke instructed the dog to do various tricks, everything from rolling over to playing dead, much to the delight of the audience. She even stood up on two legs and danced with Zeke.

The scene was so incongruous, and so heartwarming, that Julia naturally found herself laughing along with the others. She wouldn't acknowledge the annoyance she nursed at being interrupted, knowing it was beneath her to do so.

But after the show, as soon as Zeke put Tip back in his truck, he made a beeline for the table where Julia and Bryan sat.

He grinned, yanked his tie loose, clasped his hands behind his head, and put his feet on the table, crossing his legs and tipping the chair a good three inches off the floor.

Despite herself, Julia relaxed, feeling a definite sense of security when she was with him.

Immediately, alarms sounded in her head. She couldn't forget her Great Scheme. Bryan was sitting right here. Bryan didn't set off alarms.

She couldn't end up as her mother had been. Alone.

Zeke wasn't her father, she reminded herself. But she couldn't shake the fear. For all the good things Zeke was, he was also a blue-collar worker, and would remain so. He would have to struggle to make ends meet all his life.

It sounded selfish, and maybe it was. But she was thinking of the children she wanted to have. Children who would have a better life than Julia had as a child. They would never know what it was like to be deprived of life, though surely with Zeke, they would have love.

And still the fear persisted.

"How are you feeling?" Zeke asked quietly, sliding a glance at Bryan. "Everything okay?"

She pasted on her best smile, but it felt counterfeit, and by the look on Zeke's face, it must have shown. Nevertheless, she assured him she was fine.

Just fine.

Suddenly Thomas ran from the kitchen, a stricken look on his face. He studied the room, and then rushed toward Julia.

She was on her feet, moving toward him with Zeke right behind her, before Thomas reached the table.

"What happened?" she asked hastily.

"It's Evy. Please—come." He was breathing hard and his eyes were wide with panic. "She fell."

Julia didn't ask any more questions. She quietly followed Thomas into the kitchen, not discouraging Zeke when he slipped his large, comforting hand into hers and laced their fingers together.

Evy was on the floor, crouching against a counter and grasping her stomach with both hands.

Slipping her hand out of Zeke's, Julia knelt next to her and put a hand on her shoulder. "Evy, I need you to tell me what's happening. What are you feeling?" She kept her voice low, even and confident— she hoped.

Evy needed her now. She had to be strong.

Zeke, standing just behind Julia, jammed his

hands in his pockets, feeling powerless to help. What could he do for a pregnant woman in distress?

He admired Julia for her strength and courage. He doubted she knew much more than he did about pregnancy, but she was trooping along, taking control of the situation and comforting Evy in the process.

Evy leaned toward Julia's ear, but Zeke still heard what she said. "I'm bleeding. Bad. I was reaching for something in the cupboard, and I—"

"Okay." Julia took her by both arms, silently demanding her attention. "You're going to be all right, Evy. Do you hear me? Jesus is with you *right now.*"

She nodded, wrenching in pain as she did so.

"Has Thomas called for an ambulance?"

"I—" Evy began, then stopped as a contraction overtook her. "I don't know."

Thomas, bouncing on his heels, jammed his fingers through his thick brown hair. "I didn't—uh, I'll go right now."

"Stay with your wife, Thomas," Zeke interjected, already moving toward the door. "I'll make the call."

It felt good to have something useful to do. He trod heavily toward the hallway where the nearest phone was located. In moments, he'd made the call and was back in the kitchen with Evy. And Julia.

Evy looked worse than when he'd left her, but there was nothing he could do until the paramedics arrived.

Nothing he could do. Except pray.

* * *

Julia stood outside the church, barely even noticing the crisp, cool foothill wind brushing the back of her neck. She'd wanted to follow the ambulance to the hospital right away, but there were many details she had to attend to first. They couldn't just leave the women alone at the church without a by-your-leave. Excuses had to be made, at the very least.

So she'd wrapped things up as quickly as possible, explaining as best she could what had happened to Evy, trying not to scare the women. Evy's baby wasn't due for eight weeks yet.

She felt rather than saw Zeke come up behind her. Without a word, he placed his hands over her shoulders and rubbed lightly, kneading the knots of tension from her taut muscles.

His tender touch was exactly the encouragement she needed. With a muddled cry, she whirled into his embrace, wrapping her arms around his deep chest and clinging to him as if anchoring herself to him.

"Poor Evy," she said, her words muffled by his shirt, which he now wore untucked. His bow tie was long gone, and his shirt wide-open at the neck, tufts of curly blond chest hair peeking from the top. It was the Zeke she knew, and she rejoiced in the woodsy, manly smell of him. His nearness—his strength—gave her comfort, and that was enough for now.

A small group of HeartBeat staff gathered on the sidewalk. They appeared to be looking to Julia. She extricated herself from Zeke's embrace and gathered the group together.

"Evy's baby is coming too early. Apparently, she was reaching for something and fell over. The stress of the impact brought her labor on. The doctors are saying that the baby is coming tonight."

"Shall we gather together and pray for Evy and the baby?"

Julia might have expected Father Bryan to suggest such a thing, but it wasn't Bryan's voice.

It was Zeke's.

With little commotion and less ceremony, Zeke pulled the group together into a small circle and reached for Julia's hand.

It was quiet for a moment after a chorus of *amens,* and then Julia broke the silence. "We need to organize how we're going down to the hospital. There's no telling how long this baby will take to come. Maybe there is something we can do for the Martins. I don't know."

Everyone burst into speech at once. It was quickly decided that they would all go down to the hospital and do what they could for the Martins.

Zeke offered to drive, though he only had three seats, and his proposal was quickly taken by a young couple who worked in counseling at HeartBeat.

Julia wished she could go with him, but knew there was hardly room in the cab of his truck for three adults, never mind four.

She flashed Zeke a grateful smile, and he nodded in response. His big blue eyes were shining with compassion, and Julia swept in a breath.

She was left to ride with Bryan, along with a young woman named Sarah and her six-year-old son, Troy. She supposed she should be pleased to have the chance to spend more time with Bryan, but she felt dubious and troubled instead.

The moment Julia was settled into the front seat of Bryan's sedan, Sarah, sitting in the back seat with her son, burst into tears, sounding almost hysterical.

"How can I help you?" Julia asked softly, turning in her seat.

"Troy was early," she explained haltingly. "I really know what Evy is going through. I didn't know if Troy was going to live. I was terrified beyond belief. He was so small—only four pounds."

Julia reached back to where Sarah sat hunched over her seat and grasped her hand tightly.

"Sarah, how did you get to Grace Church tonight? Did you drive?" Bryan's high, melodic voice was firm and reassuring. Julia took comfort in it, and hoped Sarah could do the same.

"I took a bus. I don't have a car of my own right now." Sarah wiped her eyes with the tissue Julia offered.

Bryan nodded. "I think I'd better drop you and Troy off at your house now. Is that okay with you?"

Sarah nodded miserably and gave him her address. "I want to be there for Evy, I really do. But I know it would be too hard on Troy to be at the hospital for an extended period of time. It's already past his bedtime."

She stopped and sniffled. "I'd really like to be there for Evy, though," she repeated.

"You can pray," Julia said gently. "God can do more for Evy than any of us can."

It took a few minutes to reach Sarah's house. Sarah and Troy waved goodbye, and Julia promised to call and keep her updated.

"Well, I guess it's just the two of us, then," Bryan said amiably, pulling the car onto the freeway.

Julia started as if a sheer bolt of electricity had run through her. Even her hair tingled, a prelude to her suddenly exaggerated senses. Her stomach turned in waves that approximated nausea.

She glanced in Bryan's direction, not nearly as taken by his dark, eaglelike profile as she thought she might have been. Perhaps *ought* to have been. But she would consider that later.

She was alone with Bryan.

Evy and her baby lay heavy on her heart, but she thought to remind Bryan of what he'd been about to say to her earlier—to pick up the trailing end of their interrupted conversation.

She felt distinctly uncomfortable, and shifted in her seat. It seemed almost criminal for her to be concerned with her own problems at this time. Guilt assuaged her, and she readily accepted the thorny feeling as well deserved.

"What should we do when we get to the hospital?" Julia asked, striving for a way to make conversation, and saying what was foremost on her mind.

"Depends." Bryan neatly pulled the car onto the off-ramp.

Julia could see the hospital lights, and her stomach knotted uncomfortably. "I wonder how everyone is doing?"

"Zeke will probably be able to give us a status report."

Yes, Julia thought. Zeke would have things well in control. Big, strong and compassionate. He was a natural leader whether he recognized it or not. She hadn't recognized his potential until this very evening. She wondered if he even knew the gift he possessed.

Chapter Seven

Julia couldn't shake the shadowy feelings that settled over her as she prayed silently for Evy's premature baby.

Several members of the HeartBeat staff hovered; some speaking together in low voices.

Zeke was pacing back and forth in the labor and delivery lounge, looking every bit as anxious as a new father. He stopped pacing and turned to them as Bryan and Julia approached.

"I'm glad you're here." He combed his fingers through his thick blond hair apprehensively. His face was grim.

"They had to take the baby by C-section," he said without preamble. "Evy is recovering now, but the baby…"

His voice cracked, and he stopped talking.

Without thinking, Julia dropped Bryan's hand and bulldozed Zeke, burying her head in his chest.

"Is he dead?" she whispered, her heart aching with pain for her friends and the dear, sweet baby who'd come into the world a bit too early.

Zeke kept his arm around her, but stepped back and tipped her chin up to face him. His eyes were wide with alarm. "I'm sorry, Julia."

She squeezed her eyes closed against the bad news, but tears leaked out despite her efforts.

At the sight of her tears, Zeke's heart hit the ground. Once again he'd flubbed up his words and hurt someone.

Not just someone. Julia.

He grit his teeth for a moment, trying to find the words to right the wrong he'd done. Words were not his tools of choice, and he floundered helplessly.

"No, Julia. Please don't cry. I did a lousy job of explaining things. It isn't like you think." Zeke's apology was low and coarse, but strong enough to give him the satisfaction of seeing light come back into her beautiful green eyes.

He shrugged sheepishly. "The baby's not dead. Why don't you take a seat, and I'll try to explain what's going on."

Julia nodded mutely and took the seat Zeke offered. He crouched before her, wanting to be on the same level, face-to-face with her as they spoke.

"The baby's not a he, she's a she," Zeke began.

"A little girl?" Tears lined her voice again, and Zeke cringed, wondering if he put them there.

He nodded, focusing all he felt in his heart into his gaze. "She's going to be okay. But she's going to be in the hospital for a while until she gains some weight. I guess her lungs aren't fully developed yet, so she's hooked up to some machines. I'm warning you now—it looks a lot worse than it is."

He took a deep breath. "Do you want to see her?"

"Can we?" Julia exclaimed.

"Take us to her immediately." Bryan apparently didn't realize Zeke's question had been addressed to Julia. But there was no help for it.

"Right this way," he said evenly, allowing Bryan's terse words to slide away unchallenged. With a comforting arm around Julia's shoulders, he led her to the window of the intensive care nursery, and let demanding Father Bryan follow them as he willed.

He moved them along at a crisp pace until they'd reached the intensive care unit for the newborns. Zeke wanted Julia to see Chantelle as soon as possible.

Through the window, they watched a tiny, three-pound infant fighting for the right to live. It was a heart-wrenching scene, and it choked him up even now, the second time he'd peered intently through the glass to see the blessed child.

He shot a look at Julia to see how she was handling things. She hadn't said a word, but he knew from watching her that her emotions ran deep. This emotional situation couldn't help but affect her.

Julia's heart had, indeed, instantly gone out to the baby girl. Unlike the typical infant nursery where the babies lay comfortably swaddled under warm lights, this baby was surrounded by an oxygen tent, and was attached by wires and tubes to several blinking monitors. IV tubes extended from the veins near the temples on her tiny head.

"What's her name?" Julia whispered.

"Chantelle Evelyn Martin," Zeke whispered back, though the glass was soundproof. "Isn't she beautiful?"

"I don't know about *beautiful*," said Bryan doubtfully, shaking his head.

Zeke threw Bryan the surprised look Julia was feeling. Then he glanced her way, and their eyes met and held, sharing their exasperation without needing to speak a word.

There was no need for words, Julia realized. She connected with Zeke on a deeper level. He always seemed to understand what she was thinking.

And at the moment, she, like Zeke, was questioning Bryan's sanity. What an awful thing for Bryan to say, especially at a moment like this.

"Well, she isn't beautiful," Bryan replied defensively when he saw their combined looks. "Certainly not in the typical sense of the word. She looks like a wizened old man, or an elf, or something."

Julia met Zeke's gaze again, and he winked.

"It's only my opinion," Bryan continued. "The

Bible says children are God's blessing, so I expect her parents think she's pretty special."

"I expect so," Zeke agreed. "That's where the rubber meets the road."

Bryan shook his head. "Where do you get your metaphors, Zeke? At the five-and-dime store?"

Zeke clenched his jaw and looked away.

"There's nothing more special in this whole world than new life," Julia murmured, ignoring the men's repartee in favor of the tiny, struggling infant.

"Umph," said Bryan. It was unclear whether or not his response was an agreement. "What I need to know is what room Evy is in." He thumped on his Bible for emphasis. "Can't do anything for the baby."

And there, thought Julia, was truly where the rubber met the road. Bryan wanted to minister, and he couldn't help little Chantelle. That was why he was so edgy, perhaps.

"Evy was in the recovery room when I last checked. We'll be able to see them as soon as the doctors give her a room. Maybe even now."

Zeke put a hand on Julia's shoulder, and she marveled once again how gentle the giant of a man could be. His heart was in his touch.

"Would you like to stay here with the baby for a little longer?" he murmured close to her ear.

Julia nodded, her heart stretching back to the baby, knowing she *could* do something for little Chantelle.

She could pray.

"No," Bryan barked, almost like an order. "I want her with me."

Zeke shot a startled and not altogether friendly glance at Bryan.

"I want her to help me out with Evy, that is. I insist."

"*You* insist?" Zeke parroted.

Julia, as surprised and offset by Bryan's behavior as Zeke was, laid a restraining hand on Zeke's forearm. Bryan certainly wasn't turning out to be the man she'd expected. She sighed inwardly. There was so much to consider. Like Evy. Her first inclination, to stay watching and praying over the tiny infant melted away, replaced by a burning need to see Evy.

I'm only trying to help, she coached herself. It couldn't hurt that Bryan had been the one to ask.

Though Bryan hadn't exactly asked for her help. Ordered would be more like it. But Bryan was no doubt wound up given the circumstances, and she mentally offered him the benefit of the doubt once again. This was, after all, the first opportunity for them to minister together in an emergency.

Zeke wouldn't have acted that way.

As she followed Zeke down the hallway, she studied the back of his broad shoulders and set her jaw in thought. It was difficult not to notice the differences between the two men.

Bryan was slim and dark and handsome in a classical way. He demanded attention, and commanded leadership—with his mouth, if necessary. He knew what he wanted and he went for it, at any cost. He was a man of vision, the kind of guy you just knew would make his dreams come true.

Zeke was twice the size of Bryan, and in his own way was quite intimidating, yet she was certain he would never demand his own way. Though he was clearly a man others would be inclined to follow, he led with a quiet, easy confidence she found easy to respect.

More, she wouldn't admit, not even to herself.

Zeke took a deep breath and tried to calm the inferno raging within him. The way Bryan ordered Julia around was beyond comprehension, not to mention common courtesy.

No doubt it was none of his business, but Zeke couldn't help but want to fix the problem. It was his way to work through crises with action.

Hoping Julia didn't notice, he clenched his fist and vented his frustration with a subtle but effective pumping action. That it was Bryan's neck he was mentally wringing wouldn't go further than his mind.

At least that thought made him smile.

Bryan grabbed Julia's elbow and forged ahead of Zeke. "Let me tell you what I want you to do."

Zeke wondered if the deep crease between Bryan's dark brows was worry or annoyance.

Annoyance, he decided, and then prayed for forgiveness for being petty. Someone had to rise above this situation, and Zeke decided firmly it would be up to him to take on that role. But that didn't stop him from eavesdropping on what Bryan was saying to Julia.

"I'm going to counsel Thomas with the Scriptures." Bryan waved his Bible. "You see if you can do the same for Evy. Shall I give you a list of relevant Bible passages?"

Zeke mentally cringed for her as he watched the struggle mirrored on Julia's face. She had obviously caught the inherent slight in Bryan's words every bit as much as he did. But her expression quickly flitted from irritation to compassion and determination.

"I know the Bible well, Bryan. I'll do what I can for Evy."

"Perfect." Bryan nodded in satisfaction.

Zeke spoke quietly with a nurse at the desk, then led Julia and Bryan to the room where Evy was recovering. He couldn't help but note that Bryan continued to hold Julia's arm, nearly pinching it.

Frowning, he turned his gaze away and focused his thoughts on poor Evy and Thomas. And baby Chantelle. They needed every prayer he could utter, and every good thought he could give them.

Zeke forgot everything the moment he laid eyes

on Evy, and it was evident Julia felt the same way, as she rushed to the bedside and took the woman's hand.

Evy's face was pale and translucent, making her eyes seem huge, disproportionate to the rest of her face. Her usually shiny, immaculate blond hair plastered her forehead from the sweat of her exertion and lay around her shoulders, wet and strawlike. She clenched her hands convulsively, her shoulders hunched and shaking.

It was a terrible scene, any way he looked at it. But what Zeke noticed most of all was the blank stare Evy maintained. It troubled him that he could do nothing more than stand and watch, helpless to be able to bring aid and comfort to her. He shifted from foot to foot, anxious to find something practical to do.

Bryan was already with Thomas, leading him to a seat at the table in the corner of the room. His gaze shifted back to Evy, but clearly it was more appropriate for Julia to be with the inconsolable woman than for him to try to assist her.

Zeke was no doctor who could help Evy. He was no pastor, to offer words of comfort to Thomas.

He was a big, lumbering carpenter with nothing to give.

He crossed his arms and leaned against the nearest wall, not knowing what else he could do and tired of pacing around.

Julia seated herself softly on the bed next to Evy and reached for her hand.

"Evy, it's Julia."

Evy didn't respond, but continued to stare at the ceiling with hopeless, clouded eyes.

"I can't get her to snap out of it," said Thomas, agony lining his voice. "I've tried to tell her the baby is all right, but it's almost as if she can't hear me at all." Thomas, too, looked pale and exhausted.

Bryan caught the attention of the weary husband by slapping his Bible onto the table, patting it lightly as if the Book itself would lend aid. It was clear that would be the extent of Bryan's assistance.

Zeke grunted softly. "It figures."

Not that the Word of God wasn't appropriate right now, but Thomas needed good, old-fashioned human help from God's people, as well. Like Julia was doing with Evy.

He shifted his gaze back to Julia. When their eyes met, Zeke realized there was something he could do here.

He could support Julia.

Her eyes were wide with panic, and she was swallowing convulsively. This was a tough situation, and she was under a lot of pressure to help her friend.

Zeke moved to the sink, filled a bowl with warm water, and removed a bleached white washcloth from the polished chrome rack in the cabinet above.

Silently, he wet the washcloth and handed it to

Julia. Tears of gratitude in her eyes, she took the cloth and gently stroked Evy's forehead, murmuring soothingly all the while, almost as if Evy were a small child.

Evy's shoulders gradually relaxed, and Zeke squeezed Julia's arm in support.

When Evy's eyes weren't quite so wide, Julia leaned forward and took Evy by the shoulders.

"Evy Martin, you listen to me."

Zeke watched in fascination as she forced the woman to meet her gaze, and held it there. "You've got a beautiful daughter down the hall who needs her mommy. Chantelle can't do this alone. She needs you. You've got to be strong for her."

Zeke wanted to interrupt, to stop Julia from what sounded to him like an overly harsh accusation. He trusted Julia's discretion, but perhaps she was too distraught or overtired to think rationally. Weren't gentleness and compassion the proper tools for this situation?

Evy shifted into a semi-sitting position. Stunned by her reaction, Zeke thought he saw light flicker on in her eyes.

Maybe Julia did know what she was doing.

"Evy, I know you can do this," Julia stated, her voice firm and strong. "Reach into your heart and muster your strength. I know you're feeling weak right now, but you know God uses our weaknesses and turns them into strength."

Evy hiccupped once, then threw her arms around Julia's neck and sobbed wildly. Julia held her until she'd finished crying, gently stroking her hair as she would a small child.

Zeke watched, mesmerized, as Julia took the situation into control, with a gentle reserve of strength and love she probably didn't even realize she possessed.

Finally, Evy had worn out her tears, and lay shivering and hiccupping. Thomas joined his wife on the bed, carefully seating himself so he could wrap her in his arms.

Bryan, still seated across the room, looked grave and thoughtful. He leaned back and crossed his arms, making no move to come to Evy's bedside.

"How are you?" Thomas whispered hoarsely, and Zeke found his own throat clogging with emotion.

Evy smiled weakly, but there was a stubborn, life-giving spark in her eyes. "With God's help, we're going to be okay." She hiccupped and swallowed. "All of us."

"God bless us, every one," Zeke quoted hoarsely.

Julia smiled compassionately. "With God's help, Evy, you and Chantelle will make it through just fine."

To Zeke's surprise, she reached up and took his hand, pulling him close to the bedside and giving him a tight squeeze.

"God's help," she repeated. "And your friends' help, as well."

Chapter Eight

Julia woke the next morning with a tremendous headache throbbing just behind her right eye. She was happy for the Martins and baby Chantelle, who were all stable and recuperating nicely.

But socially speaking, last night had been nothing less than an unmitigated disaster.

She stared dolefully at her reflection in the mirror above the bathroom sink, leaning forward to examine the black shadows around her eyes. Yes, it was official.

She looked as bad as she felt.

Bryan had been furious with her for *interrupting his personal time with Thomas.* Never mind that Evy needed Thomas to support her, and that things moved forward rapidly from there.

Did it matter at all to him that Evy was doing much better, and that Chantelle was holding her own?

As if his insult wasn't enough, he'd kept up a

sulky silence the whole drive home. She was beginning to feel Bryan, the man she'd carefully selected to marry based on a specific and rigid set of criteria, was actually nothing more than a spoiled child.

Maybe she'd just picked the wrong pastor. Surely there were others not quite so full of themselves. It figured she'd picked Bryan. He just hadn't been that great at the hospital.

The clear winner in the respect department was Zeke, who'd been calm and strong all night long. And when she'd needed him, he'd been there for her, no questions asked. She had a connection with him, something internal and impossible to explain. But she didn't want to marry him.

Someone thumped several times on the door, and the pain in Julia's head hammered sharply with every knock, swelling like a tidal wave and making her insides dip and sway.

Julia groaned and shuffled back toward the bedroom. Whoever it was would just have to wait. But of course, whoever it was promptly began another round of persistent banging.

"I'm coming, I'm coming," she howled, glaring in the direction of the front door. She tossed on a pair of purple sweatpants and an ripped old blue T-shirt, then moved toward the bathroom, thinking to at least run a brush through her tousled locks before answering the door.

She stomped to the door and swung it open. It

took less than one second for her to realize her day had definitely gone from bad to worse.

Father Bryan stood glaring, arms crossed and feet braced, in the threshold. There was an agonizing moment as his gaze took in her hair and mussed clothes, his face expressionless.

When their eyes met, she realized with horror she was still wearing the remnants of yesterday's mascara. She cringed. She didn't suppose is could get much worse than this.

Bryan didn't smile. His lips slowly turned down at the corners, as if he'd sampled some food that disagreed with him. His overall demeanor suggested someone had gone and ruined his perfectly good day.

Probably her.

She winced, and her face flamed. She brushed her hair down with the flat of her hand, only to feel it *poing* back up to its original points with resolute tenacity.

Just as quickly as it had appeared, her embarrassment faded, her hackles raised with righteous indignation.

What had ever possessed her to consider Father Bryan Cummings as marriage material? He was a conceited snob who only thought of ministry as it benefited his own career, or his ego.

She wanted to shake herself for being so daft as to even consider planning so dire a fate as marrying a man like Bryan. She almost shivered. What had she been thinking?

It was then that she saw Zeke. He stood just behind Bryan, his arms loaded with boxes.

Zeke's blue eyes gleamed with amusement, the corner of his mouth twitching as he struggled to keep his even features composed.

If that man laughs at me, I swear I'm going to scream, Julia thought, once more wallowing in embarrassment, but appreciating the smile his humor brought to her lips. She looked from one man to the other and experienced the fleeting childish desire to stick out her tongue at the both of them.

With that thought in mind, she smiled.

Zeke smiled back at her as if sharing the joke. Bryan continued to scowl.

Under the circumstances, she could only think of one viable alternative.

She closed the door. Hard.

Zeke snickered.

"What are you laughing at?" Bryan barked, turning to face Zeke with a scowl. "I hardly think this is a funny situation."

Zeke divested himself of the boxes he held, squatted down against the opposite wall, pulled his baseball cap low on his forehead and settled in to wait. He'd wait all day for sweet Julia.

In freezing drizzle. Fortunately, the day was partly cloudy and not too unbearably cold.

Zeke ran a hand down the beard on his cheek and tried not to smile. "To have the door slammed in my face by a beautiful woman? I think it's hilarious."

Bryan grunted and shifted from one foot to the other. He didn't say it, but Zeke could see the *you would* in his stance and gaze.

"We didn't call first," Zeke reminded him, though he knew his logic fell on deaf ears.

"What does she expect us to do out here? Just stand here and freeze until she deems to open the door again for us?"

Again, Zeke couldn't help but laugh. "Pretty much."

Bryan grumbled under his breath and leaned his shoulder against the door.

Five minutes later, Julia opened the door, welcoming them in with a singsong voice.

Bryan, who'd leaned his full weight against the door, catapulted into the room, stopping just short of a somersault on the living room floor.

Zeke yawned and stretched, giving the impression of a man ready to nod off to sleep. But when Julia approached, he smiled and extended his hand. "Help me up?"

"As if I could," she said, laughing, but she reached for his hand. He pulled himself up, giving her hand a quick squeeze before releasing it.

Their eyes met and held. Zeke's mouth went dry and he couldn't swallow. He cleared his throat. "I'll just get these boxes. Will you hold the door?"

He was aware of her watching as he carefully and single-handedly balanced three large boxes in his arms, praying they wouldn't tip over and make a fool of him. The boxes were loaded to the brim, and he sure didn't want to crash and burn in front of Julia.

Bryan didn't offer to help, of course, except for directing Zeke to put the boxes in the kitchen. Zeke didn't take offense—it wasn't worth the mental energy to bother.

Julia cornered him as he stacked the boxes neatly on the kitchen counter. "Okay, guys, what's this all about? Or am I supposed to guess?"

"Where's Lakeisha?" Bryan asked, ignoring Julia's question. He peered down the hallway curiously. "Is she still sleeping?"

"Lakeisha?" Julia repeated. "She is still sound asleep. We won't see her until noon at the least."

Zeke chuckled. "A night owl, huh?"

"Classic case. I think she was up until after 2:00 a.m. reading."

"Well, that complicates things," Bryan said, sounding annoyed. Which he probably was, Zeke thought. Every little thing bothered the man, if it was out of his control.

"Bryan, the ladies had no way of knowing we were coming," Zeke reminded him in a stage whisper.

He flashed Julia an apologetic smile. "Bryan and I were trying to think up some practical ways we could help the Martins. We thought you and Lakeisha could help us brainstorm." He waggled his eyebrows. "Give us a female viewpoint, you know?"

Julia chuckled. She was still unsettled about the men's unannounced appearance at her door, not to mention being disconcerted by the casual, all-male way Zeke leaned on the kitchen counter, looking adorable with his ruffled hair and sleek beard. He looked as if he belonged there, in her kitchen, every bit as comfortable as her salt and pepper shakers and the cookie jar.

Only infinitely more dangerous.

"I'm free today to help you, but I can't speak for Lakeisha, since I don't know if she's made plans for the day."

She peered through the hand hole of the nearest box. "What's in here?"

Zeke lifted the lid on the first box, which was heavily laden with food—a bag of flour, one of sugar and a box of biscuit mix. The second box contained milk, eggs, bread, meat and other perishables. The third box wasn't covered, and contained laundry soap, disinfectant and a whole host of cleaning supplies.

"We wanted you ladies to see what we'd acquired, so you could give us advice on what you still needed."

Bryan took a seat at the head of the table and threaded his fingers together. "Seeing as I'm the minister here, I'll be in charge of this operation," he proclaimed out of nowhere.

"What operation?" asked Julia, confused.

"Operation Baby Chantelle, of course," said Zeke with a chuckle.

Julia grinned at him as the idea sank in.

"Could we please be serious here?" Bryan exclaimed, his melodic tenor sounding stilted, as if he were clenching his teeth.

"Sorry," said Zeke, looking adorably repentant as he slid a wink at Julia.

"We're on our way to the Martins'. We thought we could cook and clean or…something," Bryan finished slowly.

"Do either of you men know how to cook?" Julia queried.

"Well, no, of course not," said Bryan. "That's why you and Lakeisha have to come with us."

"Speak for yourself," howled Zeke, sounding genuinely offended. He pulled himself up to his full well over six-foot height and pulled on the collar of his blue-plaid flannel like a man preparing to give a speech. "I'll have you know that I'm an outstanding gourmet cook. Though we probably won't be cooking any gourmet meals today."

"It's a good thing you can cook, Mr. Gourmet," said Julia with a laugh, "because I can't boil water."

"You...can't?" She wished Bryan didn't sound quite so flabbergasted. It wasn't the Dark Ages, for crying out loud. Hadn't he ever heard of *take-out?*

"I'm a firm believer in fast food and the supermarket deli section, if you must know," she explained reluctantly.

Bryan shook his head, as if he couldn't believe her words. "Well, cook or no cook, we're planning to meet at the Martins' house this afternoon. We want you and Lakeisha to join us." He sounded as if the issue with Lakeisha were settled, if not to his satisfaction, then at least as best as possible.

"Again, I can't speak for Lakeisha, but I'll be there." Julia paused and swept her hair back with her hand. "Any updates on Chantelle?"

Zeke nodded. "I called the hospital this morning. She appears to be holding her own. But we need to keep praying."

"I'm glad you thought to include me in your mercy mission," she said softly, catching Zeke's eye. She knew this operation wasn't the brainchild of Father Bryan, no matter how he scowled at being left out.

She smiled, trying to include a sulky Bryan in the gesture, but her gaze continued to be locked with Zeke's. Completely unnerved, she strove to continue her dialogue. "It helps to have something constructive to do."

"Yes, it does," Zeke agreed with a smile that was for her alone. It made her toes curl.

"I guess I can pack up these boxes, then, since you can't help me with recipes." He winked at Julia before replacing the covers on the boxes and bundling them into his arms. "See you this afternoon."

Julia's breath caught. "Of course."

It was like a huge, blaring signpost that Bryan didn't offer to help Zeke carry anything. He merely tucked his ever present Bible underneath his arm and waved a hand at Julia. Zeke might have been a burro, for all the attention Bryan paid him.

Julia bristled. She tried to play the good hostess and smile, but knew that with Bryan it was more like a grimace. She had a lot of thinking to do, where Father Bryan was concerned. But right now, she just wanted everyone out of the apartment so she could have some room to reflect on recent circumstances.

"Until this afternoon, then," she said cordially, then shut the door and leaned against it with a sigh.

She hoped Lakeisha would decide to come with her. She didn't know if she could spend an entire afternoon in the company of Zeke and Bryan without going completely crazy.

As if thinking about her had wakened her, Lakeisha appeared in the kitchen, yawning and rubbing her eyes. She took a good look at Julia and chuckled.

"And I thought I had a late night." Lakeisha

flopped onto the sofa and stretched. "Who was that at the door?"

"Would you believe it was Father Bryan and Zeke Taylor? They wanted to enlist our help cleaning and cooking for the Martins this afternoon."

"Ha," Lakeisha snorted. "They obviously don't know of your considerable talent in the culinary field."

Julia sniffed and stuck her nose in the air. "I informed them of my...deficiencies. And they want me anyway."

Lakeisha raised her eyebrows. "I'm sure they do."

Julia blushed. "That's not what I meant and you know it." She flopped down in the armchair across from the couch, tucking one knee up under her. "You may be interested to hear I have officially given up on the Great Scheme."

That got Lakeisha's attention. "Yeah? I'm ecstatic. You've finally come to your senses."

Julia shook her head. "It's simply that I've decided Bryan and I are...incompatible."

Lakeisha roared with laughter. "Now that's an understatement if I ever heard one."

"So do you want to come with me today, or what?" Julia asked, quickly changing the subject.

"Poor Evy," Lakeisha said. "I'd be glad to have something constructive to do for her."

"Me, too. I always feel like my hands are tied in

these kinds of situations. My heart goes out to them so much, but I can't do anything to ease their pain."

"You said Zeke will be there today?" Lakeisha asked just a touch too brightly. Julia didn't blame her. It was hard to think about Evy's situation.

"Yes. Why?"

Lakeisha gave her a pointed look. "Why do you think?"

"Can we not go there?" Julia asked, irritated.

"Oh, stop being grumpy," Lakeisha replied lightly. "Do you like him, or don't you?"

It certainly didn't take any effort to conjure up his handsome face. "He's okay," she agreed reluctantly. Julia studied her cuticles in order to avoid meeting Lakeisha's eyes.

"Better or worse than chopped liver?"

"Oh Lakeisha," Julia exclaimed, laughing. "I like Zeke okay. It's just that…"

What? Just what?

"Just?" Lakeisha prompted.

"He's just too much like Daddy—um, like my father." A spark of anger went through her at the thought of her encounter with her father last night, but she pushed it aside.

"Big, brawny, delicious Zeke? Mmm-mmm, girl-friend, not even close. How do you mean, like your *father?*"

"Oh, I don't know," Julia admitted with a sigh. "His job. Mostly. I guess."

"Zeke's a carpenter, for crying out loud," Lakeisha squeaked, sounding exasperated. "How is that anything remotely like a deadbeat dad?"

"He's a blue-collar worker," Julia replied promptly, knowing very well how judgmental and thickheaded her answer sounded. "I can't help the way I feel, Lakeisha. I know it's dumb, but I've always had it in my head to marry a minister. Who better to raise my kids. I don't want my children's lives to turn out like mine did with my blue-collar worker dad. I couldn't live with myself if that happened."

"I can't fault you there, girlfriend," Lakeisha said earnestly. "And I sure won't be the one to throw the first stone."

Julia sighed inwardly. Clearly Bryan wasn't the hoped-for answer to her problems, but now she didn't know if there was an answer. At least with Bryan there'd been a pitiful sense of hope. There were other pastors, she supposed, but right now that sounded like a pretty grim prospect.

All she felt now with regard to plans for her future was a vast, gaping emptiness.

Was that what she had to look forward to? Emptiness?

Without Bryan, she'd probably fall head over heels in love, and get married for all the *right* reasons.

And then die miserably when the love of her life found greener pastures and moved on.

Like her mother died at the uncaring hand of her father.

A feeling—not butterflies, but more like a family of kangaroos—bounced around in her stomach in every which direction.

She couldn't let herself fall in love.

Chapter Nine

It was difficult to understand God's ways sometimes, Zeke thought as he sat straight-backed on the edge of the Martins' couch. He knew it sounded like a cop-out to some, but he believed everything God did was for good. Even the early and traumatic arrival of baby Chantelle was nestled in the hands of a loving God.

It was just that God didn't always explain His motives. Like when a parent said *"Because I said so,"* to an unruly child who didn't know what was really best for himself.

But it was hard to swallow even with faith, and he wondered how Evy and Thomas were coping. He also wondered where Julia and Lakeisha had gone. He shifted uncomfortably and rested his arms on his knees.

He jumped and bounded to the front door when he heard Lakeisha impatiently pounding on it with her fist. "Get out the scrubbers and cleaners—your work crew is here!"

Zeke immediately opened the front door and gestured her in, his heart not settled until his darting gaze landed on Julia and affirmed she was present. "I'm glad you're here," he said sincerely. "I was beginning to think no one was going to show up."

"What, and miss the party?" Julia joked, tugging on the hem of her purple sweatshirt.

"Speaking of which," Lakeisha added, "Where *is* the party?"

Zeke shrugged. "A group of ladies from Heart-Beat came in and whisked through the house with the cleaning stuff. Not that there was much to do. Evy keeps her house spotless."

Julia's face fell. "Oh, then there's nothing left to do to help Evy?"

Zeke ran a hand along her shoulder. "Sure there is. Actually, we get the good stuff—the real practical part of the job that will make a difference for Evy when she gets home."

"Where's Father Bryan?" Lakeisha asked.

Zeke noticed the pointed look she gave Julia, but brushed it off as nothing. He wasn't into the mind-reading business. He grinned wryly. "Bryan decided his talents lent themselves to reading the Scriptures with Evy and Thomas at the hospital."

Lakeisha barked out a laugh. "Now, why am I not

surprised? Scrubbing toilets is just not within Father Bryan's capacity."

Zeke agreed. The Martins needed grunt labor to help them out today. And that, Zeke would bet, were he a betting man, was something Father Bryan Cummings would never condescend to do.

For the first time, it bothered Zeke a little that he *was* the kind of man people called when they needed handiwork done.

And for a brief moment, he admitted, if only to himself, that he was jealous.

Father Bryan was the kind of man Julia would want to spend her life with—a slick, well-dressed young man with a great education and a good future ahead of him.

Zeke couldn't hold a candle to him. Not in looks, for sure. He was nothing but a bumbling giant in dirty work clothes. The only future he could give a woman was love. No fantastic career. No big nest egg for retirement, though he had some money tucked away.

Sweet Julia deserved so much more than he could ever hope to offer.

He frowned and stroked his beard. When had this dream formed, the one where he and Julia could be together? He'd been happy with his life as it was, and hadn't really considered how it might look to a woman. To Julia.

His head was swimming with emotion by the time

he reached Julia, and he didn't know what to do. He wasn't used to experiencing emotion with any particular depth, and certainly nothing in his scope of his experience had ever compared to this. He was a man of action.

But when he was with Julia, he didn't know his head from his toe, a jigsaw from a chain saw, or even which end of the nail to pound. He felt stone stupid and soaringly brilliant all at the same time.

Zeke mentally shook himself back to the present moment and the work ahead of him. "Do you want to flip for chores? Heads I do laundry, tails I cook. What do you think?"

His gaze was aimed at Julia, but Lakeisha quickly broke in. "I think you'd better come up tails, Zeke, or Evy's going to get a week of boxed dinners."

He chuckled. "Okay, then, ladies, let me help you find the washer and dryer."

"Well, that should do it," said Julia, wiping a drop of perspiration off her temple with the corner of her oversize sweatshirt.

The Martins' laundry room was nothing more than a small, drywalled corner without even a single window to shed light. The sixty-watt bulb dangling from the open socket overhead did little to illuminate the humid darkness.

"One load to go, and we're out of here. I never knew folding cloth diapers could be so tedious. Can you imagine having to do this every other day? I can't imagine why Evy chose cloth diapers. I'd have a diaper service, at least." She chuckled.

"I hope Zeke is faring better than we are," Lakeisha said with a groan, muffling a yawn behind her hand. "I, for one, am thoroughly exhausted."

Julia's stomach swirled at the casual mention of Zeke's name. She'd heard him clumping around upstairs and wondered what he was doing. She almost wished she *had* chosen kitchen duty. Diapers were the ultimate in monotony.

Lakeisha yawned again, as if to prove Julia's point. "This day hasn't been so bad," Julia said, voicing her thoughts.

Lakeisha laughed. "You thought it would be bad?"

"Awful," Julia admitted. "Who wants to spend the day cleaning?"

It was for Evy, and she'd thrown herself with a vengeance into washing, drying and folding the huge piles of laundry, and it had helped her work off some of the anger, confusion and other emotions swirling inside her. She felt like a bottle of carbonated soda pop that had been thoroughly shaken and was ready to explode the moment someone twisted the lid.

"Anyone for a hamburger?" called a booming bass down the stairwell.

Julia and Lakeisha took one look at each other and dashed for the stairs, each trying to be the first to reach the kitchen. The one issue the roommates consistently agreed on was food—and hamburgers topped the list for both of them.

"I'm starving," Lakeisha said, reaching the landing first. "It's about time you fed us poor, work-worn souls, you big lug."

"Hey!" Julia exclaimed, pointing to the telltale bags littering the kitchen table. "These hamburgers are take-out!"

Zeke grinned sheepishly and shrugged. "I was tired of cooking."

"Cheater," Lakeisha admonished, reaching for a burger.

"I'm appalled, Zeke. I thought at the very least we were going to have an opportunity to sample your fine gourmet cuisine. Instead, we get take-out. I'm sooo disappointed." Julia ended her sentence on a sigh.

"We should boycott him," Lakeisha suggested. "Eat at a separate table."

Zeke frowned dramatically. "And I thought I was getting you a special treat," he said with a shrug. "Oh, well. I guess I'll just have to drink all these chocolate milkshakes by myself. Seems a shame."

Julia immediately moved to his side, teasingly curling an arm around his waist. He didn't appear to mind.

"Did someone say chocolate milkshakes?" she purred. Stretching on tiptoe, Julia reached to peek into the bag Zeke held, but he only grinned and lifted it higher, above her reach.

"Ah, ah," he teased. "I'm not sure you *deserve* a milkshake."

"Sorry, Lakeisha, but I'm changing allegiances," Julia declared, still reaching for the bag Zeke held teasingly over his head.

"Concede?" he asked in an equally husky tone, his intention clear.

Julia felt her cheeks warm as Zeke pinned her with his gaze. She knew Lakeisha was watching every action, and was no doubt amused by the scene. Zeke stood motionless, the bag over his head like a mistletoe offering, amusement glowing from his eyes.

Her heart hammered, even as her mind told her this was just a ridiculous, flirtatious game and nothing more.

But it didn't feel like a game as she stood on tiptoe, pulling on Zeke's flannel collar to get his face on her level. The sweet, alluring scent of sawdust brushed her nostrils, and she could feel his heart beating under her palm.

Taking a deep breath, she closed her eyes and brushed her lips across the coarse roughness of his cheek just above the line of his beard.

Lakeisha applauded, Zeke chuckled and Julia blushed to the roots of her hair.

"Chocolate milkshake," she reminded the grinning man with his arm still half around her.

"A woman after my own heart," he teased. He lowered the bag and presented each lady with their prize dessert.

"How are things in the world of laundry?" Zeke queried lightly.

"We're never going to get done," Julia groused. "I had no idea one baby could have so many items of clothing. Not to mention diapers."

"I'm finished up here," Zeke said just before he took a bite of his hamburger. "I mean, everything is prepared and most of it is in the oven. I just have to keep track of the time so I can finish baking the other dishes."

Lakeisha's black eyebrows shot up under the line of her wiry bangs. "You're joking, right?"

Zeke's grin was all male, that *man conquers world* look that sent such tremors through Julia's heart. She laughed heartily.

Lakeisha switched her gaze to Julia, and Julia didn't like the gleam she saw in her roommate's eyes. It meant trouble, the kind with a capital *T*.

"What?" she queried softly, knowing she didn't want to know.

"Well, it just occurred to me," Lakeisha said with a light gesture of her hand, "that I have some things I need to do at home. I have some important paperwork I need to finish. And I think I need to clean my room," she added for good measure.

Julia knew full well Lakeisha's room was spotless, as was their whole house. Lakeisha was an obsessive housecleaner. "What are you doing?" she whispered frantically.

Lakeisha winked at her roommate. "You'll see."

Zeke, who'd been unable to comment due to the hamburger he was chewing, swallowed and spoke up. "You know, Lakeisha, since I'm done with the cooking, I can help Julia finish up, and you can go ahead and leave."

Lakeisha's grin amplified by a million watts. "Are you sure? That would be fantastic."

"No problem," Zeke agreed with a nod. "We'll be fine here by ourselves."

She turned her shining gaze on Julia. "That, my dear roommate, is what I was *doing*. Enjoy."

Before Julia could so much as swat at Lakeisha for completely humiliating her, Lakeisha was out the door and revving the engine on her car.

So much had gone on the last few weeks, and so many emotions whirled through her, that she was almost afraid to turn around and face Zeke. He was a good man. She didn't know what to do with him, how to categorize him in her mind and heart.

In short, he frightened her.

But when she turned and her gaze met Zeke's, a dash of hope sprinkled over her. Hope driven by the cool, calm strength and steadfast faith reflected in the pools of his huge blue eyes.

Hope.

She clung to that feeling. With her world going haywire, and her father trying to steal his way back into her life, practically stalking her like a criminal, she needed all the hope she could get.

Chapter Ten

"Did I hear a touch of worry back there, Julia?" Zeke queried gently. He'd moved to stand directly behind her. His breath lightly fanned her hair, and his hands lightly spanned her waist.

She whirled to face him, not sure to be angered or relieved that he had noticed. His gaze met hers in a compassionate, unwavering gaze.

"I guess so," Julia admitted, exhaling sharply. "My father being in town is stressing me out." She hadn't voiced that thought before, and it frightened her. "Not much I can do about it, though."

Zeke stroked her cheek with the backs of his fingers. His hand felt rough against her skin, yet oddly reassuring. She wanted to reach up and press his hand there, holding the moment, but it was only a thought, and one she would never act upon.

"Sometimes it's tough dealing with past feelings and issues, especially with loved ones. With family."

Moving away from her and giving her much needed space, he turned one of the kitchen chairs around and straddled it, resting his chin on his thick forearms.

"You sound as if you speak from experience," Julia said, following his example and seating herself at the table, albeit forward on her chair.

"I do." He didn't elaborate.

Julia was on the verge of asking him what he meant, when they were interrupted by a loud whirring sound, which punctuated itself from time to time with thumps that sounded much like metal on metal.

Their gazes met, and her eyes widened in surprise.

"What do you think?" Zeke asked, his voice low and his lips hiding a smile.

Julia laughed, and they both raced for the stairs, jostling each other in their haste to be the first to the basement.

It was immediately evident that the washing machine was the originator of the terrible sounds. With every turn it knocked from side to side. Smoke and sparks rose from the rear of the machine. Soapy lather spouted in rhythm from the interior and splattered all over the floor, popping up the lid as if the machine had taken on a life of its own.

Julia turned to Zeke, waiting for his response, but he simply stood with his arms crossed over his massive chest, literally gaping at the spewing appliance, his blue eyes shining with amusement.

"Aren't you going to do something?" Julia demanded, grasping a handful of blue flannel on his sleeve and shaking his arm.

"Huh?" It was the first time she'd ever seen him look apprehensive. Stunned, even.

"What is it you want me to do?"

"I don't know! You're the carpenter."

"Precisely," he agreed hastily. "I work with wood. I don't know the first thing about electrical appliances."

"Men!" Julia exclaimed with an aggravated howl. She stomped toward the machine and pulled at the timer handle.

Nothing happened.

She pulled again, and the knob came off in her hand. The machine continued to rumble and sputter, unscathed by her advances.

"Terrific," she protested loudly over the noise of the machine. "Now what?"

She waved the knob at Zeke, almost shaking it at him. "*Do* something!"

His only move was in his expression, as he lifted his eyebrows in question. "What exactly would you suggest?"

"This thing is going to set the house on fire if you don't hurry."

Zeke was amused. So much for the battle of the sexes.

The washing machine was broken. And she expected him to fix it. Never mind that he didn't know anything more than she did about washing machines.

Less, perhaps. He mimicked the tenor of his thoughts, screwing one eye closed and biting on his lower lip in an imitation of Popeye.

The most ironic, hilarious part of the process was that he knew what to do with the machine. He'd known all along.

But he liked to watch Julia with her feathers ruffled. She was adorable. She made his heart catch in his throat.

But she did have a point. The dragonlike, soap-spewing washing machine needed to be conquered, and he, apparently, was the knight errant in shining armor who could perform the noble task.

With one quick sweep, he leaned over, wrapped his hand around the cord, and deftly unplugged the machine from the wall.

Instantly the spewing and flaming ceased, leaving in its wake only the quiet fizz of popping soap bubbles.

"Your dragon is slain, fair lady," he teased.

Julia pinched her lips together, and Zeke thought she might be angry with herself for not having thought of the wall plug. She was definitely a Type

A woman, always needing to be in control of everything.

He'd probably done her a service. Given her the opportunity to see her own inadequacies. He chuckled aloud at the wry thought.

"What are you laughing at?" she demanded, and then pointed at her feet. "Did you happen to notice that our feet are covered in soapy water?

Surprised, Zeke followed the direction of her gesture and suddenly realized they really were standing ankle-deep in soapsuds.

He hadn't even noticed. His work boots kept out the moisture, but surely he should have been aware he was slapping around in the water when he moved.

Julia looked as if she might laugh, scream, or even cry, and all of the sudden their situation didn't seem so funny.

Or maybe it was. He just had to convince Julia to see the absurdity of the situation.

"Submerged sneakers," he commented wryly, letting his amusement show on his face. "Well, at least we don't have to worry about burning the house down."

Julia gave a shaky chuckle, and then put a hand to her throat and began to laugh in earnest. "Only getting electrocuted."

Arms akimbo and hips cocked to one side, she pasted Zeke with a saucy look that made him stop breathing, then tilted her chin and asked, "How come you couldn't fix that machine?"

Zeke copied her movements. He placed his hands on his hips and said in his best falsetto voice, and in an exact replica of the tone she had used, "How come you thought I *could* fix that machine?"

"I don't know," she said, sounding defensive.

Zeke shifted his posture, wondering how to deal with a woman whose moods shifted faster than the Colorado weather.

Julia removed her hands from her hips and crossed them over her chest. "My father could have fixed it."

Zeke bristled. "Oh, I see."

Again, he followed her movements, amplifying the motion as he crossed his arms over his chest. "So I don't measure up to Daddy's standards, do I?"

"I thought…" She stammered to a halt, then tried again. "Daddy—my *father*—is a jack-of-all-trades."

"Who knows how to fix washing machines," he finished for her.

"Well, y-yes," she stammered.

"You've discovered my weakness," he joked with a shrug. "I am helpless before fire-breathing electrical appliances."

So much for a knight in shining armor. He relegated himself to squire in her eyes.

"You did all right with this one," she argued

softly, patting the now quiet machine. "See? He's not even breathing smoke anymore."

Zeke tried to smile, but it came out as a half grin pinched on one side of his face. "I'm an expert builder, and I can cook a gourmet meal, but I'm completely useless in the electrical department."

"Where'd you learn how to cook?" Julia asked, sounding genuine and friendly, and obviously trying to lure him into a more cheerful subject.

Brimming with genuine and distinctively feminine compassion and sincerity, this was the Julia that Zeke knew.

And loved.

He cleared his throat rapidly, forcing his mind to answer her question, to dwell on facts and not feelings. "I learned to cook in a soup kitchen, believe it or not. I work downtown in one of the homeless shelters on Tuesday nights. They wanted me to cook. Once I discovered I had a knack for it, I started experimenting with gourmet cooking on my own. Following along with those television guys, you know?"

He grunted and shook his head. "I never thought about it before, but I suppose gourmet cooking is a pretty strange hobby for a carpenter, huh?"

She immediately made a sound of denial in her throat and waved him off with her hand, swishing it through the blond hair cascading down her shoulders.

Zeke swallowed hard. It was hard to focus sometimes. Julia's inner and outer beauty sometimes struck him hard, right between the eyes.

Like right now. He labored to catch a breath.

"I'm jealous," she admitted softly. "I can't cook a single thing. Not to save my life."

He winked. "I'll have you over some night and give you cooking lessons."

As soon as the words were out of his mouth, he realized how awful they sounded. Like he was coming onto her or something. He cringed inwardly, desperately wanting to take the words back.

Unfortunately, there was no way to eat his words and regain the camaraderie they'd previously shared.

Afraid to look at her, but needing to express his remorse, he slowly turned his gaze to her.

She surprised him, taking his words at face value, as they'd been meant. "I'd like that, Zeke," she agreed softly, then smiled and reached for his arm, a brief, soft touch that did more to reassure him than a thousand words would have done. "In the meantime, though, I'd like to hear more of what you do at the soup kitchen."

"I'm happy to tell you, Julia," he said, more earnestly than she'd ever know.

She laughed; a light, ringing sound that delighted his ears and made him want to laugh, too.

"No time like the present. But I think we better talk over a couple of mops. What do you think?" She winked at him.

What he thought was that his heart had stopped dead in his chest, but outwardly he kept moving, as if he weren't walking a figurative foot off the ground.

He found two worn sponge mops and a bucket in the utility closet. He handed a mop to Julia and kept one for himself. He tried to place the plastic bucket on the floor, but it floated, so he placed it on the now silently contrite washer.

"We'd better get busy if we want to have this mess cleaned up by Christmas."

With Christmas only three weeks away, Zeke wasn't being overly sarcastic, Julia thought wryly. She applied herself to her mop, vigorously plying and squeezing dirty, soapy water into the bucket, which one of the two of them dumped into the sink on a regular basis.

As they mopped, Zeke told her of the homeless men and women he'd met, and how hungry they were, not only for food, but also for an answer to their problems.

Julia hurt for them, even as she heard about them. She wanted to be like Zeke. She wanted to help the homeless, just as she wanted to help women in crisis pregnancies. There were so many needs, and she felt for them all.

She wanted to help everyone.

The knowledge that she wasn't capable of such philanthropy was part of what had given birth to her now defunct *Great Scheme.* Marry a pastor. Help all kinds of people. Work right on the front lines.

A little like what Zeke was doing.

The thought surprised her, and she filed it away to reflect on later. "Tell me more," she urged.

"Seeing the little children at the shelters is the hardest part," Zeke said, squeezing his mop into the bucket. "Can you imagine being a homeless, abandoned mother with nowhere to shelter your baby? The little ones…" He stopped short.

Julia's heart swelled until her chin felt taut with emotion. "Could I go with you to the homeless shelter sometime?"

Zeke stopped mopping and looked at her full in the face. "I'd like that," he whispered huskily.

Their gazes met and held, and Julia read a symphony of emotions in Zeke's warm blue eyes.

Quite suddenly he broke his gaze away, scooping up the full bucket and dumping the water into the sink. "What are you doing for Christmas this year?" he asked with a casual smile.

That smile had her heart dancing a tango across her chest. She was alarmed by the strength of the feelings that passed between them. She wasn't certain she wanted to analyze the thoughts in her head and the emotions running through her heart.

Sometimes it was better not to think too much. This was one of those times. She turned her attention to her mop and the hopelessly wet floor.

"Lakeisha and I always spend Christmas together," she said softly. "We haven't bought a Christmas tree yet, though. We get a small tree—something less than four feet tall. The little ones fit better in our small apartment. But I always get a real tree, not one of those fake jobbies. I love the smell of fresh pine, don't you?"

Zeke apparently chose to ignore her babbling, and honed in on her first sentence. "No family?"

"Nope." Julia frowned, a storm once again brewing. "Well, not anyone I'd care to spend Christmas with, in any case."

Zeke stopped mopping and turned to her, his eyebrows raised in question.

"You're wondering why I don't spend the holidays with my father," she said dully, knowing it was a statement and not a question.

Zeke nodded and leaned his palms onto the top of the mop handle.

Julia hadn't told anyone about her father, except for Lakeisha, and even then, she'd kept her explanations minimal. Lakeisha had seen. She knew. But Julia had never talked about it. The need to share the entire story with someone suddenly seemed too overwhelming a burden to bear. Zeke's compassion, the quiet way he reached out to her, seemed to be the freedom she'd been looking for.

The words poured out of her mouth as quickly as the tears poured down her cheeks.

"I feel kind of foolish," she said, quietly dabbing at her cheeks with the corner of her sweatshirt.

Zeke chuckled softly at her action and handed her his handkerchief from the back pocket of his jeans. His hands easily spanned her waist as he propped her up onto the washing machine, where they'd be face-to-face as she spoke.

"It's not like my story is unique or unusual in this day and age," she protested.

Zeke leaned in on her, one hand on either side of her hips, until his nose was inches from her own and he had her gaze tightly locked with his. His warm breath was the cool sensation of polar ice.

That frightening thought made her try to pull away from him, but he wouldn't let her go. His arms were like steel bands beside her. He wasn't technically even touching her, but she had nowhere to wiggle away from his grasp.

"The issue isn't whether or not your relationship with your father is unique or unusual, Julia. It's *your* story."

The way he said it, combined with the firm, gentle look in his eyes, broke down her reserves. "Okay, but you'll probably be sorry you asked."

"Let me be the judge of that," he said gently, tipping her on the end of the nose with his finger.

"Okay. Well, let's see…my mom and dad married after they'd known each other two weeks."

"It sounds like you should start this story with 'Once upon a time.'"

Julia made a sound that was half a surprised laugh, half a snort. "Doesn't it, though? It gets worse."

Zeke made a sweeping gesture with his arm.

"They met at a country club. She was a debutante, and he a waiter. He swept my mother right off her feet with his charm and good looks. I'm sure teenage rebellion played into it, too. I was never allowed to meet my maternal grandparents, so I couldn't say. My mother tried time and again to mend fences, but my grandparents never reneged."

"Poor little rich girl makes good with the waiter of the country club," he said thoughtfully. "But he married her, so he must have thought he loved her."

"Oh, I'm sure," she agreed, knowing Zeke could hear the derision in her voice. "In fact, I'd wager he'd still say he loves her, if he was questioned on the subject. Carrying a banner for her all the years she's been gone. It's probably what he's come here to try to tell me, not that I'm going to stay around long enough to listen to him."

Zeke frowned. "Then why—"

"Do I detest the man so much?"

"If he loved your mother—"

"You know, that's just it. Everyone around here, you and Lakeisha included, seem to think that if you have love in your relationship, everything else just falls into place."

Zeke opened his mouth, but Julia held him off, extending her hand palm out.

"I'm here to tell you, it isn't so."

From the way Zeke's eyebrows hovered low over his eyes, Julia thought he looked ready to argue, but when he didn't open his mouth, she continued. "My father *loved* my mom, but he couldn't keep a job to save his life. My mom might as well have been a single mother, for all the help he gave her. He'd keep a job for two weeks, sometimes three. And then he'd disappear."

"Disappear as in completely?" Zeke asked, sounding genuinely amazed.

"Disappear as in until his money ran completely out," Julia modified. "Then he'd show up again, walk in the door as if nothing had changed."

"And your mother?"

"My mother never said a word. Not once. At least not in my hearing. I refuse to believe she never chewed him out in private.

"Mom was a Christian, and I believe it was her faith that got her through. She went to counseling, I know. She'd run off without a penny to her name, so she hadn't attended college and couldn't now, with a little girl to support."

Julia's eyes got misty in remembrance of the striking, golden-haired angel whose green eyes were always watching over her. "She left me with the neighbors at night and stocked shelves at a discount store. She was always there for me when I was awake. I think the only sleep she caught was when I was in school."

"Wow," said Zeke, with a low whistle. "She was very dedicated to you, Julia."

"Yes, she was," she said fiercely. "And she saved every penny she earned so I could go to college and get a good education."

"And here you are."

"And here I am. But my mom worked herself into the grave getting me here, so what difference does it make?"

She tore her gaze away from him, looking anywhere but into his warm, compassionate eyes. She didn't need or want sympathy for her situation. She just wanted a better deal for her own kids.

"So why is your father here now, do you think?" Zeke didn't force her to look at him, but the long, comforting strokes of his hand on her hair reminded her all too strongly that he was here. And that he cared.

"I couldn't tell you." She snapped out the words, feeling like she wanted to throw something. "And to tell you the truth, I don't want to know. He left the day my mother was buried six years ago, and he never looked back. I'll tell you one thing—I have nothing to say to him."

Zeke nodded and shifted his weight to his heels, leaning his thick shoulders against the bare, crusty drywall with no quandary about the dust settling onto his shoulders, making white streaks on his blue flannel. She recognized he was thoughtfully giving her the space she needed.

Julia slipped off the washer and looked at her sopping sneakers, trying to focus on the discomfort of her wet feet rather than the furious squeezing of her heart and throat. She picked at a piece of imaginary lint from the sleeve of her purple sweatshirt. She studied her pinched fingers as if she'd find an answer there.

Zeke moved to her side and took her gently in his arms, stroking her hair and murmuring softly under his breath.

For the first time since her mother's death, Julia allowed herself to cry. Sobs gushed forth, wave after wave in pounding fury.

Zeke's flannel was soon soaked, but he didn't seem to notice. He simply held her, tightly yet gently, and let her vent, until finally, there were no more tears.

Julia was amazed at how she felt. Talking about her childhood had been surprisingly good therapy for her, but finding within her heart the ability to cry—well, Zeke had given her a gift, something she'd never be able to repay.

She sniffled, focusing on regaining her composure.

"Sorry," she apologized at last, her voice cracking. "I got your shirt all wet."

Zeke smiled tenderly. "I don't mind."

He pulled away from her, pausing only to run a finger down her nose, slowly over her lips, to the line of her chin.

Then, suddenly, he backed away, hefting his mop and returning to his job. "I think I can finish up here by myself. There isn't much to do besides mop this mess up. I can't do anything about the washer today. I'll have to call someone to come out and fix it. Why don't you go pick up that Christmas tree you've been talking about and surprise Lakeisha with it."

Julia smiled and thanked him. It wasn't every day you made a friend like Zeke Taylor. But thank God she had.

Chapter Eleven

Even without a family to celebrate with, Julia loved the Christmas season. Peace on earth and goodwill toward men. The snow-covered Rocky Mountains glistening like diamonds in the Colorado sunshine.

Snowmen.

Children laughing.

The sluicing of ice skates as they cut across a frozen pond. Carolers strolling down the Sixteenth Street Mall, their tunes warming the crisp evening air. Christmas shopping at Larimer Square.

The crackle of a winter's fire warming her woolen-sock clad feet as she toasted a marshmallow to a crispy dark brown.

So many happy childhood memories, blissful days full of baking cookies and wrapping presents she'd made especially for her mother. Sometimes she even saved enough change to buy something small and delicate for her small and delicate mother.

Julia whistled a Christmas hymn as she wrapped tiny flickering lights around the lovely little pine she'd purchased at a lot on the way home from the Martins' house.

She inhaled the crisp, lingering scent of fresh pine needles and stepped back to survey her work.

The colored lights twinkled merrily against the deep-green background. The tree tipped to one side about six inches from the top, so the shimmering angel she'd placed there was likewise tilted.

But Julia didn't mind the flaws. Flaws gave a tree character, separating it from its artificial counterparts. Again she inhaled deeply, planning the execution of the numerous decorations ladening the boxes piled around the usually immaculate living room.

First, she decided, she'd pop some corn to string. Then she'd tie Victorian ribbons into fancy bows around some of the branches. After that, she'd garnish the whole thing with a multitude of icicles that would reflect the twinkling lights.

As she strung pieces of popcorn through a long string of thread, she allowed herself to ponder recent events. She immediately recalled the tender look in Zeke's eyes as she'd related her story, the way the two of them connected without words.

He listened without judging her, even when she herself knew she deserved judgment. Never in her life had she opened herself up to someone the way she had to Zeke. It seemed natural to reveal her true heart.

She *trusted* him.

He was the kind of man a woman could depend on. He had an inner strength that matched his outer might, and he wasn't afraid to share that intensity with others.

But he's not the right man for you, Julia reminded herself.

Money would always be an issue. And she knew firsthand how big an issue money could be in a marriage. Zeke was a hands-on man. What if he got hurt or killed on the job? What if they had to move around a lot so he could find work?

Still, it was getting harder and harder to convince herself there wasn't something between them.

The truth was, she was terrified of the possibilities Zeke brought to light.

She plunged the needle through a piece of popcorn and straight into her finger. She watched silently as a tiny dot of blood pooled where she'd poked herself. The finger began to throb, and she fought the urge to thrust it into her mouth, as a small child would have done.

As the cool water of the kitchen sink bathed her sore extremity, she considered where her own work had brought her. Heartless. Calculated and presumptuous.

She'd chosen Bryan so she wouldn't get hurt the way her mother had been hurt, by falling in love with an imperfect man. She was only now beginning to understand that all men were imperfect, in one way or another.

She'd have to revisit her Scheme with new eyes.

With Zeke she was too vulnerable. She couldn't keep secrets from him. He knew instinctively what she was thinking and feeling. And she certainly wasn't comfortable with the feelings he aroused in her heart. Just thinking about them made her want to panic, to bolt and run.

Bryan was safe. Boring, perhaps; but safe. Besides, he was a pastor.

He was also an egotistical, self-centered piece of work.

She'd never been more confused in her life. She supposed she could scrap the whole thing and start over. Bryan wasn't the only young, single pastor in the world. But the thought of starting over only made her stomach turn. Everything she thought she was, wasn't, and all that wasn't suddenly shone with such potential she could hardly bear to think about it.

As she dried her hands, someone heavily thumped on the front door, waiting no more than three seconds before thumping again. Repeatedly.

Not today, Julia thought, her whole body tensing. *Please, God, no bad surprises today.*

Bryan stood in the corridor, awkwardly attempting to hide a large pot of poinsettias behind his back. A thin smile lined his usually serious face.

"What lousy weather," he announced as she opened the door and ushered him in.

"Come in, Bryan," she said, nearly rolling her eyes at his negative mood and trying not to stare at the profusion of red petals peeking from behind his back.

Father Bryan Cummings catapulted into the room, his face in its usual eagle scowl, the front lock of his fine black hair dividing his face. "Julia, I've got to talk to you about something.

"Are you by yourself? I need to see you *alone* for a few minutes," Bryan announced without preamble. He set the plant he'd been holding aside, as if forgetting he'd even brought it. "It's important, or I wouldn't ask."

As if he had—*asked,* that is. She supposed she should be shocked by his abruptness, but the awful truth was that she expected him to act just the way he had.

How had she ever conceived such a silly notion as to want to ally herself with Bryan? It was a question, she realized, that she should have asked herself months ago. It gave her a chill to realize that in her zeal to find someone she could join in ministry, she'd overlooked one very important point.

Character.

Reluctantly, she turned her attention to Bryan, willing herself to continue her charade; which, she now knew, was exactly what it was. *All* it was.

Bryan's scowl lessened as he pulled up a stool next to her. "Julia," he began, "I have something very important to ask you. I'm sorry it took so long for me to get here to see you. I was busy with the Lord's work, you know."

"Of course," she conceded, though she wondered what *Lord's work* would keep him from visiting a friend. She refrained from asking, and Bryan didn't elaborate.

"I don't know that you've noticed, Julia," he said, punctuating her name, "but you and I work well together in ministry."

Julia nodded, tapping her fingernails on the countertop. This was some kind of cockeyed dream turned into a nightmare. It couldn't be happening.

"Well, I think it's time we became partners in the Lord."

Julia, trying to sip at her water glass, gagged and sputtered. Water went down the wrong pipe, and she swallowed hard, gasping for air. The pain and burning probably served her right, she thought grimly.

She coughed several more times before she could speak. "Come again?"

When he smiled, his lips looked out of place with the rest of his dark features.

"My graduation from seminary is coming up in May." He smiled grandly. "I'm planning to start a new evangelistic ministry—the Bryan Cummings Evangelistic Ministries."

He let that sink in a moment before continuing. "I'm going to travel all over the country, and of course internationally. I'm going to speak to huge crowds of lost and unsaved people, and win thousands of souls to the Lord. Can you see it, Julia? Can you catch my vision here?"

Why stop at thousands, she wanted to ask, obstinately desiring to stick a pin into his inflated ego; but she reluctantly stifled the childish ambition, and attempted to quell her stirring anger.

"I'm going to need an advertising and publicity executive, and of course I immediately thought of you. You're perfect for the job."

The advertising and publicity manager for an international evangelistic ministry.

It was a tempting offer, the kind of step up in her career that she'd been searching for. She had no doubt Father Bryan would be a huge success in his effort. He was wholly devoted to his career, and he had the Midas touch in everything he tried. If his stories were anything to go by, he'd been starting and operating successful ministries since high school. She could ride the wave of ministry with him—help who knew how many thousands of people every year.

It was certainly the opportunity to help people on a much broader scope than she was operating on now. Her internal paintbrush was already painting the colorful canvass for her.

Wasn't that what she wanted?

She felt as if her lungs were ready to explode. All her goals, dreams and desires—nearly everything she'd been working for and dreaming about, were being handed to her on a silver platter.

She was being given the opportunity to be a part of something bigger than herself. To be in a position where she could really count. To use her God-given gifts to work in a *big* way for the cause of Christ, instead of the small, life-by-life ministry she was experiencing now.

Her thoughts slammed to a halt like a freight train on brakes.

Her goals—and her dreams—had *changed,* she realized with a start. She didn't know what the future held, but she suddenly knew in her heart, with the kind of peaceful assurance that only comes from God, that her future—and her heart—weren't in touring the world with Father Bryan Cummings.

"You don't have to answer right away," Bryan assured her. "I know this is going to be a big move for you, from a small, local agency to a worldwide ministry. But don't worry. I think you're up to it."

"Actually, I'm not," she retorted, more than a little offended by his patronizing tone.

"What?"

"Your offer—the position—sounds wonderful, and I'm honored that you thought of me. But I'm afraid I'm going to have to decline. I don't think working for you is God's best plan for me right now. I'm sorry."

She was thinking about the local soup kitchen,

and the women at HeartBeat—the young teens and frightened wives. A person didn't have to be great in order to touch lives.

Only big. Bighearted, like Zeke.

Father Bryan looked dumbstruck. "You don't want to pray about it first?"

"I don't believe my answer would change, Bryan. God is taking me in a different direction right now, and I've got to follow His lead."

"You're sure?"

"Yes. Absolutely. But again, I appreciate your thinking of me."

"All right, then," Bryan said, abruptly standing and clearing his throat noisily. "I'd better leave now. You know how it is. A pastor's work is never done."

She watched without emotion as he let himself out of the apartment. Maybe it was shock, but she couldn't dismiss the tiny inkling of relief emanating from the general area of her stomach.

There were still many things to work out, but at least she'd pitched her Great Scheme in favor of finding God's way for her. "A man plans his way, but his steps are the Lord's."

Zeke crouched low, his back tight against the cold concrete. Bryan Cummings strode from Julia's apartment and within five feet of Zeke, but the pastor never saw him hunkered there.

Zeke's right hand clenched the bouquet of pink

carnations he held on his lap. He wanted to hurl the wretched flowers over the edge of the landing and let them fall heedlessly where they would, but something inside him stopped him from the action.

Father Bryan had beaten him to the punch. Zeke had no sooner exited his truck, than he'd seen Bryan striding purposefully up the walk, a large pot of poinsettias in his hand.

Zeke knew exactly where he was going, and he could guess why. And that *why* made his carnations insignificant.

Pink carnations, for crying out loud. Why hadn't he been more romantic, more thoughtful?

Poinsettias? Julia would love those. And Bryan had known.

Zeke had merely wanted to buy Julia something as an expression of their growing friendship, and perhaps as a hint of his own growing feelings for her.

Not roses, the clerk at the flower shop had said. Not unless you mean love.

He did, but he didn't want to be pushy. With what Julia had told him about her past, the last thing he wanted to do was appear too forceful.

Now he wouldn't appear anything at all.

What was he thinking? That he could win the love and devotion of the kindest, sweetest woman he'd ever known?

If only love were so easy.

Chapter Twelve

"Does Lakeisha need a ride?" Zeke asked as he gave Julia a lift into his truck. Julia hadn't seen him in a week, and was surprised how much she'd missed him.

"No," she responded with a laugh. "Lakeisha sleeps until the last possible moment, then cranks it in gear all the way to church. We'll see her there without a moment to spare."

"Hopefully not with a speeding ticket in her hand," Zeke joked under his breath.

She slipped a glance at him, her straight-toothed smile so clear and bright that his breath caught in his throat.

"That's why I called you for a ride when I knew my car was going to be in the shop this weekend. I needed someone dependable."

Zeke tensed, squeezing the steering wheel with both fists. *Good old dependable Zeke.* Was that all he'd ever be to her?

And yet, she had phoned *him,* out of all her friends and acquaintances, for this little favor. Did he dare read anything into the action?

When they arrived at the church, Julia indicated her usual preference of the second pew from the front. Zeke suspected it had something to do with being close to Bryan, who always helped serve the Eucharist.

He hoped he was wrong.

Zeke mentally shook his head, extremely annoyed with himself. Here he was in the sanctuary at church, and his mind was on the potential situation between Bryan and Julia. He knew he should quiet his roaring mind and focus on worshipping God.

He fidgeted in his seat and slid to his knees, hoping prayer would set his mind on things above. But as he glanced to his right where Julia sat, he knew it was beyond him to do. He prayed God would forgive him for it. After all, He had made Julia in the first place. And He must know He'd made her irresistible to this simple carpenter.

There was one sure way to put himself out of his misery, he realized as he slid back to his seat on the pew next to her.

He could ask her out. On a real date.

He stretched his arms out on either side of him as he lounged back in the pew, his Rockies baseball cap clasped in one fist. He was suddenly aware of his clothing, his red flannel shirt, fastened at the neck with a black cotton tie that felt way too tight all of a sudden.

He cleared his throat and pressed his hand upon Julia's shoulder, a casual attempt to get her attention.

She quickly turned her smile upon Zeke, and his words froze on his tongue.

It only took a moment, but a moment was enough.

Father Bryan slid into the pew in front of Julia and leaned toward her, his gaze quickly capturing hers. Zeke knew Bryan would have no trouble with his words.

Father Bryan looked as formidable as always in black clericals and his trademark scowl firmly in place.

But Bryan didn't speak. He only looked at Julia for a moment, then stood and cleared his throat, a clear prelude to a speech.

"I've got an important announcement to make after the service today," he said, loud enough for everyone around them to hear.

Bryan slid Julia a knowing look in the process. He tilted his chin in the air in what Zeke thought was a high-hat manner, even for Father Bryan.

Julia broke eye contact and looked away, and Bryan's scowl deepened. With a loud huff of breath, he turned and stalked away without explaining what his wordless conversation was all about.

Zeke knew now wasn't the time to press the issue

of wanting to be near Julia, but he still found it hard to concentrate. He had much to be thankful for, and the familiar liturgy of the service drew him in.

Even so, by the end of the service, his heart had migrated to the right of him, where Julia sat. He was bursting to ask her out, to make his feelings official, and found it practically unbearable to have to sit quietly in the pew.

Immediately following the benediction, and with a hearty *Thanks be to God,* Zeke reached for Julia's hand, determined to make this day the day things changed—before he lost the courage to do so.

"Excuse me, everyone." Bryan moved to the pulpit and spoke into the microphone attached to his alb. "Will you please remain seated for just one moment? I've got an important announcement to make."

Zeke heaved a sigh of impatience, feeling almost as if Bryan was purposefully throwing stumbling stones at his feet.

Bryan leaned into the pulpit, peering into the congregation until he was certain he had everyone's undivided attention. Then, maximizing his propensity for drama, he stepped out from behind the right pulpit and walked to the middle of the aisle.

"This is a very happy day for me," he said without flavor. "I would like you all to share my joy."

Zeke choked. Was he announcing an engagement? To Julia?

He slid a glance in her direction, but she was rustling through her purse. He couldn't see the expression her face.

Bryan's next words gave him a temporary reprieve. "This week, I incorporated the name Bryan Cummings Evangelistic Ministries."

Zeke let out the breath he'd been holding. Everyone applauded politely, and Bryan basked in the glow for as long as he could milk it.

Lakeisha, who'd appeared out of nowhere at the end of the service and had slid into the pew next to Julia, squeezed Julia's hand.

"This is it," she whispered loud enough for Zeke to hear. She sounded excited, and Zeke couldn't help but be curious about the meaning of her words.

He didn't have long to wait.

Bryan's smooth tenor voice eased through the sanctuary. "My ministry stands to make a great difference in the world, winning many thousands of men and women to Christ, both here in America and internationally. We'll be headquartered in Palm Beach, Florida, so I'll be leaving Grace Church and HeartBeat at the end of this term."

Again, he waited for the stir to die down.

"Today, I'd like to publicly ask a particular woman, someone right here in this congregation, to join my team. I want her to be the first to say she'll relocate to Florida to help serve the Lord at BCEM."

Julia.

Zeke didn't wait around to hear the words said aloud. He rolled from his seat and stalked from the sanctuary as fast as he could, not caring if people wondered at his action.

Not caring.

Please, God, not caring.

Julia was convinced no one could miss the way Bryan pierced her directly with his sharp stare. If she could have turned herself into liquid and drained through the floorboards, she would have gladly done so. A gigantic porcupine was rolling around in her stomach, sending pins and needles of pain into every extremity.

That her plans concerning Bryan could have come to such an implausible conclusion, and with such dreadful timing, was unthinkable.

Thank the Lord she'd come to her senses before she'd set off on a wild-goose chase called Bryan Cummings Evangelistic Ministries. Serving dinner at a soup kitchen was much more to her liking, especially with Zeke by her side.

And she would be working for the *right* reasons this time—because she loved God and *wanted* to help others, not because it was some kind of spiritual requirement she had to meet.

She realized Bryan was staring at her, and she lifted both eyebrows, wondering what he was waiting for. Was he expecting some kind of reaction from her? To stand and be recognized?

The effects of the moment were far-reaching, she realized, the porcupine turning to a knot deep in her stomach. If Bryan publicly asked her to join his team, she'd have a difficult time turning him down. People would assume she wanted the position. It would be awkward and embarrassing to explain amidst congratulatory wishes, and she was certain that was exactly what Bryan had in mind.

The fact that she'd already turned him down once didn't seem to faze him. He wasn't the type of man to take rejection well.

Evidently, he didn't take rejection at *all*.

Bryan had to know he was forcing her hand.

She sucked in a breath and caught her bottom lip between her teeth. Every nerve vibrated against her skin as she waited for the words that would create an entirely new set of difficulties, and complicate everything in her life a hundredfold.

Lakeisha, evidently sensing and misunderstanding Julia's tension, again squeezed her hand. Lakeisha saw the opportunity here, even if it was Father Bryan making the offering.

She sighed and closed her eyes, unable to look to her left side, where Zeke sat. She could imagine all too well what he must think.

"And so," continued Bryan after another extended pause, "I want you all to congratulate my new Executive Coordinator of Publicity and Advertising, Miss Julia Evans!"

Julia stood to the applause, then took a deep breath and moved to Father Bryan's side. With a wave of her hand, the small conversations around her ceased.

"I am flattered," she said slowly, carefully choosing her words, "by the generosity Father Bryan has shown in selecting me to be one of the key members of his new team at BCEM. I believe this ministry will have a profound impact, and am excited by the direction Father Bryan is taking it."

Her church family applauded warmly, which only served to tighten the knot in Julia's gut.

"While I'm honored," she continued, keeping her voice steady even when her hands were shaking, "I will not be able to accept this position."

Any lingering conversations came to a quick halt, and the sanctuary echoed with silence.

"Bryan's organization appeals to me in many ways, but I believe God would have me stay here in Denver. With HeartBeat. And with you at Grace Church. I'm very committed to the ministry here, and after searching my heart, I truly believe that's where God wants me to stay right now."

To Julia's surprise, there was much supportive applause amidst the confusion and titters of conversation. She didn't blame the congregation for not understanding what was going on.

She blamed Bryan.

It gave her something constructive to do with her mind, figuring out a hundred different ways to torture the man. With a last nod, she smiled shakily and sat down hard on the front pew. She felt as if she'd broken out in a sweat, but knew that was just her imagination working overtime.

People flooded forward, offering Bryan their best wishes. Julia didn't budge an inch from her seat. Zeke had disappeared somewhere. She was certain he believed she would—maybe should—take the position. She wanted him to know she'd be staying around.

But she wasn't moving from this building until she'd had a chance to speak her mind to Father Bryan. He slid her the occasional sidelong glance, perhaps hoping she'd take off and save him the embarrassment.

He could nurse his hope all he wanted. It was possible she'd let him off the hook. It was possible pigs would learn to fly.

Just not very probable, she thought with a tight-lipped smile. Lakeisha asked if she should stay, but Julia waved her away. This was between two people and only two people, not the entire congregation, as Bryan would have it.

Eventually, the crowd ebbed and Father Bryan loosened his alb and started gathering his things together. Julia waited until everyone had cleared the sanctuary, but then she wasted no time moving to his side.

"What exactly were you trying to pull back there?" she snapped, though keeping her voice low in the acoustic echo of the church.

Bryan looked straight at her, his brown eyes wide with surprise. "What would that be?"

She lifted a sardonic eyebrow. "What do you suppose I'm talking about?" The man was either obtuse or plain stupid, but Julia doubted either.

Bryan took a deep breath and scowled, his dark eyebrows meeting at a sharp point just above his eaglelike nose. "Why did you embarrass me like that?"

"Excuse me?"

"I just offered you the best position you'll ever get the chance to take, and you publicly humiliated me in my own church."

Julia pulled in a deep breath to steady her thundering heart. "No, Bryan. You've got that wrong. You offered the position to me the other day, and I *turned you down.* How could you have forgotten something that important? Or were you trying to goad me, to force my hand?"

"I was trying to make you see what's good for you," Bryan retorted. "You didn't know what you were saying. You hadn't had time to pray about it."

"I knew exactly what I was saying," Julia assured him blandly.

Bryan whirled on her so quickly she didn't have time to react. She winced as his fingers clamped on to the tender flesh of her upper arms. "Don't make the biggest mistake of your life, Julia."

"Oh, I won't." Her eyes widened as she realized just how true that statement was.

Bryan's eyes gleamed with excitement. "Then you'll join me in ministry?"

In his zeal, he was shaking her by the shoulders, though Julia doubted he realized he was even holding on to her. "No, Bryan. That's not what I meant."

"But you have to—"

Julia tried to pull from his grasp, but he tightened his grip and pulled her close to his face. "I have to succeed in this," he hissed desperately.

"Let her go."

Bryan's grip turned into a vise at the command of the deep, imposing voice.

Zeke.

She'd never been happier to see anyone in her life. She had no idea why he'd returned to the church, but she was definitely glad he was here.

He strode to her side and broke Bryan's grip from her arms in one quick, smooth movement. And then she was safe in Zeke's arms, those tight bands of steel wrapping around her and offering her the support she hadn't even recognized she'd needed.

She started shaking. At the time, she hadn't realized Bryan had actually frightened her, but now, belatedly, she was acutely aware of her heart pounding in her ears.

"If you try to manhandle Julia again," Zeke said through clenched teeth, "I *will* find out about it. And you will answer to me."

Bryan's face drained to a deathly white.

"Do we understand each other?"

Bryan tried to speak, but only stammered unintelligible syllables. He pulled his Bible to his chest like a shield and beelined for the sacristy of the church.

Julia felt rather than heard the deep rumble in Zeke's chest. She wasn't sure if it was a growl or a chuckle, but he was definitely following Bryan's retreat with interest. His heartbeat was regular and familiar, and she clung to him a moment longer, until her pragmatic nature took over and reminded her that she had her face buried in a man's shirt.

His shirt smelled good, too—*he* smelled good. The familiar scent of wood and man that was distinctly Zeke enveloped her every bit as much as his arms did.

He, too, apparently took stock of their situation, for he cleared his throat and stepped away, leaving only one hand on her shoulder for support.

"Are you okay?" he asked gruffly, his fingers softly toying with the hair curling at the nape of her neck.

She shivered, and thought it probably wasn't due to her close call with Bryan.

"I am now," she whispered. He wrapped both arms around her, and she allowed him to pull her back into his embrace. The steady beat of his heart was more welcome than he would ever know. "Now that you're here, everything's fine."

Chapter Thirteen

For several minutes, Julia stood staring at the large red Christmas flowers she'd placed on her mantel, unable to categorize her feelings. With a disgruntled growl, she tossed the innocent flowers into the trash bin by her desk.

Her entire life had turned upside down in a single morning. How was that possible?

Or maybe it had been longer than that. Maybe she'd known what was coming this morning, and had instinctively prepared for the grenade Bryan threw in her direction. Prepared, as in run like crazy and dive for cover.

Sighing audibly, she pulled the rumpled flowers from the bin and placed them back on the mantel. It wasn't the poinsettia's fault men were so difficult.

Easily diverted on this lazy afternoon, she stared blankly out the window, admiring the frost-covered pines surrounding the apartment complex, when

Lakeisha whirled into the apartment, her arms full of shopping bags.

"Hell-o, girlfriend," Lakeisha exclaimed with a laugh.

She was a study in animation, her dark cheeks flushed rose from the crisp evening air. She dumped her parcels onto the sofa, grunting from the effort.

"Been shopping, I see," Julia said, responding to Lakeisha's light manner in kind, glad of the deep relationship they shared, where sometimes words were not needed at all.

Julia wondered at her friend's apparent happiness, and privately admitted to being more than a little jealous. Lakeisha was a good-natured woman in general, but today she was full to bursting with brilliance and energy.

Julia watched with wry humor as her roommate flopped onto the blue Victorian armchair, wrenching her boots from her feet and tossing them in the general direction of the front closet. She stretched and yawned, her lounging movements reminding Julia of a spoiled exotic kitten.

"Sit with me," Lakeisha suggested, pointing at the worn sofa. "I have news—I won't be here for Christmas."

Julia felt as if her stomach were doing somersaults. If Lakeisha left, she would be completely and utterly alone over the holidays.

Talk about abandoned...

"Why?" Julia asked softly, although she already knew in her heart.

Lakeisha's eyes brightened, and the slow flush that had begun to recede now reappeared on her dark cheeks. "Girl, I'm so excited! My mom is actually staying home this year, instead of traveling all over the world and back. Christmas in America. What a novel concept."

Julia swallowed hard and bit back tears, but Lakeisha didn't appear to notice her distress.

Her roommate laughed gaily. "You know she's been seeing that Robert Martin guy, the historian? Well, I guess it's getting serious. It was his idea, actually, I think. *They* want me to drive out to Wisconsin to spend the holidays with the both of them, Mom said." She swept in a big, happy breath and encompassed the room with the broad gesture of her arms. "At *home*."

Julia did her best to smile, but knew the effort was absorbed by her protesting heart. Just thinking back to their small, shared hometown in Wisconsin was enough to bring tears to her eyes. She hadn't visited since the day she graduated from high school. "How nice for you."

The words sounded stilted, even to Julia. She was happy for her friend, truly she was. But...

Lakeisha sprung from the armchair like a cat, the rosy flush turning to red splotches. She closed the distance quickly and threw her arms around Julia's shoulders, dancing them both around in circles.

"I think he's going to ask Mom to marry him," she confided joyfully.

Of course. It made perfect sense. Meet the family. Pop the question. In this cockeyed day and age, when a man wanted to meet a woman's daughter...

She felt as if she were losing a sister, even though the rational side of her brain reminded her how silly she was being.

"What's that smell?" Lakeisha asked, changing the subject.

"Smell?" Julia was grateful to her friend for accepting the gesture and changing the subject, but she had no idea what her roommate was talking about.

"Flowers or something." Lakeisha sniffed the air, turning toward the fragrance of the poinsettias. "Where'd you get these?"

"Bryan."

Lakeisha lifted an eyebrow. "Way to go, girl. It isn't a dozen red roses, but it's a great start to that Great Scheme of yours."

"Ugh." Julia cringed. "Please don't remind me that I ever considered marrying a man like Father Bryan."

Lakeisha belted out a laugh, and then jumped as sudden knock startled both of them.

"Who is it?" Lakeisha called.

"Special delivery for Julia Evans."

Lakeisha shrieked merrily. "More flowers for you, Julia, do you think?" she teased, an amused gleam in her eye as she whipped the door open. "Do you think they're from Father Bryan or Zeke?"

Zeke send her flowers?

Shaking her head at her own silliness, she swallowed the lump that had formed in her throat, and moved to the door, wondering why Lakeisha had suddenly grown silent.

Her roommate seldom gave up the tease without nursing it for all it was worth.

"Julia isn't here."

Lakeisha's words startled Julia so that she moved in the direct line of door. "What do you mean I'm not here?"

Before her roommate even had the opportunity to huff out a breath and give her *the* look, Julia knew exactly what she was talking about.

She fervently *wished* herself *not here.*

"Julia, I've come to apologize about the other night," her father said from just outside the door. "I've brought you flowers. Pink carnations, your favorite."

Now how did her on-again off-again father know that private and very personal information? A swift frost gathered at the top of her neck and raced down the tendrils of her back.

Lakeisha hastily threw herself between them.

"Julia has made it crystal clear she doesn't want to speak to you."

Greg Evans grinned rakishly. "Call me persistent."

That was enough to bring a groan from Julia's lips. And enough to help her make her mind up.

When Lakeisha opened her mouth to speak, Julia stepped forward and reached for her hand. "You've been a great friend in this," she said, with a grateful squeeze. "But I think it's time I had him in and got this over with, don't you?"

Lakeisha's eyebrows disappeared behind her black bangs. "It's your call, girl."

Julia shrugged. It was enough to send her skeptical roommate back to her own room, grabbing a muffin on the way.

Greg Evans grinned jauntily at his daughter, then swept his still-blond hair off his face with his palm, and presented the bouquet of pink carnations with a flourish, a small wrapped Christmas gift still tucked under his arm.

"Save it," Julia rumbled, before whirling on her heels and tramping back into her living room. If he followed, he followed. It was no concern of hers.

The door closed softly. Julia froze, her hands clenched at her sides. Despite her best intentions, her whole awareness was in questioning whether or not her father had followed her inside. She needed to know.

And then, suddenly, she did know.

He was there, in the room, just behind her. She couldn't see him, but she could feel him standing there, silently watching her.

"I'll get a vase," she said, her voice hoarse. She moved decisively to the counter, a blatant effort to avoid having to look at her father.

"That would be good," her dad said quietly. "You look stressed," he added, then cleared his throat.

Stressed? After the day she'd had so far, *stressed* didn't even begin to describe what she felt. "You could say that."

"Sorry," he apologized abruptly, and then blew out a breath.

She returned with the vase and took the flowers from him. He was still standing. "Forget about it," she replied glibly. "You're only part of the problem. Feel free to sit down if you want."

Her dad took a quick seat in the nearest chair, the stiff blue upright Victorian armchair. He set the present on the corner of the end table, and then shifted several times, looking every bit as uncomfortable as Julia felt.

With a silent prayer for guidance and strength, she pulled herself together and sat down on the couch, opposite her father, and looked him in the eye. The proverbial gauntlet had been thrown, and she deftly picked it up.

"I'm listening," she said sharply. "Talk."

Her father's smile slipped for a moment, but he caught it and twisted his mouth into a sporty half-grin. "You're so much like your mother, Julia. It astounds me. Your beauty, of course. The way you handle yourself. Your composure and self-confidence. All that comes from your mother."

Julia cocked a brow. "I think you should take some of the credit," she said wryly. "For my poor qualities, at least."

He barked out a laugh. "Okay, a little."

Julia found herself relaxing just a little in his presence. It wasn't as hard as she'd imagined it would be, sitting in a room and talking with her father as if he were—well, her *father*.

But she was still a far cry from forgiving and forgetting. That, she thought she might never be able to do.

"I still don't understand why you're here," she said softly, absently pinching the skin between her thumb and forefinger. The discomfort was a welcome distraction.

"I'm here to make amends, Julia. I'm a changed man, and I want to be your father."

"I told you before—I don't want, or need, a father. I'm a grown woman now, and am managing quite nicely on my own."

"I recognize that," Greg agreed immediately. "I don't want to get in your way. I just want to see if it's possible to be a part of your life."

Julia blew out a breath and shook her head. "What? Until you leave again? Until the sweet siren of another job in another town lures you away?"

He nodded sagely. "That might happen."

Julia made a sound half between a laugh and a snort. "That *will* happen. This much I know." She turned her gaze on him, all the anger and frustration of years of abandonment showing in her eyes. "You still can't hold a job for more than a month now, can you?"

He jammed his fingers into the soft curls of his hair and frowned, the first time in very long time Julia had seen such an expression on her father's face.

"Some things don't change."

"Hmmph." Julia shook her head and looked away.

"But my heart is changed, Julia. I found the religion—the relationship—you and your mother treasured so much."

Julia's heart gave an irregular beat, and her breath lodged in her throat. "You're a Christian?"

He nodded rapidly. "Can you believe your old man found the Lord?"

It was a difficult concept to consider. The man who'd trailed in and out of her mother's life, breaking her heart every time he walked out the door, was professing belief in the religion he'd once mocked? The man who'd laughingly made light of his daughter's needs?

Julia shook her head. "I need time. I can't deal with this. I need to think about what you've said, to sort this all out."

Her father stood and nodded, that cocky grin once again perched comfortably on his face. "No problem. You want space, you've got it. But Julia?"

"Hmmm?" she said absently, refusing to meet his eyes.

"Take me seriously."

She balked inwardly. He'd never taken her seriously, so why should she offer him any mercy?

The answer immediately came to her, wrenching her heart in two. *Because that's what Christ would do.*

Chapter Fourteen

The quiet *tick-ticking* of the clock on the mantel bored into Julia's head. She stared again at the present her dad had quietly left on the end table. She hadn't opened it, and wasn't sure if she ever would.

She squeezed the bridge of her nose, dispelling the pressure she felt there. If she didn't get out of here, that clock would drive her insane. Or at least give her one doozy of a headache.

It was too quiet. What else could explain why the generally unobtrusive ticking of the clock was so apparent, and so annoying?

Lakeisha had been gone for nearly a week. She'd bounded off for her trip to her mother's without a single glance backward. Julia wasn't certain her friend had even been aware of her, as caught up as she'd been in the preparations.

Not Christmas preparations. *Leaving* preparations. Not that she blamed her. Who wouldn't want to go home for Christmas?

But now it was Christmas Eve, and Julia was completely and utterly alone.

She was looking forward to the evening, when she would attend Grace Church's traditional Christmas Eve candlelight service. It never failed to warm her heart to hear the revered Christmas story as the Bible told it, gently interspersed with favorite hymns and lovely, majestic pieces performed by the sanctuary choir.

This year, the children were creating a live creche, complete with a donkey and a sheep. Even the baby Jesus would be a living, kicking, perhaps even squalling infant in his mother Mary's arms.

Her mind shifted to Chantelle, who would be coming home to her own mother's arms in just a couple of weeks. God *was* good.

She smiled to herself despite her melancholy. She wasn't the first person to find herself alone on a holiday, and she certainly wouldn't be the last, she told herself firmly.

And she wasn't truly alone, was she?

Didn't God say He'd never leave her or forsake her? Now was as good a time as any to cash in on that holy promise.

Warmth rushed through her. How could she have forgotten God at such a time as this?

Feeling better, and determined to *do* better, she

decided she needed to stay busy, and not simply mope about the house. It was several hours before the service, yet.

She would go stir-crazy if she remained bottled up in her apartment. Cozy was one thing, but she felt as if she were being suffocated by her surroundings. She curled up on one end of the rumpled sofa, staring out the balcony window toward the snow-glistening Rockies and wondering what she ought to do.

Ice-skating. The abrupt bolt of inspiration surprised her, but she embraced the idea anyway. It had been a good, long while since she'd skated, but what was to stop her from making up for that deficiency this very day!

After all these years, she knew she wouldn't be comfortable enough to skate in front of others, so the local indoor rink was out, but there was that nice pond she'd found tucked in the trees just behind Grace Church, and with the temperature having taken a nosedive in the past few days, she was sure it would be perfect.

She loved to skate. She'd always loved to skate.

Against her will, her mind transported her back to a time deep in her past. How she had begged her father for ice-skating lessons, like all the other little girls in her class were taking. She had such glorious, romantic dreams of becoming a world-famous figure skater, like the ones she'd seen in the Olympic Games on television.

That is, until her father shattered that one tiny ray of hope in an otherwise common existence. Even now, she could hear her mother's words echoing through the recesses of her mind.

There's not enough money this year. Maybe next year, when your father comes home.

But next year hadn't been different, nor the year after that. She'd finally settled with teaching herself the basics with secondhand skates someone in the church had passed down to her when she was fourteen.

Julia stood and stretched, shaking the bittersweet memories from her mind with a wave of her head. Her melancholy mood wasn't going to improve by drudging up old memories.

What would help was going ice-skating. She might not be that world-class figure skater, but she knew enough to have a good time. What better way to spend a lonely winter afternoon?

It had been a while since she'd been on skates, but the movements came back to her with remarkable ease. The crisp bite of the wind in her face, the way her arms floated and bobbed as she turned—it was reminiscent of an earlier, more innocent time.

Julia did a pirouette, laughing when she wobbled and almost fell.

She closed her eyes, reveling in her peaceful surroundings. For a moment, she could almost believe that she was, indeed, a world-class skater. She let her imagination go full force to envision her routine, before finishing with a tuck and bow. In her dream, she could hear the crowd roar their applause. She curtsied right, and then left, the warm spotlight glaring upon her. This standing ovation was more than she could ever have dreamed of.

And then she froze, forcefully yanked out of her fantasy by a sound.

There *was* an ovation, albeit singular applause. She spun about, searching for the origin of the all too real appreciation of her efforts.

Zeke Taylor lounged a thick shoulder against the trunk of a solid pine, clapping his approval.

"Bravo," he called enthusiastically. "Encore!"

He appeared genuine enough, but not nearly enough to stop Julia's face from flaming, first from embarrassment at being caught, and then with utter infuriation.

How dare the man interrupt her private moment, and then have the gall to stand there and ridicule her?

Julia very ungracefully stomped off the ice and straight toward Zeke.

"You—you—" she stammered, too flustered to complete her sentence.

Only marginally resisting the urge to thump her

finger into his thick chest, she balled her fists on her hips. "What on earth are you doing here?"

Zeke's grin widened. He enjoyed her display of temper, knowing she'd merely been caught off guard. He hadn't meant to intrude, but he wasn't the rascal she made him out to be, either.

Not entirely, anyway, he thought, grinning. "You know you're adorable when you're angry, sweetheart?" he teased lightly.

Julia's jaw dropped open in astonishment, and he was certain he'd struck a chord within her.

"You know," he continued, his throat dry. "You were pretty good out there. Did you have lessons?" He grunted as he slid his back down the jagged tree trunk until he was seated on the wet, snow-packed ground.

Julia shook her head, but didn't speak.

"I enjoyed watching you." The words were quiet and honest.

She stared at him for a moment before answering. He gazed back at her, waiting patiently for her to answer.

"I wanted lessons," Julia said in hushed tones, dropping down beside Zeke and arranging herself primly on the snowbank. "Daddy didn't make enough money for me to have lessons. Of any nature."

Zeke nodded. "That's tough. My folks didn't have much extra money lying around, either."

Julia scowled suddenly, and shrugged. "Yeah, well, that's in the past now."

With a low sigh, she turned to the burnished sapphire of the glistening pond, her gaze distant and unreadable. Zeke studied her profile, at once struck by her beauty, and aching for the pain she suffered but wouldn't share.

What could he do? Zeke wondered. What could he say? Again, he came up against his own ineptness for words. In the end, he remained silent.

After a moment, she turned back to him. "What are you doing here?"

Zeke took her change in topic in stride, realizing she needed to get away from whatever menace was following her. He hoisted one foot into the air and pointed to his worn black ice skates.

"You're a retired figure skater?" she asked in a teasing tone, the sparkle returning to her glorious green eyes.

Zeke gave a loud chuckle. "I used to play hockey when I was a kid. I haven't been ice-skating in a while, though. It seemed like a good idea today, for some reason."

"Oh." Julia couldn't think of anything to say, so she just shrugged.

"I didn't mean to disturb you," he apologized in a low, rough voice. "It was just an idea. I can come back another time."

"No!" The word was out of her mouth before Julia

could consider the wisdom behind it, but belatedly, she realized her rapid response had been right on the money. "Please don't leave."

She *did* want Zeke to stay out here with her. She didn't tolerate Zeke's company—she enjoyed it. She laughed a lot when he was around.

More to the point, up until the moment Zeke arrived, she'd been feeling completely cast aside. That feeling went away when he smiled at her. And it helped a little to know that here was an equally solitary, if not lonesome, human being in the world.

She stood and smiled at him. "There's more than enough room on this pond for the two of us."

Zeke returned her smile with his own wide, bearded grin and leaped to his feet, an action remarkably graceful for a man of his size.

"Race you to the far end," he called, already skating out over the pond.

"Hey! No fair," Julia shouted, quickly pumping her legs to catch up with him.

With his strength, combined with his head start, Zeke was lounging at the far end of the lake, casually practicing a hockey warm-up, by the time Julia glided up, huffing and puffing in the crisp air.

"That's hardly fair," she complained, laughing until her sides hurt. "If anyone should get a handicap here, it's me."

"With a name like mine, you think *you* should

get the handicap?" he asked pleasantly. Zeke, she noticed, did not seem the least short of breath.

"Why? What *is* your full name?" she asked, suddenly curious. She was surprised to see the color heighten on his face above his beard.

Her heart flipped over, leaving her even more short of breath. But he'd been the one to bring it up. She wouldn't back down now. Besides, she really wanted to know.

He pinched his lips together and fidgeted uncomfortably, breaking their locked gaze to look at his feet. "I've never divulged that information before. To *anyone.*"

"Why not?"

The deep splotches lining his cheeks reddened. "It's stupid."

"It can't be that bad," she encouraged softly.

"It's bad. Promise you won't laugh."

Julia reached for his arm and gave it a soft, reassuring caress. "I'm shocked that you think so little of me," she teased. "Of course I won't laugh at you. I'd never do anything so awful."

Zeke cringed. "Famous last words."

She took that as a personal challenge. "You think so? Try me."

He stared at her a moment, then sighed and shrugged grandly. "Oh, all right. Ezekiel Habakkuk Malachi Taylor."

Julia's eyes widened, though she tried desperately to keep her reaction from showing on her face. Laughter bubbled in her throat, and she swallowed. Hard.

Zeke frowned ominously as he searched her expression for any sign of mirth. His twinkling eyes belayed his offended expression, though; the typical paradox of Zeke Taylor. Ezekiel *Habakkuk Malachi* Taylor, she mentally corrected herself, still trying without success to hide her amusement.

For Julia, seeing his dark look was the final straw. She burst into fits of laughter. "Oh Zeke, how could they?"

Zeke sniffed and planted his hands on his hips, looking all the more masculine for his overstated feminine gesture. "My mother is very fond of the prophets."

"I should say so." Julia hiccupped, still attempting to control her outburst. It seemed she was constantly laughing when Zeke was near.

"And you?"

"I beg your pardon?"

"I confided *my* middle name—names."

"Marie."

He nodded as if satisfied.

"Don't even think about telling anyone else about my name," he warned as he slid back onto the ice, gliding in ever widening circles across the pond.

As Julia sped by him, she called out, "I like your name."

It was the truth. Zeke was a strong, masculine name, matching the brawny man bearing it. When he reached out his hands, she took them in her own.

"You'll have to name your kids after the Biblical kings or something," she suggested with an impish grin.

He bellowed out a laugh. "What if I have girls?"

She thought for a moment. "Well, the wicked queens are out, so I guess you'll have to go with the more godly Biblical examples of womanhood. Stick with the tried and true, you know? Like Mary Elizabeth or something."

He cocked his head and grinned at her, at once taking in her measure and appearing as if he didn't quite believe what he saw.

Suddenly, his gaze locked with hers, he began swinging her in a slow circle. His mouth was pinched in a tight line, and his brow dropped low over his forehead. It was an expression of intense concentration.

Intense emotion.

He pulled her close, and they promenaded in lazy circles. She was eminently aware of his arm around her waist, of the way his breath mixed with hers as they skated in perfect time with one another.

He didn't speak, and Julia couldn't think of anything to say. But words weren't necessary. It was enough just to be here.

Together.

Suddenly he whirled around in front of her, spanning her waist with his large, gentle hands as he skated backward, pulling her along with him.

"Julia, I..." His breath swirled in the mist as his sentence dangled into nothingness. He pulled her closer, and she realized only belatedly they weren't skating anymore.

Slowly, they skidded to a stop, but Zeke didn't let go of her waist, nor did his intense blue-eyed gaze leave hers, even for a moment.

She knew he was going to kiss her a moment before he cupped her chin in his hands and leaned down to her level.

"Stop me if you..." His mouth hovered close and warm over hers. His voice was low, hoarse, and full of longing.

That hesitation, the simple kindness that made Zeke Taylor the man he was, brought the desperate emotions in Julia's heart to the surface, and it was she who covered that last half-inch, million-mile distance to his lips.

He groaned when their lips met. His kiss, like his touch, was soft and tender, yet she could feel the sheer masculine strength barely constrained beneath the surface.

Zeke might not be a man of words, but he was a man of deep passion, in his faith, in his life and in his love.

Love.

She wondered how long her heart had known what her mind was only now beginning to comprehend.

Her heart pounding loudly in her head, she broke away, skating as fast as she could for the far end of the pond, afraid to look back and see the havoc she'd wreaked by her errant actions.

Her errant heart.

How had this situation gotten so completely out of control? More to the point, how could she ever hope to fix it?

She had to get away. She couldn't face Zeke until she'd had time to calm down. To think. To rationally work through the complications. To straighten out her hopelessly tangled emotions.

She aimed for a small nook where ducks and geese often waded. Perhaps she'd see some today, though the lake was frozen over.

Her mind frantically occupied with trying to get herself out of her awful predicament without hurting Zeke, she didn't even notice the black smudge mottling the otherwise clear surface of the lake until she was right on top of it.

The last thing she remembered hearing before her head started whirling was the terrifying sound of ice cracking under the blade of her left skate, and a deep, alarmed voice screaming her name.

Chapter Fifteen

Time shortened, marked only by the sound of Julia's rapid breathing. Zeke had noted the weak ice earlier, but hadn't thought to mention it to Julia when he was skating with her.

He hadn't been thinking at all, only feeling, from the moment he'd taken Julia into his arms. He mentally kicked himself a million times over for his lack of foresight as he sharply bladed toward Julia.

He knew the danger inherent in black ice, and the knowledge made him pump harder. If he could reach Julia before she fell into the frigid water, they might have a chance.

She hit the ice only moments before he skated to her side. Gritting his teeth and praying desperately, he changed his course and set himself in a straight line for her.

He'd heard the ice crack.

With a final surge of strength, he plowed across

the black ice. It broke underneath his blades. With all his might, he catapulted forward, awkwardly grasping Julia in his arms and throwing all his weight in the direction of solid ground.

For a moment, he wasn't certain they'd make it. Then, suddenly, the ground appeared to come up to meet them.

With a grunt, he twisted his body so he took the brunt of the landing, sheltering sweet Julia in his arms as they rolled.

They were safe.

Relief washed over Zeke, and he breathed a prayer of thanks. Reluctantly, he gently released Julia onto the hard ground and rolled onto his back, throwing his arms over his head. The solid, frosty ground felt reassuring under him, and he lay still for a moment and closed his eyes, motionless except for his heaving chest.

He heard Julia beside him as she sat up and rustled around, apparently stretching her own bruised body. She groaned, and his eyes shot open.

"Are you all right?" he asked. He cleared his throat against the scratch in his voice.

"I think so," said Julia, timidly poking at various muscles. "How about you?"

Zeke stood slowly, testing his muscles as he went. "Nothing broken, but I'm going to be sore when I get up in the morning."

Julia also tried to rise, but fell back with a shriek

of alarm. Her face paled markedly, and she squeezed her eyes shut.

"Julia?" Zeke crouched by her side and gently caressed her arm. "Where does it hurt?"

She cringed, giving him no suggestion of from where her pain initiated. "I'm sorry."

"Don't be." His heart swelled. She was so fragile, and she didn't even realize her own limits. Even now her courage showed, as she bit her bottom lip and tried to act as if she weren't in the tremendous pain he knew she was.

Again, she tried to stand, but Zeke pushed her back down. "Where does it hurt?" he asked a second time.

Her gaze met his, tested his, and for a long moment she remained silent.

"My ankle," she said at last, pointing to her left foot. "I must have twisted it when I fell."

He gently probed the area with his fingers, and unlaced her skate as delicately as his big, ungainly hands could manage.

She jerked her leg from his grasp when he touched a tender spot, letting out her first real howl of pain. Then she grew silent, her lips pinched as waves of pain assailed her for her hasty movements.

Zeke again reached for her ankle. "I know this hurts, sweetheart, but I've got to see what you've done to this ankle of yours."

He continued to probe deeply, making mental notes when she winced or complained.

For a moment, his exploration ceased as he searched the back pocket of his faded blue jeans for his pocketknife. Taking her foot in a firm grip, he methodically cut the sock away.

"That way I won't have to move your ankle so much," he explained as he worked.

Julia's eyes widened, but she kept still, panting deep breaths in order, Zeke surmised, to keep from yanking her leg from his grasp.

"How bad is it?" she rasped.

"I don't know yet," Zeke answered, gently removing the last bits of her sock. With infinite tenderness he replaced her foot on the cool ground, gently packing snow around it to keep it stable.

He'd procrastinated long enough, and Julia was waiting. He crouched down by her and took her hand in his. "Don't panic, now, sweetheart, but I think it's broken."

Julia only nodded sullenly.

"I'm going to drive my truck back here so you won't have to be moved so far," Zeke said firmly.

"You can do that?" she asked, gritting her teeth against the pain.

He forced a grin. "One of the many benefits of a four-wheel drive. My truck can go almost anywhere." He paused, and then chucked her lightly under the chin. "Try not to move any more than you have to."

Zeke wasn't gone more than a couple of minutes before Julia heard the welcome sound of his engine revving and his boots crackling over the uneven, snow-packed ground.

Moments later he was again by her side, scooping her up as if she weighed nothing, and tucking her into the warmth of his chest. The muscles of his arm contracted and expanded beneath her neck. He smelled fresh and clean, with just a hint of sawdust. A thoroughly masculine scent, she thought dizzily.

Her heart flooded with relief, an emotion she didn't question. She was just so glad Zeke had been here with her. If she'd been alone…

The memory that she'd almost chased Zeke off the pond made her stomach turn over. That she'd been running—skating—away from him at the time of her accident seemed irrelevant now. She gazed up at him, trying to corral her feelings, trying to express her appreciation.

No words came. "Zeke, I—" she began, but clamped her mouth shut, unable to continue as, to her chagrin, tears pooled in her eyes.

Zeke's solemn expression turned from compassion to an emotion she couldn't name. His deep-blue eyes sparkled as he, too, fought for words. "When I saw you skating for that black ice, I…"

Julia nodded. She wasn't surprised or alarmed

when Zeke suddenly leaned down to her, claiming her lips in a sweet, sensitive kiss. This time, there was no doubt of the rightness of the action in Julia's heart. Their kiss allowed both of them to express feelings they were unable to voice.

But just as suddenly as he'd kissed her, he withdrew, and Julia wondered if he was remembering their earlier encounter on the pond. Regret filled her for her foolish actions.

He didn't back off physically. His arms were still firmly clutching her to his chest. But his gaze became distant, and his jaw was taut with tension. In a low, gruff voice, he whispered, "I'll try not to hurt you."

He cradled her close in his arms as he lumbered back to the truck. When they reached the big blue work truck, she saw he'd already opened the passenger side door. He deposited her gently onto the seat, taking his time swathing her ankle with a woolen blanket.

His silence was unnerving. Julia tried to read his eyes, but he refused to meet her probing gaze. The tension in the air was thick, punctuated by the tendons straining in his neck.

"Zeke?" she queried gently, just as he was about to close her door.

He froze in his tracks, and then leaned his elbow against the hood. He looked at her then, his gaze full of regret.

"Julia, I apologize," he said in a coarse but even voice. His throat constricted as he swallowed. Again, he looked away. "I had no right to kiss you. Not out on the ice, and not now. Please forgive me."

He didn't give her time to respond before slamming her door closed and trudging to the driver's side of the truck.

Nor did she have a response to give. If Zeke's kiss was puzzling, his withdrawal was doubly so. She hadn't protested the second kiss. She had, in fact, responded to his touch.

He spoke not a word on the drive to the hospital. Julia puzzled over his reaction and discreetly watched his profile out of the corner of her eye. He was clearly tense. Not that his death grip on the steering wheel was indicative of his overall mood or anything. Or the way he clenched his jaw, for that matter.

In her pain, Julia saw little reason not to direct her pique at the confusing, perplexing man sitting next to her. Maybe it was his fault she could barely think to put two sentences together when she was around him anymore. Maybe it was his fault her knickers were in a twist, and she couldn't figure out right from left, never mind her feelings.

She knew every name she called him was wrong, every accusation false. Did she have to ask forgiveness of someone if she only insulted him in her head?

From time to time he would glance in her direction, and she would look away. She couldn't bear to read the hurt look in his eyes, and know that she was responsible for putting it there. She wanted to scream out an apology, tell him it was all a big mistake, but she was relatively certain he wouldn't respond to such tactics.

Zeke's expression was grim and determined as he scooped her into his arms and carried her gently into the emergency room. The haunted look in his eyes had disappeared, replaced by concern.

He was quick and methodic in his efforts, depositing her in a wheelchair before signing in at the triage center. He didn't leave her side for a moment.

Julia didn't say anything, but she took great comfort in his presence. His large, bulky frame felt like a shelter to her, and his immense heart a wellspring. She prayed he wouldn't leave, but didn't know how to voice her thoughts. Or maybe she was simply afraid.

When the nurse began wheeling her in for examination, Zeke began to follow, then lagged behind, looking from her to the floor and back again. Finally, he halted completely, stuffing his hands in the front pockets of his jeans and watching with wide eyes as the nurse began to wheel her through the emergency room door to the back of the hospital.

"Zeke," she cried, lifting a hand to him, suddenly not caring how it looked to anyone. She was terrified of being alone right now, and Zeke was her only friend.

Relief pouring from his heart, Zeke rushed to her side and took her hand tightly in his, giving it a gentle squeeze to let her know in a tangible way that he was there for her.

He'd started to follow her earlier, only to realize he really had no right. And since Julia hadn't said anything, he'd stopped in his tracks.

"Don't leave me," she begged quietly as he and the nurse helped her up onto the examining table.

"I won't, sweetheart. Just don't move that leg," he reminded her.

His heart was swelling, but his expression was grim. He didn't want his sweet Julia experiencing even a moment of pain, and he suspected she was in for a night of it.

He meant what he said. He wouldn't leave her side.

The nurse bustled around, taking Julia's pulse and blood pressure. "Julia, the doctor will be here in a moment to examine you. And we've already put in a request for you at X-ray. Some nights, waiting for an X-ray takes forever."

She smiled kindly, and then turned to Zeke. "Are you her husband?"

Zeke felt blood rush to his face, which only intensified at Julia's stunned expression. He cleared his throat. "Uh, no, ma'am. I'm not her husband." He nearly choked on the word. "I'm just a friend."

"Not *just* a friend," Julia corrected quietly.

Zeke's gaze rushed to hers. What did she mean by that? Was she just teasing? Or could she mean that her feelings ran deeper than friendship?

He yanked his red bandanna from his back pocket and mopped the back of his neck. Man, it was hot in here.

The nurse chuckled. "Well, I'll let you two work that one out between yourselves. The doctor will be in shortly."

Zeke turned to Julia, ready to ask her just what she meant by that earlier statement. She'd been light and teasing with the nurse around, but now he saw just how pale her face was, and the distinct shine of pain in her eyes.

There would be plenty of time later to find out if her feelings matched his. For now, he would do as he'd promised, and be there for her—heart, soul, mind and body.

Julia was in the corner of the emergency room, curtained off from the hustle and bustle of the doctors and nurses around her. She'd requested to see Zeke the moment she was out of surgery, and he was reassuringly quick to return to her side.

"How's it feel?" he queried gently, a relieved smile lining his bearded face.

Julia thought he might be hiding a pair of dimples behind that beard of his. That notion made her smile in return, despite all she'd recently been through. "I don't feel anything at the moment. But I have to stay cooped up here until the anesthesia wears off."

Zeke cringed. "It'll probably hurt like a doozy then, huh?" he asked, enveloping her hand in his large one.

"No doubt," Julia agreed. "They put pins and staples and who knows what else in my ankle. I think they said they taped my torn ligaments. Do you suppose they use duct tape?"

Zeke chuckled. "Probably."

Their conversation wore down to an awkward silence for a few minutes.

"I guess we're missing the Christmas Eve service tonight, aren't we?" he asked in a transparent attempt to keep the conversation neutral.

"Oh, Zeke, I'm sorry. You don't need to stay here with me. If you leave right now, you'll still have time to catch at least part of the service."

"No." Zeke surprised her by the vehemence of that single word.

She crooked an eyebrow, waiting for his explanation. *If* he'd give one. He was notorious for his silence.

He grinned crookedly and said more gently, "I want to stay here with you. Besides, you need a ride home. You didn't bring your car. Remember? And I'm not sure you could drive it now if you had. Do you have a stick shift or an automatic?"

"Automatic," Julia replied promptly. "I never learned how to drive a stick shift. Which is apparently a good thing for me, huh?"

He chuckled. "I guess."

"Well, I'm glad you're with me anyway, Zeke." She gestured around her. "Emergency rooms make me nervous."

"Me, too," Zeke said with a relieved laugh. "I broke my arm once playing football. While I was getting it fixed up, they wheeled in a man who'd had a heart attack. It was just like in the movies—everyone was scrambling around and slamming his chest with those electric pads."

"How scary for you." Julia squeezed his hand. "How old were you?"

"Twelve. But at least my mom and dad were with me then."

Julia frowned. If she'd been hurt, she doubted if her father would have bothered to be with her, though of course her mother would have been.

No, that wasn't quite honest. It *had* been her father who'd been by her side during her infrequent childhood illnesses. She remembered him dressing in a silly hat and calling himself *Nurse Daddy*. He did goofy things like that. It was responsibility that was his weak suit. Her heart clenched in pain.

Zeke squeezed her hand, his face a mask of concern. "Are you hurting?"

Julia shrugged. "Yes. But not my foot. My memories. Let's talk about you."

Zeke cocked his head and stared at her as if looking for something. Finally, he capitulated. "Okay. What about me?"

"Your mom and dad. Are they…" She let her sentence trail, unsure of how to complete it delicately.

"Oh, no," Zeke exclaimed with a nervous chuckle. "No. I'm grateful to God that both of them are alive and kicking. So much so that they're out on a Christmas cruise to Alaska at this very moment."

"They went on a cruise instead of spending Christmas with their son?" Julia demanded, surprised at the surge of righteous indignation flowing through her for the emotional state of her friend.

Zeke chuckled again. "Sons, plural. I have two younger brothers, but they're spending the holiday with my Aunt Burma in Palm Springs. Aunt Burma's a little too much for me."

"So you're all alone this Christmas?"

Zeke nodded affably. "Yes. But that's my own doing. I'm the one who bought the tickets for the cruise. It's something my parents have wanted to do for years. Now just seemed like the right time."

"You can afford a *cruise* on a carpenter's salary?" Julia burst out, and then clapped her hand over her mouth, mortified that her uncharitable thoughts had reached her lips.

"Don't sound so shocked," he protested with a

smile, not seeming to take offense. "I didn't make the money in a week, you know."

"I apologize," Julia choked out through a closed throat. "I can't believe I said that. It was none of my business to begin with." Heat poured into her cheeks, and she laughed shakily.

Zeke reached over and tipped her chin up with his finger. His eyes were clear and smiling. "I don't mind your asking," he said firmly. "I'm not touchy about my job. Truth be told, I do make a good living, though I did save for a few months to come up with the cruise money."

He paused and gave her a friendly wink. "Besides, I don't have a family to support. It's just me, and I don't eat all that much."

Julia chuckled, but Zeke's eyes had clouded over, so she quieted. She was unused to seeing his mood change, especially so quickly. He was so often the friendly and open carpenter. Now she was seeing how multifaceted he was, and she was intrigued.

"Why…how did you come to be a carpenter? Is that what your father does?"

Julia watched as his attention shifted from his thoughts to her question. "What? No, my dad's an electrical engineer." Zeke paused and swiped a hand across his face and down his jaw.

When his gaze returned to Julia, the gleam in his eyes that was at once so heart jolting and yet so reassuringly familiar had returned. "This may surprise you, but I have a liberal arts degree."

"You do?" Julia's mouth gaped in spite of herself. Then, realizing how she must look, she immediately apologized. *Again.*

"I'm sorry. I just thought you didn't need a degree to be…" The end of her statement faded into a self-conscious silence.

Zeke chuckled. "You don't have to be afraid to say it. *Carpenter.* Jesus was a carpenter, you know. It's not such a bad vocation, all things considered."

"Why did you go to college, then? I mean, if you didn't need to? Or did you decide to become a carpenter after you finished your degree?"

Zeke thrust his large, callused hands out for her inspection, palms up. They were the strong, worn hands of a man who worked hard for a living.

"I've always been good at making things with my hands. I was the kid on the block who spent most of his time in his dad's workshop. I was always good at math, too, which is important for a carpenter." He stopped and winked at her. "It's an exact science, you know."

A blush warmed her cheeks.

His grin widened. "By the time I was a teenager, I was refinishing antique wood furniture. And making some good money at it, too, which I later used to put myself through college."

Julia marveled that such large hands could be so

gentle and nimble with wood. And with animals, like Tip the Wonder Dog.

And especially with people, she reminded herself. She'd have drowned today if it weren't for Zeke.

Hesitantly, she reached out a finger to trace the calluses on one of his palms. He quivered, but didn't remove his hand from her grasp.

"I went to college for my own benefit," he said with a catch in his voice. "I always knew that when I finished I would return to my first love, carpentry."

"You are very fortunate, then," Julia said, feeling the peculiar urge to kiss each worn callus and make it better. "Not many of us have the faintest idea what we want to do with our lives, even in college."

She shook her head. "I wanted to be in an occupation where I could help people, but my forte is art, wouldn't you know. I'm glad you have the opportunity to do what you want to do."

The most surprising thing about her statement was that she really was glad for him.

A *carpenter.*

"I make a good living," he repeated, his eyes warming. Lifting his hands away from her, he shoved them in his pockets and jingled his change as if for emphasis. "I'll be able to take care of a family when the time comes."

When the time comes.

Chapter Sixteen

Zeke couldn't believe he'd let her talk him into going back to the church to retrieve her car. She'd been quite adamant about it, on the verge of hysteria, Zeke thought, and he sure didn't know how to deal with a hysterical woman.

She kept muttering something about having Lakeisha gone, and Julia needing the car in case of an emergency. As if *this* wasn't an emergency.

She had fallen asleep moments after he'd tucked her soundly into his truck, and she'd slept all the way from the hospital to the church parking lot. Her head had slipped comfortably onto his shoulder, and he hesitated to disturb the pretty scene she made.

Sometimes his heart just ached, full as it was with his love for Julia. If only he could find the words to tell her how he felt.

He turned off the engine and flicked off the lights, but didn't wake Julia immediately. The parking lot was much as they had left it, but there were signs of the many people who'd come to worship at Grace Church that evening.

Festive green and red bulletins littered the parking lot here and there. A few used candles were strewn across the side of the stairs.

"I'm sorry you missed it."

Zeke nearly jumped out of his skin at Julia's soft, compassionate whisper.

"Missed what?" he said, noting the coarse, sandpaper quality of his voice.

"Christmas Eve."

"I didn't miss Christmas Eve," he objected. "It's right here in front of us."

"I meant the service, and you know it," she said, playfully poking him in the rib as she sat back up and stretched. "I really wanted to be there tonight."

"I'm sorry you missed it," he said, reaching out to brush back a lock of stray hair that had fallen over Julia's face.

"I wish I could at least go in and pray for a minute."

Zeke brightened. "Merry Christmas."

"Merry Christmas to you, too."

"No. I mean, I can grant you your wish."

Her gaze narrowed on him in the soft darkness of the night. "How?"

He pulled his key from the ignition and jangled the key chain in front of her. "Your wish is my command." And he was happy to do it, for in bringing Julia happiness, he found it himself.

He helped her out of the truck. She wanted to try walking on her new crutches, but Zeke would have none of it. Not with the number of ice patches shining on the asphalt.

Besides, why should she walk when he could easily carry her in the comfort of his arms?

She squealed as he scooped her up. "Did I hurt you?" he asked, creasing his forehead.

"Hurt me? No," she said with a small laugh. "But you startled the living daylights out of me."

"Sorry." He did his best to look repentant, and knew he'd failed when she laughed.

He brought her into the church and headed for the sanctuary.

"Why do you have keys to the church?" she asked suddenly. "I mean, I'm not surprised, but I didn't know you performed in some official capacity here."

"I don't," he said evenly. "It's nothing official. I just do the odds and ends repairs over here, so they gave me a key."

Julia nodded. She'd suspected it was something like that—official capacity wasn't Zeke's style. Yet he did twice as much for others as most official ministers she knew.

"Where do you want me to put you?" Zeke asked, flipping on the lights to the sanctuary.

"Well, I can't kneel," Julia said. "In fact, the

kneelers are going to be hard to manage, even without kneeling."

"I guess that leaves kneeling at the altar out, too, huh?" Zeke asked, looking around for a solution.

"Just deposit me in the front row," Julia instructed.

"Can I take you back with interest?"

"What? Oh..." Julia's face flamed at his gentle teasing.

For all his banter, Zeke was quick to leave her alone in the sanctuary. Alone with her thoughts, and her feelings, all of which banked up against each other like puppies raring to get out of their pen.

She stared up at the cross on the wall, then down at the remnants of the nativity scene across the base of the altar platform.

As always, the contrast of the scene struck her heart. A king who was born a pauper. God made Man to die for man, a thief's death on a Roman cross. And yet tonight was for celebrating, gifts given to loved ones in remembrance of Jesus' great gift to mankind.

Grateful tears coursed down her cheeks as she realized she wasn't alone, and hadn't ever been alone, even when she was at her loneliest. Surely a baby born in a manger must have known many tears.

He knew.

She closed her eyes. She wanted to release all her

fear and sorrow, but even now she was afraid. How could she possibly deserve what God freely gave?

"Are you hurt?" Zeke asked from somewhere in the darkness, his voice lined with concern. "Is it your leg?"

Julia laughed dryly and swiped at her tears as Zeke came forward into the light. "No, not my leg. My heart." She hiccupped a breath. "But I'll be fine, now. I'm not alone."

"No, you're not," Zeke agreed gruffly as he swept her back into the warmth of his arms. "Never alone, Julia. Do you understand?"

"I think I'm beginning to." She paused for a moment. "How did you know I was crying?"

He squeezed her tight to his chest. "The acoustics in the sanctuary are pretty good."

"I guess."

He paused and set her down on the front steps as he turned back to check the lights and lock up the place.

For after midnight, it wasn't cold. The building and surrounding trees blocked any gusting wind. Julia swept in a deep, clean breath of air, and then let it out with a sigh.

"Still sad?" Zeke asked, slipping down next to her on the stairs.

"Not sad," she denied softly. "Though I still wish I could have been here when they lit the candles."

Without a word, Zeke stood and hopped over the

side rail. Julia's jaw dropped in astonishment—the drop was four feet if it was an inch. She heard him rustling around and assumed that meant he wasn't hurt.

Hurt? The man was made of steel. She crooked a smile at the thought of the worry that had coursed through her when he'd disappeared over the railing.

"Are you sneaking off without me to leave me to freeze in the snow?" she called into the blackness of the night. She wished there was a moon, so she could see better.

Suddenly he was beside her, one hand behind his back and looking very pleased with himself, and her. "No, not leaving."

"What, then?" she asked, smiling at his secretiveness, her heart beginning to pound with a childlike sense of anticipation.

He pulled his hand forward. It contained two candles, apparently discarded after the candlelight service earlier.

Her breath caught and held as he gently opened her palm and placed once of the candles in her hand. With a soft touch undergirded by his strength, he wrapped her fingers around the stem, then turned her hand until he could brush a soft kiss against back of her knuckles.

She couldn't see his expression in the darkness, but she could clearly see the tender, reverent look in his eyes, as he fished in his pocket for a box of matches, and then scratched one, sending a single bright flame flickering around his face.

The breath locked in her throat let out in a whoosh as her heart expanded to fill every gap in her chest. Quietly, reverently, Zeke lit his own candle, and then blew the match out.

He put his free arm around her and brought his head close to hers, so close his warm breath fanned her cheek.

He looked as if he were preparing to say something, but at the last moment, he simply tipped his candle into hers, so that their flame became one as her fire was lit with his.

She watched the flames for a moment, thanking God for this time, for Zeke, for Jesus, the Baby and the King.

It was Zeke who broke the silence. She'd never heard his voice sound more regal or majestic as when he offered the simple song of gratitude up to God.

Reverently, lovingly, she joined in.

"Silent night, Holy night…"

Julia awoke to the crackling sound and pungent aroma of bacon frying on the range. At first her foggy brain registered little other than the tantalizing suggestion of breakfast.

For a moment, she almost believed she was still a child, and the homey sounds coming from the kitchen were those of her mother joyfully cooking the family's traditional Christmas breakfast: blueberry muffins, scrambled eggs and bacon, all washed down with fresh orange juice.

Her father would call her down to breakfast, and she'd race down the stairs, anxious to begin tearing into the gifts than surrounded the fresh-cut Christmas pine. Most of the gifts would be hers.

"Mmm," she said, yawning and stretching. Instantly, she froze her movements, not so much because of her aching muscles, of which there were many, but because of the sharp pain that pierced up her left leg.

Reality thrust its ugly nose into her pleasant childhood memories, reminding her forcefully that she was now an adult. And she was alone on this Christmas morning—or at least, she was supposed to be.

Who on earth was in her kitchen? She was curious, but not frightened. Burglars didn't fix breakfast.

Perhaps Lakeisha had returned early. She set her jaw against the continued throbbing in her ankle and turned onto her back, resting her head in the crook of her arm.

"Good morning, sleepyhead," called Zeke from outside her closed bedroom door. "I borrowed your key and let myself in this morning. I thought you might like to have a nice breakfast for Christmas morning. Can you get yourself up to the table?"

Julia jolted when she heard a male voice on the

other side of the door, sending her heart racing, and bringing a smile to her lips—at least until she tried to move.

The first attempt brought a shock of pain, and she groaned. With effort, she managed to slide to the edge of her bed and wrestle her protesting body into a sitting position. She was still wearing the faded jeans and red shaker sweater of the night before. At the time, it had seemed easier to sleep in her clothes than to change.

She'd been exhausted when Zeke had dropped her off the night before, and, after taking a pill for the pain, had fallen into a dead sleep the moment her head hit the pillow, despite the cast on her leg. Zeke, she assumed, had let himself out.

"It smells wonderful," Julia called back, taking a deep whiff of what she was sure was fresh-baked blueberry muffins. "I'll be along as quickly as I can."

"No rush," he called. "Whenever you're ready."

She could hear him whistling "Joy to the World" as he worked, pots and pans clamoring, followed by the familiar high-pitched *ting* of plates and silverware meeting.

Julia reached for her crutches and made the painful journey to the bathroom, muttering under her breath at her pallid skin that amplified the black shadows resting under her eyes. She scrubbed her face vigorously with a warm, damp cloth, hoping to restore some color, then debated whether or not to apply makeup.

Her growling stomach won out over the desire to look pretty for Zeke. The tantalizing smells reminded her all too well that she'd missed supper the night before.

Besides, Zeke had already seen her both without makeup and at her worst. If he couldn't handle it, he probably would have already left, she thought with a smile.

The first thing she noticed upon entering the alcove that contained the dining room table was the huge vase of bright-pink carnations—at least two dozen of them—that nearly overwhelmed the modest round table.

Zeke stood at the kitchen sink, his back turned to her, Tip resting quietly at his feet. She didn't resist the urge to lean her face into the bouquet and take a deep whiff of the intoxicating scent. As she straightened, she noticed a small card attached to one of the stems.

She swept a furtive glance at Zeke, but he was still busy at the sink. Balancing on one crutch, she opened the tiny envelope. The card read, "May your future be running over with God's blessing."

She swept in a breath and held it as she read the simple signature—*Love, Zeke.*

Julia stared at the card for a full minute before placing it gently on the table before her. Here were the pink carnations she'd been waiting her whole life to receive, a token of sentiments she had once fervently vowed she wanted nothing to do with.

And yet, she thought, her heart giving a regretful twinge, this wasn't how it was supposed to be at all. Zeke Taylor was too good a man for her Great Scheme.

Somehow, Zeke had known her preference for pink carnations. Or maybe it was a fluke. But either way, the flowers signified some indication of his feelings for her. Didn't they?

Julia's mind was in a muddle. Zeke was a dear friend, perhaps the best one she'd ever had. He listened. He cared.

And so, she realized, did she.

"Zeke, these carnations are lovely," she said, wincing at the betraying squeak in her voice.

Zeke turned from the sink, holding his wet arms at shoulder level.

Julia immediately burst out laughing.

"What's so funny?" he asked, cocking a hip and pretending offense. He was dressed in his usual blue jeans and a black flannel shirt. But what caught her eye the most was her own white, frilly, lacy apron draped around Zeke's shoulders, barely serving to protect the center of his chest, dwarfed against his upper body.

"Now don't you go thinking I'm getting soft and

frilly on you," he drawled, throwing his wet hands to his hips.

"Of course not," Julia agreed. "I'd never think of suggesting such a thing."

And she wouldn't, either. The frilly apron was funny precisely because it looked so ridiculous on Zeke's masculine frame. Zeke was, she admitted frankly to herself, without a doubt the most attractive, masculine man she had ever met.

And she *was* attracted to him. Not only were his features handsome, but his quiet, gentle strength and faith, and the integrity with which he lived, gave him a distinct appeal that the other men she knew lacked.

She fervently wished Lakeisha hadn't run off to her mother's for Christmas. Julia definitely needed a friend to talk with right now. Her life was becoming more complicated by the moment.

If, emphasis on *if,* she was falling in love with Zeke, she was headed for sheer disaster, and she didn't know how to apply the brakes. Not that Lakeisha was an expert on love, but at least she was a true believer in love, and insisted on the benefits of having love catch you off guard.

The most frightening thing of all was that falling in love was beginning to sound like a winning deal. When she thought about Zeke, it became appealing to follow the whims of her heart, and her Great Scheme be burned.

Chapter Seventeen

"**D**ig in," Zeke encouraged with a crooked grin. She looked nearly as dazed as she had when she'd first appeared in the kitchen.

He knew he was taking a big chance in coming here this morning, but it was a risk he had to take. He well knew he was stepping over the boundaries she'd laid. She'd have every right to be angry with him if she wanted to be. He'd even brought his dog without asking.

But there was no one here to care for Julia, and it was Christmas morning. No one should be alone on Christmas morning.

Not even him.

With the first bite, Julia began eating ravenously, if in her usual elegant manner. "This breakfast is just what the doctor ordered," she said in between bites.

They ate heartily, both having missed supper the night before. Even Tip dug into her small plate of bacon on the floor. Julia kept up a steady stream of small talk between mouthfuls, hardly letting him get a word in edgewise. That suited Zeke just fine. He liked to listen to the melodic sound of her voice. And he didn't know what to say, anyway.

His heart welled in his chest, until he thought he might burst with the feelings Julia fashioned inside him. He prayed desperately for control. As much as he loved Julia, he wanted first to glorify God.

But hadn't God put these feelings for Julia in his heart? Peace and joy washed over him as he realized it was true. There was no barrier between him and his love for Julia.

Except, perhaps, Julia herself. He knew she felt something for him, but was that something strong enough to stand the test of time? Last night, they'd shared the most intimate moment of his life. He could only hope she felt the same way.

But it wasn't enough to wonder. Suddenly, and with all his heart, he had to know.

He pushed back his chair and stood slowly, then stacked the empty plates. "Julia, I need to talk to you," he began, feeling as out of breath as if he'd run a marathon. "I have something to tell you."

He struggled to keep his features composed as he brought the dirty dishes to the sink. He wanted to grin like a schoolboy. But he paced himself and turned, setting his jaw with determination.

She needed to know how he felt. Now.

"I know it's Christmas morning and all, and neither one of us got a good night's sleep. Still, we're alone here this morning, and I feel I've got to speak while I'm still able to do so."

He lumbered to her side. With another grin, he lifted her softly and placed her on the couch, and then crouched before her. He wasn't even aware he'd been holding his breath until his lungs began to burn from lack of oxygen. He gulped for air.

"What's up?" Her usually sunny soprano was stilted, a sure sign that her throat was constricting around her words.

He swallowed hard. He was a man of action, not words, and especially not talking about relationships and feelings. He was way out of his element.

He wanted to tell her how he'd been attracted to her by her honesty and lack of guile. How he'd watched her serve others without a thought to herself. Her kind heart and commitment to God would make any man's heart melt. She was a woman a man would be proud to stand by, to love and protect and serve.

His heart hammered so strongly in his chest he was certain Julia must be able to hear it. Would that she'd be able to hear his thoughts, also, so that he would not have to go through the painful process of making them words.

She sat patiently, varying emotions fighting for prominence in her expression. A sense of unreality enveloped him, making his head swirl. None of this was planned.

"Zeke, don't," Julia protested suddenly, her voice cracking. "Please don't."

Zeke put up his hands, palms out, as if to ward off a blow. "No. Don't stop me. It's something that needs to be said, to clear the air between us. After that, I promise I won't say another word about it."

Julia, for once, was struck completely dumb.

"I'm in love with you, Julia. I think I always have been. I love everything about you. Like how your cute little nose perks on the end."

Despite herself, she raised a hand to shield her nose from his view.

Zeke chuckled.

So many feelings welled up in Julia she thought she might twist away like a tornado. Every little thing was out of control, and panic surged through her.

"But even more than your outer beauty," he continued, "I love the beauty of your soul, which tells me so much about your true heart for God."

A tear ran unheeded down Julia's cheek, leaving a slight, glistening trail in its wake. Zeke reached across the open space between them and gently wiped the streak away with the corner of this thumb. It was the lightest of caresses, yet it sent shivers down Julia's back in a way cold air could never do.

"It would give me the greatest pleasure on this

earth to have you for my wife, to hold you and cherish you the way you deserve to be cherished, every single day for the rest of my life. My work would be an extra joy just to be providing for you. I'd give you everything I have. Everything I am."

"Oh, Zeke," Julia begged, her heart wrenching with every word he spoke. "Please don't. Not now." There were too many questions unanswered, problems unsolved.

She couldn't seriously think about a significant relationship with Zeke, with her relationship with her father—and her heavenly Father—at such cross purposes. She was terrified. He was asking her to marry for love.

She squeezed her eyes shut against the pain throbbing in her temple.

"Why not now?"

"I have…other issues I need to resolve. There's someone else I—"

"I'm not asking you to marry me," Zeke interjected hastily. His gaze took on a glazed distant quality.

Julia tried to speak, but it came out a croak.

He strode to the front closet and reached for his coat. "I just wanted you to know how I feel. I love you. I always will. If you ever need anything, I'll be there for you. You don't even have to ask."

She knew with a stark certainty the truth of his

words. He *would* be there for her, as he had been since they'd begun their friendship.

She watched him walk away, his steps sturdy and firm. She longed to call for him as he swung through the door, to beg him not to leave. To ask the question her heart so wanted to answer.

But something deep inside smothered her words before they could reach her lips. She wouldn't—couldn't—ask, or answer, even though she knew that as Zeke walked away, he took her heart along with him.

Julia had apparently dozed off on the couch, her head resting in her hands. She woke suddenly when the door to the apartment crashed open.

Lakeisha stumbled in the door, looking entirely too cheerful. Her normally neat black hair looked windblown, though the day was calm.

Julia stood abruptly, apparently forgetting in the rush, her broken ankle. But the pain shooting up her leg was clearly a sharp reminder, and she sat back, her face pallid.

"What happened?" Lakeisha burst out, rushing to her side. "Are you okay?"

Julia laughed shakily. "That depends on your definition of *okay*. My ankle is broken."

"Oh, you poor baby." Lakeisha gave her a big hug, patting her back like a mother would a child.

"I think my heart is broken, too," Julia admitted softly. "And that hurts even worse." She ceased speaking when hot tears sprang to her eyes.

"What happened? Tell me everything," Lakeisha demanded.

"Wait," she inserted hastily. She'd wished for Lakeisha to be here, but now that she was, Julia wasn't sure she could talk about what had happened. "Why are you here?"

Lakeisha snorted. "Well, that's a fine how-de-do. I'm glad you missed me."

Despite herself, Julia chuckled. "That's not what I meant and you know it. Why are you back *early?*" she modified.

Lakeisha waved her hand in a brushing motion. "Mom and Robert got married. Hitched. On Christmas Eve. It was so great!"

"I'm happy for them."

"So am I," Lakeisha agreed. "But then I figured they needed a honeymoon, so I came home. I sure didn't expect to find you all laid up."

Julia shrugged. "It's not so bad. How *did* you get home, by the way?"

"I stood on standby forever and caught the earliest possible flight, which, let me tell you, was no easy feat—not with all the holiday traveling. Good thing I had my credit card."

"I guess," Julia agreed mildly. "There's still some warm blueberry muffins left in a basket in the kitchen, along with some bacon, if you're hungry."

"Great! I'm famished," Lakeisha exclaimed, already on her way to the kitchen. "You cooked with a broken ankle?"

Julia took a sudden interest in examining her cast. "Zeke cooked me breakfast."

"Zeke Taylor cooked you breakfast on Christmas morning?" She let out a low whistle. "Just look what happens when I leave for a couple weeks."

"It's not that big of a deal," Julia said, and then cringed with the lie.

Lakeisha sauntered back into the living room, nibbling on a muffin with a smug, thoughtful expression on her face. "All right, girlfriend. What gives?"

Julia smiled. She related the story of her ice-skating adventure and how Zeke had rescued her, leaving out the fact that he'd kissed her, as well as their time at the church, which felt almost sacred. Those secrets were too private to share, even with her roommate and dear friend.

"You're blushing," Lakeisha said wryly. "Which brings me to the question that has been gnawing at my mind since I barged in here earlier."

"What?"

"Something happened. Something big."

"Sort of," Julia admitted, unable to hide her confusion.

"Big *how?*" Lakeisha asked, her eyes narrowing like a detective closing in on a big case. "What did he do, propose?"

Julia knew Lakeisha meant it as a joke, which made it that much more of a shock to her system. "Not exactly," she hedged.

"He *proposed* to you!" Lakeisha exclaimed, dancing about the room with a muffin in each hand. "You and Zeke! I just knew it. I knew it all along. Didn't I say it would happen? Zeke's the man for you, I said. I called it from the first. Oh, Julia, I'm so happy for you." She embraced Julia so firmly that it sent shooting pains up her cast-covered leg.

She groaned. "I hate to burst your bubble," said Julia, thoroughly exasperated and in no small measure of pain. It had been a *long* day. "But it occurs to me to point out that I have no intention of marrying Zeke Taylor!"

"What?" If Lakeisha had almost screamed before, her voice definitely raised a few decibels now. "What do you mean you aren't going to marry him? Are you crazy?"

"Probably," Julia agreed shakily, sinking back into the warmth of the sofa. "I don't think I am meant to get married at all. To be honest, I don't know that what I feel for Zeke is love. But I will admit there is something between us. I care very much for him. But I'm not going to marry him. I'm sorry if this hurts, Lakeisha. But people who marry for love get hurt, and that's a fact. I'm not going to make the same mistake my mother made."

"Zeke isn't your father, Julia," Lakeisha said quietly. She rested her arm across the back of the sofa and tucked her legs underneath her. "And even if he *was* like your father, which he's not..."

Julia held her hand up, but Lakeisha pressed on.

"I know you don't want to hear this, Julia, but your Mom was in love with your father, with all his quirks and faults. I think if you search deep within your heart, you'll find that you love Zeke Taylor.

"If you're honest with yourself, you'll realize that you two have exactly what it takes to build a lifetime relationship. Something different and better than what your parents shared. And something completely different than your *Great Scheme,* which was nothing more than a way to ease your conscience and satisfy the ticking of your biological clock. You have a chance at true happiness, Julia. All you have to do is let it happen. Zeke would never hurt you the way your father hurt your mom. And I can tell you one thing—if a man of Zeke's caliber ever proposes to me, I'm not going to be wearing that long look covering your face."

She paused, shaking her head regretfully. "Not me, honey. I'll be packing my bags for my honeymoon."

Chapter Eighteen

The next few days saw a steady stream of visitors to wish Julia well. Many people from HeartBeat and Grace Church stopped by, often bringing flowers or balloons or meals to help her out. Even Thomas and Evy Martin dropped in, promising they'd bring Chantelle over when she was released from the hospital in a few days.

Zeke stopped by daily, but never stayed long, and never attempted to corner her alone or bring up the subject he'd been so intent on Christmas morning.

Which was a good thing, for Julia was on her guard against such a circumstance occurring. She was determined not to give Zeke the opportunity to propose.

If he didn't ask, she wouldn't have to endure the blinding pain of turning him down.

She was getting heartily tired of always having to be waited on. She felt like an invalid on crutches.

This wasn't supposed to be a big deal, was it? Didn't people break their legs every day?

But after a week, she still wasn't able to do much other than move back and forth between her bedroom and the living room sofa, and even that was with little grace. She felt like a hog-tied calf, so awkward were her movements.

Sighing loudly, she reached down and picked up the present her father had left when he was here. She'd tried to open it several times, only to change her mind and put it down untouched. She just couldn't bring herself to see what was inside, to find what her father considered a present to a daughter he barely knew. Now, again, she fingered the clumsily wrapped gift. The midnight-blue paper boasted angels trumpeting the birth of Christ, and again Julia remembered her father's halting confession of faith.

Could it be true?

The present felt like a book, except that it was too soft around the edges. Curiosity overcame her. Biting the edge of her lip, she tore into the paper, and then gasped in surprise as tears sprang to her eyes.

Her mother's worn leather Bible, just as she remembered it as a child. Years washed away as she pictured her mother curled in an armchair, the Bible open on her lap.

She stared misty-eyed at the gold-embossed words on the cover.

Holy Bible.

It had been her mother who'd passed down the faith of the fathers to her. She swallowed hard.

Jesus was supposed to be her rock, her fortress in times of trouble. In her mind she had known that for years, yet the words had never touched her heart.

Not until this moment.

If ever there was a time when she needed a rock to cling to, it was now. She was drowning in a sea of her own making.

She flipped idly through the pages, wondering where to turn for help. All the precious words, the chapters, the books, were entirely familiar to her, and yet so completely foreign.

She ruffled the gilt-edged pages. There were so many words. How would she find what she needed?

God help me, she prayed desperately. God was her final hope in sorting out the mess she was in. She prayed silently, ashamed that He had been the last place she'd turned in her trouble.

Perhaps her walk with the Lord wasn't everything she'd convinced herself it was, even, maybe even in spite of, her constant search to do more for Him, to be more for Him.

As she meandered through her mother's Bible, her gaze alighted on a small red rose petal flattened between the pages in the book of Ephesians. With it was the corner of a torn and time-stained piece of stationary.

Without considering whether or not she should,

she flattened the Bible so she could read the faded words.

To Greg, my love.

She swallowed hard. It was a love letter, written long ago by her mother, and to her father. She knew she was trespassing into private territory, yet she found herself unable to stop reading. Further memories of the many wonderful years with her mother engulfed her.

It was almost as if her mother had reached down from heaven and caressed Julia's soul as she read her mother's words to her father: "I'll cherish every moment God allows us to share. Know that every moment we're apart, my heart is yet with you."

Julia's tears wet the seasoned page, further blotching the ink. She turned the sheet over hastily, wanting to preserve the precious memento.

Her mother hadn't been blind to what her father was. She'd loved him through it. It turned Julia's understanding of her parents' relationship over on its end. If her mother had known and forgiven Greg Evans of his faults, could she, Julia, do any less?

Her eyes lighted on a couple of verses in the second chapter of Ephesians, words that had been highlighted with a bright yellow pen: "For by grace you have been saved through faith, and that not of yourselves, it is the gift of God, not of works, lest anyone should boast."

The words were not new to Julia. They were the

first verses she had ever memorized—for a contest in her junior high youth group. She closed her eyes, able to see the words clearly imprinted in her mind. She hadn't forgotten those verses in all these years.

Or had she?

Not of works, lest anyone should boast.

The words echoed over and over in her mind.

Not of works.

Not of works.

The verse was talking about salvation. Salvation was the free gift of God in Christ.

But what about afterward? What about now?

Her head throbbed and pounded. Hadn't she been trying to *do* for God? Wasn't she working for Him? Or had she been trying to collect brownie points for heaven?

Her Great Scheme might have been just another notch on her Bible.

She felt the tingling of a thousand tiny shivers running up her back. The answer she'd been searching for was right here before her. She read the words again.

Not of works.

She didn't have to carry the burden she'd been bearing all this time. Christ was waiting to take it from her. It was as if the sun had risen after a moonless night, so clear did her mind and heart suddenly become.

Being a Christian was a relationship with God, not fulfilling a *Things to Do* list.

She closed her eyes again, this time savoring the warmth and peace running through her. How had she possibly forgotten her love for God?

But now it was back. She was back. And she knew most assuredly that she could face whatever problems and trials now assailed her. She was ready to take advantage of all the good happening in her life.

Julia was finally ready to accept what her heart had been telling her for weeks.

She loved Zeke Taylor.

And he loved her.

That she could be so magnificently blessed caused her heart to swell into her throat, and she sent silent prayers of thanksgiving heavenward. She and Zeke would spend their lives together, and have a beautiful family together.

She wondered how many children Zeke wanted. Julia herself had never given that much thought to children, but now the prospect of a family of little blond-haired, blue-eyed children that resembled their father wasn't so very daunting.

No matter what, she knew they'd be happy.

Outrageously, wonderfully happy. As her parents had been in their own way, if she'd only opened up her eyes and looked. Only they would do it better. That was her father's gift to her.

The power of her emotions nearly overwhelmed her. She thought blithely that they'd have to start their family right away; otherwise her heart would surely burst from the love bubbling inside. Her children, *their* children, would be further outlets in which to pour out her happiness and love.

She couldn't wait to tell Zeke.

But first, she had a phone call to make.

Someone thumped loudly on the door, and Julia stirred from where she lay on the couch, her mother's Bible propped open in her lap. It had been two days, and so far her plans had come to nothing.

"You sure are popular," Lakeisha complained, scuffling from the bedroom. She waved her hands back and forth, her fingers spread wide, looking rather like she was attempting to conduct a symphony.

"Just painted your fingernails?" Julia guessed correctly, with a laugh.

"And they are going to smudge when I answer the door, thank you very much," quipped Lakeisha, who nevertheless grappled for the doorknob. "Come in, come in. Welcome visitors, and all that."

Julia's father swept a ball cap off his head and entered the apartment, just as Julia struggled to a sitting position from where she reclined on the faded and quite lumpy sofa. She had never before noticed how the worn inner fibers had bunched over time, leaving the sofa bumpy and abrasive on her tender skin.

It was just enough to put her out of sorts, she thought, were she not so glad to see her father.

Lakeisha looked dazed, as if unsure whether to invite the prodigal father in, or to slam the door on his face.

"Come on in, Dad," Julia called to ease Lakeisha's burden. She thanked God for a friend who cared as much as Lakeisha, who understood and reflected her own feelings. But now her feelings had changed.

Her father's gaze brushed over her before resting on her cast. He looked ready to drop from exhaustion, Julia thought, noticing the dark circles under his eyes, the exaggerated crow's-feet around his eyes.

He looked so much older than she remembered the last time she'd seen him.

Yet in spite of his fatigue, he moved with the agility and grace of a much younger man as he rushed to his daughter's side, awkwardly grasping her hands in his.

"Julia, baby, what happened?" The years and empty space between them dissolved, he curled her into his chest just as he had done when she was a child, a time when she had truly believed Daddy could heal all her wounds.

For a brief moment, Julia allowed herself to believe it again.

"It was nothing," Julia said, clumsily removing herself from his embrace. She proceeded to fill him in on her accident.

They sat in awkward silence for several minutes. Julia was more than a little concerned about her father's haggard appearance, but was unsure how to voice her thoughts. It had been too many years, and she'd kept too much distance between them. How would she ever bridge the gap now?

A few weeks ago she would have blurted her thoughts right out, probably in anger. But things had changed for her over this short time.

She had changed, she realized in astonishment.

The front door opened quietly, causing both of them to turn. Julia's father stood haltingly, his eyes widening at the apparent familiarity with which the giant of a man entered the apartment.

Zeke let himself in, then turned, startled to find himself face-to-face with the older man. That Julia had company was no big surprise, but that it was the familiar face of the Grace Church janitor—Julia's father—stunned him to the core.

He glanced at Julia, and she nodded in response to his unspoken question.

"Greg," he boomed out, extending his hand. "How are you?"

"Zeke," Julia's father replied, flashing a friendly smile. "Are you here to see my Julia?"

Zeke saw Julia bristle, and encouraged her with a wink.

"Yes, sir, I'm here to see Julia," he said easily. Speaking to Julia, he said, "I let myself in. I thought you might be dozing."

He also knew how stir-crazy she was, and he thought she might just chuck her pillow at him.

"How are you feeling, sweetheart?"

Julia blushed at the use of his familiar pet name, and his smile widened. He shouldn't tease her like this, but it was just too good an opportunity.

Her father seemed to be taking it in stride, reseating himself on the armchair, which left open the opposite side of the sofa from where Zeke stood. The seat right next to Julia.

Before being seated himself, he asked politely, "Is this a bad time for me to be here, Greg? I know you haven't seen your daughter in a while. I can always come back another time."

"Not at all, Zeke. We'd like you to join us, wouldn't we, Julia?"

Zeke seated himself without waiting for her answer, though he thought she'd be happy to have him there. As far as he knew, she still wasn't on speaking terms with the man.

With Zeke to break the tension, the three spoke easily of her father's recent traveling experiences and Zeke and Julia's ice-skating escapade. Her father roared with laughter at Zeke's description of his own role as the knight in shining armor. And his eyes narrowed with concern as Zeke described spending Christmas Eve in the emergency room of a hospital.

Julia was finally beginning to relax in her father's presence, very much due to Zeke's easy manner with Greg. As usual, Zeke knew all the right things to say to put anyone at ease, including her father.

After several minutes, Julia's father cleared his throat. "I'm sure you'll understand if I request to see Julia alone for a few minutes," he said without preamble. "It's important, Zeke, or I wouldn't ask."

Zeke wasn't too quick to jump when Greg requested it. He gave Julia a long, hard look, apparently trying to access her feelings on the matter. She couldn't mistake the ardent devotion in his gaze, not even if she wanted to, and knew he would stay here with her if she so much as nodded.

Of course, he couldn't know she'd invited her father here herself. "Please, just go," she whispered, a ragged tone to her voice.

For a moment, Zeke's face registered a kind of hurt surprise, but then he locked his featured into a clear line. Even then, his smoky blue eyes held a glimmer of his intent. He wanted to remain her protector, and she was, in a very real sense, sending him away.

She didn't miss the way he slammed the door behind him. Her heart ached as if a door had slammed there, as well.

"So, then, what's the deal with Zeke?" her father questioned, reminding Julia of a similar question from her roommate's lips. It was a question that continued to haunt her late at night when she was unable to sleep.

"What about Zeke?" she echoed testily, not wanting to blurt out something foolish to her father.

"Just wondering if there's anything serious going on between the two of you," he answered, point-blank.

"Yes," she answered before she thought better of it. "No," she amended hastily.

Her father chuckled. "Which is it? Yes or no?"

Julia groaned. "I wish I knew."

"That bad, huh?"

"Worse."

"Love never comes easy, hon," her father said softly, his head bent. "There's always a price."

Julia's gaze riveted to him, but he wouldn't look up and meet her eyes. She'd always pictured him as the aggressor, the one who administered the pain, but now she saw him as he was, a man filled with pain and regret for actions he couldn't take back.

She'd hated this man. Now she felt only pity. And love.

Reaching for her mother's Bible, which was still lying open on the coffee table, Greg Evans reached out and ran a finger across the highlighted verses in Ephesians.

"These were your mother's favorite verses," he said, a catch in his voice. "That's why I put the note and rose petal between those pages. The words always remind me of your mother."

Her father's words heightened her joy. Julia's heart swelled with love for her departed mother, feeling her love reaching out to her even through the distance of eternity.

"I don't know how to tell you this, so I'm just going to tell you," her father blurted suddenly, tearing Julia from her thoughts and memories.

"What?"

"I'm leaving."

She'd known the words were coming, but that didn't stop the wrecking ball from taking a swing at her midsection. She closed her eyes against the pain. "When?"

"I don't know. Soon." He blew out a breath and slicked a hand through his hair. "I'll come back and see you often, I swear I will."

She nodded mutely.

"I tried to keep an honest job here, Julia. I really did. I want to be near you. But I've got this inner call to see the world. It haunts me day and night. Staying here, and working one job, isn't what I was made for."

Julia knew. It was why her father looked so ragged. The sweet siren of new sights and sounds beckoned. Of course he was going to follow.

"Can I make one request?" she asked softly.

"Shoot."

"Bang."

Her father looked startled for a moment, then laughed.

"Stay for my wedding?"

His eyes grew wide. "Come again?"

"Well, I'm not positive I can still convince the big lug that just left that I'm marriage material, but he seems to have taken a liking to me. I can't seem to live without him."

"I'll be there," Greg promised.

"Oh, and there's one other thing."

"Name it."

"Could you help me move from this awful, lumpy couch to the armchair? I don't have my crutches handy, and my back is killing me."

She'd only meant for him to give her a hand, but with a wide, endearing smile, her father scooped her into his arms, proving himself in as good a shape as a younger man.

As he gently seated her on the armchair, he paused. "Can I get you anything before I leave?"

"No," Julia mumbled, feeling suddenly exhausted. Her father's beaming smile was genuine. He really cared for her.

Perhaps it was time to bridge the chasm she'd formed between them and voice what she only now discovered she felt.

"Daddy?" she said as he turned to leave.

"Hmm?" he asked, looking back from his path to the door.

"I love you."

His lips quivered for a moment as he fought for control. Then a lone tear escaped from the corner of his eye and meandered down the lines of his cheek to bank off the crease of his jaw. His cloudy blue eyes cleared, gleaming in a way that made him look years younger than he was.

"I love you, too," her father croaked before dropping to his knees by her side and crushing her in his strong embrace. "Oh, baby, I love you, too."

Chapter Nineteen

Julia had spent the dark hours picturing how Zeke would grin when she told him she loved him, a thought that had sent shivers down her spine, though she'd been toasty warm under her electric blanket.

Like the strong and compassionate man he was, Zeke had willingly stepped out of the way in order for her to pursue what he must have believed in his heart would make her happy.

But now she was going to rectify that error.

"Please help me find Zeke," Julia implored Lakeisha, grabbing her roommate by both hands as she passed the lumpy couch where she was once again ensconced. "I've got to talk to him right away."

"Don't you think you've put him through enough, girl?" Lakeisha asked blatantly. "You know he's in love with you, don't you? Don't hurt him more by chasing after him when you don't mean it."

"Hurt him?" Julia exclaimed. "Hurt him? I want to *marry* the man, not hurt him."

At Lakeisha's astonished look, she nodded. "You're right. I've been an idiot. I've been in love with Zeke for a long time. I was just too foolish to realize it." Her eyes penetrated into Lakeisha's, imploring her to read the honest intensity of her heart.

Her roommate's gaze narrowed, and then she nodded. "Do you know where to find him?"

Julia shook her head. "He could be anywhere."

Where would Zeke go? Her mind blanked. She'd called him, but he was either not home or not answering the phone. The last time she'd tried, the number had come up as disconnected, which is what put her in such a panic now.

She was about to throw her hands up in despair when it suddenly hit her. "The pond behind the church."

"The *pond?*" Lakeisha questioned, sounding as if she believed she hadn't heard Julia correctly. Then, with a dramatic sigh, she shrugged. "Okay, girl. What I won't do for the cause of true love."

It took fifteen minutes for the two women to get Julia down the stairs, into the car, and to make the short drive to the church. Getting to the grove of trees behind the church was another matter. They were hampered at every step by Julia's amateur use of her crutches, particularly when they began moving across the loose-packed snow.

Julia's heart fell as she neared the pond. It was too quiet. Zeke must have gone somewhere else. Her intuition had been wrong.

At this rate she'd never have the opportunity to explain. Her mind explored all of the horrible possibilities. What if he left town before she had a chance to speak to him?

Forget speaking to him. She wanted to plant a kiss on him he'd never forget. One that would leave him wanting more for the rest of his life.

When Lakeisha suggested they return to the car, Julia begged for a few minutes alone.

"You're sure you can make it out here? It's pretty slick."

"I'll be fine. I just need a few minutes alone." To let her heart break in solitude.

"Okay. I'll be waiting for you in the car."

Lakeisha moved off, leaving Julia alone with her thoughts and her crutches.

She sucked in a big gust of crisp, clean air, another by-product of the recent snow. Denver, like most large cities, had a brown cloud of pollution that choked the oxygen out of the air. But with the snow came relief, and for the moment, Julia gloried in the very act of breathing, letting the cool air brush the cobwebs from her head and the hot sting of her heart.

Working her way carefully to a spot near the water's edge, she leaned her head back against the tree, welcoming the feel of the scratchy bark against her scalp.

Her heart turned to God, and she willed herself to pray, to offer her burdens and her shattered heart up to God. Out here, God seemed so much closer, more approachable. She observed His handiwork all around her, from the scratchy pine at her back to the bristling of a chipmunk who had inadvertently run across her path.

When she opened her eyes again, she was amazed to see the outline of Zeke's sturdy frame. She rubbed her eyes to be sure he wasn't a mirage formed from a desperate heart.

He stood at the edge of the pond with his back toward her, his hands thrust into the front pockets of his blue jeans. He didn't have a coat, but seemed oblivious to the frigid winter air.

She slowly became aware that she was trespassing on something infinitely private, and felt her cheeks warm in spite of the fact that her intrusion was unintentional and as yet unnoticed.

She thought he might be praying. Part of her wanted to leave, but something greater compelled her to stay. She sat quietly at the base of the tree and watched him for a moment.

His Rockies cap was pulled low over his brow, complimenting his sharp, bearded profile. He was gazing over the lake, his breath coming in short puffs of white.

He looked so strong and handsome with the winter sunlight forming a background to his fine physique. Her heart swelled with tenderness as she considered what he must be suffering unnecessarily.

He looked so unhappy.

"Zeke," she called quietly, almost afraid to break the silence.

He turned slowly, his big blue eyes widening. "Julia," he gulped. "What are you doing here?"

Zeke's heart, already pounding loudly from the exertion of the hike he'd just made, doubled its rate. He smiled grimly and walked to where Julia sat. The skin on his face stung with the flush of effort. The crisp air caused his breath to come out in heavy puffs spewing from his laboring lungs.

It stung, and he was glad.

"Julia," he said in greeting. "I didn't see you."

Though he was flustered by her presence, he struggled not to show it. She was a welcome friend, not an intruder.

She patted the ground next to her. "Have a seat. I'd offer coffee, but I didn't think to bring any."

"Don't mind if I do," he said, flopping down on the snow across from her. He stretched out onto his side and leaned onto his elbow. After a moment, he broke the silence. "What are you up to?"

"I came here looking for you. But when I didn't see your truck in the lot, I decided I needed a few minutes alone to think," she said, her voice earnest.

"I came here to think, as well," he admitted gravely. "Nothing like fresh air to put things in perspective."

"Me and my pathetic problems," Julia lamented.

He reached out and tucked a lock of her hair behind her ear, brushing the soft sweetness of her cheek with his fingers as he did so.

"What's troubling you?" he asked, his voice unusually low.

"My father, partially," she answered, but Zeke didn't think she was telling the whole truth. Her expression was shaded.

"He's a good man," Zeke said quietly.

She nodded slowly. "Yes. I guess I'm beginning to realize that."

"I've spoken with him several times at Heart-Beat."

"He'll be leaving soon," Julia said in a monotone.

Zeke cleared his throat. "I'm sorry to hear that. Have you worked things out with him?"

"Yes, in a way. I think I'm beginning to understand my father. I don't agree with his methods, but I think I can finally accept him for who and what he is."

"I'm glad." Zeke stroked her arm, offering reassurance. "I like to see you happy. This thing with your father has taken more out of you than I think you realize."

"How so?"

"Sometimes the problems we have here on earth affect our relationship with God."

"That hasn't happened with me," Julia immediately protested, and then quickly clamped her mouth closed.

Hadn't she been having problems praying lately? And her priorities were all confused, of that much she was certain, and she hadn't the faintest idea how to fix the problem. And all along, Zeke had known.

She looked across at Zeke, focusing instead on his handsome face. He looked worn, his blue eyes troubled.

"I was thinking about you," he said as if in answer to her unspoken question.

Julia's gaze shot to Zeke's face. He had risen to a sitting position, his arms clasped around his knees, and was staring back at her, his features even.

"About me?" she echoed weakly.

"I just want you to forget all about what I said on Christmas morning, okay?"

"What? Why?"

"It doesn't matter."

"What do you mean it doesn't matter? Is that why you've had your phone turned off? Because you don't love me anymore?"

He gave her an odd look. "I didn't have my phone turned off. You must have called a wrong number."

Julia looked away as her face flamed. But she

couldn't help the words that tumbled from her lips "I love you, Zeke."

He stood abruptly, his hands clenched into fists at his side. "Julia, don't," he pleaded, his voice cracking with emotion.

Her words thrown back at her, however unintentionally. She cringed as she fumbled with her crutches in an effort to stand. "Listen to me," she implored, reaching her arms to him. "It's always been you. I was just too blind to realize it."

He brushed her hands aside as he walked past her, back up the hill.

"Zeke, please." She'd beg if she had to. He'd been through enough pain on her account—it was no wonder he mistrusted her now. But she couldn't very well chase after him, so she had to make do with her words. "Just hear me out."

When he froze midstride, she took that as a good sign, and plunged in with the truth. "I love you. I have for a long time. I had all these foolish plans, and I was all mixed up."

She ground to a halt.

When he turned, his expression was laced with pain, but Julia could see the hope shining from his clear blue eyes. She allowed all the intensity of her love to flow from her heart and through their locked gazes. Surely he could feel the sincerity of her love.

He smiled in that crooked way he had, and her heart turned over.

"I love you, too," he said, his voice low and raspy.

With a growl of happiness, he pulled her into his warm embrace and kissed her. He marveled at the way his arms fit so perfectly around her, as if they'd been made for each other. But then again, he mused in amazement, they *had* been made for each other.

And if he had his way, she wouldn't spend a day out of his arms, not for the rest of her life.

After a few minutes, Zeke broke the embrace. "We've forgotten something important, sweetheart."

"What?" Julia asked, looking dizzy and rumpled and thoroughly kissed.

Zeke dropped to one knee in the snow, and she clutched her hand to her heart.

"Julia Marie Evans, will you marry me, funny name and all?"

Julia composed her features into an expression of serious contemplation. "Ezekiel Habakkuk Malachi Taylor," she said, a small chuckle escaping her at the mention of his middle names, "I would be honored to become your wife."

He stood and whooped with joy, throwing his Rockies cap into the air, and hardly noticing when it caught up on a high branch, sending a shower of snow to baptize them like rice at a wedding reception. "Now don't you go repeating that name in public," he warned.

Julia wiggled back into the comfort of his arms.

"Well, there is one way you could keep me from talking," she suggested coyly.

He laughed and obliged her upturned lips.

They stood silently for a minute, enjoying the quiet perfection of the moment. "Julia, sweetheart?" Zeke whispered into the freshness her hair.

"Hmm?"

"Is there anyone you'd like me to…you know, ask…I mean, for a blessing on our marriage?"

Julia leaned back and smiled full into Zeke's face. "This won't come as a surprise, I don't think, but it would be nice to ask…my father."

Epilogue

"Julia, girl, you outdid yourself," Lakeisha said with a happy chuckle.

"I'll say," agreed Greg Evans, who was seated in a wicker rocking chair, contentedly rocking a newborn baby in the corner of the room. After two years, Julia wasn't sure she'd still be in contact with her father, and yet here he was, sharing her joy. *Their joy.*

"Where did you get her name, anyway?" Lakeisha asked, breaking into Julia's thoughts. "Esther Naomi Ruth. It's beautiful. Long, but beautiful."

Julia's heart welled at the thought of her newborn, and the man who was now the proud father. She shared a knowing smile with Zeke.

Zeke's arms were also laden with a newborn baby.

"Or *his* name, either," Lakeisha continued, reaching out to jiggle the baby boy's hand. He gurgled, and Lakeisha chuckled.

"Matthew Luke," Zeke pronounced heartily.

Julia rejoiced that her dear friend—and her father—shared this special day with her and her beaming husband. The secret of the names, they'd keep between the two of them.

Lakeisha kissed the boy's forehead, then turned and kissed little Esther's fair cheek.

"Esther Ruth Naomi and Matthew Luke," Julia pronounced with a mother's smile. "Twin blessings. And that's the gospel truth."

* * * * *

Dear Reader,

Have you ever done the right thing for the wrong reason?

Julia Evans wanted to serve God with her whole heart, but in her zeal, in her reliance on her own abilities and resources, she was tempted to do God's work on her own. In the process, she almost missed God's best for her!

I don't know about you, but I often get so busy that I don't wait on the Lord. I jump from project to project like a wild kangaroo, and never take the time to rest and seek God's best for my life. Yet it is when Christ works through my weaknesses that I am truly strong.

I hope you'll take a moment now to stop and wait upon the Lord. Depend upon God, dear reader. Only through His power can we be effective for Him.

I pray God's best for you, today and always.

I love to hear from my readers. Let me know what you thought about Zeke and Julia's story, and how you've sought God's best in your life. My address is P.O. Box 28140 #16, Lakewood, CO 80228-3108.

God's Best,

Deb Kastner

THE CHRISTMAS GROOM

Therefore if the Son makes you free,
you shall be free indeed.
—*John* 8:36

To the LORD my God, with grateful thanks.

HOW TO VALIDATE YOUR
EDITOR'S FREE GIFTS!
"THANK YOU"

1 Peel off the FREE GIFTS SEAL from the front cover. Place it in the space provided at right. This automatically entitles you to receive two free books and two exciting surprise gifts.

2 Send back this card and you'll get 2 Love Inspired® books. These books have a combined cover price of $11.50 for the regular-print and $13.00 for the larger-print in the U.S. and $13.50 for the regular-print or $15.00 for the larger-print in Canada, but they are yours to keep absolutely FREE!

3 There's no catch. You're under no obligation to buy anything. We charge nothing—ZERO—for your first shipment. And you don't have to make any minimum number of purchases—not even one!

4 We call this line Love Inspired because every month you'll receive books that are filled with joy, faith and traditional values. The stories will lift your spirit and warm your heart! You'll like the convenience of getting them delivered to your home well before they are in stores. And you'll love our discount prices, too!

5 We hope that after receiving your free books you'll want to remain a subscriber. But the choice is yours—to continue or cancel, anytime at all! So why not take us up on our invitation, with no risk of any kind. You'll be glad you did!

6 And remember...just for validating your Editor's Free Gifts Offer, we'll send you 2 books and 2 gifts, *ABSOLUTELY FREE!*

YOURS FREE!
We'll send you two fabulous surprise gifts (worth about $10) absolutely FREE, simply for accepting our no-risk offer!

The Editor's "Thank You" Free Gifts Include:

- Two inspirational romance books
- Two exciting surprise gifts

YES!

PLACE FREE GIFTS SEAL HERE

I have placed my Editor's "thank you" Free Gifts seal in the space provided above. Please send me the 2 FREE books and 2 FREE gifts for which I qualify. I understand that I am under no obligation to purchase anything further, as explained on the opposite page.

❏ I prefer the regular-print edition
105/305 IDL FJLP

❏ I prefer the larger-print edition
122/322 IDL FJLP

Please Print

FIRST NAME

LAST NAME

ADDRESS

APT.#   CITY

STATE/PROV.   ZIP/POSTAL CODE

Chapter One

Colin Brockman was late to his first day of school. More accurately, his first day *back* in school.

He crept as casually and quietly as his big, squeaky-tennis-shoed feet would let him into the muted twilight tones of his Child Psych auditorium classroom. Gym shoes were far more comfortable than navy dress shoes, but Colin found that, for a moment, he missed the familiarity of the spit and polish, the recognizable click of the heels as he walked.

At least he knew what to expect from navy issue. He hadn't a clue what to expect from this day.

With a relieved huff, he slid into a seat that, while made with an adult in mind, certainly didn't take into account his considerably large frame. He shifted backward and forward, left to right, knocking his knees against the bottom of the desk, raking his elbows against the steel hardware and knowing that with every movement he continued to draw unwanted attention to himself and his dilemma.

Didn't these desks adjust for height somehow? Or had he just picked one meant for a third-grade kid?

When no bolts loosened under his fingers, he changed tactics, turning, stretching and curving himself as smoothly as possible into the seat, mentally comparing himself to a piece of artist's molding clay.

Mashed, rolled and squished into the creation of the Master's form.

Despite his discomfort, Colin grinned at the mental picture he'd created of God pounding and kneading him into shape, and knew he wasn't so very far off. He was a work in progress, potter's clay in the Master's hands. He trusted God could make more of him than he could of himself—he'd gone that route already, and anyone with an eye could see where that had taken him.

He continued his slow, steady movements until he was certain he could breathe and stretch his long legs, which appeared to be his two greatest problems at the moment. That, and maybe the ability to actually reach the desk with his hand in case he wanted to take notes on a class that was rapidly moving along without him.

Pushing the hood of his oversize gray sweatshirt off his head with both palms, he used his fingers to scrub through the tips of his fine blond hair. It had been years since he'd grown his hair above a military buzz cut, and no one had mentioned how terribly it would itch and bother him.

Still, he thought he might live through it if he could grow it past the Chia Pet stage.

He smothered another grin. He didn't mind, not really. In the big scheme of things, it was a pretty small annoyance. At least he had the choice of whether or not to grow his hair out, to make his own decision about something even as minimal as that, for a change.

The navy, for all its many benefits, didn't give a man many choices, and Colin was eager to make up for lost time now that he was his own man.

Eager to begin his career as a student, he jammed one hand into his backpack, digging for a fresh spiral notebook and a pen or a pencil to write with. He was positive they were to be found somewhere in the depths of his bag.

Or at least thought they were there.

He was almost certain.

He bit the corner of his lip and made another pass at it. His hand closed over several items, which he grasped and discarded—a fork, a sock without a mate, a baseball, a stud finder he'd been using earlier in the day on his apartment wall in order to hang pictures.

He cringed, squeezing his eyebrows down close around his eyes as he called himself every kind of idiot. It was his first day of school. Surely he had remembered to throw in something to write on. And to write with.

At length, he found the notebook he wanted, but his blue ballpoint pen, the one he'd purchased especially for this new school year, eluded him, until he remembered suddenly he'd shoved it into the back left pocket of his jeans before he left.

So he wouldn't forget where it was, naturally.

Settling restlessly in his seat, he took a moment to look around, tapping his newly found pen on the top of his notebook as a rich female voice resonated warmly from the front of the room, speaking of classroom procedures, what to expect from the course and what homework assignments would be like.

Colin listened with only half an ear. He knew he should be paying more attention, especially on his first day, but he was more interested in his fellow students than what was going on at the front of the room.

Who were these people, and what were they in for? He didn't expect to fit in with a crowd of kids coming straight from high school, exactly, but...

Oh, man.

Old man was more like it. Was he really ready for this?

He was astounded at the profusion of young men in baggy pants, young ladies with fuchsia and other

Easter colors striped in their hair, ill-concealed Game Boys peeking out of pockets, coats, dresses and purses. Bodies of both genders were pierced in places Colin didn't even want to think about.

Oh, man.

Where were the people like him? Where were the people who hadn't figured out they needed to go to school until they were—what was a nice way of phrasing it?—well past their adolescent prime?

Looking around him, he felt worlds older than the youngsters in this class, though that was hardly the truth. He was thirty, which wasn't exactly over the hill.

He was probably only a decade older than most of the students. But in experience, he was an antique compared to the young men and women sitting around him.

Or at least he felt that way.

His gaze wandered down to the floor of the auditorium, where a couple of professors, young ladies, were taking turns speaking. The muted sunlight made it hard to see that far down, but Colin's vision was excellent.

He smiled as his gaze shifted from one of the female professors to the other and riveted upon her.

He was much closer in age to that pretty little parcel with the gorgeous long legs, sashaying back and forth in the front of the room.

Much closer.

He didn't know why he hadn't noticed the attractive twenty-something woman earlier. He had to be really nervous to have missed that bright beacon of light in an otherwise shadowed room, for it was her warm voice lighting up the darkness.

And to think he hadn't even looked to the front of the room until now! Not to look for potential assignments or anything. He hadn't even glanced at the prominent overhead projector illuminating the middle of the room.

To think he'd almost continued on blissfully unaware of the lovely angel who would most certainly transform this class into something, if not pleasurable, then at least palatable.

He grinned. He couldn't help it if he liked a pretty face. He hadn't seen enough of them in the navy. His ambition to become a chaplain didn't make him blind to a pair of pretty eyes or make him immune to the scent of a beautiful woman.

He might not have a lot of relationship experience of his own to draw from, but he'd been around. He'd been there to watch firsthand when his beloved twin sister fell for the love of her life. He knew how it worked.

And to be honest, he wouldn't mind so very much if *it* worked on him.

In his opinion, God had saved the best for last. Women were the highlight of God's creative efforts, and when He'd finished Eve, He'd had good reason to pronounce His work *very good.*

He tossed his pen down on the desk and leaned forward in his seat, intent on a better view. Now that he'd noticed the pretty prof, he couldn't take his eyes off her.

She had long, thick dark brown hair that gleamed with red highlights as it shifted when she walked. And her eyes were a dark, rich green, and the color of Christmas velvet.

Her sharp gaze was, he noticed with a blast of electric shock, pinned directly on him. He had no doubt whatsoever that she hadn't missed his tardy entrance to his first class on his first day of school, or of his subsequent fidgeting around in his seat as he unsuccessfully attempted to get settled.

He cleared his throat aloud.

That could be a problem.

She was obviously his teacher.

His *professor,* he mentally corrected. This was college, not grade school.

Miss Prof. Or was that *Mrs.?*

He flashed her his most charming grin. Surprise flashed across her gaze and her pretty, full lips hinted softly at a grin; but then the moment was gone. She frowned and lifted one eyebrow in silent question.

What was he up to?

He swore he saw the corners of her sweet lips

twitch as she shook her head, looking put out and disappointed in that unique way elementary school teachers had of making their students feel guilty for misbehaving in their classroom.

Colin's back went up in a moment, his spine stiffening in stubbornness. If she was looking to make someone feel *guilty,* she was looking at the wrong student. This wasn't elementary school, and he wasn't a child anymore. He was paying good money to attend the seminary, and to take these university classes on the side.

This was his planet, his continent, his day, hour, minute, and he wasn't even counting seconds.

He was here because he wanted to be, and he'd arrive and leave when he wanted. He wouldn't purposely do anything to disrupt the class or bother any other students, but he wouldn't hand over any of his freshly minted independence, either.

He knew his philosophy sounded a good deal like a bad attitude, but it wasn't. He happily extended his generous outlook to the rest of the world, if they wanted it, which he very much doubted. He'd always thought himself a bit of a maverick.

In truth, he just wanted to find out what it meant to be footloose and fancy-free. He'd never had the chance to do that, even in his youth. And now that he had the time and opportunity, he wasn't going to give it up, even to a pretty professor.

He turned his attention to the first lecture, scribbling illegible notes on the first clean, crisp page of his notebook.

Colin was soon lost in thought and note-taking as he attempted to follow the lecture. Ms. *Gorgeous Legs*—he clearly needed to find out her real name— was talking a mile a minute, and very animatedly, about something called the Hierarchy of Needs that some famous psychologist guy named Maslow had come up with.

Projected onto the screen at the front of the auditorium was a diagram in the shape of a triangle. A person, especially a child, the lovely woman explained, was unable to focus on obtaining or meeting the needs on the higher levels until he or she had fulfilled the lower-level needs, the base needs, if you will. Things such as finding food, warmth and shelter.

Colin frowned at the diagram he'd traced onto his paper. The more ethereal needs were indeed placed exclusively in higher rows.

But what about the search for God? Didn't that transcend even the most basic need barriers? As a future navy chaplain, he experienced the insatiable desire to know more, and quickly scribbled his own ideas in the margins.

Since he assumed he'd missed the part of the lesson on how the class was run, he wasn't certain how to go about getting his questions answered. He had no office hours or phone numbers to call.

"Serves you right, Brockman," he mumbled under his breath.

He started to raise his hand, then pulled it back down, deciding he'd ask his question at the end of the class...if he could remember it for that long. There was a lot of stuff to think about, and this was only his first class of the day.

He'd always considered himself a smart man, but not necessarily good at book learning. If he was going to make it in college, he was going to have to apply himself, especially since he hadn't been to school in years.

"Your first assignment is going to feel like a big one," said the beautiful woman in the front of the room, her thick sable hair swishing hypnotically with each movement. Colin pressed his chin in his hand, scratching at the stubble. "But it's important that you take this project seriously, and have it completed by next Monday."

Colin paused in his note-taking and scowled, shaking his head in silent dissent.

"Great," he whispered under his breath. "A term paper on the very first week of school."

He was completely serious in his opposition, but the three-hundred-pound jock next to him bellowed out a deep-throated laugh.

"Something funny, gentlemen?" The sable-haired woman in the front of the room was eyeing him again. He bit his bottom lip against a smile. He really needed to learn her name.

"No, ma'am," he called out, and the boy next to him sniggered. Her lovely green eyes grazed over the younger man and landed squarely on Colin. Her gaze glimmered with amusement, though her posture was tight and her expression grim.

He resisted the urge to straighten his shoulders and couple his hands on the desk as he'd been taught to do in military school. Rather, he slid down in his seat just about as far as his large frame could fit.

Maybe his question could wait. Maybe he could simply disappear altogether.

"Your assignment," announced Holly McCade, deciding her best strategy on this first day of a new year of student teaching was simply to ignore the snickering, juvenile troublemakers in the back, "is simply this. Find somewhere you can observe a situation in which children are struggling to meet their basic needs. There are dozens of examples I could give you on where to find these children, but I leave that part up to your discretion and creativity. Please feel free to come see me for help and/or suggestions if you run into any trouble with this part of the assignment."

She paused, struggling, for a moment, with her phrasing. "You must observe those children for at least two hours, but the more time you spend with them, the better of an understanding you will walk away with."

She held up her own three-ringed notebook. "Taking notes would be a good idea, but you are not required to do so. You will be required to hand in a one-page paper telling me who you selected, where they are located and how much time you spent observing."

"Is that all?" asked a surprised young lady in the first row. The girl was obviously just out of high school. She was wearing too much makeup, and wore her boyfriend's high school letter jacket around her shoulders.

Holly laughed. "Yes. That's all."

A surreptitious glance at her watch signaled a frenzy of activity as students packed up their books and got their things together.

And she hadn't even said the word *go,* she thought, smothering another smile.

"Remember, if you have any questions, I'll be here for another ten minutes."

A couple of students responded to that call. One obviously wanted to get in good with the teacher and make sure Holly knew who he was. The other was a typical overachiever obsessing about whether or not Holly would give an A+ on the assignment when the student in question was only allowed to turn in one page.

"Take it easy," said a rich, laughing baritone from

somewhere behind Holly's left shoulder. "You make it sound like you *want* her to make us write a term paper or something."

"I…well…I…" stammered the girl, and then picked up her books and darted out of the classroom without another word.

Somehow Holly instinctively knew to whom the voice belonged even before she turned around. She was certain it must be the man she'd noticed sitting at the top round of the auditorium. The man with sparkling blue eyes and an untidy bit of light blond hair.

It felt strange for her, as a student teacher, to be teaching someone older than she was, although the man could hardly be called her grandfather. She guessed him to be around thirty, only two years or so older. Not much of an age difference.

Older people returned to college all the time in this day and age. She'd taught a retired couple last semester and hadn't seen anything strange about that. So it wasn't such an oddity for this man to be enrolled in her class.

But it certainly felt like an oddity, especially when the character in question had spent the study hour cracking jokes with an eighteen-year-old boisterous jock. She would have thought a guy this man's age would have respect for the classroom, if not the teacher.

"Can I help you?" she asked testily.

His grin slipped. "To tell you the truth, ma'am, I don't know."

Was he toying with her? She searched his face, but saw no hint of his intentions. His expression gave her no clue whether he was serious or not.

But dealing with potential class clowns was part of student teaching, and she sighed inwardly, even as she steeled herself to be graceful under adversity, no matter how handsome the package.

With effort, she smiled. "Do you have a question about the assignment?" she asked, rephrasing the query.

"Question, comment, statement," Colin said. "My name is Colin Brockman, by the way." He thrust out his hand with a wink and a grin.

He already knew her name, at least if he'd been paying attention in class. Since he probably hadn't been, and because she didn't want him to keep calling her *ma'am,* she responded.

"Holly McCade," she answered. She hadn't missed a beat in their conversation, but her heart missed several beats as she shook his hand. He had large palms, smooth fingers and a firm but gentle grip.

"My question has to do with that triangle thing you talked about in your lecture," he said.

"The Hierarchy of Needs," she supplied. "The one suggested by Dr. Maslow."

He nodded vigorously. "Well, the thing is, Miss…

Mrs.…uh, Holly," he stammered, then stopped for a moment and tried again. "I believe there's a bigger base than the one you've—Dr. Maslow's—given."

Intriguing. He *had* been paying attention. "How do you mean?"

"I mean God, ma'am. I think there should be a new bottom row—one reserved for God alone."

Holly's heart stirred. As a Christian, she shared similar feelings, but of course could not teach those beliefs openly in a public classroom. Besides, Dr. Maslow's theory had been used in the psych classroom for years.

"Do you mean," she asked slowly, "in the place of eating and sleeping?"

He frowned and shook his head. "No."

"Please continue, Colin. Keep in mind that Maslow did make room for metaphysical thinking at higher levels of the triangle, addressed after the basic needs have been provided for."

His eyes narrowed in thought, and he stroked the stubbly line of his jaw. Shaving hadn't, apparently, been the reason he was late for class.

"The more I think about it, the more I wonder if God should really occupy a level at all," he said, sounding surprisingly contemplative, considering his scruffy appearance.

He continued, sounding more confident with each word. "God isn't a system, something you think about or organize with. He's not Someone you can compartmentalize or graph. I guess what I'm trying to say, and not very eloquently, is that I think He's a relationship. *Without* boundaries, or format. He transcends the triangle."

"Maybe He *is* the triangle," Holly suggested quietly. "By and in and through everything—every need, every want, every desire."

Before Holly could catch a breath, Colin pounded a nearby table with his fists and hooted with glee. "That's it! Hot diggity-dog."

She chuckled nervously, brushing her fingers through her hair as she covertly looked around to see if anyone had noticed his outburst. To her relief, the room was empty except for the two of them.

"Ain't life just grand?" he asked with a smile. "Don't you just love it when you *get it?*"

She'd never thought about it that way, but she supposed she did enjoy the thrill of discovery. His childlike enthusiasm was contagious, and she found herself smiling back at him.

And she found herself modifying her initial opinion of her unusual scholar. Colin might, after all, be precisely the type of student she wanted to teach. "Do you know where you're going to go for your assignment?" she blurted without thinking.

He shook his head, his blond hair fluffing out every which direction. He reminded her of a little boy growing out his summer haircut, or maybe of a wild turkey, she wasn't sure which.

Either way, he looked adorable.

"I have a couple of ideas, if you'd like to join me," she offered tentatively, unsure why she was reaching out to him. She wasn't sure she was supposed to be interacting with students on this level. She wasn't even sure she liked him.

"The Christian Relief Center is open to visitors. We could go there," she suggested.

"These are street people?"

"Yes. CRC caters to women on the street who are there due to divorce or battering. There are always lots of children to observe. CRC tries to sweep these women and children off the street and, well, meet their lower hierarchical needs."

"That's a mouthful," Colin said. "Hierarchical. Try saying that three times fast."

Holly felt the heat rush to her face. "You don't have to go with me if you have somewhere else to go."

His gaze flickered with amusement. He reached out and lightly chucked her under her chin. "I have no place else to go. Lead on, fair Holly, and I will follow."

Chapter Two

Holly McCade switched her position on the university park bench, crossing her left leg over her right and stretching her right arm across the back of the bench. She turned her head, taking in the landscape all the way around her. Colorado was gorgeous in the fall, and Greeley was no exception. Though it was too early for the aspen leaves to turn their traditional shades of yellow, orange and gold, the day was still vivid with color.

Greeley lay on the eastern plains, and Holly could see the green and brown patchwork of farmland and ranchland from where she sat. And though there were one or two taller buildings marring the view, she could even see the front range of the Rocky Mountains in all their majestic splendor, far enough away to require a plan, but close enough for a drive.

Students milled around between classes, talking,

studying or playing Frisbee on the lawn. Birds chattered from the trees, and there was even a big brown squirrel helping himself to lunch from a convenient garbage barrel.

It was all very nice, and she might even have enjoyed the morning sunshine and the lovely views, except that she wasn't sitting here to spend half her Saturday watching university students play games and hungry squirrels rummage for food.

She was waiting for Colin Brockman.

With a loud sigh, she glanced at her watch.

Again.

She didn't know why she'd offered to do this—meet with a man she hardly knew and wasn't completely sure she liked. Probably she was under some misguided, philanthropic notion that she could help him broaden his horizons on his way to a better understanding of child psychology.

And to have waited over an hour for him—she must really be losing it. She wasn't the young woman with low self-esteem who'd do anything for a man she might have been in her youth. Anything but!

She should go. She could be busy with something else. Her time was important, and Colin obviously didn't respect that. Or respect her, for that matter.

She should have gone with her first impression, she decided. Colin was nothing more than an overgrown kid with mischief in his heart.

She suddenly recalled all those little things she

noticed about him that clinched her first opinion—
the cut of his uneven hair, the day's growth of beard
on his face. Even his clothes looked like he'd thrown
them on from where they'd once lay crumpled, probably on the floor of his bedroom.

He was a rascal, all right.

A *late* rascal.

Anger and frustration welled up inside her heart.
Anger at herself. Why had she bothered waiting?

She sighed and reached for her bag. She already
knew the answer to that question before she asked
it of herself.

First impression of him notwithstanding, when
she'd spoken with Colin two days ago in the auditorium and he'd voiced his very clever and fervent
thoughts on Maslow's theory, she'd sensed something exceptional about him, something that drove
away every thought of his scruffy appearance and
reeled her in to his charm. He fascinated her with
the inkling that there was something more to him
than his outward appearance.

Something extraordinary.

His eyes. His beautiful, sea-blue eyes. When he
spoke about anything, they danced with happiness
and amusement. When he spoke about God, they
blazed with love, fire and excitement.

She couldn't help but want to find out more about
the man. She wasn't ready to pursue a relationship
with anyone, but she could use all the friends she

could get. And she wanted to get to know more about Colin.

It wasn't as if she were attracted to him or anything. Not *that* way. He was hardly her type. *Her* type of man was a stylish, well-dressed, aggressive overachiever who cared more about himself and his career than he did the woman he supposedly loved.

Which was exactly why she was swearing off the whole gender. One-hundred-percent cold turkey.

Except for Colin. And it appeared *he* was swearing off *her.* She glanced once again at her watch and decided she'd waited long enough.

She gathered her bag, concluding it was pointless to stay any longer. He was obviously not going to show up, and the longer she waited, the more she was going to hurt herself.

Maybe he never planned to come in the first place. And since she hadn't thought to give him her cell phone number, he wouldn't have been able to contact her if something important *had* come up, and he couldn't make it for legitimate reasons.

"Fair Holly, your carriage awaits."

Even as her heart skipped a beat at his fairy-tale teasing, she whirled around on the bench, her gaze narrowing in on the errant charmer. She was determined to give him a piece of her mind before she lost her nerve to the tune of his sweet words.

With a pointed glance at her watch, she stated the obvious. "Colin, it's 11:15."

He chuckled. "Thank you, *Ms. Big Ben,* for the update."

"Oh, and *Mr. Late* ought to be the one to talk. Should you be in kindergarten instead of college? It's apparent you can't tell the time."

To her surprise, he agreed. "I probably should be in kindergarten, at that." He pulled up the sleeve of his black Mickey Mouse sweatshirt and bared his arm to her perusal.

"Showing me your muscles?" she teased.

"Showing you my watch. See?"

"You aren't wearing a watch."

He broke into a grin, as if she'd made some great discovery or major breakthrough, with his help.

"Exactly," he confirmed.

"Exactly...what?" she asked, suspecting she really didn't want to know.

"I don't wear a watch."

"I think we've established that fact." If his goal was to get her laughing, and she thought it might be, he was succeeding admirably.

But there was still the issue of his standing her up for an hour. "We agreed that we were going to meet at 10:00 a.m. sharp, as I recall. If you weren't going to meet me here when you said you were, why did you bother to mention a specific time at all?"

"I didn't mention a specific time. You did. Besides, I'm here now. Isn't that what's important?"

"Isn't keeping your word important?" she shot

back, annoyed, but she regretted her hasty words when his face colored scarlet.

He had the nerve to look angry? Indignation rose tightly within her. She pinched her mouth closed, her heart pounding rapidly in her defense. *She* was the one who'd been injured here.

"Yes, ma'am, keeping my word is very important to me," he replied gravely, his golden brows bridging low over his eyes. "I guess I should have told you up front that I—I don't live by my watch," he stammered.

His gaze met hers, then he looked away. "I expected to arrive much closer to our scheduled meeting time than I did. I do apologize for that."

She was intrigued. There was a story here he wasn't telling her. Why would a man forswear a watch, particularly when he was in college, where time was so very much of the essence?

"So tell me, Colin…how do you make it to all your classes without knowing what time it is? Since you don't wear a watch."

He shrugged, and his face pinched up so it looked almost like a cringe. "Well, I know you saw me sneak in late to your class the other day, so I guess I can't deny it. My system's not perfect."

"Oh, it's not *my* class," she corrected, heat warming her cheeks at his assumption. "I'm only a student teacher at the moment. For my doctorate, you know? There are two of us team-teaching the child psychology class this semester, under a full professor's guidance."

"Oh? I thought you were a full professor." He slid down to sit beside her on the bench. "You certainly talk the game. Imagine my surprise when I arrive at my very first college class only to discover that my university teacher is cuter than I am."

Her face was now utterly flaming. He might not be the best-dressed man she'd ever known, but he had the silver tongue of a devil in disguise. She'd have to watch herself around his blatant flattery, or she might just wind up believing him.

"So what about your system? Do you just guess what time you're supposed to be in class?" she asked in a rush of breath, trying desperately to turn the subject away from herself.

"More or less. I do have an alarm clock. On school days I usually haul myself out of bed in time to make it to my first class."

He grinned and gave a casual shrug. "From there, it's just a matter of moving from building to building. The timing is about right for me to make it to my next class with extra to spare, and my courses at the university are all in a row, so I don't have any downtime."

"Not even for lunch?"

"Nope." He winked. "I brown-bag it. Eat in one of my classes. Not yours," he added hastily.

"For some pathetic reason I believe you," she said,

shaking her head. "But that still doesn't explain why it took you so long to get here today."

He flashed her a twisted grin but kept silent.

She wasn't about to let him get away with it, even though he was silently begging her for mercy. "You know you're going to tell me, so you might as well just spit it out and be done with it."

He probed her soul with his gaze, looking as if he were about to refuse to say a word. Then, suddenly, his gaze grew clear, and he relented. "I rescued a litter of kittens."

Holly made a little squeaking sound out of the back of her throat—the best she could do for speech at the moment.

He cleared his throat. "I found them abandoned in the Dumpster at my apartment. What could I do? Just leave them there to fend for themselves?"

She couldn't help it. Her heart went soft, and no amount of coaxing could harden it up again. Colin Brockman was a hero, and what was more, he didn't even like admitting to the fact.

Unless he was just teasing her, testing her resistance to the romantic.

"You're kidding, right?" she asked, secretly hoping he wasn't.

His sea-blue eyes widened as he scrubbed his hand through his tousled blond hair. His mouth puckered in a reluctant half smile, and he shifted his gaze back to the ground. "What do you think?"

She sighed and reached for his arm, sliding her palm up to the breadth of his shoulder. Her fingers didn't miss the depth of muscle hidden beneath his cotton shirt. Colin was every bit as strong as he looked. "I think I'm a sucker for kindness. How many kittens were there? And what did you do with them?"

"One question at a time, please. There were six little kittens. Newborns. Four black, one white and one little guy, the runt of the litter, with black and white patches all over him."

Holly made a tender, choking sound in her throat and Colin lifted an amused eyebrow.

"They were stuck in a shoebox with a lid on top. Someone had taped the box shut with packing tape and tossed them into the Dumpster. I just thank God I walked by when I did."

"Poor little things," Holly cooed. "How could some terrible person abandon a litter of newborn kittens? Who would be so awful?"

"Too much trouble, I guess. Some people can't own up to their responsibilities."

"I'll say," she agreed, righteous indignation coursing through her. Poor little things. "So what did you do with them?"

"Well, I'd like to say I found nice homes for all of them. Someplace with little girls to tie bows around their necks and give them milk when they purred."

He smiled grimly. "But I did the next best thing—took the little nippers to the local Humane Society."

She could tell he was choked up about it, though he struggled not to let it show on his face or in his low voice.

"You did the right thing," she assured him, "although I know it must have been tough to let them go."

He laughed, but it was a dry, echoing sound. "You could say that." He looked around, rubbed his palms together and stood abruptly.

"So...where are we off to today?" He'd switched from melancholy to cheerful in an instant.

She stood and met his gaze, expecting to see the truth hiding under the surface; but his eyes were a clear, bright smiling blue. She couldn't keep pace with him. His erratic hairpin curves in emotion were more than she could navigate.

She took a moment to collect her thoughts. "Actually, we can walk there from here, so we won't be needing that carriage you mentioned," she said, feeling her tone might be a little too bright.

"I thought we were going to a rescue mission or something."

"That was my original plan, but as I was thinking about it, I wondered if we couldn't go a different direction for your assignment. Do something the other students might not think to do."

He smiled, and it lit up his whole face. "That

sounds good to me. I'm not exactly your typical student, as if you hadn't noticed. But you know, that brings up another question."

"Yes?"

"Why are you helping me?"

Holly froze inside. She didn't know the answer to that. "We can go the rescue mission if that's what you want to do."

"You didn't answer my question."

She pulled her book bag into her chest, using it as a shield. "No, I didn't."

His voice softened. "Why not?"

"I…" she began, and then her voice trailed off as her throat tightened. "I suppose I thought you might need help."

Colin tilted his head, silent for a moment. Then he slapped his hand against his thigh and roared with laughter. "I look that bad, do I?"

No, he didn't look bad. He looked wonderful. He'd also looked like a lost sheep that first day in class. Completely out of his element. And she'd always been drawn to the pariah. Perhaps that's why she'd responded to him the way she had.

It was as much a mystery to her as anyone.

"I didn't mean that in a bad way," she amended rapidly. "Actually, I'm just as interested in the topic as anyone."

"I hope so, considering you're a grad student," he pointed out wryly as he reached for his bag. "Is it okay for you to be helping me, Mrs. Prof?" he asked softly as he slung his bag over his shoulder.

"Ms. Prof, thank you very much. And I should think so," she answered, realizing she'd consciously set aside taking into account the ethical implications of her helping one student over the others. Would it be considered fraternizing for her to be here with Colin?

She hoped not, and for more reasons than one.

"I'm a student, too, Colin," she reaffirmed, as much to herself as to him. "I'm helping out the child psych class because my doctorate thesis is in the area of child psychology, but I'm not a full professor. So I don't see any hindrance from us exploring the first assignment, or any other, together."

"Okay," he said easily. "I'm glad."

His simple, straightforward statement took her aback. He could be frighteningly direct at times.

"What's your doctorate thesis about?" he asked as they walked, sounding, to her surprise, genuinely interested in what she had to say.

She laughed. "You don't really want to know, do you?"

He grinned back. "Why not?"

She playfully jostled his shoulder. "Because it's long and complicated. I'll tell you, if you really want me to, but not right now."

"Okay," he conceded, falling easily into step with her. "Later, then."

"Sure. Later. Right now, we'd better set our minds on *needs hierarchies*."

"The triangle is already forming in my mind," he teased, holding one hand to his temple as if he were conjuring the image as he spoke.

"You have some good ideas about where God fits into human need," she said on a serious vein.

"They're just thoughts," he corrected. "I've been mulling it over, but I'm not satisfied with my conclusions. It's a complex topic."

"You sound like you're trying to make it into a theological principle or doctrine of the faith," she teased. "I'd almost think you were trying to set this thing in stone."

"Maybe I am," he confessed with a ready smile. "I'm no scholar. I'm sure you've figured that out by now. But I do know that everything I learn here I'm learning for a reason. I'm also attending Stanton Seminary at the same time as the university."

Holly shook her head, shock reeling through her. As nice as he was, she just couldn't see Colin as pastor material. "You want to be a pastor?"

He laughed. "Oh, no. Not this man. A navy chaplain."

Seminary? A *navy chaplain?*

He would have done better to have left it at pastor. A navy chaplain, Holly could picture. But regret filled her. She'd been enjoying getting to know Colin. And she already knew she couldn't be a part of *this* man's navy.

Chapter Three

Colin wasn't sure what he'd said, but Holly looked as if she were ready to take a nosedive, or lose her breakfast, or maybe both. Her complexion turned white and clammy, and she was clasping her canvas bag to her chest as if it were a lifeline.

Or a shield.

He made a quick mental backtrack. He was sure he hadn't done anything inappropriate, and all he'd said was that he was training to be a navy chaplain. It was as if she'd frozen at the word *chaplain,* though moments earlier her voice had sounded teasing when she'd asked him if he was going to be a pastor.

She'd already made it clear to him she shared his faith. So what could be the problem?

He swiftly reached a hand to her to steady her, but she brushed him off with a scowl. Both literally and figuratively, he suspected.

"What did I say?" He asked the question gently, but that didn't stop her from cringing.

"Nothing." She snapped out the single word, steadfastly refusing to look at him and stepping away as if he were invading her space.

"Come on. Something I said or did made you angry." He set his backpack on the sidewalk and gestured to her with both his hands free.

She shook her head, almost vehemently. "I'm not angry."

"Then what?" he coaxed gently, adding his most winning smile for effect. Surely his immense manly charm wouldn't be lost on her, he thought sardonically.

It had always worked before.

His grin widened just as her frown narrowed. "Have you charmed your way out of *every* difficult situation you've ever found yourself facing?" she asked curtly, propping her free hand on her hip.

He scrubbed his fingers through his already-tousled hair, debating with himself how much honesty was called for in such situations. Finally he shrugged. "Mostly, yes."

She turned on her heel and faced him off with the spit and polish of a drill sergeant. "Well, it's not going to work with me, Colin Brockman."

He pulled in his smile, but knew it still tugged persistently at the corners of his mouth. Her eyes were sparkling with challenge, and he was determined to see them brimming with mirth.

With that lofty goal in mind, he lifted a hand to her cheek and slowly ran his index finger down the line of her jaw. It was extraordinary, how the rough calluses on his finger felt against the silky smoothness of her skin, as if the two were made for one another.

Callus and cream. Direct opposites, and yet the sensation of his hand on her skin was all the more breathtaking for its very contradiction.

Holly didn't speak, not even to turn him away, so he leaned into her ear and whispered, "Don't be so sure about that. I can be charming when I want to be."

Her reaction was classic, and not totally unexpected. Huffing loudly, she began marching in a direct line away from him. She didn't look back, not even to level him with a glare.

And—another point in his favor—she didn't swing her book bag at him, though he could tell the thought crossed her mind.

Laughing, Colin caught up his own bag and followed, loping to catch up with her long strides. "So where are we going?" he asked easily, as if the unusual moment between them hadn't taken place at all.

It was his way, to go on and not dwell on things. He hoped she'd follow his lead.

He'd make a point to find out later what had gotten her so ruffled. Sometimes it paid to wait until emotions had calmed before addressing matters of that nature, anyway.

Not that he was an expert. He strode to keep up with her quick pace.

They walked in silence for a moment, and then her gaze swung sharply up to him. She looked apprehensive, as if she was concerned he might be joking again, and she didn't like that prospect. He smiled to assure her he was on the up-and-up.

"The university has an extension program that works with children who have special needs," she began, putting on her teacher's voice, which Colin thought was for his benefit.

Or maybe for hers. He bit back a smile.

"It's called Marston House."

"I think I've heard of it. They take care of Down's syndrome kids and stuff, right?"

She shook her head, but her eyes were laughing. "And stuff. Oh, Colin, you're hopeless! What am I going to do with you?"

"I can't wait to find out," he quipped.

"You wish." She nudged him playfully on the arm. He grinned, happy that the easy camaraderie was back between them.

"Anyway," she continued, "I've arranged it so the children you'll be meeting today are all deaf. They take special classes to learn sign language and lip-reading, among other things. Eventually many of them learn to speak by themselves."

"Pretty impressive stuff," Colin said, uttering a low whistle. But just as he spoke, he caught the gist of her words and froze to the spot, reaching for her elbow so she wouldn't walk away without him.

"Did you say meet the kids?"

She whirled on her toes, teasing surprise registering in her eyes. "Of course I mean kids. You're in a child psychology class. And that's the assignment. Or have you managed to squirrel that away *out of sight, out of mind,* as well?" She tapped her temple with her index finger.

He grinned wryly. "Something like that. Actually, I was referring to the *meet* part of the sentence. I'm positive you didn't say anything about meeting or interacting with the children we monitor when you gave out your very specific and succinct instructions. The word I remember is *observe.*"

She looked flustered for the briefest moment, and Colin grinned. For some reason, it gave him a kick that he could do that to her.

That she could fluster him just as easily was completely irrelevant.

"Observe means to watch, view, scrutinize, monitor," he said as blandly as a walking dictionary.

"I *know* what *observe* means," she snapped, moving rapidly from flustered to annoyed. And while he enjoyed setting her off-kilter, he wasn't so sure he wanted to cross the line.

An angry woman was a volatile woman, and that he didn't need.

"It's no big deal," he said, fibbing through his teeth.

She crossed her arms and raised a dark eyebrow. "Colin Brockman, I haven't known you that long, but anyone with half an eye to see can tell you're not telling me the truth."

He slouched away from her. "How's that?" he asked defensively.

"Classic symptoms. Won't look me in the eye. Hunches away from me. Fiddles with the zipper on his jacket." She smiled, her eyes gleaming with amusement. "I'm a psychologist, remember?"

In the space it took her to say the words, he'd dropped his hand from his jacket, pulled himself to full rigid military attention, looked her straight in the eye and jammed his fingers through his hair just for good measure.

Holly chuckled, but her eyes were serious. "What's the problem, Colin?" she asked, more gently and softly than he would have expected, or maybe even thought that he deserved.

He knew he wasn't making any sense to her. He didn't make any sense to himself at times. She had every right to be annoyed with him.

Still, he wasn't one of those open, sensitive guys

who bared their souls on the first date, and Holly was hitting a nerve. Thanks to God, he'd made many resolutions in his life and in his personal relationships, but he still kept his emotions tucked safely away.

Not even this pretty psychologist was going to pull his true feelings out of him, though, if anyone could do so, Holly might be the one.

"I don't like children." He knew it sounded harsh, but it was better than admitting the real truth, that he was afraid of them.

Holly made a sound from the back of her throat that was close to a snort. That was about as much nonsense as she had ever heard from a man, and she told him so.

"You don't have to meet the kids if you don't want to, but I think you may surprise yourself. From everything I know of you, I believe you'd be good for them. They could really use your attention."

Colin raised his eyebrows, and a shield dropped over his eyes. He smiled with obvious effort. "All right, then. Bring them on."

Holly wanted to laugh at his forced bravado, the gravelly sound in his voice making it sound as if he were walking the plank.

But found she couldn't laugh at him. Colin was obviously hiding something, and though she wanted to share his burden, she decided to say nothing and let this hand play out on its own.

Sometime soon, she would discover what was haunting him. What was the mystery, the hidden crisis he veiled so well behind his casual demeanor?

It might be the psychologist in her that wanted to know the truth, but Holly suspected it was the woman.

Very much the woman.

As they entered the school facility at Marston House, Holly greeted the administrator, who led them to a large playroom filled with equipment. A large, multicolored plastic jungle gym took center stage, surrounded by various-sized rubber balls, a teeter-totter and a number of gymnastics devices, including rings, parallel bars, a balance beam and a gymnast's horse.

To one side, a group of elementary-aged children sat in a circle on the floor, practicing their hand signs in an animated display.

Colin stepped so close behind Holly that she could feel his warm breath prickling on the back of her neck, even before he spoke. As if he'd done it a million times, he placed his hands on her shoulders and rubbed his thumbs gently against her sore muscles.

Her own breath caught so suddenly in her throat that she was afraid to speak, for fear he'd be able to hear the emotion in her voice and comprehend how his nearness was affecting her.

"Do you know any of that stuff?" he queried

softly. For once, she heard no hint of merriment lining his voice. Awe, perhaps, and a little fear, but not the laughter that was his captivating trademark.

"Stuff?" she parroted, wishing he would step away from her, but not finding it in herself to make the move on her own.

He wrapped his arms around her and demonstrated with his hands in front of her chin.

"This," he said, touching his index fingers together.

"And this." He touched his right middle finger to his left palm, and then reversed the action.

She was impressed. He'd been paying attention.

"And this." He wiggled his fingers in a nonsensical manner. She felt rather than heard laughter frothing to the surface.

She laughed and turned out of his grasp. "The first, I can tell you, means *to.* The second sign is *Jesus,* which is obvious, when you think about it."

"The nails in His hands."

"Right. And as far as the third sign goes, I'd have to say you need to learn how to finger spell."

"And here I thought I was so close." He wiggled his fingers again in nonsense language.

Holly ran down the finger-spelling alphabet with him, amazed at how quickly and accurately he picked up each letter sign.

"Hey, wait a minute," he broke in, midalphabet. "This is a university-run school."

Holly nodded, but didn't comment, not knowing where he was going with his point.

"Why are the children learning how to sign *Jesus?* Isn't that a breach of separation of church and state or something?"

Holly would have bristled at the question, were his tone not so reverent and sincere.

"These kids have to learn everything they need to survive out in the world. Part of that world is faith and God and church. So the kids learn the signs they'll need to know to follow along with the praise songs and hymns, not to mention the sermon. I don't know about you, but my pastor preaches about Jesus a lot."

Colin chuckled, remembering the cantankerous old hellfire-and-brimstone navy chaplain who'd helped him see the light. What if he hadn't been able to hear the old man's preaching? It was so easy to take God's gifts for granted.

There and then he prayed silently in gratitude for his own blessings, and resolved himself to brighten these courageous young children's hearts in some way this day.

His heart felt heavy with their burden and light with God's peace at the same time. It was a funny, choked-up kind of feeling, and Colin wasn't sure what he should make of it.

"Do they have special deaf churches?" he asked in an attempt to cover his own discomfort.

"No." Holly took Colin by the elbow and nudged him toward the group of children. He offered a token resistance, but it was no more than that.

He knew it was a ploy, and he suspected she knew it, as well.

His cover was blown. He did care.

"Most of these kids go to one of the larger churches around town, one of those that offers an interpreter for the deaf. Greeley's a good town to grow up in if you're deaf. The college draws in students wanting to learn to work with the hearing-impaired, so there is no shortage of eager interpreters."

"That's good to know," Colin said, but his focus had already shifted to the children.

It was obvious the moment they got the go-ahead to break out of the group and play. Children scattered like a flock of chickens with a fox in the coop. Smiles and laughter abounded all over the place.

"It looks and sounds just like a regular playground," Colin murmured in awe and wonder. "This is absolutely incredible."

"What did you expect?" she asked softly.

He looked down at her warm, velvet-green eyes and shook his head. "I've learned not to have expectations." His voice lowered and he frowned. "Somebody always gets hurt."

She slid her palm over his forearm, intensely aware of how his muscles tightened under her touch.

"'Somebody,' meaning you?" she queried gently, keenly aware of the risk she took in asking.

He shoved his hands into the front pockets of his jeans, effectually brushing her hand away from him. "Sometimes."

It was little more than a whisper. Colin obviously didn't want to talk about it, but Holly didn't realize how much until he abruptly turned and strode away from her, taking refuge with the children he'd earlier professed to dislike.

He singled out a young boy who was tossing a rubber Four Square ball against the wall in an empty rhythm. He was all alone in his corner of the room, and he appeared not to notice when Colin approached him.

Holly cringed inwardly. Of all the children to pick, Colin had to go and choose the one least likely to respond to him. He was in trouble again, and he didn't even know it yet.

She started to follow, but her determination to save Colin from himself came to a screeching halt, as did her feet, when Colin appeared to strike up a conversation with the young boy.

It was impossible.

Well, perhaps *impossible* was too strong a word. But highly unlikely, from a large, untrained, blustering hulk of a man like Colin Brockman.

The boy was nine-year-old Jared Matthews, a mildly autistic boy counselors had as yet been unable to reach with any effectiveness. He wasn't deaf, but he often fled reality for a world of his own, somewhere deep inside his head where he could make sense of a life that flew by too fast, too strong and too loud for him.

Like many autistic children, Jared was very smart and clever, amazing others with what he could do. Music was his forte. Without any instruction whatsoever, he could play any instrument given to him. He had a natural ear for music, and played beautiful songs he made up in his mind.

But that was only when he could pull himself from his autism, and it was becoming increasingly difficult for him to do so. More and more, he retreated into a world of his own making, rather than living in the real world.

The fact that he had been shifted from foster home to foster home during his young life didn't help. He'd been all but abandoned by parents who didn't want the trouble of an autistic son, and Holly was certain it wouldn't be long before the parents made it official.

She hoped—prayed—she was wrong.

Parents didn't abandon their children, even those with disabilities. She'd been raised to believe that family took care of their own.

Her heart welled up, as it always did, for the boy and his terrible, tragic situation, especially knowing there was nothing she could do about it.

That was the worst part, knowing she could only help so many, when there were so many more in need.

Colin crouched down to the boy's level, his movements painstakingly and laboriously slow. With even more care, he gently reached toward the boy, and when Jared didn't protest, he tousled the boy's inky black curls.

To Holly's great surprise, not only did Jared not pull away from Colin's touch but, within moments, he'd focused his gaze on the man, and was playing against Colin in a game of Two Square.

Impossible!

Chapter Four

Holly was dumbfounded. Colin was playing Two Square with an autistic boy as though it were no big deal. As if he were an expert in the field. As if he didn't have a care in the world.

This from a man who professed a blatant dislike—or more accurately, as Holly suspected, a *fear*—of children. She didn't know what Colin had done to put Jared at ease, but in her mind, it was nothing short of a miracle, quite literally a work of God.

Surely Colin would have to realize what a special gift he'd been given. And if he didn't know, she fully intended to be the one to tell him. She suspected he'd only deny the truth, but she was compelled to confront him with the obvious.

Someone had to tell him he had a gift, or he might wander aimlessly for the rest of his life. He was a strong man with much to give the world, and if she didn't miss her guess, especially to give needy children.

All that was left was for him to figure that out for himself.

She started across the floor, her pace quick and determined. Her movement alerted Colin, whose gaze switched away from Jared to her. Their gazes met for only a moment, but it was enough for him to realize her intentions, or at least to guess at them.

It was as if she'd pushed his panic button. Alarm sparked from his sea-blue eyes, and in a moment, he was off and running.

Literally.

It was a clear attempt to avoid her, but for some reason, she didn't take it personally. She'd always had a penchant for the tousled stray—this one just happened to be a man. She'd catch up with him sooner or later.

Holly chuckled when Colin began walking hunched over like a big gorilla, touching his toes and making hooting noises. And she wasn't as surprised as she might have been when Jared followed, placing his hands on his toes and echoing the high-pitched monkey sounds.

He mimicked Colin yet again when Colin threw his arms in the air and waved them wildly, whooping like a man gone wild.

The comical little parade didn't stop when Colin

braved the balance beam, pretending to waver in the middle and making all kinds of funny faces.

And it was not only Jared aping his antics. One by one, each of the deaf children joined the line, smiling as they pretending to waver in the middle of the balance beam, just as Colin had done, making the same faces he had made.

In and out of tunnels, up and down the slides they went, one by one. Over the vaulting horse and somersaulting across the mats they flew.

Colin led and the children followed. And the merriment didn't end until the regular teacher signaled the close of the session by flickering the lights, so the children would know it was time to return to class from their play.

Colin, his face flushed, and dabbing at his sweaty temples with the edge of his shirtsleeve, looked absolutely elated.

"Did you see that?" he asked, sounding amazed and grateful, and not the least bit superficial.

"I told you, you're a natural," she teased, unable to stop herself from rubbing it in just a little bit. "Do you want to come back again sometime and play with the *children* again?"

His eyes widened, full of emotion she was certain he didn't want her to see.

"Yes." He nodded.

"No." He shook his head.

He halted abruptly, his mouth hanging open,

before he swallowed hard and jammed his fingers through his hair, sending it spiking every which direction. "I don't know, Holly. I don't really know what just happened."

His voice sounded strained, as if he were under a tremendous amount of pressure. And maybe he was.

Holly linked her hand through the crook of his arm and accompanied him out of the school. "You'll figure it out," she said gently. "You connected today."

"Do you think?" He sounded genuinely amazed, and more than a little choked up.

"Jared, the young boy you were playing with, seldom responds to contact. What you did today was a major breakthrough for him. The counselors at Marston will be thrilled."

She slid her hand down his forearm and linked her fingers with his. "I think God has given you a special gift, Colin."

He squeezed her hand and cleared his throat. "I'm humbled."

Holly hadn't expected such a reaction, and her throat closed around the unnamed emotions pounding through her chest. Colin was so strong, his navy background giving him squared shoulders and a powerful bearing; yet for the moment, she sensed a quietness in his soul, a new and tender sensitivity that only served to enhance his masculine image in her mind.

"I don't want you to take this the wrong way," she said slowly, her grip on him subtly tightening, "but I'm proud of you."

A slight flush tainted his tanned cheek, and one corner of his mouth tipped up in a grin. "Do you think?" he asked, his eyes gleaming.

"I think," Holly agreed, her voice scratchy with unspoken thoughts and unnamed emotions. She laughed as she pictured Colin being innocently followed by all those children. "You know what?"

"What?"

"I also think you are a veritable Pied Piper."

Colin stepped into the door of his small studio apartment. Dirty socks hung over the backs of the chairs and clothes were strewn haphazardly around, as if a tornado had blown through. Unwashed dishes were piled high in the sink, and books and papers littered the floor.

He took one look at the utter chaos he'd left in his living quarters and sighed deeply.

It was good to be home.

The last few weeks had proved incredibly busy, as professors and students alike shifted into high-learning mode. He hadn't been ready for the chaos on the high seas of academia.

Go to class.

Take good notes.

Read the textbooks.

Study for exams.

Colin barely knew what to make of it. He hadn't been in school for years, and had certainly never taken such a heavy academic load. He felt as if he were scrambling to keep up. At his best, he'd never been a model student and he didn't feel remotely close to his best at the moment.

It was the first time in his life he'd really wanted to succeed in school, but he felt as if he was not achieving the levels of accomplishment for which he was aiming.

A weekend of PT and reserve training was a welcome relief. The physical training was a terrific opportunity to stretch his idle muscles stiff from hours of cramped study, and the navy structure a good break from his self-imposed anarchy.

He'd also hoped his reserve work would give him some distance, some perspective on his thoughts, for no matter how hard he tried, or how much he studied, he couldn't seem to get Holly McCade out of his mind.

He'd seen her now and again over the weeks, passing in the halls, before and after class, always greeting one another and promising to get together for coffee, but never quite making the connection.

And he wasn't positive it was all coincidental. On a subconscious level, he thought he might be avoiding her.

Which was ridiculous. He ached to be with Holly. He thought about her every waking moment.

Yet he was obviously avoiding every opportunity to be alone with her. And it was possible she was doing the same with him.

No. He couldn't blame it on her.

He was at fault, and it was about time he acknowledged it, though he guessed that by now Holly might be blaming herself for the fact that they hadn't connected. His limited knowledge of women, mostly from his twin sister, Callie, made him believe they were prone to shoulder the blame in most circumstances, and this was probably no exception.

He only hoped he hadn't inadvertently hurt her. And he kicked himself for only now realizing that as a possibility.

He wasn't even quite sure why he was running away, except that his life was a tangled mess right now and he felt he needed to sort out the pieces before he spent any more one-on-one time with Holly.

Being with her was a roller-coaster ride in itself, without all these other things going on in his life. He was too confused to add his unquestionable attraction to Holly into the equation.

Callie was bugging him to come up to Oregon to be with her and her husband, Rhett, for Thanksgiving, but he wasn't sure he was up for the trip. Being with Callie would simply reopen old wounds about his family.

Bathed in the love of her new husband, Rhett Wheeler, Callie had succeeded in putting the past behind her, where it belonged. Colin knew what he'd find at Callie's—a traditional Thanksgiving dinner with all the fixings, followed by a jaunt to the church for a Thanksgiving praise service. God at the center, family most important and children all around.

Rhett and Callie had two children—a teenage son, Brandon, who was Rhett's from a previous marriage, but whom Callie loved as her own; and a capricious baby girl who was the apple of Rhett's eye.

Between the two of them, there was enough noise to drown out Puget Sound. And more happiness and giggles in one place than Colin thought his heart could bear right now.

He was happy for his sister, but he was envious of her, too. And he wasn't sure that now was a good time to rub his own nose in his shortcomings.

He didn't blame Callie for trying to get everyone together for the holidays. In fact, he appreciated that she always thought to include him, knowing he had no one else and nowhere to go; and no doubt realizing how much she now had, how much God had blessed her in her husband and children.

Colin unbuttoned his dirty blue shirt and twisted out of it, not caring where it dropped. He pulled on his T-shirt to stretch it out, but he didn't remove it. It might be sweat stained, but it was comfortable.

He shifted, grimacing. Neither he nor Callie had many family traditions to pass down to their children.

Oh, his mother, when she was alive, had always prepared turkey with all the trimmings. She'd forced the festivities and brought out the best china. But his father always managed to ruin everything. Sometimes he complained about the food, but more often he complained about Colin. Colin cringed at the mere memory of his father's harsh, grating voice.

You're a complete failure, son. You disappoint me every time I turn around.

Callie should have been born the boy. At least she got good grades and stayed out of trouble.

You're nothing but trouble.

Nothing but trouble.

Colin squeezed his eyes shut and pushed the memories away, burying them in the black recesses of his mind, where they belonged. He shouldn't have gone there, even for a moment.

It did no good to dwell on the past. But it did help him make his decision.

He'd stay home for Thanksgiving and order a pizza. Callie would understand.

He scrubbed a hand over his eyes and tried to concentrate on his future. One thing he *did* know for certain—God was working through all the things that had happened in the past few weeks, including bringing Holly McCade into his life. Colin sensed that He was changing the whole course of his future, not to mention his ministry.

His Child Psych class had started out as nothing more than a requirement on his transcript, and not one he was particularly keen on completing. Now, it had suddenly become the focus of his life, in more ways than one.

Little autistic Jared Matthews was often on his mind, and always in his heart, as he figured out new and original ways he could help the boy. Though he didn't call attention to the fact, he'd visited Jared almost daily since that first time.

Sometimes, he thought he might be making a difference in the boy's life. Often, he felt there was little he could do for the lad.

Except be there. He could do that.

Because of his work with Jared, Colin had also started considering the children of military parents, those he'd be working with as a navy chaplain, those like the ones he'd grown up with.

He desperately wanted to find something he could do for them when he reenlisted. If he could reach the children…

Finally, he felt as if he had some real direction, a place to focus his energy, as he studied and struggled to become a navy chaplain. His work at the seminary and university took on new meaning, and he found it wasn't quite so difficult to pay attention to his studies as it had been before.

He was slowly unraveling one of the most complex strands of his life, and it was exhilarating.

Motivating.

And most of all *confusing*.

The most pressing question of all still loomed in his mind. It was the main reason he'd worked his body so hard this weekend, trying to sort these things out in his mind.

Where did Holly McCade fit in?

On one hand, Colin pictured her as an angel from heaven, and not just because of her beauty. She'd taken the time to help him, to rescue a poor, helpless student when he'd been floundering, even though she didn't have to do a thing.

And somehow, she'd known just what he needed.

She'd discovered his heart, and pegged him right into his future before he himself had a clue. How had she *done* that?

With an almost deliberate intent, she'd forced him into a situation beyond his experience and control. She had lined him up with a real live child, face-to-face, where he was compelled to look into the boy's eyes and confront his own fears.

And discover his destiny.

She was incredible.

She brought out the best in him, and he thought he might be a good influence on her, as well. Was it his imagination, or did she shine a little brighter when she was in his company?

Unfortunately, that was the problem.

Holly McCade was a monumental distraction. Right now and always. He didn't trust his head when he was around her. Or his heart.

Who knew if she might steal it clean away?

He unlaced his spit-polished black boots, groaning as he took them off his feet. If his hard weekend workout wasn't enough to clear his mind, he was in a whole heap of trouble.

He couldn't stop thinking about her.

It occurred to him on more than one occasion that he might want more from his relationship with Holly than mere friendship. But that was a concept so new, he hardly dared explore it.

With the singular background of a navy career out of high school and his own poor upbringing as a child, he'd never before in his life given thought to having a real, romantic relationship.

He'd dated his fair share of women, but only on a social, casual basis. He'd not taken the same woman out more than a handful of times, and even then, he never remembered feeling remotely as he did now with Holly.

Now he was toying with the concept of making a commitment to a woman. Holly deserved no less, and he wanted above all to give her everything she deserved, the world on a platter.

A real, accountable relationship. Something permanent. Grown-up, even.

It had only taken him until he was thirty years old to meet a woman extraordinary enough to prod him into acting like an adult. Go figure.

He was treading on new territory, and he hardly knew where to begin. He struggled to compose his thoughts.

Women, in his experience, were friends. Occasionally, they'd become innocent diversions. He'd stolen more than one kiss over the years, but nothing memorable.

Shaking his head, he grunted in frustration. A kiss was one thing, but a committed relationship was something entirely different. When he looked at Holly, he heard wedding bells ringing in his ears.

Colin slammed his hand down on the table, slicing through the silence like a knife. He hadn't so much as kissed her yet, and here he was mentally standing at the altar in a tuxedo, holding matching wedding rings in his palm.

He took a deep breath and let it out, relaxed his posture and chuckled aloud.

First things first.

He had to steal a kiss.

Chapter Five

❧

"Holly. Holly McCade. Earth to Holly. Come in, Holly."

"I'm sorry. What?" Holly asked, reluctantly pulling herself from her thoughts.

Sarah Rembrant, her friend and co-student teacher, shook her head and belted out a laugh, loud enough to cause Holly to take a fleeting look around the room to see if anyone had noticed the outburst.

Fortunately, students were only now beginning to arrive for class, milling around with the cluck and gaggle of a coop full of chickens.

"Where were you?" Sarah asked.

"What do you mean?" Holly asked, confused. "Where was I when?"

"Just now. You were a million miles away. If I didn't know better, I'd say you were somewhere in the vicinity of cloud nine. Tell me the truth now. Have you been holding out on me? Are you in love?"

"Don't be ridiculous," Holly snapped back, agonizingly aware of the color rushing to her cheeks even as she said the words.

Sarah's jaw dropped in astonishment. "You *are* in love."

Holly scowled at her friend and waved her off. "It's about time to start class."

Sarah nodded, but the look in her eyes assured Holly this subject wasn't closed.

It should be, Holly thought, crossing her arms about her like a shield. She wasn't in love. No one fell in love at first sight, except in the movies.

This was real life. Savvy women dated awhile before they made a commitment, and even then there was generally a long engagement.

It made sense to take her time to get to know a man, to discover his true character and whether or not she would be compatible with him. Know all his quirks and his faults, not just the charm that made a woman forget her own head.

Then, perhaps, armed with all that knowledge, it would be safe to fall in love.

She wouldn't know. She'd never been remotely close to falling in love. She was no expert in matters of love, by any means. Sarah's teasing notwithstanding.

Reluctantly shifting her mind into teaching mode, Holly let Sarah carry most of the class, and tried not to let her gaze wander too often to the blue-eyed, ruffled-haired, heart-stealing troublemaker seated in his usual seat in the back row.

Class went quickly, to Holly's surprise, and it wasn't long before the bell rang signaling the end of class. And she hadn't looked at Colin more than a handful of times.

She'd just started gathering her notes when she heard a familiar deep, teasing voice speaking to her just over her right shoulder.

"Got a minute?"

How had he managed to sneak behind her when she wasn't looking?

Holly flashed a silent distress call to Sarah, whose eyes widened noticeably at the sight of the good-looking man who cupped his hands on Holly's shoulders and turned her gently but firmly around.

"She's got all day," Sarah said, nudging Holly toward Colin, closing what little distance lay between them.

So much for friendship.

"Thanks a lot," muttered Holly under her breath, but Sarah didn't seem to notice—she was too busy smiling and crooning at Colin, acting like—well, like a woman behaved around an attractive man.

A surge of jealousy coursed through Holly, for which she was totally unprepared, quickly followed by a rush of mortification, flooding through with the force of a deep river current.

Which was ridiculous. She wasn't the jealous

type. Not to mention the fact that she had nothing to be jealous about.

She had no claim on Colin. She couldn't keep him from flashing that charismatic grin to all the pretty women he met, nor would she want to. Certainly his charismatic smile would work as well on other women as it did on her, and she was hardly going to be the one to stop it. The Dodgers baseball cap he wore low on his brow did nothing to hide the inherent happiness in his smile or the joy in his eyes.

But there it was, even if she didn't want to admit it, even to herself. Holly didn't like the way Colin and Sarah connected through their gazes, as if they were sharing a private joke meant only for two.

Then the moment was over, and Colin was once again smiling at her. It was funny how he could look at her and her surroundings just melted away. He had a way about him that always made her feel as if she were the only one in the world.

Or at least the only one in the world for him.

"Well?" he queried lightly.

"Well, what?"

"You haven't answered my question yet."

Sarah cleared her throat. Loudly. "I think I better go pick up my notes off the overhead projector," she announced in an obvious attempt to leave Holly alone with Colin. Her wink in Holly's direction was an unnecessary addition to the melodrama.

But it helped nonetheless. Relief washed through Holly along with the realization that Sarah posed no threat, to whatever it was inside her that was feeling threatened.

She steadfastly refused to even *inwardly* acknowledge why it should bother her at all, never mind try to put words to her feelings. It was a free country, and Colin was too handsome a man not to be noticed by the women around him.

She took a breath, but it caught in her throat. Her relief was short-lived, and was quickly replaced by panic as she looked up at Colin's sparkling, mirthful gaze and lazy half smile.

"Your friend is nice," he commented, gesturing a nod to the retreating Sarah.

"Yes, she is," Holly agreed mildly, watching Colin's face for a reaction and relieved when there was none.

He turned his warm gaze on her and smiled his enigmatic grin, and her heart did a back flip despite her reservations. Any thoughts of threat or panic dissipated like a bad dream in the daylight. Colin's smile alone was enough to make a woman forget her own name.

"Busy Saturday?" he asked, casually pushing a stray lock of her hair away from her face.

Instinctively, a lie sprang to her lips, a defense against the truth. She immediately set about the task of conjuring up something interesting to say she was doing. Something other than spending the weekend alone.

But before anything plausible came to mind, Colin broke in. "I hope you'll say you're free for the day. I have something I want to show you at my apartment. Something I think you'll like. A lot."

Anything she'd been about to say was immediately lost in her interminable curiosity about all things Colin. If she were the proverbial cat, she most certainly would have expired by now.

"I'm free," she reluctantly admitted. She didn't have time to regret the words, for his eyes lit up like sparklers on the Fourth of July, glittering with delight and amusement.

"I promise you won't be disappointed."

Somehow, she didn't think she would be.

"Why don't you come over in the morning and stay for lunch? I'm a lousy cook, but I'm a whiz when it comes to speed-dialing Chinese food."

"This surprise of yours will take that long?"

His half smile appeared again, along with a healthy shade of red across the top angle against the soft scruff on his cheeks. "Aw, shucks, ma'am." he said bashfully. "You caught me red-handed."

She laughed despite herself. "How's that?"

"Well, I hoped I could persuade you to stay long enough to help me brainstorm a few ideas for my big research project in your class. You gave me a great start on your course with our first excursion, and I thought maybe you could help me out again."

She caught his gaze and held it, questioning him with her eyes. What was really behind this half serious, half flirtatious question?

What did he really want of her?

Somehow, she knew there was more behind his outwardly simple request than met the eye.

"Oh, come on," he pleaded, grabbing her right hand and placing it over his heart. "You wouldn't want your favorite elderly student to fail your class now, would you?"

She chuckled. Aged he was not. "What do you want me to bring?" she said on a sigh. "I make a grand tuna salad, if you're interested."

His blue eyes sparkled like a mountain stream in the sunshine. "Just bring your beautiful self. We'll let the lunch plans take care of themselves."

"Colin," she objected, "you are completely incorrigible."

"I was going to say *adorable*," Sarah inserted as she sashayed by with a load of textbooks in her arms.

"Thanks for the compliments, ladies," Colin said, tipping off his baseball cap and swinging it around in a grand gesture. "I'm going to have such a big head my cap won't fit."

"You consider *incorrigible* a compliment?"

"You don't?" he asked, sounding genuinely surprised.

She nearly choked on her laughter. "Not in the general scheme of things."

"Oh, now, come on! Who wants everything to be the same all the time?" He punctuated the statement with a wide, confident grin that made Holly wave her hands and roll her eyes at him.

"You never know what to expect when you're with me, right?"

That, at least, was the truth.

"It's always an adventure when you're with Colin Brockman," he asserted smugly. "Always fun and games. Something new around every corner."

"You make that sound like a good thing," she muttered under her breath.

He froze in his tracks for a moment, watching her keenly and looking as if he couldn't quite figure out what he was seeing.

She wasn't surprised. She and Colin were as different as day and night in every way.

And yet there was that *adorable* thing.

Colin was that, surely, and Holly hadn't missed the fact. She had to admit she was attracted to him, but she was terrified of him, too. Jumping off cliffs without knowing if there was an ocean beneath her just wasn't her style.

Not anymore.

She gritted her teeth and closed her eyes against the dark memories threatening to surface. Now was not the time to drudge up past mistakes.

She needed to stay with the program. Stay in control of her life and her feelings.

But with Colin, she just couldn't say no.

When he smiled, his whole face smiled. His whole *body* smiled. And when he opened his arms to her, she didn't resist. He was tall, and strong, built like a fortress, and navy tough. And he smelled wonderful—a clean, soapy scent that tickled her nostrils and made her want to inhale deeply.

She could feel the rumble of his chest on her cheek as he spoke.

"We'll stick with *incorrigible,* then," he said softly, next to her ear. "The good kind."

"If you say so," she mumbled into his shirt.

"I do," he agreed with a nod. "So hold on tight, sweet Holly, and get ready for the adventure of a lifetime."

Chapter Six

As Saturday arrived, the bright Colorado sun shone high in the sky, promising another fine fall day in the shadow of the Rocky Mountains majesty. Colin whistled under his breath as he searched for his key to his apartment door, happy, for the moment, just to be alive and breathing.

That is, at least until his gaze rested upon Holly, leaning impatiently against his front door and looking as if she had a few choice words for him. He didn't know exactly what time it was, but he guessed by the exasperated look on her face that she'd been waiting for him a good long while.

He *had* said to meet him here in the morning, he realized with a prickly brush of hindsight that left him feeling genuinely chagrined. Jumping into motion to cover his mistake, he jammed the key into the lock, stumbling over himself as he tried to express how apologetic he felt at having left her waiting.

In the end, he could only state the obvious without blathering on like a complete idiot. "I'm sorry. I know I'm late."

Holly lifted her forearm and gazed pointedly at her watch. "*Very* late."

Colin shrugged and motioned at his wrist. "I don't have a…"

"Watch," she completed for him. "Yes, I know. We've been over this before. Otherwise I would have left a long time ago. As it is…"

"I didn't mean to make you wait," he said, rubbing his palm across her shoulder, brushing back the soft, sable curl of her hair.

She chuckled. "I know you didn't. I came prepared this time." She pulled a paperback book out of her purse and waved it under his nose.

"Something for your doctorate?" he queried, lifting an amused eyebrow.

She flipped the cover to reveal the title. He recognized it to be one in a mystery series, one with a cat as the main character.

"I suppose I should be studying my psych books," she admitted with a grin. "But I thought I'd take a break today, it being Saturday and all."

"Works for me." Colin unlocked the door and gestured her in. "I'm all for taking a break whenever you can squeeze them in." He looked back at her and grinned. "Saturday. Monday. Wednesday…"

He stopped short when he surveyed his apartment, and Holly plowed right into his back, mumbling something under her breath about "brick walls."

He had more pressing matters weighing on his mind. What would she think of him when she saw his living quarters?

If anything, his front room looked *worse* than it usually did.

Was that possible?

He'd been meaning to give his present barracks a thorough scrubbing down this morning, but then an opportunity had come up that he just couldn't pass up on, and he'd gone off without giving another thought to the state of his dwelling.

And now, he was going to live to regret that easy dismissal.

Holly was practically openmouthed as she stared at his living room, arms akimbo as she confronted the slapdash, careless environment that was the true indication of his chaotic lifestyle.

Hopefully she wouldn't judge him too harshly. The mess didn't make the man, did it?

He cringed inwardly and struggled not to demonstrate his discomfort on the outside. He wanted to wiggle and squirm like the worm he was, living in a hole filled with dirt, or at least dirty laundry.

Holly turned to him, her face a mixture of emotions. "The socks strewn across the top of the furniture give the place a certain kind of ambience, don't you think?"

It was the last thing he could have expected her to say, and it threw him off for a moment. "I…uh… that is…"

"I know, I know. Your maid hasn't been here yet today." She moved to the orange patterned couch that looked—and probably was—from the seventies. With a gentle smile, she casually brushed the clutter aside, seating herself straight-backed and elegant, as if she didn't have a care in the world, and wasn't bothered at all by the disorder around her.

He recognized what that action cost her. He'd known her long enough to know she was the queen of order. If her meticulous appearance wasn't a dead giveaway, her scrupulous school notes and flawless handwriting would be enough to suggest her tendency toward, if not perfectionism, then at least chronic neatness. She was stretching herself for him, and he appreciated it more than he could express.

With a grin, he sprawled on a green armchair across from her, kicking one leg over the arm of the chair and propping one elbow on his thigh. He might not be able to voice his gratitude, but surely she'd be able to see it written on his face.

"So where were you today?" she asked, pulling

her legs beneath her and leaning back against the cushion. "Or is it a state secret?"

He chuckled. "No secret. I was over visiting Jared Matthews at Marston House. I try to get by and see him every day, if I can."

Her eyebrows hit the ceiling. "Michelle Walker, the principal at Marston House, mentioned in passing that you'd been visiting Jared occasionally, but I had no idea you were growing so close to the boy."

He looked away and shrugged. How could he explain the feelings he had toward Jared?

In some way, that brave youngster represented the struggle Colin had gone through himself as a boy; and, in turn, every wretched mother's son trying to make the most of a tough situation.

He found he wanted—*needed*—to do something to make Jared's life better, to help him find a little happiness in the world. The kind of happiness Colin himself had missed as a boy.

He couldn't change his own circumstances or his past, but he would do what he could for Jared. It was the least he could do. And the most.

"Do you think you are getting through to him?" she asked softly. "Is he making any progress?"

Again, Colin shrugged. "Sometimes. Other times it's like he's completely locked away in his own mind, and all I can do is sit quietly beside him and wonder what he's thinking inside."

He crooked his elbow on his knees and gazed out

the glass double doors that led to a small wooden balcony overlooking the apartment parking lot. Jared Matthews grabbed at something in his heart. How could he express what he felt, when he wasn't even sure he could put it into words himself?

"Whenever I get through to him," he continued, "I feel like I make a genuine connection. Like the two of us have something special."

He paused and scrubbed his fingers through his hair. "Other times, I just sit and visit with him, talking about all kinds of stuff even though he doesn't respond to me. I'm not completely sure he knows I'm there."

"He knows." Holly's sweet, gentle voice soothed the ache in Colin's heart.

"Yeah," he agreed quietly, closing his eyes to hold on to the comfort. "I guess he does."

"It's too bad Jared's in such a bad situation," she remarked regretfully.

The hair on the back of Colin's neck brushed to attention. He had the distinct impression she wasn't talking about Jared's autism when she mentioned his *situation*.

He cleared his throat. "How's that?"

"You don't know?"

He shook his head.

"I would have thought Michelle or Janice at Marston House would have told you, since you're seeing Jared so regularly."

"Told me what?"

She pinched her lips together before answering, her velvet-green eyes awash with compassion. Colin suspected that emotion might extend to him, as well as the little boy in question, and he didn't know what to make of it. He swallowed hard.

"Jared was just removed from his ninth foster home. He's having a great deal of trouble staying in a foster home setting, and foster parents just don't seem to know what to do with him."

He blew out a low whistle. "Oh, wow."

"Yeah. It's bad. He can't seem to find a good match with a family, and I think he's just miserable. The worst part is that his real parents hardly ever come see him."

"You're kidding." Colin emitted a low growl. He knew what it was like to have a father who paid no concern to him.

"I wish I was." Holly shook her head. "They've practically abandoned him to the state, though they haven't made any formal petition. I have heard they've indicated to the staff at Marston House that they can't handle a little boy with autism. Isn't that sad?"

Colin didn't answer. He was lost in his own thoughts, his mind going back to the moment in his own life when his dad ordered him to leave the house, to attend military school in another state.

Because his father couldn't handle being around *him* anymore.

"What kind of parents abandon their kids, even when they have problems? Can you even imagine?" she continued.

He could imagine.

He looked up at her, biting the inside of his lip until it bled in to control the emotions roiling through his belly. He was plunging into deep water here.

He hadn't told Holly the truth, or at least not the whole truth. The only ones who currently knew anything about his past relationship with his father were his twin sister, Callie, and her husband, Rhett.

And they never talked about it.

Neither did he.

But he was going to talk now. He didn't know why, but he sensed, somehow, that it was important for Holly to understand where he was coming from, why he believed the way he did about children. About families.

And that meant breaking his self-imposed code of silence.

He cleared his throat. "When I was sixteen, I got into trouble with the law."

He heard her sudden upsweep of breath and grinned mildly. At least he could be sure he had gotten her attention.

"I was arrested for shoplifting at a grocery store.

It was on a foolish teenage dare with my twin sister, Callie, and it was only a candy bar."

He waited for her response, but she remained silent, staring at him with wide eyes brimming with disbelief.

He laughed. "I promise I've never done anything as remotely stupid before or since," he assured her.

Her facial color had heightened to a healthy rose, and he wondered if she regretted being here with him now. Was she going to spend the rest of her life staring at him as though he were a common criminal?

He cringed at the thought that he might have impeded on their friendship by sharing such information. Had he said the wrong thing again?

"What happened?" she whispered coarsely, clearly aware that the black moment in his story was yet to come. She sounded a little like a small child eager to hear the ending to a good story.

But at least she didn't sound judgmental. He found the courage to continue in that.

Colin ran a hand down his jaw, reluctantly remembering the moment. "My father hit the roof, and was as close as he'd ever been to hitting *me*."

Holly made a strangled noise in her throat, and he moved over to sit by her, draping his arm over the back of the couch. She leaned in to him, laying her sweet cheek on his chest as if trying to find his heartbeat.

If she *was* trying to find his heartbeat, she'd find it racing. He focused his mind on continuing his story, and found his thoughts difficult to collect.

"My dad was so angry, he threatened to send me away to a military boarding school. I thought he was kidding. Or maybe I hoped he was just threatening me in anger, and didn't really mean what he said. But the next day, he was on the telephone, calling around to find me a boarding school. He was looking for something as far away as possible. Out of state, at least. Something in the next galaxy, I think."

He blew out a breath. He thought he'd dealt with all his anger, but it was still difficult to look back to the trauma he'd experienced in his youth without some stirring of emotion. And he sure wasn't finding it easy to talk about, either.

"I can't believe a father would not want to be with his son," Holly said, anger tinting every word.

"Believe it," Colin snapped. "My father just wanted me to go away. In fact, I think he wished I had never been born."

Holly made a strangled sound.

Colin grit his teeth. "When I left home, the only thing he said was that he hoped that the military could beat some sense into me."

"Well, they clearly failed," she teased softly, and Colin's gaze flew to hers. Her eyes were full of sadness and sympathy, but she was clearly trying to lighten the mood, and Colin could have kissed her for the effort.

"So true." He chuckled wryly. "I never could seem to bend myself to appreciate the military lifestyle."

She shook her head and laughed a little too brightly. "That from a career navy man. I don't think I'll ever figure you out."

"Sounds pretty bizarre, doesn't it?"

"If I didn't know you, I'd say *yes*. But I think I understand the paradox in this case. I do want to know what happened, though," she said, once again changing the tenor of the conversation, gently nudging back toward the subject of Jared Matthews. "Having a father turn you away from home is a lot for a young man to swallow. But you turned out terrific, so you'll have to tell me how it's done."

"The word is *abandoned*. No matter how you couch it in other terms, the fact is that he abandoned me. Intentionally."

"Yes," she agreed mildly. "That's exactly what I'd call it. And I'm sorry, Colin."

Her gaze met his, warm and reassuring, and for a moment he let down his defenses, let himself feel once again the pain of rejection.

But this time, he had someone here with him. Someone to commiserate. Someone to care, to comfort him.

He squeezed his eyes closed, gratefulness washing through him as she gripped his hand, linking her fingers through his.

"I can't help being curious...." she said softly, pulling him back to the present.

He opened his eyes, gazing down at her and enjoying the novelty of the soft feelings swirling through his chest. "What?"

"How did you handle yourself when you found yourself in military school?" she asked with a smile that let him know her question wasn't entirely innocent. "Did you make yourself hard to live with? Refuse to concede? You simply don't strike me as the kind of man to give in without a good fight."

"Oh, I fought, all right," he agreed, torn between a smile and a frown. A dull ache started at the back of his neck and throbbed mercilessly into his head.

"What did you do? Act up in class and get kicked out of school? Beat up on other kids and take your anger out on them? Run away from the dorm and get chased through the woods by a pack of baying hounds?"

He blew out a breath. "In a way, I guess, I did all of those things. I certainly got in my share of fights. I tried to get kicked out, and ended up on K.P. or running the obstacle course at midnight in the pouring rain. I learned pretty quickly to keep my mouth shut and my opinions to myself."

"Keep going," Holly urged. "This story isn't over yet."

Colin snorted. "Hardly. I did my time. But my

father didn't even bother to come to my graduation ceremony. My graduation." He drew his left hand into a fist, but stopped short of punching it into his right palm. "I decided right then and there I never wanted to see him again, not as long as I lived. I decided to disappear and never be seen again. Someplace my dad would never find me. Somewhere he'd never think to look."

"So you...?"

He unclenched his fingers and ran a hand across his stubbly jaw, concentrating on the prickly feeling against his skin. "I joined the navy."

She laughed and shook her head. "I knew you were going to say that. But it still seems odd to me that a man who disliked military school so fervently would join the navy."

He reached out and pushed a stray lock of soft, sable hair from her cheek. Touching her grounded him, reminded him that he was his own man, thirty years old and not a boy. And he was sitting beside a beautiful, sensitive woman who at times appeared to understand him better than he understood himself.

He had a future to embrace.

But he knew that no matter how personally agonizing it might be, he was obligated to finish his story. Only then could Holly really understand where he was coming from, and what made him the man he had become.

"My joining the navy seems like the action of a

crazy man. I know. I've thought about it a million times since that day in the recruiting office, wondering how I could ever have made that decision."

He snorted and shook his head. "All I can say is that it made sense at the time. It might not have been rational, but I did have my reasons. The military lifestyle was familiar to me, however disagreeable it was. And I knew I could disappear quickly into the navy. My dad would never think to look for me in the military."

He paused thoughtfully. "Not that he would think to look for me at all."

"What about your twin? Callie, right? Did you tell her where you were?"

"No. I never told her anything. I didn't make contact with her at all." He chuckled dryly. "She was pretty angry with me when I finally got around to looking her up."

Holly grinned wryly. "I can imagine."

"You probably can," he agreed. "Fortunately for me, she's a kind, forgiving woman, and Rhett's a good, supportive husband. Thanks to him, I didn't have to live in the doghouse too terribly long before she welcomed me back home."

"I'll bet that's a great relief to you."

"It is. I really love my sister. I'm glad we could reestablish our relationship. I've always had a special bond with Callie, her being my twin and all. When we were younger we used to say we could read each other's thoughts. And I think it was pretty near true."

Holly smiled again. "I'm glad for you."

"And in consolation, the navy's been good to me. I've been stationed on both coasts and in the Far East. I've met a lot of good people, some of whom mentored me and introduced me to the love of Christ. And I have a lot to look forward to once I've reenlisted as a chaplain."

"It worked out for you, didn't it?"

"God had it all in His capable hands," Colin stated emphatically, realizing after he said it, that what he said was true.

"He does, doesn't He?" Holly parroted softly.

"Which is what we've got to remember as we pray for poor Jared," he said, stealthily refocusing the spotlight. "I'm sure that his parents feeling the way they do about him couldn't have helped his autism."

"I think you're right about that. He sometimes retreats completely into himself, as you've no doubt seen when you work with him. He generally doesn't want to interact with anyone. Especially men."

She smiled gently and nodded in his direction. "And yet here you are, Colin. You have had the most success of anybody here in getting through to Jared, and in so little time, too."

He supposed he should feel proud, but he was humbled by the statement.

"I…" He cleared his throat and ran a hand over his mouth. "I…really care for the boy."

"Oh, Colin!" Holly launched herself at him, wrapping her arms so tightly around his neck he could barely breathe. "I knew it."

"Knew what?" he queried, his voice muffled by the arm of her sweater.

"I knew you'd realize your own potential. Your calling."

"My calling," he parroted, breaking her embrace as he stood and moved toward his bedroom door. He couldn't continue all this serious talk. He'd had enough talking and *feeling* for one day.

If he could *do* something, he'd do it. But he didn't want to talk about it.

He opened his bedroom door, and a scruffy little black-and-white ball of fur pounced into the living room, then rolled around and around, reaching for his tail.

Holly squealed in delight. "You didn't tell me you had a kitten."

"I didn't have a kitten, at least up until a few weeks ago. Remember our first date?"

Holly's heart jumped when Colin referred to their first meeting as a date, but she quickly reminded herself how unpredictable Colin was. He no doubt meant the word *date* in a generic sense.

"I remember you were late," she said.

He grinned and nodded. "Right. But do you remember *why* I was late?"

Holly's heart swelled as she recalled the circumstances surrounding his tardiness. She'd been so angry with him at the time, and yet he'd managed to win her over with his pathetic excuse.

And his boyish charm. "You were rescuing a litter of kittens, as I remember. You found them in a Dumpster or something."

"That's right."

"I'm sure I remember you saying you'd taken them to the Humane Society, so they would be adopted out to good homes."

He picked up the wiggling kitten and pulled it in next to his chest, slowly stroking over the small feline's back until he settled down and began purring contently in the big man's arms.

"I did. All except Scamp here. I just couldn't find it in my heart to give him away," he admitted in a low, husky voice.

Scamp. The name fit the rascally black-and-white-patched kitten. And maybe the moniker fit the man the cat had obviously adopted, as well.

"I think you two need each other," she remarked thoughtfully, studying the man and feline together. Scamp was still purring, and had curled into a ball, looking as if he was preparing to take a nap right there on Colin's palm.

"Don't let Scamp hear you say that. He thinks he is king of the world."

She laughed as Scamp pawed at Colin's scruffy chin. "He sure acts like he's king. And I'll bet you spoil him rotten, too, don't you?"

Colin chuckled, and his cheeks colored.

"I thought so."

"I'm not admitting to anything on the grounds it might be incriminating."

Holly reached forward, stroking the kitten on his ears. "Your very first kiddo, huh, Colin?"

"Hah!" Colin threw up his free hand, waving her off almost frantically. "That may be. But Scamp is the first and *only* kid I'm going to have in *this* family."

Chapter Seven

"What is that supposed to mean?" Holly snapped, more severely than she would have liked. She knew she sounded desperate, but he'd surprised her.

In a quick, defensive move, she swept Scamp away from Colin and cuddled him under her chin. He purred and rubbed his nose against her.

"Are you saying you don't ever want to have a cat again?"

She hoped.

He winked and shrugged. If he noticed her discomfort, he wasn't showing it. "Kittens are okay. I just don't want to have kids."

"You're joking!"

"After what I just told you about my own youth, you think I'd subject that kind of heart-wrenching agony on a child of my own?"

She wanted to point out the obvious, that it wouldn't *be* that way with a child of his own, but it was patently evident he was already finished listening to her.

Ignoring her attempt at conversation, he had dropped to his knees and was hissing at Scamp, who obliged by hissing back.

Colin's revelation amazed and stunned her. From what she'd seen and heard, he would make an excellent father. He was kind and compassionate, and full of the type of boyish charm that had Holly picturing him wrestling on the floor with a handful of small children.

Granted, right now it was more like a mangy, half-starved black-and-white kitten.

As bad as his childhood had been, Holly knew he was making the mistake of a lifetime to rule out becoming a father someday.

Why it should matter so much to *her* was beside the point.

Somehow, she decided with a strength of resolve that she didn't want to question, it had become her responsibility to make stubborn, thickheaded Colin Brockman see the error of his ways.

Children were a gift from God, not something to be feared and avoided. They were the very image of one man's love for his wife, and in that love, the image of God Himself.

Holly struggled to see Colin's viewpoint, to understand how he could feel as he did. Children were her livelihood, of course, so she was biased on the subject.

But more than that, she realized, children were her greatest dream.

Marrying Prince Charming and raising a house full of her own laughing children had been her heart's desire since she was old enough to understand what harboring such romantic notions was all about.

And those feelings hadn't faded over time. If anything, the older she got, the more she clung to her fancy.

At her age, it was probably no more than wishful thinking to believe she would—or even could—bear a houseful of children. Men weren't exactly clamoring to play the role of hero and father.

Or more accurately, not the right kind of man.

She peered down at Colin, who was lying on his back with the cat perched on his chest. They were both meowing at the tops of their lungs, and Holly couldn't quite decide who was outhowling whom.

Colin could be her Prince Charming, she realized with a start. If he combed his hair, tied his shoes and stopped slouching, it was possible she could picture him galloping into her heart on a white steed, with a shiny coat of armor dazzling brightly in the sunlight.

She caught her breath and held it, nibbling softly

on her bottom lip. Maybe *that* was why she cared so much what he thought.

It was an unsettling notion.

"Do you want to work on your term paper?" she asked briskly, standing. Her head was reeling, and she scrambled to anchor herself back in reality. "That is why you asked me over here, isn't it? To brainstorm topics for your paper?"

He rolled over onto his knees. "I already have a topic."

"But I thought…"

He rose to his feet and grinned. "Okay, you caught me red-handed. I'll admit it—I invited you over here on false pretenses."

"To meet the cat?"

He slid a surprised look at Scamp. "What? Oh. Well, partially, I guess. Mostly I just wanted to spend some time with you."

Her heart picked up pace, sending little, tickling flutters down her neck. "I'm honored. I think. I enjoy spending time with you, too."

She narrowed her gaze on him, giving him her best *severe teacher* look. "Are you really that far along on your term paper?"

He chuckled and ran a hand across his scalp, making random points of his thick white-blond hair stand at attention. "I didn't say that. I said I had a topic. It's not the same thing."

She wasn't the least surprised. "Well, I'm glad to

hear you've done that much on your paper, anyway. I'm sure it's better than some students have done, though as your teacher, I would highly suggest you motivate yourself in the near future."

He chuckled.

"Care to share?"

He sat up and crooked his arm around one knee. His sea-blue eyes sparkled with excitement. "I thought you'd never ask, Teach."

She sat down Indian-style before him. "Please, Colin. Professor lectures are all over for the day. I promise. I'm here as your friend."

He smiled slyly and ran the back of his index finger down her cheek and across her chin. "Are you?"

She had no idea what he meant by that comment, but her throat went dry and she found she couldn't swallow. "I... Just call me a casual observer, then. I know you've put a lot of effort into this class, and I suspect you've come up with an interesting theme for your class project. I can't wait to hear it."

"A casual observer, huh?" He chuckled. "I'll just bet you are."

She frowned. "What's that supposed to mean?"

"Oh nothing." His smile told her just how far from *nothing* he meant.

"Colin, you have five seconds to..." she threatened with a smile.

"Okay. Okay." He pulled some papers from under

the scratched and chipped oak coffee table that looked as if it might have come from a secondhand store, or maybe a garage sale. "My notes are right here. Somewhere."

"So there's a method to your madness," she teased with a giggle. "And here I thought you were living in complete, unsystematic chaos."

"I can find what I'm looking for. Most of the time." He shuffled the papers and cleared his throat. "See? Here it is."

"Please proceed." She slipped softly into an armchair and leaned forward, wrapping her arms around her knees. "I'm all ears."

"My goal in completing this class is to create a program I can implement when I return to the navy as a chaplain. As you know, I've been drawn to the plight of children recently."

He paused and grinned at her. "Anyway, I began to think about the military kids I've run across while in the navy. I'm not a military kid myself, but I think there's a lot of need within the system as it stands today. These children move around a lot as their parents are reassigned to various duty stations. And if Mom or Dad is called in for active duty, the child may not see them at all for a long period of time."

"Wow. I'm impressed."

He grinned and winked at her. "And all this brilliant deep thinking is a direct result of your fabulous teaching."

Holly smiled, aware he was teasing her, but flattering her nonetheless. "I'm glad to hear my lessons are reaching someone's ears. Sometimes when I'm teaching I think I'm speaking into empty space. That enormous vault of an auditorium echoes back at me like I'm in the Grand Canyon. *Alone.*"

"I've been listening," he said softly, rolling to his stomach and tucking his chin into his hands. "Before I started listening to you, I hadn't ever really thought about the needs of children. I certainly didn't consider the kids much when I was working as an RPS in the navy. Of course, Religious Program Specialists get more of the paperwork and less of the interaction than a regular navy chaplain does."

"You do realize that there are outside, auxiliary operations targeting Christians in the military that have programs available for military kids and teens," Holly interjected, thinking of her own experience as a marine drill sergeant's daughter.

She knew the programs well. She was a product of them. Or was that a by-product?

Not that the programs themselves were bad. They just hadn't reached and helped a teenaged Holly when she'd been calling for help.

"So I don't need to create something—is that what you're telling me? King Solomon's *nothing new under the sun* and all that business?" His voice was rough. He sounded frustrated.

"No, no," she protested immediately, causing him

to grin at her in relief. "As much as these programs do, they don't reach the kids one-on-one, on a personal level where it really makes a difference. That's what you're talking about, isn't it?"

His blue eyes sparkled. "Exactly. I knew you'd understand where I was going with this."

"In that case, you'll be pleased to know the ball field is wide-open to your unique ideas. And to your enthusiasm."

He gave a low whistle. "It seems like a pretty wide ball field. I don't have a clue where to begin."

"Have you done any research on programs used in the past? Made a study contrasting their goals and effectiveness?"

"No, but I suspect there aren't many programs that would match the organization I've concocted. I can call one of the chaplains I worked with in the navy and ask him for help."

"Excellent start. You don't want to assume anything without doing your research, or you'll inadvertently duplicate something that's already been done."

His brows creased low over his eyes. "Good point, well-taken."

She smiled, glad to be able to use her years of training to help a friend. "You'll want to cross-examine the information you get from the navy with data you get from the other branches of service."

He glazed her with a sugary sweet look that

melted her insides and contrarily put her on the defensive in a single glance.

"What?" She leaned forward and narrowed her eyes on him.

"What, what?" he asked, his voice and features dripping with feigned innocence.

"You know *what*. That look you just flashed me. What do you want?"

He looked away and pretended to brush a speck of lint from the shoulder of his white T-shirt. "It's nothing, really."

"If it's nothing, why aren't you telling me what you want?"

"I wouldn't ask, except that it will save me a bundle of time, and you know how you've been getting on me to make better use of my time."

She chuckled. "I just want you to be *aware* of time, Colin. I don't care how you use it."

"Yes, but if you talked to your father about the marines for me—"

"Hold it right there, buster." She stood with alacrity as she cut him off. "I'm out of here."

Her heart was pounding so glaringly in her head she could hardly hear or see, and there was a funny ringing sound in her ears.

All in all, she felt like she might pass out.

Or be sick. Either way, she wanted to be out of Colin's apartment when it happened.

"You'll excuse me, please. I've got to go." Dizziness engulfed her, and she reached for the back of the couch and struggled for a breath.

Colin was on his feet in an instant, his hands on her shoulders in a strong but gentle grip Holly doubted she could break.

"Hold on a second," he said, his voice as soft and low as the purr of his cat. "What did I say?"

"Nothing. I just have to go."

"Holly, I know you better than that. I know I've said something to upset you, and I want you to tell me what it is."

Holly unclenched her teeth long enough to answer him. "I have not, nor will I ever, go to my father for help or advice. Not ever. If you want to talk to him, feel free to accompany me home for Thanksgiving and ask him yourself."

Colin didn't know which portion of her comments to address first. "Is that an invitation?" he asked, surprised.

Her eyes widened. How had she gone from bee-lining her way out of Colin's apartment to inviting him home for Thanksgiving dinner?

"Yes, I suppose it is," she agreed reluctantly. In for a penny... "I know my mom would love to have you come up to the lodge with me. Just give me a heads-up so I can tell her to set an extra place."

"Heads-up," he answered immediately, and then paused, dropping his hands from her shoulders as he took a step back. He had to wonder, now that he'd already committed himself, just what he was getting himself into.

He'd accepted this invitation from Holly without a second's thought between his mind and his mouth. And yet his original, carefully thought out plans included a day of prayerful solitude on Thanksgiving, knowing that right now he had nothing to give anyone, not even his family.

Nothing emotional, anyway.

He'd even turned down the opportunity to share the holiday with his beloved sister, Callie, not to mention the prospect of spending time with his nephew, Brandon, and his new niece, Abigail.

Why did Holly's request feel so very different to his mind and heart?

Holly.

It was definitely Holly.

Holly was watching the interplay of emotions on his face and narrowed her eyes on him when his gaze connected with hers. *For once,* her expression told him, *I caught you off guard.*

If only she knew.

His unruffled, nonplussed, ride-the-wind-and-see-where-it-will-take-you attitude couldn't hold a candle to spending a day in the presence of sweet, spectacular, solidly dependable Holly McCade.

"I'll let my mom know you'll be coming," she said. "But there are conditions, Colin."

"Be on time and wear a tie?" he quipped, trying to coax a chuckle from her.

She looked all too serious as she stared back at him. "You can start with that. My father's a stickler for those kinds of details. But it's actually my father to whom I was referring."

Colin pictured his own very intimidating version of Holly's Marine Corps drill sergeant father in his head and wondered if going to her parents for Thanksgiving was such a good idea after all.

"Should I salute?"

"Colin!"

"Sorry." He did his best to look ashamed, which earned him a reluctant chuckle. He followed with a feigned salute that Holly slapped away.

"Believe me, you'll feel like saluting when you meet my father. *I* feel like saluting him, and I've never been in the military."

He took a loud, sweeping breath and reached for Holly. She stood stiff for a moment, then allowed him to fold her into his arms.

She was very serious about her relationship with her father, and she didn't have to speak it aloud for him to see the tension she was feeling. He was obviously not the only one who had issues with a father. He stroked her hair and murmured soothingly.

He closed his eyes against the sudden longing in his head and heart to protect Holly from whatever it was her father had done to cause her such anxiety.

He'd long since given up the killer instinct that used to rise in him at the mention of the word *father,* but he was still inclined to distrust the title. He'd learned, living through the school of hard knocks, that not every father deliberately set out to hurt his child, but most managed to do a bang-up job in the end, intentionally or not.

Hence the reason he was so disinclined to have children of his own. He didn't want to hurt his own offspring, his own precious gifts of God, intentionally or otherwise.

He had enough to do just comforting damsels in distress over their own father's conduct.

With a shaky laugh, Holly sniffed and stepped back out of his arms. "I'm getting you all wet."

He hadn't known she'd been crying. She was still visibly shaken. Her fingers held a tremor as they wiped a few tears from those velvet-green eyes.

"That's okay. I'm a navy man, remember? We're used to water."

She chuckled again, this time sounding a little stronger and more sure of herself.

"You'd better hit me with those conditions while I'm still agreeable to a coat and tie," he teased in an attempt to distract her from her tears.

"It's nothing, really." She paused and took a deep breath. "Just this. Whatever you have in mind to do, or to ask my father, feel free to do it. I'm sure he'll be very helpful."

She looked over his shoulder and her velvet eyes misted once again. "Just do me a favor and leave me out of it."

Chapter Eight

Holly looked so miserable, so withdrawn, that Colin did the only thing he could think of.

He kissed her.

On hindsight, he realized it was probably not going to be the best idea he'd ever come up with, but at the moment, all he could think of was the softness of her lips, her cheeks, her hair.

Holly stiffened for a moment when his lips first brushed across hers, but she quickly melted into his embrace. With a contented sigh, she wrapped her arms tightly around his neck and pulled his face down to deepen the kiss.

Colin chuckled over her mouth. Perhaps she felt something for him after all. It was enough to make him want to shout for joy, except that he was too busy kissing her to shout.

The sensation of cradling Holly within the circle of his arms was wonderful. Everything *about* Holly was wonderful. But when he tried to express those feelings in his kiss, she backed away.

"What?" he groaned, trying to pull her back into his embrace. She resisted, turning out of his reach and wrapping her arms about herself in a manner that brooked no argument.

"Colin, what is this all about?"

She was back to her old self, serious, rigid spine and stiff shoulders. He wanted to reach out to her, to make things all right again.

He wanted to kiss her again and have her return that sentiment; but he knew from the look on her face it was a lost cause.

"I don't know what you mean," he denied, his voice low and husky. He tried to make eye contact, but she shifted her gaze away.

"We've been friends for a while, Colin, but there was no cause to kiss me."

He shook his head, disagreeing fervently. "I had a million reasons for kissing you, Holly."

"Oh, I wish you didn't." She slumped down on the couch. "This never should have happened."

Colin's mind was reeling. "I'm confused. I like you. And I think you like me. We kissed each other as a token of affection for each other. Where is the problem in that? What? You don't like me?"

She scrubbed a hand down her face, as if to wipe off the assortment of emotions she displayed there. "I don't want to get into it. I don't even know where to begin addressing the issues that kissing you raises."

She shook her head and waved him off, as if that was that. "I'm not comfortable. Can we just leave it at that?"

But he didn't want to leave it at that. She made kissing sound like some kind of legal issue, or at least a topic for a self-help book.

He merely wanted to know what was wrong. He wanted to fix the problem.

Now.

With effort, he reined in his tender curiosity and crouched before her. Infinitely careful with his touch, he reached forward, suspending his motion until she consented with her gaze. Then slowly, his breath suspended in the moment, he lightly skimmed the palm of his hand down her upper arm.

"Understand one thing about me," he said, his voice low and earnest. "I like you. I consider you my friend. A very, very *good* friend. And I would never, ever hurt a friend."

She attempted a shaky smile, but he could feel her quivering.

"I'm sorry I'm acting like a goose," she said with a wobbly laugh. "Maybe someday I'll be able to explain why I'm acting this way." She looked away, and her eyes became glazed. "But not today."

"Not today," he repeated, half to himself, and half to her.

It didn't make sense. But then, she was a woman. Men and women weren't supposed to be from the same planets, were they? He held her close. "Please don't apologize to me." He crooked a finger and tipped her chin up until her reluctant gaze met his. "You have the right to your feelings."

She pinched her lips. "I don't know about that. But I appreciate your understanding."

Understanding might be overstating it, but there must be some label for the feelings he was experiencing right now. He grinned and tapped her on the nose. "You've got it."

He might not comprehend, but he could be supportive, even if he couldn't shake the feeling that Holly thought they'd—*he'd*—done something wrong.

He summed up his feelings. "We kissed, and it was fun. End of subject."

He stood and pulled Holly to her feet. His mind was still spinning, and his muscles needed something physical to do to lighten the mood and make Holly feel better.

"Now, why don't we go down to the park and see if we can have even more fun?" he suggested with a wink. "It'll take my mind off the pressure of finishing my project for your class."

He took her hand and guided her to the door. "And if you're *really* nice, I might even be persuaded to push you on the swing."

* * *

The phone was ringing as Holly entered her apartment. Holly threw her keys down on the table by the door and raced for the telephone.

"Why didn't you tell me?" Sarah demanded as soon as Holly picked up the receiver. "It's not fair for you to keep such a hunk a secret."

Holly's heart raced, and she labored to take in a breath. "I don't know what you mean."

Sarah barked out a laugh. "Oh, right. I'm sure you don't have a clue. As if plucking the best-looking student from the classroom and claiming him for yourself is your usual style."

"I did no such thing!" answered Holly indignantly. "And you know it."

Again, Sarah laughed. "Of course, silly. *I* don't care if you date a student."

"I'm not dating him. And there's nothing in the student teacher's handbook that prohibits my seeing someone in the class."

"Exactly," Sarah agreed easily. "So tell me all about him. I already know where you met. What else is there to tell? What? Where? And when?"

Holly cringed, knowing Sarah couldn't see her. "I'd rather not."

"What's wrong? You sound shaken up."

"I am. Something happened today with Colin that I—well, I just think I'd be better off to find out a way to avoid him from now on."

"Did he hurt you?" Sarah, her voice defensive, sounded all ready to lay in to Colin, and Holly chuckled despite herself.

"No, of course not. Colin wouldn't hurt me. At least, not on purpose," she clarified quickly.

"Meaning?"

"I just want to back off. Things between the two of us are getting a little too complicated for me." She paused, easily conjuring up the handsome blond sailor. If she expelled her breath on a sigh, it wasn't on purpose.

At least that's what she told herself.

"So he's not a nutcase or anything."

"Oh, no." It was amazing, how quickly she rose to his defense. "Colin is a gentleman in every sense of the word. He's smart. And funny. And I don't have to tell you how handsome he is. I just can't be around him right now. And I can't explain it."

She swept in a breath and darted a furtive glance around the room, searching for something comforting on which to settle her gaze.

But her pristine apartment offered little in the way of consolation. She snatched a pillow from the couch and pulled it close to her chest. "That sounds crazy, doesn't it?"

"You said it, not me. Is he pushing for a commitment and you're not ready for it?"

Holly laughed shakily. "Oh, no. Nothing like that. But I do think he's pushing our relationship toward the next level, something more serious than a casual friendship."

"And?"

Holly clutched the telephone. "Sarah, you are one of the few people who really know me. You *know* why I can't be with Colin."

"I know why you're *afraid* to be with him," Sarah inserted. "Because of your past. But if Colin is half the man you say he is, he'll understand, Holly. You have to be honest with him. Talk to the man. You aren't the only one in the world who has ever done anything in their past they've been ashamed of, you know."

Holly felt her cheeks flushing with warmth. "I don't *want* him to understand, Sarah. I'll die of humiliation if he ever finds out the truth about me. I don't think I could handle that. I want to go back to the way things were before he entered my life."

"You can't do that."

"I know that. But I made a mistake in pursuing a friendship with him. He's just not the kind of man a woman can be friends with."

"Honey, I could have told you that with one look at the man." Sarah laughed. "But I don't mean to downplay how you're feeling. He wants more, and so do you. And it scares you to death."

"That's precisely the point, Sarah. And that's why you've got to promise me you'll help me steer clear of Colin Brockman, and all the trouble he brings."

"Holly, I don't think—"

Holly cut her off. "Promise. You have to. With your help, I'll be able to put that blond-haired scalawag out of my mind once and for all."

"I promise…" Sarah said. Then she finished her sentence under her breath. "Not to tell you *I told you so* when this all falls apart."

The more Colin thought about his encounter with Holly, the more perplexed he became.

Sure, he'd kissed her without warning her first, but he was positive she'd been receptive to his affection, at least at the moment their lips had first touched.

So what had happened to turn her away from him?

He'd asked himself that question a million times, and each time he'd come up blank. He'd prayed over and over for discernment, for a tiny glimpse into heaven, or at the very least into the complex and bewildering mind of a woman.

No sign, wonder or great revelation came on any front, not that he really expected it. Bright lights were his style, not God's. And Colin was too restless to be motionless enough to hear the still, small voice that might really do him some good.

Worst of all, Holly was obviously avoiding him at all costs. It had been two whole weeks, and he hadn't seen her once.

No. That wasn't completely accurate.

He'd *seen* her, all right. But he couldn't get close to her, no matter how hard he tried. Every day in class, he watched her speaking, teaching a subject that lit her internal fire. He enjoyed the sight of her thick, sable hair swishing in waves across her back, and pictured those velvet-green eyes he'd come to know so well gleaming with brilliance, though he couldn't see them clearly from the shadows of the room where he always sat.

With every breath, he longed to speak to Holly, and his arms ached to hold her, to assure her nothing was wrong between them.

Nothing was wrong.

He remembered back to the first time he'd seen her. *Ms. Gorgeous Legs,* he'd called her.

She was that, all right. The memory brought a smile to his lips.

But there was so much more to Holly McCade than her pretty face and fine figure, that he couldn't begin to name them all. And there was so much more Colin wanted to learn about her.

It was an insatiable yearning, to know everything about her a man could learn. He knew this much— he connected with her on a level that had made her his closest friend, while paradoxically becoming the greatest mystery of his life.

Holly was kind and sensitive, with a sense of humor that matched his own—except for those few times he couldn't figure out. She was strong in a feminine sort of way. She knew where she belonged, and where she was going.

But she was hiding something. Some kind of secret that was keeping them apart. That was the only reasonable explanation he could fathom.

He'd glimpsed her in a hallway once and had started to approach her, but as soon as she'd seen him—and she *had* seen him—she'd turned and fled in the other direction like she had fire at her heels.

He had no doubt she was running away from him, that *he* was the proverbial fire nipping at her heels. The only question was, *why?*

What exactly had he done to strike the match?

Colin wasn't the type of man to sit back when there was a challenge to be met, and he wasn't about to let Holly run out of his life without a fight. She was the closest friend he'd ever had, except for his sister, and since Callie was related by blood, he could hardly count her.

He was going to get Holly back into his life. No argument about it.

Like the military man he was, Colin planned his strategy carefully. He would begin with Holly's friend Sarah, who had been so bubbly and flirtatious before, and had practically shoved Holly in his direction with her encouragement. Sarah now stood as staid and stoic as the walls of Jericho around Holly, acting like a fortress between her bewildered friend and Colin.

When he approached Sarah about Holly's noticeable absences in class, and the way she tactfully avoided him whenever she *was* there, Sarah cheerfully chatted around the issue. When he pressed her, she stoned up.

The walls of Jericho.

Clearly, Sarah didn't know how *that* particular story ended.

If he couldn't go to the source, he would find out through other means what was happening with Holly. Colin waited for the right moment, after class when Sarah was busy cleaning up. Sarah wouldn't run as far and as fast as her friend and colleague Holly. He could feel it in his gut.

When he advanced, it was a full-scale attack. He even sent a couple of figurative spies, in the form of jocks that sat near him in psych class whom he'd made acquaintances with, to spy out the land. They kept Sarah occupied while the classroom exited, luring her off to the side where she would be more vulnerable.

He waited in the shadows until the trumpet was sounded.

Then he charged.

Sarah saw him coming, rapidly interpreting the determined expression on his face, if her flare of panic was any indication. She scurried for her notes and books, but put them down again when she realized there was no immediate means of escape.

Where was there to run? Colin would only follow, and probably cause a scene.

Colin squared his shoulders. He was taking no prisoners. No matter what he had to do.

"I don't even know what I said," he declared boldly, taking a calculated risk that Sarah knew the whole story and would not mistake his meaning.

There was an awkward moment where the air crackled with electrical silence. She narrowed her gaze sharply upon him.

Then, all at once, the walls of Jericho cracked, and started to crumble.

With a vengeance.

"Said? What you *said*? It's what you *did,* you dumb, overgrown sailor."

Her insults didn't bother him, but her accusation cut to the quick.

He'd never knowingly hurt Holly. And Sarah of all people should know that. Was it only two weeks earlier that she'd been pushing the two of them together?

Women.

"What I did," he repeated, trying to keep the frustration he was feeling out of his voice. "And that would be *what,* exactly?"

"If you don't know, I'm not going to tell you. You'll have to take that up with Holly."

"In a second," Colin barked back, seething with annoyance. Was it just with him, or did women always talk and not say what they meant? "Except, as you well know, Holly isn't speaking to me."

Sarah shrugged, and Colin thought he saw just a hint of concession in her eyes. "I did tell her she ought to talk to you."

The walls continued to crumble. He grinned. This was one battle he was determined to win.

"I'd never hurt Holly. Sarah, if you listen to one thing from me today, this is it. You've got to believe that."

She pinned him with a fierce, protective glare that spoke louder than words. He already *had* hurt Holly.

"Maybe not intentionally."

He scrubbed a hand through his hair. "Look, I'm trying to fix the problem, whatever it is. Whatever I have to do, I'll do it. If she'd just tell me what's wrong, I'd have a lot better shot at making it better."

He shook his head fervently, his determination to make things right with Holly renewing with every breath he took. He *would* make this work. "At least I'm *trying* to work things out with her, which is more than you can say Holly is doing right now."

Sarah nodded. "I'll admit, that's commendable." It sounded like half truth, half cynicism. She continued to eye him closely, taking his measure.

She was a good friend to Holly, Colin realized, but while he appreciated her loyalty, he also wished he could cut a break with her here. Anything would be better than what he was feeling right now.

It was now or never to blow the ram's horn and shatter any remaining bricks. He cleared his throat and flashed her his best pleading gaze. "Sarah. Please. Give me a break. Help me out."

She narrowed her eyes on him. "I'd like to do that, Colin, but I'm not sure I can. I have a division of interests here."

"No you don't," he replied immediately. "Sarah, we're all on the same side here. You, me and Holly. We're striving toward the same goal. You've got to see that we are."

He pinched his lips together in a straight, determined line. He wasn't going to stoop to yelling at Sarah, but he figured he wasn't beyond a little begging. "Where is Holly now?"

She wavered for a moment before answering, her eyes flickering with uncertainty. "She's back in the psychology office. Doing research, if I'm not mistaken."

"Good."

"I'm sure she doesn't wish to be disturbed."

He waved her off with a shake of his head. "Take me there." It was more of a command than a request.

Sarah flipped her long hair to one side and perched her hands upon her hips. "And then what?"

Colin shrugged. "I guess we'll figure that out when we get there."

* * *

"Got a minute?" Colin peered suddenly around the side of the office door and flashed Holly a toothy Cheshire cat grin.

Holly put a hand to her chest to still her pounding heart. He'd startled her, popping in unannounced as he had; but if she were honest, that wasn't the only reason her heart was beating so rapidly.

It was the man himself. And she had no desire whatsoever to speak with him.

He knew it, and she knew it. He was purposefully backing her into a corner, and she mentally scrambled for the best way to react to his unwelcome presence.

"For you, anytime," she said, then wondering how her lips could so easily form such a falsehood. She tried to smile, and knew it looked more like a grimace, but Colin didn't appear to notice. Or if he did, he was resolutely ignoring her discomfort.

He swirled into the office like a whirlwind, pulled up a wooden, straight-backed chair, turned it backward and straddled it, leaning forward on his arms.

"So what are you up to?"

Obviously not what was really on his mind. Not even a particularly good opening line, from friends who hadn't seen each other in a while.

Holly steepled her fingers and leaned back in her seat, a big, black leather office chair that creaked when it moved. "What do you really want?"

Colin raised both his eyebrows. "You know me so well."

"Ha-ha."

"That wasn't a joke."

Holly groaned. "Everything's a joke with you, Colin. This much I know."

"You've got it all wrong," he protested.

"Do I? There is no ulterior motive for your visit today? Nothing you hoped to accomplish?"

He colored. "Well, there is that matter of Thanksgiving dinner."

"See? I told you so," she crowed, delighted at the opportunity to see Colin squirm a little bit.

"Did anyone ever tell you," he replied mildly, leaning his chin on his arms, "that it's not polite to gloat when someone's begging?"

Holly's breath caught in her throat. "You're begging?"

His clear, sea-blue gaze caught hers and held. "Do I need to be?"

She looked away. "No," she said around the catch in her throat. "I guess not."

He smiled so gently, and so completely without gall, that she instantly forgave him everything. Even stealing a kiss.

"Are you sure?" he continued, standing to his feet and yanking his chair out of the way so that the legs scratched against the tile floor. "Because I can get down on my knees right now."

Holly held both of her hands in the air, mortified. "Please don't."

He didn't. Instead, he held his hands out to her, pulling her out of her chair until she was standing face-to-face with him, a little closer than she would have liked, but not so close as to make her back off.

"Am I re-invited for Thanksgiving dinner?" he asked in a teasing tone.

"To my knowledge, you were never uninvited," she reminded him.

"Not technically, maybe."

"Not at all."

"We're going to have to talk, you know." His words were soft, but their meaning was unmistakable. He wanted to know why a kiss could send her off the deep end.

"Do we have to talk now?"

He chuckled. "No. Just sometime."

"Sometime, then." She'd put *that* moment off for as long as possible. Now that she was in Colin's presence again, she remembered how much she liked being around him, and she wasn't quite ready to give that up.

Which she'd have to do when he found out the truth about her. He wouldn't want to be around the kind of woman she was.

"Sometime it is."

"You really want to come?" she queried softly, squeezing his fingers.

"I really do." His gaze told her how much. "I need to speak with your father, remember?"

She did remember. And she thought she should feel insulted, for him to remind her of that. Maybe with another man, she would be.

But with Colin, she somehow knew that while he did need to speak with her father about the marines, he was really coming along to spend the weekend with her. And for now, that was all she needed to know.

Chapter Nine

One look into Colin's sea-blue eyes and Holly's common sense must have floated away. That was the only possible explanation.

And now, on Thanksgiving Day, she had to pay for her moment of weakness.

Holly straightened her jacket and slid a glance sideways at the handsome man standing beside her on her parents' front porch.

He looked straight ahead, his bearing tall and strong. He didn't appear to be looking in her direction, but just the same, as she turned her glance away from him, he reached out and grabbed for her hand, giving it a reassuring squeeze.

She smiled softly. She didn't know whether the reassurance in his grip was more for her benefit, or for his.

It was the first time she'd ever seen Colin look nervous. She thought, given the circumstances, that she might be basking in the pleasure of watching him sweat, but she was more taken in by the moment's witness of sheer humanity.

He wasn't always one hundred percent in control, after all. The knowledge made her like him even more.

Holly was a bit amused by his looks. His jeans and sweater looked as if they might have been ironed. It looked as if he'd bought a new pair of running shoes for the occasion, for the supple white leather wasn't marred by a single scuff.

He'd even combed his hair into a semblance of military precision. Not a single strand of his white-blond hair was out of place, no doubt thanks to a good slathering of gel.

She looked up at him and smiled. She wasn't at all sure she wanted him here with her today, but there was no sense in making him suffer any more than was absolutely necessary. Not that there was any doubt on that point.

He *would* suffer.

Her father would see to that, however shrewdly he crafted ways to turn the screws on Colin. It was going to be an agonizing weekend for everyone concerned, and for her most of all.

Holly made up her mind at once not to be the cause of any of Colin's difficulties. At least not today.

She closed her eyes and sent a silent and uncomfortably overdue prayer of forgiveness heavenward. It wasn't Colin's fault she had a sordid past she was struggling to keep hidden, especially when she was the one who hadn't been up-front with him in the first place. Maybe if she had been…

Stealing a kiss was not a crime.

She might even have enjoyed it, were circumstances different.

But they weren't.

She shifted uneasily. Her parents were taking an inordinate amount of time answering the door. On purpose. To keep them squirming.

Holly knew she'd eventually have to talk to Colin, and tell him the truth. Even if they never took their relationship beyond the friendship they had now, he deserved to know.

But knowing would change everything. And she would put that moment off for as long as she could. She had already waited too long to bare her soul to him, at least with any hope of his understanding. He would want to know why she hadn't been up-front with him.

And to be honest, she didn't know the answer to that question anymore. She wished she *had*.

She wasn't going to kid herself with anything but the truth. He was going to turn around and walk right out of her life when he found out how she'd spent her teenage years, what kind of person she'd been back then.

A shiver ran through her. There wouldn't be any more stolen kisses between them to worry about.

Which was all the more reason to enjoy whatever time she had left with him. She squared her shoulders. She had a lot of memories to make, something she could treasure later.

After.

She glanced sideways to see if Colin was feeling half as impatient with the wait as she was. He wasn't his usual talkative self, if that was any indication.

But when he met her gaze, all her doubts disappeared. The smile Colin gave her was anything but apprehensive, edgy or even impatient, for that matter. It was his usual careless, confident grin, and it immediately made her feel better inside.

Funny how he could reassure her even when he wasn't trying.

Her father swung the door open, and she knew in an instant he'd been making them wait on purpose.

Anger flared in her chest, but Colin squeezed her hand again, as if he knew what she was feeling, and her resolve to make the best of things strengthened. She wasn't going to let her father get the best of her. Not now that Colin was here with her.

"Dad, this is Colin Brockman, the man I told you about."

Holly's father, Ian, his hair cut in a characteristic military crew, and his T-shirt a marine green, pinched one eye closed in that grizzled way he had, then pursed one side of his lip and spoke out of the other. "Navy man, my girl says."

Colin squared his shoulders and looked the man directly in the eye. "Yes, sir. I'm out of the service now in order to attend college and get my master's degree, but I plan to reenlist upon my ordination to the ministry."

"Good man," the sergeant barked, clapping Colin on the back. "Rather you were a marine, but military's always welcome under this roof."

Colin grinned as casual as ever. "Thank you, sir. I'm glad to be here."

"Mrs. McCade will be sorry she missed the chance to be here to greet you, but she had some last-minute shopping to do." Sergeant McCade grunted. "Put a roast in the oven and took off like a whirlwind. Don't know what got in her craw."

Holly giggled and shared an amused look with Colin. She had told him a little bit about her sweet, quixotic mother, and it was just like her to run off at the last minute for some frivolous reason or another when she had guests coming.

She probably wanted to impress Colin, Holly thought, smothering another laugh. Impress him with a new red-checked tablecloth, or turkey-shaped salt shakers or Mother-only-knew what else.

More likely, when her mother did finally see him, Colin would be the one impressing *her*. It wasn't every day Holly brought a devastatingly handsome and charming man home to supper. Mom was in for a shocker.

With the tender consideration of a true gentleman, Colin placed a hand at the small of her back and accompanied her inside. Without hovering, he remained close to her side, his broad shoulders serving as a protective and very effective barrier between Holly and her father until she was ready to face him.

"Hello to you, too, Daddy," Holly said, giving Ian a perfunctory hug and a kiss on the cheek. He looked older than she remembered, and tired.

Or maybe *she* was the one feeling old and tired. At this point it was hard to tell.

"Sweet Pea."

She blushed at the use of her father's pet name for her. If he was trying to embarrass her, he was doing a wonderful job of it.

"Holly, why don't you go on down to your room, and I'll bring your things along to you shortly. Colin, grab your gear and follow me. I'm putting you up in the spare room."

He paused and looked back severely. "The one on the *opposite* end of the house from Holly, if you take my meaning."

Colin chuckled, but his smile, for once, did not reach his face. His blue eyes were like ice cubes. "That will be fine, sir."

Holly held back in astonishment that Colin didn't

bark back at her father for such insensitivity. He'd had no right, and Colin was his own man.

Sure, he was easygoing, but no man enjoyed being pushed around, and she thought Colin, most of all, would get his back up at being ordered about.

She half expected—*hoped,* she recognized suddenly—that Colin would stand up to her father in the way she'd always wanted to but never had the nerve.

Instead, he was rigidly polite, and clearly military. To his credit, he didn't say a word when provoked, except a brisk, military sanction.

Still, it could happen. Her drill sergeant father was a master at provocation, and Holly was pretty sure he wouldn't let up on Colin, if for no other reason than that she had brought him home.

Hit the right button, and every man would go off.

Even cool, cavalier Colin Brockman.

Colin was obviously a master at maintaining his composure, or else he had an arctic demeanor that was a part of him she hadn't seen before. Evidently, he had some way of shielding his true thoughts and feelings from the world, more than just the carelessness or even world-weariness she'd observed in him earlier.

Had the military given him this rigid self-possession? Or had his youth—his father—cast these scars?

"Young man, there's another thing we'd best get straight about your stay here," Ian continued, as if

Colin's icy eyes weren't boring into him. "Something very important. Pay attention."

Holly tensed, anticipating the explosion. Either it would be her father's words, or Colin's temper.

"If I find you so much as in the same hallway as the one where my little girl sleeps, I'm going to tan your hide from here to Texas."

Colin flashed a suddenly warm, amused glance in her direction before he grinned at the sergeant. This time, the smile was real, even a little bit cheeky. Holly knew it, and she knew her father knew it. "Yes, sir, Sergeant McCade, sir. I understand completely, sir."

"What?" snapped the sergeant when Colin looked as if he wanted to say more.

"Well, sir, I was just thinking…"

"Get on with it."

"You've warned me about visiting your daughter's hallway, sir."

"What's your point?"

Colin's gaze met Holly's, his eyes sparkling. "I think it's only fair that you warn her off mine. Or you'll tan *her* hide all the way from here to Texas?"

"Colin Brockman, you are treading on very thin water," Holly warned, holding out one hand and swinging her purse like a weapon.

"Are you being impertinent, son?" Ian McCade asked at the same time.

"I dare you," Colin said to Holly, his eyes brimming over with laughter.

When his gaze shifted to her father, Holly took the opening and nailed him in the rib cage with her purse. Colin was on it in a moment, hooting with triumph as he wrapped the strap around his wrist. He used the momentum of the swing to yank Holly off balance and pull her under his arm, where he tucked her snugly.

"Yes, sir," he said, nodding at her father. "Completely impertinent."

The sergeant roared with laughter. "Glad to hear it. Welcome to the McCades, son. Home away from home."

Colin unpacked his bag and settled in to the small but comfortable room he'd been given. It was sparsely but tastefully decorated in masculine colors of red and blue. The twin bed looked a good deal more comfortable than the naval bunk to which he was accustomed, so he couldn't complain.

Keeping the room neat would be a trial, but not an impossibility. He'd managed in the navy, and he would manage now.

Using the small bathroom to wash up and run a comb through his already-tousled hair, he quickly adjourned to the den, where a roaring fire was blazing in the hearth. It was quiet, dark and cozy, and

Colin found himself able to take his first real, deep breath in over an hour.

He covertly scanned the room. He could hear bustling sounds of pots and pans coming from the kitchen from whom he assumed was Mrs. McCade, and there was a black Labrador retriever dozing by the fire, but to his relief, Holly was nowhere around.

Colin had a mission to fulfill, and the sooner he got it over with, the better.

He'd realized as soon as he saw the stern, commanding drill sergeant that the older man had a noticeable soft spot in his heart for his little girl. But he highly doubted Holly had ever recognized that kind of affection from her father. Ian wasn't the effusive type, unless you called barking orders effusive.

For his part, Colin wasn't going to let himself be intimidated by the gruff old man—he'd seen enough hype in the military to know just what Sergeant McCade was trying to pull.

Colin grinned. A little bellowing wasn't going to keep him from asking Holly's gruff father a very important question.

Sergeant McCade was relaxing on a leather easy chair with his sock-covered feet propped up on a stool. He puffed with satisfaction on a black pipe, his black reading glasses propped on his nose as he perused the daily newspaper.

"Good afternoon, sir." He stood before the armchair as he greeted Holly's father, trying to be convincingly amicable and categorically unmilitary, knowing he succeeded at neither.

Ian grunted and waved toward the sofa, then buried his nose back in the newspaper.

Colin crouched on the edge of the cushion, elbows across his knees, his hands gripped tightly together. "I was wondering, sir, if I could talk with you. If you have a moment. If it's convenient."

He clamped his mouth shut before he said anything else stupid. Before he rambled anymore.

Sergeant McCade pinched the rim of his glasses between two fingers and pulled them halfway down his nose. For a moment, he merely eyed Colin over the rim, then grunted again and returned his glasses to the bridge of his nose, shaking his paper noisily.

Colin took that as a yes.

"Well, it's like this, sir," Colin began, tightly lacing his fingers in front of him. He was careful not to clench his fists. "Lately, I've been spending a lot of time with your daughter, and I want you to know I think the world of her."

Ian grunted harshly. "That so?"

"The truth is, I really like her. But I can't seem to get close to her. She's not the easiest person to reach. Maybe you know what I mean."

He cleared his throat, but found he couldn't look away from Sergeant McCade's stare. He was frozen to the spot, unable even to breathe.

Holly's marine drill sergeant father narrowed his

gaze on Colin the way a panther pinned down his prey. His eyes gleamed gray in the firelight. "Close."

"Close, sir, meaning getting to know her better, becoming good friends with her," Colin clarified, finding his breath, and his voice, with alacrity. "I want you to know up front that I'm a good Christian man, sir, and I'm committed to staying—" Colin felt himself stammering. "That is…being—"

Ian actually chuckled. Colin felt the tension ease from the room, and smiled back at the older man. Although he wasn't quite sure what Sergeant McCade found so funny in the situation. While Colin was sweating bullets, Ian was as cool as the proverbial cucumber.

"I get your point," the sergeant replied acerbically. "And while I don't know *why* I believe you, I do believe you."

"You do?" Colin asked in surprise, his face flushed with elation.

"Yes," Ian answered briskly. "I do." He steepled his fingers and tipped them to his chin. "So, then your problems concerning my daughter are merely in the…*spiritual* realm then? Is that correct?" he asked with an amused twist to his lip.

The flush in Colin's face increased until he was sure his skin was flaming red. He cleared his throat against the pressure choking him. "Uh, not exactly, sir."

"Meaning?"

"Yes…w-well." Colin stopped, realizing he was stammering again. That would never do, not with a marine drill sergeant. He'd best just say it like it was and get it over with, since he'd come this far. "The fact is, sir, I kissed her."

Ian didn't budge. Colin expected him to frown, or chuckle or shoot him dead right there on the spot. Ian was a rock, showing not an ounce of emotion.

He did have a few words, however.

"What about your commitment to—" Ian cleared his throat, a little overdramatically, if you asked Colin, but then, drill sergeants were given to the overdramatic.

"Frankly, sir," Colin said, deciding to be blunt, "it seemed like the right thing to do at the time. As a general rule, I don't see anything wrong with stealing a kiss now and again."

"And is that what you did?" Ian's words were straight and wry. Still no bona fide reaction, though, not even in his expression. His gray eyes were as cold as ever. "*Steal* a kiss?"

Colin thought back to the moment he'd kissed Holly, how she'd melted into his arms, how right it felt to hold her and feel her heart beat with his.

"Yes, sir," he said at last. She *had* reacted, but he hadn't given her any hint of his intentions. He'd shoulder the responsibility.

"There's your problem," Ian said with the solemn

authority of a father. He steepled his fingers again and looked wise—and unapproachable.

"What's that?" Colin asked, confused. "My problem is that I kissed your daughter? That sounds like just the sort of advice a woman's father would give."

Suddenly the rock broke. Amusement spilled like a water from a broken dam from Ian's gray eyes. "No, young man. Pay attention to what I'm saying. Your problem is that you *stole* a kiss. Like a thief."

Colin's eyebrows met the crook of his nose. "I don't understand."

Ian chuckled. "No, you certainly don't, my boy." He ran a grizzled hand over his wrinkled, clean-shaven cheek. "I think maybe you don't know my Holly well enough to be kissing her."

Colin bristled. "I know her well enough. And if she'd let me—"

Ian silenced him, laying a fatherly hand on Colin's sweatered shoulder and giving it a squeeze. "Take it from her father, my boy," he said in a surprisingly gentle tone. "Holly doesn't want to be trifled with by any young man, most especially a man in uniform."

"Trifled with? Oh, but, sir—"

"I know, son. But trust me. She doesn't see things the way you and I do." He pinched his lips together tightly, obviously pausing in order to choose his words wisely and thoughtfully.

After a moment, he continued. "She's had some—bad experiences in her life."

Colin frowned.

"I'm sure she'll tell you about them when she's ready for you to know. But do yourself a favor in the meantime. Don't steal any more kisses."

"Sir, I would never trifle with Holly." His voice was an octave lower than normal. He was surprised by the fervency burning in his heart, how much he meant what he was saying.

Where had this strength of emotion come from?

He would never have guessed he had it in him, to feel like this. It was a invigorating revelation, but a sober one.

He'd never expected this conversation to take such a serious tone. Nor for his heart to have taken such a serious turn.

He squared his shoulders and looked Ian straight in the eye. "I wouldn't hurt Holly. Not ever. You have my word on that."

"Good." Ian nodded firmly. "But don't tell *me*. Tell Holly."

He swept in an audible breath and turned his gaze away, looking distant for a moment before returning to the present.

He gave Colin a grimace that was an old man's close rendition of a smile. "Holly is good at keeping things deep inside that pretty head of hers, but I can guarantee you she's worrying about it."

"I'll get right on it, sir." Colin stood and nodded

at the grizzled soldier, feeling almost as if he should salute.

"Don't push her."

"No, sir."

Ian leaned back in his chair and returned his pipe to his mouth. As he fluffed his paper back to where it had been, he spoke one more time.

"You're the kind of man Holly needs in her life, sailor. A man who faces up to his challenges."

Colin nodded to the older man, but since the sergeant was clearly already engrossed in the newspaper, he decided to go back to his room. As he walked, he mulled over what Ian McCade had said about facing up to challenges.

Colin had been faced with many challenges in his lifetime. Now, with God's help and a great deal of his own determination, he had faced up to every challenge he'd encountered, even the lingering pain of his father's mental abuse, which he knew would never quite leave him alone.

But this—this was new to him.

Being with Holly was a challenge unlike any other he had faced. He paused in the hallway and closed his eyes for a moment, restoring his equilibrium and evening his breath.

He smiled, knowing what lay before him would be worth whatever effort he had to expend; for winning the love of a woman, Colin thought, his chest swelling with newly hatched emotion, must truly be the biggest challenge a man would ever face.

And the biggest triumph he would ever know.

Chapter Ten

Holly didn't remember a Thanksgiving dinner quite as unusual and uncomfortable as this one was turning out to be. She shifted in her seat, vitally aware of the energy crackling in the air. The tension was so thick she thought she might be able to reach up with her hand and touch it, and be physically shocked by the sheer electricity of the moment.

Her father had asked—though it had sounded more of a gruff command than a question, coming from her father's lips—for Colin to say the grace.

The request was met with a smile, as Holly knew it would be. Everyone knew he was a future navy chaplain. This was probably the first of many such requests.

Colin's prayer was simple and elegant, but the words he spoke had Holly wondering what planet she was on. Were these people really her parents?

Was the grinning man sitting across from her really the man she had brought home for the holidays?

Thanking the Lord for food, family and friends had been what Holly considered in the normal realm of things, typical Thanksgiving fare. But then Colin started going off on the oddest tangent—something about thanking God for people who chose to forgive, to give old friends a second chance at friendship, and how precious they were in the eyes of God.

She could have sworn she heard her father smothering a laugh.

Her stern, taskmaster father laughing during prayer?

Impossible!

She looked from one stiff-spined military man to the other, but could find no clues in their expressions. She picked at her meal, no longer feeling hungry.

She didn't like the notion she was missing out on some kind of inside joke between everyone else. What was going on in this house?

Colin didn't appear to have any misgivings about his own meal. He greedily gulped down enormous bites of food, between equally large quantities of conversation. He appeared completely at ease with her parents, much more so than she herself felt at the moment.

Or ever, for that matter.

And her father was watching her. She could feel

his eyes upon her whenever Colin was speaking. But if he thought to intimidate her or make her feel funny for bringing Colin home, he'd have to think again.

She reminded herself that she was no longer the small girl trying to win her daddy's approval. She had nothing to prove here today. She was simply eating a holiday meal with the family.

And she'd brought a friend home with her this year. Her mother, at least, was pleased by Colin's obvious enthusiasm for everything around him, the food and gracious company most especially.

Holly put her fork to her plate and decided the best course of action was to concentrate on her food and let the other details worry about themselves. It was hard to swallow at times, especially whenever Colin looked her way.

All through the meal, it seemed to Holly that Colin was sending her silent messages with his smile, but she had no idea what he had on his mind. She wasn't about to ask him out loud.

Not at the dinner table. And not with her father present. He'd tell her in his own good time, whatever it was that was pressing on him.

She didn't have long to wait. When her mother rose from the table and began stacking the plates, Colin charged into action, charmingly and literally disarming her mother of the dishes, insisting he would do them on his own, since he was the guest.

Holly rose, intending to follow his lead, but he shook his head. "No, no. No dishes for you."

But when she turned away, he was equally as adamant. "No, no. Don't leave. Follow me," he said as he led her into the kitchen. "I just want you to sit and keep me company," he explained as he dropped the dishes onto the counter with a clatter, scraped out a stool from the breakfast bar and gestured her into it.

"What's this about?" she asked as he filled the sink with hot, sudsy water.

He shrugged and set a stack of dirty plates in the water. "I just thought I should do a little bit to help out, since your mom spent the whole day in the kitchen creating that fantastic culinary masterpiece we just consumed."

"That's not what I was talking about, and you know it."

Colin didn't answer.

She changed the subject. "I expect my father is happily ensconced on his favorite chair in the family room by now, puffing on that silly old pipe of his. I've tried to get him to quit, but he's a stubborn son of a gun."

Colin didn't answer, busy as he was scrubbing at the dishes. It was amazing how masculine he looked, his sleeves pushed up, and hunkered over a sink of dirty dishes, a towel slapped over his shoulder.

She shook her head and laughed softly, resuming her soliloquy. "And if I know my mom, she will be sitting at his side, cross-stitching or reading a novel. They've had the same after-dinner routine for as many years as I can remember. It was one of those odd family habits that made life feel the same, even when we moved around the world as a military family. They always made me do the dishes, which I highly resented, of course. Just Dad, Mom and me. Funny, how I remember it so clearly just now."

"I've been smoking this pipe longer than you've been alive, missy," Colin mimicked in a surprisingly accurate rendition of her father, from his low, scratchy voice, all the way down to how he pinched one eye and half of his mouth closed as he talked.

Holly laughed, truly delighted. Her throat was still tight with emotion, but Colin's antics had helped. At least now she could swallow.

Colin chuckled with her, then nodded as he wiped a plate clean. "I've seen him puffing at that old pipe. He's a man with a mission. I don't think I'd want to mess with that kind of dedication."

"When did you see my father with his pipe?" she asked, surprise jolting through her at the odd sensation that something was not quite right.

She hadn't seen Colin and her father together a handful of times since they'd arrived at the lodge; and then never in the den, which was the only place her mother allowed her father to smoke his pipe.

"I saw him with his pipe at the same time he told

me why you're so afraid of me," Colin said, his voice soft and even.

Holly blanched. "What?"

Her father had told Colin about her teen years? When she'd rebelled against God and everyone? When she'd run with a loose crowd, both figuratively and literally?

He wouldn't do that to her. Would he?

"I don't believe you."

"It was a good conversation, Holly. We both felt it was very productive."

She stood and turned away from Colin, grasping the back of a chair for support. How could her father betray her trust in so cruel a manner?

And why to *Colin?*

Why not just blare it out over the military megaphone to the whole world and have it over with?

All she'd struggled to build through the years was crumbling down around her in a big messy heap. This was her worst nightmare come true.

Colin knew the truth. He had *sought out* the truth. But she couldn't blame him.

She was the one living a lie.

"He told you all about me, then," she acknowledged, her voice sounding flat to her own ears. But better flat than panicked.

"I already knew everything I need to know about you before I ever talked to your father, Holly McCade," he whispered softly, just next to her ear.

Somehow he'd moved behind her without her knowing. His steady, warm breath both soothed and ruffled her at the same time.

Holly closed her eyes tightly. She couldn't bear to think of Colin picturing her at the height of her immaturity, and she certainly didn't want to see the look on his face right now.

But she'd always known she couldn't hide the truth forever. Purity was something she'd embraced in her early twenties, too late to take back that precious gift God gave only once between a man and a woman.

She'd desperately wanted to believe the lie, as a teenager, that love and sex were the same thing. By the time she'd realized the truth, it was too late to turn back the clock.

If she ever were to marry, it would have to be to a man with a big heart.

Like Colin.

Her own thoughts burned through her. She hadn't realized…hadn't recognized…

"He didn't tell me any state secrets," Colin assured her, running his palms across her shoulders before turning her firmly around to face him. "He was helping me with *my* problem."

"And what would that be?" Holly blurted, eager to turn the spotlight away from herself, even if it were only for a moment. The rush of relief she felt was on an equal par with her curiosity to know what he considered his own quandaries.

"Well...*you,*" he admitted wryly as he grinned down on her.

"Me. Since when did I become a problem?"

"Holly, what do you want out of life?" he asked, answering a question with a question.

"More than I can probably get." She looked away, ashamed of the cynical streak that ran through her, but unable to take back the words.

"Meaning?"

She let out an audible sigh. "What most women want, I suppose. A husband. A dozen kids. A home of my own to keep them in."

"With a lock on the bathroom so you can find some privacy," Colin inserted, the gleam in his eyes both teasing and caring.

"That, too." She chuckled.

"What else?"

"What else? Oh, I don't know. The usual. A career. I want to help people, you know?"

He tucked her under his chin and held her there against his chest, where she could hear the strong, even beating of his heart. "Yeah, I know."

"Isn't that what you want?" she asked quietly, her voice muffled against the softness of his sweater. "A home? A family? Eventually, I mean."

She felt his muscles stiffen, though he didn't move

away. She slid her arms around his waist and gave him a strong hug.

"I somehow don't think that's what God's got planned for me," he said, and she could hear the tension in his voice.

"Why is that?"

He pushed her away from him enough that he could gaze down into her eyes. "You know better than anyone how bad the military lifestyle is on children. I wouldn't be so brutal as to subject my own kids to that kind of torture, never mind my wife."

"It doesn't have to be that way." She was amazed by the words coming from her own mouth; yet in the same moment, she knew what she said was true.

Her own experiences as a child of military parents didn't preclude the possibility of someone else making it work. And she and Colin had turned out all right despite the problems.

She could make it work.

She could raise military children. She already knew all the pitfalls. She could avoid them herself, and help her own children over the humps.

Of course she would never admit such a thought, most especially not to Colin.

He had returned to the sink and was noisily stacking dishes. His back to her, she covertly admired his broad shoulders and muscular physique.

"Do you think I trifle with you?" Colin didn't give any indication he'd spoken. His words were so low and velvety soft that it was almost as if he hadn't spoken at all.

But that didn't stop the bolt of electricity that sparked through her at his words, nor the heat rising to stain her cheeks in protest.

"Trifle? What do mean, *trifle?* Who uses a word like *trifle* these days?"

The answer hit her just as Colin turned, looking at once amused and sheepish. She blushed to the roots of her hair.

"Colin Brockman, *what* has my father been telling you?"

Chapter Eleven

A week later, Colin still wasn't sure how he'd gotten out of Holly's query about her father without losing his humor or his head, though Holly had threatened both and more.

But now that he was tightly ensconced in his own comfortable—if messy—apartment, he could relax, even if he couldn't quite forget about the close call. He was sprawled on the floor in front of the coffee table, a large, daunting stack of papers and books spread around him.

He had no idea where he should start. The ominous pile gave him a gut feeling that was at least as overwhelming as the one he'd experienced in his first week in boot camp. Only, this time, there was no one yelling in his face to get the job done.

He was so far behind on his studies that he thought he might never be able to catch up. It was amazing what a pretty face could do to a man's mind. Last weekend, at Holly's parents' lodge, his mind had been on Holly alone. He hadn't even thought to crack a book.

Now, when he knew he had to either get with the program or face the consequences, he was *still* having trouble concentrating, keeping his mind off a certain sable-haired beauty with velvet-green eyes that made a man's insides turn to mush.

He flipped open the book on the top of the pile and tried to read, but he couldn't help reminiscing, even so.

It had been an amazing weekend. Sitting with Holly's mom and dad and having a real old-fashioned holiday meal had been the highlight. That, and his talk with Ian, who had shed some light on Colin's relationship with Holly.

He was especially grateful to Gwen, Holly's mom, who had come into the kitchen to see how the dishes were progressing. If she hadn't stepped in at just the right moment, Colin may have been forced to reveal his hand.

And he hadn't studied his cards yet.

He grinned and chuckled. How providential could a man get?

He'd slipped away without having to say a word. Without answering Holly's query on the word *trifle*. Without admitting how far her father's conversation had gone, how much he now had to think about.

For in truth, he was beginning to think seriously

about Holly, wondering if God might have meant for her to be his life's partner. The Man Who Would Be Single was now contemplating matrimony—if not seriously, then at least with some degree of significance.

Marriage.

It wasn't as frightening a concept now that Holly was in his life. If it wasn't for his own fear—that of becoming a man like his father—he'd probably have whisked her off to the altar already.

Any sane man would have.

He chuckled under his breath and tossed aside the book he'd been reading. He picked up the next book nearest his reach. Sliding down to one elbow on the carpet, he yawned widely and forced himself to open the book, wishing not for the first time that he was a better student.

Though he'd never gotten much above C's and B's in high school, he knew he could be a good student if he put his mind to it. If he'd learned one thing during his years in the military, it was that he could improve himself, but he had to work harder.

He creased his brow, determined to buckle down.

He'd found his spot in the history book he held, and had read maybe three-quarters of a page when there was a knock on his door.

He groaned. Was he doomed to fail the semester? He was never going to be able to follow his dream of becoming a chaplain this way.

"Just a second," he hollered as he rolled to his feet. He half staggered to the door on legs that had fallen asleep on him, muttering under his breath about not being as young as he used to be.

Still grumbling, he yanked at the knob, determined to send whoever was on the other side of the door running for cover, so he could get back to the mind-numbing tediousness of his own work.

But when he opened the door, all thoughts of books and study were swept from his mind by the sight of Holly, her eyes sparkling with excitement. She shifted, almost bounced, from foot to foot, clearly in anticipation of the words that looked like they were about to bubble right out of her mouth.

Colin grinned and gestured her in. He'd never seen Ms. Straight-Arrow like this, and to say his interest was piqued would have been an understatement.

She made it two steps inside the door before she ruptured.

"Oh, Colin, I'm so excited," she burst out, whirling to pull him in the doorway and close the door. She gave him an impromptu hug that sent them both careening, until he uprighted them with a good show of strength.

He laughed loudly and swung her around. "I can see that. What gives?"

"You won't believe it."

"Why don't you sit down and tell me about it? Do you want a soda or something?"

Holly took off her coat tossed a load of books from an armchair to the floor. "A cola would be great, thanks. With ice, if you have it."

"Coming right up. Make yourself comfortable."

"There's plenty of padding," she teased, "what with all these socks and jackets lying around."

"What?" he squawked in protest. "But I cleaned this week."

Her high, tinkling laughter filled the air, and his throat closed tightly. She sounded like a spring fairy, flittering from flower to flower and laughing joyfully all the while.

Of course, if he told Holly what he was thinking, she'd probably want to crack him alongside the head with a two-by-four. Flittering and fairy weren't probably how she would want to be described.

She was a modicum of decorum, or at least a sleek, contemporary career woman.

Not the flittering type.

Colin grabbed a soda for Holly and one for himself, then kicked the refrigerator door shut with his bare foot and went back and settled himself on the couch, his legs propped on an empty corner of the coffee table.

"So what's up?" he asked with a grin.

Holly took a deep breath, and then let it out audibly. "I've found it!"

"It?" Colin parroted, popping the top on Holly's soda and pouring the bubbling liquid in a tall, ice-filled glass.

Holly looked at him as if he were dense. "Your theme paper. It's practically written itself, thanks very much to me."

"I'm interested." He slid a glance toward the gaping pile of yet-to-be-read books on his floor. Boy, was he interested.

Holly reached out and stroked his arm. "I thought you would be."

"Go on."

"Well, it's like this," she began, as if starting an epic tale.

"Once upon a time…" he teased.

"You'll think it's a fairy tale by the time I'm finished," she promised. "Anyway, to get back to the story, I went to church on Sunday."

"How very pious of you."

"Colin!"

He frowned, trying to look penitent and humble. Kind of. He cleared his throat on a chuckle. "Sorry."

"I'm sure. Now let me get on with the story. When I attended church last Sunday, they had a special program during the service. St. Andrew's does that sometimes, in order to motivate our parishioners to be out *doing* things for God in the world instead of just sitting in the pew thinking about good works.

Pastor Freeman is a firm believer in acting out one's faith."

"Good man," Colin agreed. "Not enough people walking the talk."

Holly laughed. "You almost sound like a preacher, Colin Brockman."

"I do?" he said, genuinely and pleasantly surprised. Maybe there was hope for him, yet.

"I haven't even gotten to the good part yet. The program Pastor Freeman introduced last week is called Kids Hope," she continued, smiling. "And it's the answer to your prayers. You can thank me now or later," she teased, laughter glimmering in her green eyes.

"Kids Hope," Colin repeated, smiling just because she did. "Sounds interesting. Tell me more."

He hated to be a pessimist, but deep down, he really didn't really think she had the answer. He was becoming more and more convinced there was no answer. He'd certainly been scoping around for one, and had even tried to come up with a few unique ideas of his own, all to no avail.

Still, he didn't want to spoil her fun, so he smiled his encouragement for her to continue.

"The program joins one organization, in this case my church, St. Andrew's Church, to one public school in their area, again, in this case, Stonington Elementary, which is just down the street from the church.

"At that point, the local executive director pairs adult mentors one-on-one with a child the teachers and parents believe would benefit from this service. The adult and the child meet for an hour every week. And every adult mentor is methodically supported by a prayer partner from the church."

Colin felt pinpricks of excitement brush over his skin as energy pulsed through his veins. Could Holly be on to something? "One-on-one, you said?"

"Exactly. That's the difference. The key. Do you see what I see?"

He did. His head was swimming with the possibilities. "How do you think something like this would work out on a military base?"

"Uh, Colin, that would be for you to figure out. Do you want me to write and type your term paper for you, too, or what?"

He ignored her teasing sarcasm, and hooted in delight. "What a breakthrough! I need to start by getting the lowdown on the basic training maneuvers, and move on from there. Do you suppose I could get an appointment with your pastor anytime soon?"

Holly patted both her knees with her palms. "Done. Thursday at 4:00 p.m. I hope that time will work for you. I wasn't sure of your schedule."

Colin squared his shoulders and widened his grin. "I'll *make* it okay. I can't believe you've done this for me. You're an angel."

He stood and extended his arms to help her to her

feet. She stood slowly, almost hesitantly. He didn't let go of her hands, choosing instead to run his thumbs across the soft skin behind her fingers.

Their eyes met, and her gaze softened, but she took a single step backward, shifting ever so slightly, putting the subtlest line of distance between them.

"You're a dream," he said huskily.

"Bad or good?" she quipped as she shifted from one foot to another. She didn't quite look at him—meeting his gaze and then looking away.

He wondered what he had done to make her nervous in his presence. But even he could feel the underlying electricity in the air.

Maybe that was it. His heart was buzzing with the exhilaration of the moment, and he could imagine her heart in sync with his.

He raised her hands to his lips and brushed light kisses across the softness of her knuckles. "You're the best kind of dream," he assured her, smiling into her warm, velvet eyes. "A fantasy."

Mere inches separated them. He lowered his head to keep their gazes locked. "Is it okay that I dream about you, Holly?"

A chuckle escaped her lips, but her fingers quivered when he asked the question.

"If I can dream about you," she whispered after a long pause.

The air was suddenly thick with tension, and

Colin struggled to pull in a breath. "I wouldn't have it any other way."

He found himself drawn toward her, his gaze wandering to her gloss-shined lips. He wondered if she was dwelling on the word *trifle*.

He hoped not. Because he could no more stop from kissing her than he could make the sun move backward in the sky.

As it happened, though, he didn't have to stop, or even make the first move. Holly, in a sudden impetuous move, put her arms around his neck, grabbed him by the collar and pulled his face down to hers, leaning toward him until their breath mixed.

"Kiss me." Barely a whisper, it was half a request, half a demand.

Colin willingly complied with both. With the utmost awareness, he leaned down and brushed his lips over hers, closing his eyes as he savored the sweet, gentle contact. His senses heightened at the same moment his world focused, until there was only the taste, sight, sound, smell and feel of Holly in his arms.

He closed his eyes, wanting the moment to last forever.

Instead, the atmosphere was instantly and completely shattered by the sound of the telephone ringing. Its shrill clang jolted through Colin's brain like a spoon on a frying pan, effectively dousing his romantic mood.

Even so, he didn't move or pull away, determined despite the disturbance not to lose the moment. He knew it might be a long time before they would reach such a point again.

Holly, however, immediately attempted to push back and break their embrace, turning aside toward the sound of the telephone.

"No," Colin protested, pulling her back into his arms. "Just ignore it."

Holly looked at the telephone, and then him. It was only a moment before she made her decision, melting back into his arms with a contented sigh, just as the answering machine picked up.

"This is a message for Colin Brockman," the woman on the line began. "This is Michelle Walker, the principal at Marston House. I need to speak to you as soon as possible regarding Jared Matthews."

Colin launched toward the telephone, but was too late to intercept the call. With his heart beating in his ears, he flashed an apologetic look toward Holly, tucked the receiver under his chin and rapidly punched out the numbers Michelle had recited.

Please, God, don't let him miss her.

Holly moved to his side and placed a hand on his shoulder, offering instant and silent support. He glanced down at her, flashing her a grateful smile.

She smiled softly in return.

"This is Colin Brockman," he said when Michelle

answered, clearing his throat when he realized how low his voice sounded.

"Colin! I'm glad you called back so quickly," she blurted immediately. "I'll cut to the chase. There is a problem with Jared Matthews, and I thought, under the circumstances, that you should know."

"What kind of problem with Jared?" Colin clenched his fist around the phone cord as his throat constricted around his breath, with emotion for the boy he'd come to love.

"I'd prefer to discuss it with you in person, if you don't mind." Her voice was firm, but clearly anxious, and Colin paced back and forth as far as the telephone cord would reach.

"I'll be right over."

He hung up the telephone and reached for his coat. "I'm sorry, Holly. I really want to discuss this whole Kids Hope thing with you, but it will have to wait until later. I'm afraid I have to leave right now. I'll walk you out."

Holly didn't say a word as he helped her into her coat, pulling it tight against her chin, since it was snowing outside, and wrapping her scarf firmly around her delicate neck, against the drafts.

"What's wrong with Jared?" she asked at last, halting him from his erratic movements with a level hand on his elbow.

"I don't know," he answered hoarsely. "Not something good, I'm afraid. I'm sure going to find out as soon as I can."

"I'm going with you," said Holly resolutely as he, equally resolutely, pressed her out the door ahead of him, pausing only to lock the door.

He was about to assure her Jared wasn't her problem, at least not on this day. She should go home where it was warm, not follow him about in the cold chill of the winter afternoon. But something in the look she gave him stopped him from saying a word.

She was *making* it her problem. Because of *him*. Because of what they shared between them.

Again, his throat clouded with emotion. He had already been through a lot today, and he had the feeling the day wasn't over, not by a long shot.

Had it only been a few months ago that he hadn't been attached to a single person in the whole world? He'd been so proud of the fact that he was his own man, all alone with no one to care for, or to care for him.

How had he ever lived that way?

First there was his sister and her new family. And then there was Holly. And Jared. What was a man to do with himself?

He slid a glance toward the beautiful, loving woman at his side. He might not be sure what to do with himself, but he knew *exactly* what to do with her. He kept an arm around her waist as they left.

Together.

Chapter Twelve

Holly was surprised and pleased at how quickly
Colin gave in to her request to accompany him.

Before he'd had the opportunity to send her away,
she'd already mentally lined her arguments up in a
row.

*She'd been the one to introduce him to Marston
House in the first place. She knew Jared and his
case.* And, the clincher, she hoped: *She was a child
psychologist,* after all. A professional in her field.
Perhaps she could be of some help.

And she'd needed none of it. Colin wanted her to
be there. With him. For his own reasons.

He didn't speak the whole way to the school, but
she didn't begrudge him the silence. She could tell
his mind was on the meeting ahead. So she kept her
hands folded on her lap and tried not to think about
all the bad things Michelle Walker's telephone call
could mean.

His small blue truck was a lot newer, and a good deal fancier, than her Jeep. It held in heat much better, and had a much nicer ride.

It was funny how she'd driven a Jeep all her life, just because her father's gift to her when she'd earned her driver's license had been a Jeep.

It was one of her best memories. Learning to drive had meant something to her father. He had been so proud of her that day.

She shook herself quickly to the present. Despite the smooth ride, Colin looked like he was bouncing all over—internally, at any rate. His square jaw was locked so tight she could see a tendon straining against his cheek. And he was scowling, something so foreign to Colin, it made Holly want to cringe.

She couldn't stand seeing him look so miserable. His boyish good looks set in a frown broke her heart. It was just *wrong*.

Slowly, so as not to startle him from his thoughts, she leaned toward him, stroking his brow, gently soothing the anxiety marked there.

"Thanks," he said gruffly.

"For what?"

"For being here. With me."

She choked up. "Where else would I be?"

He tossed a grin her direction, but it wasn't more than a decent attempt, and came off more like the grimace he must be feeling inside.

She took his hand and squeezed.

They arrived at Marston House a moment later, and Colin parked, got out of the vehicle and quickly moved around the truck to get Holly's door. He lifted a hand to help her down from the truck, then linked her fingers with his as they entered the school, sending her the silent message that he needed her, that they were in this together.

She squeezed his hand, offering what little support she could. She was only beginning to realize how important Jared was to Colin, and her respect for the man grew with every moment, causing her throat to tighten as emotion swelled.

There weren't too many men who would put themselves forward for the sake of a helpless little boy, especially a boy like Jared who had special needs.

There weren't too many men like Colin Brockman.

Colin wasn't in Marston House a moment before he'd obviously spotted Jared. With a quick glance down at Holly, he lit off for the playroom where he'd first met Jared. Holly followed.

The boy had climbed up a pile of boxes and was sitting high in one corner of the room, curled up in a ball and looking as if the world didn't exist for him as he rocked back and forth, back and forth, staring into space and mumbling something unintelligible— and repeatedly.

Michelle put an arm around both adults as she

entered the room. Frowning, Colin shook her hand off and started for the boy, clearly intent on finding out firsthand what was going on.

The principal stopped him. "Wait, Colin. I know you want to go to Jared, but there are some things you need to know first."

"What things?" Holly asked. It was heartrending, watching the child's visible agony.

"Jared got some bad news this morning. He's been like this all day," Michelle explained gravely. "Our staff hasn't been able to get through to him at all. I thought of you immediately, Colin. I know you've spent a good amount of time with Jared. I'm hoping maybe he'll respond to you."

Colin's troubled gaze met Holly's for a moment, and then he bowed his head. "I'm no expert. I don't know if I can help. But I'll do my best, ma'am."

Holly realized as she watched Colin approach Jared that he hadn't even waited to find out what had happened to send Jared into a downward spiral, though that was clearly a major concern. What could have happened to make Jared revert as he had?

They would find out in due time, she supposed. In the meantime, she'd take her cue from Colin. His first and only consideration was to be with the boy.

Tears pooled in the corner of Holly's eye, and she absently wiped them away. How many men would have made such an emotional commitment to a complete stranger?

Michelle approached Jared first, but when she laid her hand on his shoulder, he brushed her away with a near-violent jerk of his shoulder. She backed away from the boy with her hands held open, giving Colin a chance to crawl up the boxes and move in.

At first Colin merely crouched near Jared, speaking softly all the while, so the boy would know he was there, but not touching him or encroaching on his personal space.

He talked continually and watched unremittingly for a long while, but he didn't shift a muscle, though the minutes wore on.

Colin sat without moving for so long Holly began to wonder if Jared would respond to him, but Colin looked confident, if concerned. He somehow appeared to know instinctively that he needed to wait the boy out, to prove his trust and friendship by his presence and not by his touch.

Any concern he might be feeling in his heart didn't show in his voice. His low, steady baritone assured even Holly, as she listened to the quiet, soothing monotone whispering nonsensically.

Lost in her own thoughts, Holly missed the moment when contact was made, but suddenly the boy was in Colin's arms, rocking back and forth and making heartbreaking little rhythmic sounds that were a lot like sobs.

Colin's gaze met hers, and together they shared a moment of grief. Jared's cry was enough to break anyone's heart; and right now, Holly distinctively heard *two* hearts fracturing.

Colin resisted the urge to move. He wanted to tighten his grip on the little boy, but he knew instinctively it would be the wrong thing to do. Jared needed the kind of tenderness Colin thought that, with his own big, bumbling body and huge hands, he might not be able to give the small boy.

Yet, it was clear Jared was responding to him, and that, at least warmed his heart.

Jared had come to *him*.

He felt a great deal of responsibility toward the boy, but for some reason that burden didn't frighten him the way he thought it should have, or even would have as short as six months ago.

Had turning thirty somehow made him grow up, mature in some way he'd missed in the past?

Or maybe it was a combination of things—joining the navy, coming to know Christ, deciding to become a chaplain, meeting Holly and then getting to know Jared. Maybe it was a combination of life's events that caused a youth to become a man.

Whatever it was, he was just glad he had what it took to make the adult decisions and adult commitments it was clear he was going to have to make. At least he was beginning to believe he had what it took.

For Jared's sake, he hoped so.

"What happened to him, to set him back?" he asked Michelle quietly.

"You know he's been in foster care for several years," Michelle said gravely.

"Yes. You mentioned that you couldn't find a good fit for him, that he'd been in several homes over that period of time. Is that what's happening now?"

"Worse than that, I'm afraid," Michelle confirmed, her voice low.

Colin's gaze slid to Holly. She put her palms together and linked her fingers in front of her as their eyes met. Her message was clear.

We're in this together.

He took a deep breath and nodded. Somehow he felt better, just knowing Holly was there.

"His mother and father have abandoned him to the state," Michelle stated without preamble. "He's now officially an orphan."

"How could they?" Holly whispered harshly, her outrage showing clearly on her flushed face. "I've never heard of parents intentionally abandoning their children to the state. Can they do that? What kind of people would do that, anyway?"

Michelle sighed. "Welcome to the world of child psychology. Mothers and fathers don't always act the way you would expect them to, especially when their children have some kind of disability."

"But to abandon them to the state? How can a mother give up her child?"

"Sometimes they believe they are doing what is best for the child, giving him to caregivers who know more about how to deal with him and treat his special needs than they do. Sometimes they just don't want the responsibility of a child who is 'different.'"

"But isn't there another way?" Holly asked, disagreeing with her scowl as well as her words. "I just can't see it."

"Maybe they are poor, Holly," Colin broke in, though he realized he was treading in deep water. He was speaking about something he knew less than nothing about, and was probably better off keeping his mouth shut.

Holly looked up at him, her big green eyes luminescent with unshed tears. "Be that as it may, I don't think I'll ever understand. Or forgive. To me, there isn't a good enough reason in the world."

Holly was quiet the whole ride back to Colin's apartment, and left for her own apartment as soon as they'd reached Colin's place.

Frankly, she didn't know what to say to Colin. He had been magnificent, and she couldn't even find words to tell him how she felt when she saw him holding little Jared in his arms.

But right now she had other things on her mind.

Like how she was going to be a total failure in her chosen field. She'd not realized until the moment she'd seen Jared all curled up, helpless and alone in the world, just what being a child psychologist really meant.

What *helping children* really meant.

It meant she'd have to face the tough cases, ones that didn't work out according to the rules of the book, or even the rules of decent life.

She supposed she'd always known that, in theory, but seeing Jared so helpless today had been all too much reality for her. She'd handled some questionable cases for the state in her college internship, but Jared stepped beyond the realm of books and into the personal.

She *knew* this boy.

And it made a difference.

She held strong feelings for Jared. He wasn't just any little boy, he was someone she knew and cared about, and would wonder what happened to when tomorrow came around.

Was there any way she could look at Jared's mother and father and not want to scream at them, force them to do the right thing, to love and serve this little boy who was such a precious gift in the eyes of God?

She closed her eyes, half in prayer, half in pain. She knew there were many ways to view such a situation, and that the way the state, or any other agency she worked for might not see things her way.

Could she handle being told to do something she didn't believe in?

She searched her soul, and found she wasn't sure of the answer to that question. Her faith was beating strongly in her heart.

She could not and would not turn her back on God. The quintessential question *What Would Jesus Do?* entered her mind.

Except she didn't know the answer to the question this time around. The issue wasn't exactly cut out in black and white.

Did she keep on with her plans for the future, doing good wherever she could and making the most of every bad situation? Or did she look for another way to serve God and the world?

Was there a way she could use her skills and be true to her faith at the same time? But was that what Jesus meant when He said to go into all the world?

She's never been more confused.

There were other avenues for a trained child psychologist than working for the state. Some were overtly religious, though she'd never before considered such a vocation. Somehow, she didn't see herself as a missionary to the children in South Africa, but odder things had happened.

She wondered what Colin was thinking. Knowing Colin, he was probably out playing basketball or something, his problems already happily forgotten in the fluky, whimsical life he led.

She wished she could throw her own problems to the wind, but she knew that was beyond her capability. She was the proverbial stick in the mud. Her troubles were bound to follow her no matter where she went.

For her, the trick was to turn around and face them head-on.

Colin was not playing basketball. He wasn't playing anything. And he definitely had not been able to put aside his problems.

He slumped back in his chair, brought his hands to his head and brushed his fingers through his already tousled hair.

As soon as he'd dropped Holly off at her car, he'd turned his truck around and returned to Marston House. An idea had popped into his mind during the silent ride home with Holly, and he couldn't shake it no matter how he tried.

He'd spent a few minutes in silent, frantic prayer with God, almost begging to be talked out of the crazy idea. But when he'd felt that gentle nudging of God on his heart, he decided to follow up right away, before he lost his nerve. And that involved speaking to Michelle.

The principal of Marston House had been surprisingly receptive to his plan, but had soon excused herself to get some papers, and was taking forever to come back to her small, sparsely furnished office located at the far east end of the school.

Colin sighed and crossed his arms over his chest, his palms resting tightly over his upper torso.

This had been the longest, hardest day of his life. Even his first few days of navy basic training couldn't compare to the strain he was feeling now.

At boot camp, they battered his body; but today, holding Jared while he grieved, sheltering the precious little boy in his arms, was far worse agony than anything the navy could dole out.

Being with Jared battered his emotions, and more than that, struck at his very soul.

He'd heard Holly's anger when she lashed out at Jared's parents' actions, and he shared in that sentiment. But his mind had been so taken over with Jared's immediate needs, he hadn't wanted to waste any energy on emotion.

What he needed were solutions.

Another foster home wasn't going to be the answer for the boy. Even if he was sent to another home, he'd more than likely be permanently sent back to the state before long.

Maybe someone could reason with Jared's parents, but Colin doubted it. The boy's parents had obviously not come to their decision overnight, and it was doubtful more counseling would change their minds about what they felt they had to do, for whatever reasons they had for making the decisions they did.

Colin couldn't help but feel that Jared, with whatever understanding he had about what was going on around him and to him, was losing hope—in the system, in humankind, maybe even in God.

Colin grit his teeth and slammed his fist down on the tabletop. He couldn't let that happen to another young boy.

Not while he was there to stop it.

Chapter Thirteen

Holly wasn't sure why her father had called her up to his lodge over the weekend, but whatever it was, it couldn't be good. He'd used his drill sergeant voice when he'd spoken with her, so there was no room to brook an argument.

And her father had emphasized the need to hurry, too, so she hadn't said goodbye to Colin, or even let him know where she was going.

She was sorry she couldn't make contact, but when she'd called his apartment there'd been no answer; and of course, in typical Colin fashion, he hadn't remembered to turn on his answering machine.

Since they spent nearly every day together these days, she knew he would probably, and rightfully, assume they'd be spending the weekend together.

Which they would be, were it not for her father's request.

Even so, she knew Colin wouldn't be angry with her when he found out she was gone, even if he didn't know why or where she'd gone. He might worry a little bit, but it wasn't in his nature to stress over things the way she did, so she didn't worry—too much—that she'd caused him undue anxiety.

She had the oddest feeling, though, that it was a bad time to leave, a time when Colin really needed a friend by his side. She knew he was broken up over what had happened to Jared, even if he hadn't expressed his feelings to her.

For one thing, he'd reverted to his rigid, military posture and stiff upper lip, both literally and figuratively. That was enough to let Holly know something was seriously amiss in Colin's world.

And all the while he was wrestling with the situation with Jared, he was trying to pull things together with his Kids Hope project for her class, which in itself was a huge undertaking. He'd been making phone calls and reading dozens of books, which she knew was not his favorite pastime.

He told her in confidence he was working on a PowerPoint presentation he could use after he graduated, even though she'd assured him he needn't go to *quite* that much effort for her class. He wanted something he could use on naval bases, and was proving himself a lot more focused than Holly would have thought.

She couldn't stop thinking about Colin the whole

hour's drive to the lodge, which was a surprise. She was still broken up about her own dilemma, to which she'd come to no decent conclusions.

More than that, she knew she ought to be pondering all the possible reasons why her parents might want to see her. At the very least she should be giving it a guess.

It could be that all they wanted to do was to lecture her about why she wasn't getting married and starting a family. Certainly, bringing Colin home for Thanksgiving might have sparked that old flame.

It was a tune she'd heard many a time before, especially from her mother, although why that should require an extra trip on Holly's part was beyond anything she could contrive.

The truth was, she couldn't think of a single reason why her parents would want to speak to her in person. A telephone call would do for most things she could conceive as a problem, and they could wait until her next visit on anything else they had to say.

Unless someone was sick. But that would mean *really* sick—fatally ill, even.

Her stomach lurched as she rolled the thought over in her head. She pulled the Jeep's steering wheel sharply to the left and slammed her foot on the brake as she executed a sharp hairpin curve on the washboard dirt road, and swallowed hard to gulp down her dismay.

Was her mother incurably sick? Had her dad, her

dear, gruff Marine Corps father, contracted some sort of serious illness?

No.

It couldn't be, and she wouldn't let herself consider it for another moment. If her foot came down a little bit harder on the gas pedal, it was purely coincidental.

And it was, fortunately, on a straight segment of road.

Despite promising herself she would do no such thing, Holly had thoroughly worked herself up by the time she'd reached the lodge, simply by *not* thinking about it. She dashed from the car, let herself into the front door and launched into her unsuspecting father's arms, her tears wetting his weather-hardened cheek and dripping onto the plain forest green of a marine-issue T-shirt.

He promptly pushed her aside, squaring his shoulders and frowning over her, though he still supported her with one arm.

"What's this, now?" he barked in his best drill sergeant voice. "Buck up, young lady. We'll have no crying here."

From habit learned in childhood, she straightened herself to military rigidity and wiped her eyes.

And it helped. She was oddly comforted by his gruff actions.

The familiarity of old habit soothed her, however rough it might seem to the outside world. This was a marine daddy with his little girl, and this was the way things ran in her world.

She knew better than to shed tears in her father's presence. In truth, she thought a woman's tears might be the one thing her tough old military father couldn't handle.

"Sorry," she scratched out, her throat dry.

"Done," her father replied with a snappy nod. He'd never been much of one for extended apologies. "But don't let your mother see you this way. You know how your tears upset her."

"Yes, sir." It warmed her heart at the way her father still protected her mother, as if the woman was made of fine china, and was not the strong, sweet woman who had devoted her life to him and was in truth, in many ways, stronger than he ever was.

"How is Mom?" she queried, hoping for information to confirm, or hopefully allow her to discard, her disturbing theories.

Her father's eyebrows creased, but his eyes sparkled with mirth. "Meddling as ever."

Her heart swam with relief, and her breath relaxed as her anxiety melted within her. "She's still trying to get you to quit smoking that pipe, huh?"

He grunted. "The never-ending battle. Maybe someday I'll just quit that old pipe cold turkey and send her into an apoplexy." He laughed good-naturedly. "But then we wouldn't have anything to fight about, and our marriage would be over."

Holly laughed with him. "It would be over? Why is that?"

He gazed at her solemnly, then ruined the impression with a sly wink. "Why, then, we'd have nothing left to talk about!"

Holly laughed with him. "Then neither one of you is ill."

"'Course not. I can't imagine where you'd get an idea like that."

She *could* imagine. And for once in her life, she was quite relieved to be wrong.

"Are you wondering why we called you down to the lodge?" he asked bluntly. "Because if that's what's bothering you, you don't have to get all in a snither about it." He picked up her suitcases and gestured her down the hallway.

She snorted her protest. "I'm not in a *snither*, Dad. But you have to admit you were rather vague about why you asked me to come up here this weekend. Is it some kind of surprise?"

He gave her a half grin and nodded. "You could say that."

For a man who spent his life being inordinately up-front with people, he sure was beating around the bush with her now.

"Is it for me? It's not my birthday," she reminded him. "Nor a holiday."

Her father looked about ready to speak when the doorbell rang. Since they'd stopped in the middle of the hallway in the intensity of their conversation, they hadn't quite made it all the way to Holly's bedroom to drop off her luggage.

In his typical, immediate military fashion, her father dropped the suitcases neatly in a row by the wall, and strode back toward the door with quick, even steps.

Curious, Holly followed, though she lagged behind her father's brisk pace. It really wasn't her business who was at the door—probably the milkman, or perhaps a neighbor calling.

"Colin," she exclaimed when her father opened the door and she caught a glimpse of the thatch-haired navy man standing in the doorway, his back ramrod straight, his broad shoulders even, the very picture of military stature.

Her heart immediately began pounding riotously at the sight of him, especially as much of a shock as it was to see him here.

The only thing to ruin the keen navy image he was obviously trying for, was the slow, lazy smile that appeared on his face. The very same grin that had driven Holly crazy a million times. The smile that said he had everything under control, and maybe, just maybe, he was keeping a secret or two from the world.

As the shock of seeing Colin at her parents' lodge subsided, suspicion bubbled up inside her.

She whirled on her father. "What is this all

about?" she queried, halfway between annoyance and confusion. "I can't believe you summoned Colin out here, too! For what? Are you and Mom trying to embarrass me? Are you trying to play matchmaker? Not like *that's* going to work."

"Missy, I have no idea what you're talking about," her father denied gruffly. "And that's no way to greet a guest in our home."

Holly's jaw dropped and her stomach curled into a knot of astonishment. "Are you telling me you didn't invite him here?"

Her father's eyes narrowed as she took his measure and he returned the favor. After a moment, he firmly shook his head. "No, ma'am."

Her gaze slid reluctantly to Colin, who confirmed it with a shrug and a grin. "No, ma'am."

With a gesture indicating she was close to pulling her hair out, she emitted a long, exasperated groan and reached for Colin's free hand, pulling him inside with her and swinging the door closed behind them.

"Welcome to my parents' home," she said smartly, flashing her gaze to her father, who pinched his lips tightly as if annoyed, though his dark, gray-eyed gaze sparkled with amusement.

She turned to Colin, who just smiled at her. She didn't feel like playing games, and Colin wasn't giving her a clue. Her emotions had been jerked around too much today already, thank you very much.

"What are you doing here?" She eyed the worn backpack he had slung over one shoulder. Clearly he hadn't planned on staying. Long.

But how had he known where to look for her? She gave him another close scrutiny.

His throat was working, but no sound was coming out of his mouth. She decided to help him.

"You were following me?" she suggested, planting her hands on her hips.

Colin didn't know what to make of Holly's audacity. She was clearly upset at someone over something. But he sure didn't know who, or what. This wasn't the way he'd planned his entrance at all.

His gaze slipped unintentionally toward Ian McCade. The man met his gaze head-on, his expression a mixture of welcome and warning.

He wasn't surprised by those sentiments. It hadn't taken long in Holly's father's company to know Ian McCade was going to protect his precious little girl at all costs, and it was a daunting thought.

He swallowed hard. Carrying out this crazy plan to fruition wasn't going to be easy.

He stopped short, wondering for a moment whether he had, once again, dived into the water headfirst without first checking for the depth of the pool. He looked from father to daughter, and thought perhaps there was no water to swim in at all.

He quickly covered the ground he'd tread in his mind, reminding himself of the reason he was here.

Jared Matthews.

When he was searching and praying for an answer to Jared's problem, the solution had come with such ease it had amazed and astonished him.

Jared needed a family. *He* would be Jared's family.

No. *They* would be Jared's family. He and Holly. Together.

In one gigantic flash of insight that was akin, Colin thought, to being hit over the head with a metal beam, clang and all, he had realized the depth of his love for Holly. It was the kind of love a man built the foundation of a family upon.

Not that the idea of loving Holly was such a giant leap for him to make. But the idea of marrying her had popped him *clear* out of the ballpark.

And yet, in that one second he knew marrying Holly was the *right* answer. The *only* answer.

He'd never felt more joy in his life than the moment he'd settled his heart on a life with Holly. And Jared.

He immediately started making plans, starting with a trip up to Holly's parents' lodge to have a man-to-man talk with her father.

It wasn't going to be easy. But he'd known that before he came here.

He just hadn't expected *Holly* to be here. Her visiting here wasn't exactly a typical occasion, from what he knew about this family, and from what

Holly had said. She wasn't comfortable here. She didn't exactly come around on a regular basis.

Which meant there was a special occasion of some kind. Or else something was wrong.

He looked from father to daughter, but neither looked grieved, or bereaved, and definitely not overly joyous—only perplexed, and maybe a little annoyed. And curious. Definitely curious.

They wanted to know why he was here. They wanted to know *now*.

And it was a *logical* question, after all.

The only problem was, he didn't have a reasonable answer. At least not one he could share with Holly and her father—yet.

He cleared his throat and prayed God wouldn't look too harshly upon him for this one little fib. "Yes," he said at last, deciding the best course of action was to follow her lead, especially as he was completely unable to come up with a feasible alternative on such short notice. "I…followed you."

Chapter Fourteen

What else could Colin do, except follow Holly's lead and hope he didn't end up in a ditch? He couldn't tell them the real reason he was here, at least not until he'd spoken to her father alone. And he couldn't think of any other sensible reason he'd be at the lodge.

"I—wasn't able to catch you at your apartment, but I was fortunate enough to see you leaving in your Jeep. So I followed you. Uh…here," he added just for good measure.

"Why?" Her hands were still perched on her hips, and her gaze eagle sharp.

He squirmed inwardly, but was careful not to let his thoughts show on his face. What he wanted to do was to blurt everything aloud and get it over with, but he knew better than to let his mouth start flapping right now. He'd insert both his big feet for sure.

If he had any hope at all of winning Holly's heart,

never mind her hand in marriage, he had to do it the right way.

Move in slowly. Plan his tactics carefully. Be romantic.

And he should definitely not embarrass her in front of the father she held in such high esteem.

Besides, Ian McCade was the first step in sealing this deal. Ian wouldn't be any happier than Holly would be if Colin asked her to marry him on the spot, without at least giving them a hint of his good intentions beforehand, and leaving a good impression on them both.

Holly audibly cleared her throat. She was still waiting for an answer.

"I'm trying to finish my term paper and I need some help," he said, grimacing at how lame of an excuse he'd concocted.

At first he didn't think Holly bought it, either, but after a moment's hesitation she shrugged and waved him along.

"Come in and sit down. I'll make tuna salad sandwiches for everyone. I can't think about school on an empty stomach." She patted her flat stomach and brushed her palm along the curve of her hip.

Colin's eyes followed her movement and his breath caught and held. She was a beautiful woman in every respect. The man who won her regard was a blessed man, indeed.

He only prayed he would be that man.

He knew he wasn't good enough for her. Holly deserved much better, a more stable man, a man who would wear a watch, who she could count on to be on time for their wedding.

But he was in love with her, and he was enough of an optimist to believe love could conquer all. One thing he knew for certain—he'd gratefully spend his whole life trying to make her happy.

And he would wear a watch for their wedding. The thought brought a grin to his lips.

Glad the invisible hand had finally let go of his chest and allowed him to breathe, he followed Holly into the kitchen. Though the winter morning held a Colorado chill, she was wearing a flowery spring dress that shifted and twirled around her long, sleek legs. He wondered if she'd brought a sweater along, but didn't voice his question aloud, knowing how much Holly valued her independence.

Besides, he hadn't thought to pack any extra clothing at all.

She chatted on about the weather, her Christmas plans and a whole host of other topics, one following closely on top of the other, sometimes with unusual overlaps in thought or subject that made Colin chuckle.

"Are you nervous about something?" he queried, observing that he, himself, was about ready to jump out of his shoes with restlessness.

"No," she denied a bit too quickly. Then she

glanced at him and their gazes met and held. Her eyes told him the truth before her lips did. "Yes, I am."

He stroked her arm with the back of his fingers. "What's up?"

She leaned forward until their foreheads nearly touched. "It's my mom and dad," she said in a conspiratorial stage whisper. "I think something's up with them."

Colin lowered his brow. "Why do you say that?" he asked in the same tone of voice she was using.

Holly took his elbow and pulled him into a corner of the kitchen, where she resumed her normal tone of voice. "Well, for one thing, they called me here, but wouldn't tell me why. I asked, but they were vague."

"That does seem a little odd," he agreed. Her parents appeared pretty straightforward to him; not the type to play games, especially with their only daughter.

"As you can probably well imagine, I was terrified at first, because as you can guess, I rarely receive a summons from my parents. For anything."

At least that explained why she was here. "A summons? You sound like you're talking about the Supreme Court. What did they do, send a courier with a missive?"

"Just about. I was sure someone was dying. Why else would they call when it wasn't a holiday?"

"Your dad seems fine."

"His usual gruff self, you mean. Yes, he is. And he assured me my mother is doing well, too. So well, in fact, that she's out shopping right now." She chuckled.

"So if it's not illness, then what?" Colin found his own curiosity growing on the matter.

"When I find out, you'll be the first to know. I must admit it's nice to see a familiar face up here. What's your trouble with your term paper, anyway?" she asked, clearly finished with the subject of her parents, and ready to swim on to bluer water.

Colin's mind froze for a moment, but his slick tongue quickly recovered. "I'm having trouble wrapping my project up for the class. It's such a big idea. I thought you could take a quick look at it for me and see if I'm going in the right direction."

It suddenly occurred to him that he might be asking too much of a woman who was still technically his teacher, at least until the Christmas holiday. He was always bugging her about this thing or that. Her other students weren't haunting her that way.

"Am I putting too much pressure on you?" he asked suddenly. "I mean, you being the professor, me being the student, and all?"

She smothered a laugh with her palm. "And you're asking me now?"

He smacked his hand against his forehead. "I've been taking advantage of the professor all semester long! I'm an idiot."

She shifted so she stood behind him, wrapping her arms around his waist and laying her head against the back of his shoulders. She stood silently for a moment, just holding him.

Colin shuddered with emotion and swallowed hard. He wasn't used to feeling this depth of love, or even of labeling the feelings he was just now recognizing as *love*.

It would take some time getting used to. A lifetime, maybe.

"Do you know that you have been the only stable thing in my life this year?" she asked quietly.

He rumbled with laughter. "Me, stable? That's a scary thought."

She was about to say something in reply when her father entered the kitchen. Holly stiffened as if to move away, but she slowly relaxed her arms and locked her fingers, sealing her arms around his waist. Colin knew it was a big step for her, and he rested his hand lightly on hers for support.

Sergeant McCade narrowed his eyes upon that spot at Colin's waist, and his lips pressed and turned at the corner, one eye half-pinched closed.

Colin held his breath, feeling like a teenager on his first date, not a grown man sharing a close moment with the woman he loved. He could sense that Holly had also stopped breathing.

"Did you want a sandwich, sir?" he offered, holding up the tuna salad sandwich he'd just finished slathering with mayonnaise.

"Sounds good," said Holly's father gruffly. "I was just on my way to the den."

"I'll bring it to you there," Colin said quickly, seizing upon the opportunity he suddenly realized had been presented to him.

Sergeant McCade exited just as quickly as he'd entered, pulling his pipe from his shirt pocket without another word to either of them.

"You're sure you want to do this?" Holly asked as soon as her father was gone, her voice muffled against the denim of Colin's shirt. "I guarantee you're going to get raked over the coals on my account the moment you walk into that room."

"Why would you think that?" He turned in her embrace and put his arms around her. "Just because I happen to have tender feelings toward his daughter?"

She broke the embrace and moved to make another sandwich. "When you put it like that, it doesn't sound so awful."

He wondered why she didn't sound happy about what he'd said. He'd been tentative in his statement, probing her feelings in his own backward way.

Could it be that her emotions did not match his? That she was not in love with him?

No. There was a connection between them. He knew it in his gut.

And if an emotionally impeded student could figure it out, surely a brilliant, stunning professor would have to be in tune with the special bond they shared.

With a forced grin, Holly handed two plates to Colin and gestured toward the den. "It's your skin. Be my guest."

He flashed his most charming grin and gave her a grand wink before heading for the den and the potentially fire-breathing dragon within.

"Sergeant McCade," Colin acknowledged as he entered. "Your sandwich, sir."

The elder man waved him to a seat, and Colin sat uneasily in the blue-patterned Victorian armchair across from the sergeant's easy chair. He sat straight-backed, holding the sandwich awkwardly on his lap.

Ian was already eating, so Colin took a big bite out of the corner of his sandwich. He chewed, but couldn't taste a thing. And the bread must have been too dry, because he was finding it hard to swallow.

He wished desperately he'd thought to bring a bottle of water with him when he'd come in. What good military man made an advance without a good supply of drinking water?

He set his plate aside. He couldn't eat, not when he was literally facing one of the monumental and significant moments he'd ever faced in his life.

Holly's father had no such qualms, and was quietly devouring his sandwich and basically ignoring

Colin, which was just as well, as it gave him time to pull himself together, to pull all his military training together to work for him on this one task.

He only prayed it would sustain him.

"Sir," he said, surprised at how full and even his voice sounded. Maybe the military had been good for something after all.

"Brockman."

"May I ask you a question?"

Holly's father gazed at him for a moment, not looking the least bit taken aback that Colin wanted to speak to him, but with a marked curiosity in his eyes.

Colin held his breath, afraid to so much as swallow or move a knuckle.

After a moment, the sergeant grunted and nodded his consent.

Colin had rehearsed the speech a hundred times in his mind, but now it came out slow and scratchy from his tight throat and dry mouth. He strained to form straight, even words, feeling ridiculously awkward.

"I—um—well, I suppose this doesn't come as a complete shock to you, but I'm in love with your daughter. I guess I have been for a while now, and I'm pretty sure that, as her father, you've probably picked up on those…uh…vibes. Since you know her so well, I mean."

Sergeant McCade didn't blink an eye.

That being the case, Colin forged on. "Sir, I would like to ask for your blessing on our marriage."

The sergeant didn't look surprised, or angry, or happy about what Colin had just said.

In fact, it was almost as if Colin hadn't said anything at all.

Slowly, with agonizing patience, Sergeant McCade reached for the pipe sitting on the table beside him. He licked his bottom lip, stoked the pipe carefully and scratched the tip of a wooden match against the bottom of his slipper in order to light the pipe.

He took a puff, then two, closing his eyes to savor the aroma. Finally, after what seemed to Colin like a lifetime, he opened his eyes, tipped his pipe out of the corner of his mouth and cradled it lightly between his thumb and forefinger.

"What does Holly say about all this?"

Colin was so surprised by the question he hardly knew what to say. He'd given this so much thought. He'd thought his battle plan to be foolproof.

He would impress the sergeant by approaching him first, in the traditional, old-fashioned way of doing things.

And then he would have the added ammunition of her father's blessing to take back with him when he went to ask Holly to be his wife.

In the back of his mind, he guessed he had half expected the rugged, commanding sergeant to want to make a decision for Holly on her behalf without her consultation whatsoever.

Not that Colin would have accepted any such thing, of course, but the thought had been there, that it might happen that way.

Of all the scenarios he'd run in his mind, though, this had definitely *not* been one of them. "Well, sir, to be honest, I haven't asked her yet."

He pinched one side of his mouth together over his pipe and said gruffly, "Don't you think that'd be a good idea?"

Chapter Fifteen

Holly stepped into her parents' stable and inhaled deeply. The combined smell of horse and hay soothed her. It was one of her favorite smells in the whole world.

She'd inherited her mother's love for horses, and she loved to ride, but didn't get much opportunity to be around horses in the city, or even a small university town such as Greeley.

It was only when she was here, at her parents' lodge, that she could shed reality and indulge her childhood fantasies of roping and racing.

This morning, she'd come down to the stable to see her mother's newest asset, a beautiful, shiny black Morgan-cross mare named Belle; but in truth, she'd also escaped the confines of the house to find someplace quiet to think about what her father and mother had revealed to her the previous evening.

Her parents were set on giving her an early inheritance.

They'd told her over dinner. With Colin in the room, like he was family or something.

For some crazy reason, her father had gotten it into his head that he wanted to be around to see her enjoy what money they'd saved up over the years.

It wasn't a fortune, they assured her, but it was enough for her to be able to dream a little bit, and it would be a much needed supplement to her measly salary as a student teacher.

Her father had made a big production of the announcement, telling her over the main course so that she choked on her broccoli and nearly made a scene, dropping her fork with a loud clank onto her plate and standing so suddenly, her chair tipped backward with an additional clatter.

She'd glared at her father, but he'd just pinched the side of his lip and looked satisfied with the way he'd goaded her into a reaction.

Of course, Colin had been there to see the whole debacle. Why her parents had decided Colin ought to be present for such a grand announcement just because he was *there* was beyond her.

And it had been his reaction Holly had dreaded most of all.

He'd merely wiped his mouth with his cloth napkin—Holly thought he did that to hide his amusement, which wasn't very effective, since

mirth was shining like a beacon from his eyes—
and leaned his elbow on the table, as if he were leaning forward in order to hear better.

Apparently, no one had ever thought to teach
Colin it was polite to keep his elbows *off* the table.
And though, in her present mood, she'd been inclined to tell him, she was too busy rectifying her
own breach in manners.

She didn't know what Colin thought of what her
parents had just revealed.

She didn't know what to think.

On one hand, she wanted her parents to spend
their money on *themselves* in their retirement. She
didn't want any of their hard-earned savings.

Yet her mother had stressed, in her sweet, under-
stated way, what a true desire it would be to give
their money to their daughter while they were still
living. They wanted to see what a difference they
could make in her life.

Being reminded of her mother brought her
thoughts back to the present, and Holly moved from
stall to stall, looking for the special Morgan mare.
As soon as she saw it, she realized what a special
find the black was, and Holly immediately fell in
love with her.

Picking up a brush and curry comb, she entered
Belle's stall. She kept up a steady stream of soft,
nonsense talk, and the friendly horse nickered softly
in return.

"You're a real beauty," she told Belle. "What beautiful little foals you'll have someday."

Belle shied away from the brush, and Holly laughed. "Oh, don't worry. We don't have any stallions in this stable."

Brushing lightly at her glossy black mane, Holly ran a hand down Belle's sleek neck to calm her, and felt the horse's powerful muscles quiver beneath her touch. "Men can be a handful, can't they, girl?"

Holly sighed inwardly. *Colin* certainly could be labeled a handful.

She still didn't know why he was really here, but she'd bet a year's salary that he wasn't here to work on his term paper. She wouldn't even be surprised if his backpack didn't even contain his books and notes. If she were to hazard a guess, she thought the pack might be toting a spare change of clothes.

Besides, he hadn't even mentioned the need to work on his paper the day before, and he'd had plenty of time to broach the subject with her if that was what was really on his mind.

Which meant he was at her parents' lodge for another reason. And that she could not guess.

Holly had just slipped under Belle's neck to brush her other side when she stopped suddenly to the sound of the stable door opening. The door had squeaked for years, but her father, who did not share his wife's love of horses, had never bothered to oil the hinges.

At first Holly thought to call out to whomever had interrupted her solitude in the stable, but something inside her compelled her to remain silent at the sound of the soft but steady footsteps in the hay.

The unidentified person moved from stall to stall, but did not pause to interact with the horses as Holly would have expected her mother to do. And there was no coarse grumbling that would signify her father's role in the life of the stable—the keeper of the chores.

As the footsteps got nearer, she recognized Colin's low baritone, nickering to the horses and laughing when they responded in kind. He walked to the stall next to Belle's and stopped for a moment.

Holly held her breath.

"Good boy," Holly heard him tell an old paint mare as he reached out to touch her muzzle.

"He's a she," Holly corrected softly, extending her head and arms over the top of the stall door and making Colin take a quick step back, surprise written all over his handsome face.

She laughed with him, both at his rookie mistake, and at the way she'd caught him off guard. "Good *girl* would definitely be a more appropriate moniker. Her name is *Contessa*."

The paint pushed against Colin's hand, searching in vain for a carrot or a sugar cube, and he patted her neck awkwardly. Evidently they didn't teach equine aptitude in the navy.

"Why don't you try this?" suggested Holly, coming out of Belle's stall and handing Colin a carrot. When he hesitated, she put her hand under his, slowly stroked his own hand open flat, showing him by example the way to feed the mare.

It was an intimate posture, and Holly was intensely aware of the way her arm brushed against his, and the way the rough skin of his knuckles felt under her palm. It was suddenly as if the world had opened up and her senses cascaded to life.

The smell of the freshly thrown hay was transformed into a brisk, delightful aroma. The sound of the horses was like a symphony.

And the sight of the tall, well-built man standing close beside her was like an artist's canvas. His thatch of blond hair blew lightly in the breeze that crept through the cracks in the wood. His face, flushed rosy from the cold, contained a heart-stopping grin. In typical Colin fashion, he hadn't bothered to shave that morning, but to Holly, his adorable, tousled mane and scruff only added to the colossal masculinity he exuded.

She struggled to pull in a breath, and nearly suffocated on the bite of the wintry air. "Keep your hand out straight and she won't mistake your fingers for that carrot," she said with effort.

He looked apprehensive for a moment, but he soon followed her directions, grinning when the old, biddable mare nibbled gently at the carrot, her lips working noisily against the flat of his palm.

"It tickles," he said with a boyish chuckle.

"She's a great little mare," Holly said, stroking the paint's floppy and multicolored forelock. "Contessa was my first horse. She's a smooth ride and a gentle spirit. I think she'll always be my favorite."

Colin was silent, as if absorbing her words. She handed him another carrot and he tentatively moved on to the next stall and Belle, who nickered gladly for the attention.

Holly didn't know what to say, and felt a little like her babbling was breaking up the moment, so she just stood back to enjoy the sight of the charming man become acquainted with her horses.

"So…what brings you out to the stable?" Colin queried lightly, asking the question as if *he* belonged here and *she* was the trespasser.

She gave him a long look before she answered. His gaze gave nothing away. He showed a mild curiosity, nothing more.

"My mother just got a new mare. I came out to see her. Actually, you're feeding her now. This is Belle. She's a Morgan cross."

"I see," said Colin, as if he did. His voice was a good deal lower than usual, and just the tiniest bit gravelly.

"What are *you* doing in the stable?" she blurted, unable to wait one more minute to find out what she'd been wondering all along. "And don't tell me you came out to see the horses, because I won't believe you."

He grinned. "Of course not, Holly. I came out here to see *you*."

Her heart leapt and started dancing pirouettes in her chest when his warm gaze met hers. Something about the way he was looking at her was *different*. Her heart knew it, as did her lungs, which had suddenly refused to work.

"I'm sorry. Did you need something?" she asked through a clogged throat.

He chuckled. "You could say that."

She leaned her back against the stall door and looked him in the eye. This probably had something to do with his school project, once again.

Bracing herself, she calmed her heart down to below roaring and prepared herself to don the role of teacher, something that was getting more difficult to do where Colin was concerned. "I'm all yours."

Again, he chuckled. "I hope so." This time he sounded nervous.

Colin, *nervous?*

She *must* be imagining things. Colin was many things, but nervous wasn't one of them. She'd never seen him this wound-up before.

He placed his hand on the door above her shoulder and leaned into her, making it more and more difficult for her lungs to discover air to breathe. She inhaled the sweet pungency of soap and man that was the distinctive scent of Colin and thought she might be a little short on oxygen. She was definitely feeling light-headed.

"Were you raised around horses?" he asked, but given the vivid gleam in his eyes, she highly doubted that was the question he wanted to ask.

And she was having trouble forming an answer. The words were in her mind, but there seemed to be an electrical short in the link between her brain and her tongue.

"No," she croaked out at last. "Not as a child, anyway. Horses have always been my mother's dream, but because of the military lifestyle, we moved around too much to own horses."

He leaned closer. "I'm glad she finally had the opportunity to fulfill her dreams. When *did* she get her first horse?"

Again, Holly had the distinct feeling he was postponing the moment when he'd blurt out what he really wanted to say.

"When she was forty-seven years old, although if you tell her I even remotely alluded to her age, she won't talk to me for a week."

"My lips are sealed," he promised in a whisper, marking a silent *x* across his mouth with the tip of his finger.

Holly smiled gently, both at Colin and at the memory of her mother. "She often tells me her life started when she got her first horse. Except for having me, of course. Though she always adds that part as an afterthought," she said with an edgy chuckle.

She wished she was able to retreat from the feel of his breath on her cheek, and his arms so close about her but not quite touching her. But the stable door didn't give way under the force of her prayer, however fervently made. And it held strong behind her back.

"What are you really doing out here, Colin?" she asked abruptly, deciding to force his hand while she grappled for the stable door handle.

"I want to marry you."

His words, though softly uttered, hit her with the force of a navy torpedo.

What could he be saying to her? She hadn't the slightest idea why he wanted to see her when she'd asked him about his motive in visiting the stable, but a marriage proposal had been about as far from her mind as the earth from the moon.

Marriage. They hadn't even talked around the word, much less seriously worked through the many aspects of their relationship. She wasn't even sure they *had* a relationship.

She pulled in a breath and held it, waiting for time and reality to smooth out her world. She looked back at Colin, focused on his smiling, expectant face, and the plain leveled.

It was *Colin* asking that ridiculous and completely unexpected question. Slowly her heart resumed beating again.

With effort, she laughed and nodded in understanding. It was his idea of a joke, but he'd caught her off guard. "Right. Now tell me what you really want."

To her surprise, *he* looked surprised. Genuinely astonished.

"No, Holly. I really mean what I'm saying. I want to marry you."

"Colin," she warned, trying to keep her voice from shaking.

He was being mean, playing a spiteful joke, whether he realized it or not. It wasn't like him to be insensitive, especially on purpose.

"Holly, how can I convince you I'm in earnest here?" he asked, his voice low and fervent. Determination glimmered from his eyes. "No, wait. I know what will do the trick."

He rummaged through his fleece-lined jean jacket pocket with his free hand. "Will this convince you I mean what I say?"

Holly swept in a breath. Colin flipped open the top of a small, black velvet box to reveal an engagement ring. A lovely solitaire sparkled brightly even in the dim light of the stable.

"I...don't understand," she whispered hoarsely, clenching her hands together in front of her.

His smile wavered for a moment, but soon his confident grin reemerged. He lifted the diamond toward her, as if somehow she hadn't seen it.

She wasn't blind. Only struck dumb by the irony of the eternal bachelor asking *her* to be his wife.

"It would be great if we could be married as soon as possible," he said, grasping her left hand in his right and rubbing her ring finger with his thumb.

Holly's heart was roaring in her head. All her feelings for Colin rose up to greet her, and she was astonished at the intensity of the love she felt.

How had she not realized this before?

She was in love with Colin Brockman.

Deciding the answer to his question—even if he hadn't quite *asked* the actual question—was one of the easiest things she'd done in all of her life.

Of course she'd marry him.

Or at least she thought she would. Until the next words out of his mouth changed *everything*.

"I've got to adopt Jared Matthews soon, or he'll be sent off to foster care again and I'll lose my window of opportunity."

"What?"

"It will be much easier to convince a judge I'm worthy as a married man. And of course I was happy to hear about your early inheritance," he continued as if she had not frozen in his arms, her jaw dropped in astonishment. "The extra money is going to be like a windfall to mention at the hearing."

The affirmation poised on her lips died a sudden, painful death. The reality of the truth washed through her in wave after nauseating wave.

Colin didn't *love* her.

He didn't really want to be married in the first place. He was doing this for the sake of a *kid*.

She squeezed her eyes closed, as the stain of her own sinfulness crept up to mock her, sneaking into her thoughts again though she thought she'd put the past long behind her.

She reminded herself quickly that God had washed her white as snow. She'd started fresh.

Besides, the rejection she was feeling now had nothing to do with what she'd done in the past, because Colin didn't even know the way she'd lived as a teenager.

But knowing that didn't stop her from embracing the feeling she wasn't good enough for a man like Colin. She couldn't help it. Years of poor self-esteem had set her up for this moment.

The pain of rejection raged through her despite all her inward protests. It seemed ridiculous to feel unwanted when she was being proposed to, but no matter how she tried to look at it, she couldn't break free of the sting of her conclusions.

It was obvious he was essentially settling on second best, asking her to marry him because she was his friend, and the most obvious choice given his present set of circumstances.

He'd do anything he had to do to take care of Jared Matthews, up to and including marrying a decent, convenient woman.

And she was that convenient woman. Money and everything.

She didn't know how she could bear the heart-wrenching pain in her chest; nor did she quite know how she would retain her dignity in the moment. She only knew she must, and she would—somehow.

Perhaps the answer lay with the word *decent*. Colin needed a virtuous and godly woman to raise his adopted son. He was looking to her because he didn't know better.

Well, he was going to know better now. He was going to know the truth. And then he would do what any good, upstanding man looking for a mother for his child would do—get out of Dodge.

"Colin, there is a lot you don't know about me," Holly began, raising her chin and meeting his gaze head-on.

"Of course, sweetheart. I know I'm rushing things, but you know I've got a good reason. And we'll have plenty of time to learn all the ins and outs once we're married, don't you think?"

Holly wanted to groan. He was so naive, it was almost scary. She wouldn't believe he was for real, if she hadn't been around him long enough to know he was the genuine article.

"I think you need to know about me now."

Colin leaned forward, so his breath was brushing her cheek. "Okay. So tell me."

She couldn't think when he acted that way. She shoved him backward with both palms. "You can't marry me, Colin. After what I'm about to tell you, you won't even want to marry me."

"There's nothing you can tell me that will make me change my mind," he vowed.

She laughed without mirth. "Believe me, I've heard that before. No man wants what I have to offer. At least no Christian man."

"And what's that, Holly? What's so bad that I'm going to run screaming from the stable?" He sounded as if he was getting angry now. That was just as well, Holly thought. Better anger than hate, or worse, revulsion.

"Let's just say I wasn't a saint in high school," she said, not knowing how to say what needed to be said, and desperate to have it out and over with. "I didn't become a Christian until college. I drank beer. I smoked cigarettes. I partied with a wild crowd."

"And?"

He was going to make her say it.

She looked away. "I'm not a virgin, Colin. Not even close."

With a muffled sob, she ducked under his arm and ran away, as fast and as far as her legs would carry her. Away from Colin, and any future they might have had.

Chapter Sixteen

Colin didn't know what kind of reaction he ought to expect from Holly after his sudden marriage proposal, but dropping what she must have thought was a bomb on him and then running frantically from the quiet stable wasn't even on the list.

Neither was having her Marine Corps drill sergeant father come raging down on him like a dog on a T-bone steak.

Teeth bared and everything.

That man definitely did *not* like to see his only daughter upset. It was a wonder Colin escaped with his skin, never mind his sanity.

Well, that wasn't quite true. While his skin was still intact, his sanity was questionable.

He hadn't been the same since he'd returned to the unaltered silence of his apartment, the sparkling new diamond ring meant for Holly buried deep in the pocket of his fleece-lined jean jacket.

He'd come home weighing a great deal less than when he'd left. There was an immense, gaping empty space where his heart had once resided.

He slumped onto the couch, groaning half in welcome, half in misery. Rascally Scamp pattered onto his lap and pawed at his stubbly chin for attention.

His kitten was right. Colin knew he looked like a wreck, his green plaid shirt half-untucked from his jeans, and his hair looking as if he'd been raking his fingers through it all day.

He *had* been messing with his hair. Not so much because it was troublesome so much as the fact that he was busting out of his bones, going out of his mind over the way things had worked out. He felt every bit as miserable as he looked.

"Whaddaya think, Scamp, ol' fellow? Did I blow it big time, or what?"

Scamp only purred in response, arranging the untucked side of Colin's shirt into a nice little kitty bed with his paw, and comfortably settling himself upon it with a contented *mew*.

"I wish I was a cat," Colin said grumpily.

Scamp licked his paw clean and swiped it over his fluffy black-and-white ear, the self-proclaimed king of the castle. Colin, on the other hand, felt like a pawn in a game a good deal larger than he was.

Where had he gone wrong?

With what he hoped was a critical eye, he reviewed the series of events that had led up to Holly's stark rejection of his proposal.

He frowned, finding it hard to concentrate. He'd been feeling unusually emotional lately. Ever since he'd met Holly, in fact.

But definitely more so this weekend. He wasn't sure he could trust himself to be rational.

Especially now.

Proposing to Holly had seemed like such a good idea at the time. He, who'd sworn off children as if he were allergic to them, had become father material the moment he'd heard of Jared's dilemma and realized he could provide a stable home where others could or would not.

The next logical progression in his chain of thought was to consider getting married, to improve his chances to adopt the boy and to provide Jared with a stable home with a father *and* a mother.

So he was a little slow on the take. It was only then that he'd realized he *wanted* to get married—to Holly—and not because of Jared, though adopting the little boy made the deal even sweeter in his mind.

Holly McCade was the right woman for him, the woman he wanted to spend the rest of his life with. It had only taken a catastrophe to goad his brain into figuring out what his heart already knew.

Holly as his wife, and Jared as his son. Holly Brockman. Jared Brockman.

Until then he hadn't put a word to his feelings for Holly.

Love.

He wanted to hoot and holler and scream and cry, all at once. His feelings were at once so incredibly simple, and so largely complicated, that it went beyond description.

He was in love with her.

And she, he decided, thoughtfully and carefully, was in love with him. She'd been the sensitive, expressive one in their relationship, and he'd been the big dolt who hadn't known enough to grab on to a good woman when he had the chance. She'd hinted again and again of her feelings in a look, a touch. Even the special meaning she placed upon their kisses should have clued him in.

But he was hopelessly dull in the romance department, and he'd never let on how he felt about her. How could he, when he hadn't known himself?

He'd decided to fix that omission as soon as possible. His heart was in the right place. All that had been left for him to do was to buy a pretty diamond ring and ask Holly to become his wife.

Unfortunately, the actual event hadn't been nearly as uncomplicated as his daydream.

At first, it appeared she hadn't understood the question. Which was highly preferable to what happened when she *did* figure out what he was saying.

She'd been so distressed. Her cheeks had turned

an alarming shade of pink, her breath had come in tight gasps and her voice was shrill. She hadn't returned the sentiment he had offered.

Instead, she'd thrown her past in his face. Reminded him of how difficult and different her life had been like before she had found a Savior.

It broke his heart to think of what she must have been through. She'd suffered much. But why bring it up now? Did she think he hadn't been through enough in his own miserable life to be able to commiserate?

There must have been something—something he'd said or done to make her run away from him the way she did. Somehow, he had the gut feeling he was responsible for how their relationship now lay in ruins.

The question was, how was he going to straighten out this big mess?

He didn't have time to ponder the answer to that question because the telephone rang.

Holly!

He rummaged frantically through the basket of unfolded clean clothes he'd left on the floor by the fireplace, sure the ring was coming from somewhere in that vicinity.

It took him three rings to find the receiver and juggle it to his ear, but he answered with a full-toothed grin.

"Holly?"

"Mr. Brockman, this is Michelle Walker at Marston House."

Colin's hopes fell into his gut like a lead cannonball. He recovered slowly. "Hi, Michelle. How's Jared?"

"Holding his own," Michelle answered promptly. "Greatly due to your assistance."

"I can't take credit for that," Colin denied with a grimace. "God's the one taking care of that terrific little boy."

"Yes, well, let us hope so. Jared is the reason I'm calling."

Colin's gut clenched, and he grit his teeth. "Go ahead."

"I've spoken to social services on your behalf. They are willing to hold a hearing on your proposition, first for Jared's placement, and then for his permanent adoption into your household."

Colin squeezed his eyes closed, as close as he'd ever been to shedding tears. This would have been good news, if only...

"I hear a *but* coming," he said wryly, his throat closed and his voice scratchy with emotion.

Michelle gave a nervous chuckle. "Smart man. Here's the thing. Before you can get that hearing, you have to meet with a team of psychologists appointed by the state. It's a five-member panel of men and women from this area who'll be, basically, judging your suitability as a father for Jared."

His suitability as a father.

Colin felt as if he'd had his legs cut out from under him. Five minutes ago, he'd thought himself about as low as he could possibly go.

Now he knew it could be worse.

He had no illusions about his chances to have Jared as his son. As a single man, it would take a miracle for a judge to even consider giving him custody of the young, troubled boy.

And that was when he had only two hearings to contend with.

But now he was looking at standing a minimum of three times up before a judge or panel, and he found he didn't quite believe in miracles anymore.

He silently reached for heavenly support, but his faith was wavering under the strain, and God's comfort seemed far away.

"Don't worry too much about it, Colin," Michelle added when he didn't answer her right away. "These are all going to be friends and colleagues of Holly. I'm sure you'll do fine."

Fine? He clenched his fists and set his jaw against the anger and torrid feelings of helplessness raging through him.

Hadn't he been questioning himself these past couple of weeks? He'd run headlong into the idea of adopting Jared because he knew in his gut in was the right thing for him to do. And because he wanted to do it.

But when the pragmatic side of him sat down and looked at it, there was a great deal more to the story than that. As long as he'd held out hope that Holly would be in the picture, at least he had her loving kindness to fall back on.

Now he only had himself. And he wasn't sure if he could do it. There were moments when he wasn't sure he wanted to do it, wasn't sure what adopting the boy would mean for his career, and now—without Holly—for the rest of his life. Alone.

Jared had special needs. Could he handle it? Could he father the boy and still attend college and seminary full-time? What about the navy after that? What about the moving around?

Could he offer Jared the stability he needed, without Holly there to help?

Colin squared his jaw and his shoulders. Of course he could. He would make it work, just as he'd worked out all the other challenges he'd faced in his life. He would do what was right, and deal with the consequences as they occurred.

Hadn't Jesus Himself said to take it one day at a time?

Slowly, his mental, physical and spiritual strength returned, and with it, his resolve to do what was in his heart. He had to try, for Jared's sake. But could it possibly get any worse?

He cringed. Somehow, he thought if it were possible, it would probably get worse. He'd never been a pessimist. But he'd never felt more alone in the world than he did at that moment.

It had been two weeks, and Holly still hadn't recovered enough to resume her normal activities, including teaching her classes at the university. She'd told Sarah she was sick—and she was.

Sick at heart.

Her parents had been surprisingly gracious, allowing her to stay at the lodge and mope around as long as she wanted. Her mother brought her dinner in her room when she didn't show up for a meal; and to her surprise, her gruff old father didn't say a single word about Colin's misspoken and untimely proposal, not even to say *I told you so,* though she was certain the sergeant knew all about what had happened.

That no one spoke of the matter hadn't kept her from thinking about it, of course. In fact, Colin was about all she thought about, locked in her room with the curtains drawn and the television humming. Every look, every smile, every shared kiss replayed in her mind, a brand of self-torture she hadn't realized she was capable of.

When she returned home to her apartment, it was with a new mind. She let herself grieve for the broken relationship, and though she hadn't been able to sweep Colin completely from her mind, she knew it was time to move on with her life.

And the beginning of any new life, she knew, was a clean house. She started by opening the blue gingham curtains wide to reveal the sunlight. She swept and mopped and vacuumed until every room in her studio apartment was spotless and sparkling.

She prayed, soul searched and found something she didn't realize she had.

Self-respect. And strength. For the first time she had to confront her past within her present reality, and though she thought it might be counted a loss, she decided to count it a win.

She was still standing.

She was ready to make a go of it. She was anxious to get back to teaching. And she was ready to start her career in social services, as well. If she'd learned one lesson from all this, it was that there was very little black-and-white in the world.

She wanted to fight on the side of the good, make whatever little dent in the world she could make.

And still there was Colin.

Because she wanted to understand, to move on, she returned to the iniquitous moment in her mind, the replay painful but necessary. She knew the words by heart, remembered every movement, every expression.

He'd never even really asked her to marry him, technically, and she wondered if he even knew. And yet, for all that, it *was* a marriage proposal, one with strings attached.

How could Colin, her sweet, sensitive Colin, have treated her with such arrogance, such mockery? After all the time and experiences they'd shared together, she'd thought Colin was her friend—in truth, her best friend, the best friend she'd ever had.

And more, she knew she loved him, though she'd never told a living soul of her feelings. She hadn't been certain of her own heart herself until Colin had mentioned marriage.

Had it only been her imagination, thinking he might reciprocate those feelings?

One would think it to have been a possibility, considering he'd proposed to her. His part of the bargain would have been to have and to hold, as well.

But maybe he wasn't taking into account his own feelings. He'd certainly acted as if her acceptance of his marriage proposal was a given, a done deal before it even started, with no regard to *her* feelings whatsoever.

As if there were no question that she would immediately fall into his arms, or at least agree to wear his ring. As if the courtesy of asking didn't matter. As if her strength and dignity could withstand his callous behavior.

How little he really knew her.

Did he *really* think she would enter into a loveless marriage with him, even for the sake of a sweet little boy like Jared Matthews?

Did he really think love didn't matter?

What kind of a wife could she be to Colin without love? What kind of mother would she be to poor Jared Matthews?

The question echoed through her head, stunning her heart back to life. What kind of mother, indeed?

Tossing the mop aside, she cranked up the stereo with some classic rock music, took a long-armed lamb's wool duster and began dusting the ceiling fans and the tops of the doorways.

Her thoughts turned to the little autistic boy who'd won Colin's affection, as well as hers, over the last few months, and she felt a flash of guilt.

What would happen to the little boy if she and Colin weren't there for him?

She didn't know when Jared had stopped being just one of many kids, and had become a personal issue, but that's how she thought of him now. As her own personal problem. The way Colin obviously thought of Jared, too.

When she'd run away from Colin that day in the barn, she'd been thinking of herself—first, and only. She'd been feeling so sorry for herself she hadn't given a thought to the plight of that little boy.

Perhaps it was to Colin's credit that he was so set on making this small, but critical, difference in the world. Perhaps she was looking at this whole set of circumstances through the wrong set of lenses. Maybe Colin had never meant to hurt her at all.

He *had* hurt her with his assumptions, but she

now acknowledged that it was possible he'd had other things on his mind that day. Noble things.

Like Jared.

Of course, when it came to marriage and a lifetime together, *she* wanted to be the first one on his mind and in his heart, after God. But a precious little boy in distress wasn't a bad runner-up.

It was saying something that Colin was willing to give up his freedom in order to save Jared. She knew how much he valued liberty. Freedom to go and do as he liked was paramount to the man. Hadn't he rebelled against anything remotely stifling and autocratic—even a wristwatch?

He'd always shied away from the idea of marriage, never mind children. He was afraid he was going to turn out like his father.

And suddenly he wanted to take on both a wife and a son?

Michelle Walker had let her know that Colin was going up before a jury of her peers, in order to determine whether a preliminary custody hearing was in order. And while she knew Colin would pass the tests of charm and integrity with flying colors, without her help, he could not produce a wife.

He could not provide the secure, white-picket-fence kind of household Holly knew the board would be looking for. He couldn't show the stability he'd never known and was desperately grasping for.

The truth was there before her, and she knew it.

Colin no doubt knew it, too. And it was no doubt breaking his heart.

No single man, no matter how persuasive and sincere, would hazard a chance of adopting a special-needs child like Jared Matthews. Her heart fell for the future of the little boy. And, to her surprise, her heart fell for Colin's future, too.

As suddenly as those emotions overwhelmed her, she knew there was another way.

She could help. She wanted to make a difference in the world.

She could. She could make *all* the difference in the life of one little boy, and Lord willing, in the life of the man she loved.

Even if he didn't return those sentiments.

It was a crazy idea. Yet once the thought had crossed her mind, she couldn't get rid of it. It nagged at her, buzzing around her mind like a gnat.

What if she agreed to marry Colin?

Was it possible God could work through the situation on Jared's behalf? Was it possible Colin might come to love her over time?

In taking care of Jared, she could use all the skills she'd spent a lifetime building. She'd always wanted to do something really special, really meaningful with her life's work. Working with Jared would fit right in with her career in social work.

And old-fashioned as it was, it appealed to her to make a home for Colin and Jared. She thought she might find great joy and fulfillment taking care of her husband and children, at least if her childhood daydreams were anything to go by.

She could build a place where love and laughter spread as much warmth as a fire in the hearth. She could make a place that Colin would look forward to coming home to, and that would give Jared the sense of safety and routine he needed to thrive. And they already had a kitten.

The dream broke through like a waterfall.

Did love conquer all?

Her past rose up to greet her, taunting her, reminding her just how far from *love* she had once drifted. Ironic, how a teenage girl gave up her virtue and her morals looking to be loved.

Really loved.

It wasn't until she'd found God's love that human love, especially between men and women, began to make any sense. Clothed in the mantle of God's love, she was finally able to recognize her own capacity to give love, and hopefully, eventually, to receive love.

A Scripture she'd learned in childhood rose up to greet her like the morning sun. She remembered it word for word, the verse chiming out in her old Sunday school teacher's bell-tone voice, clearly enunciated and ringing with clarity.

Closing her eyes, she smiled at God's wisdom.

There is faith, hope and love. But the greatest of these is love.

It could work. It could really work!

Chapter Seventeen

Colin was sweating. He was *really* sweating, not just politely perspiring. And he knew the droplets forming against his temple and dripping onto his eyebrows weren't helping him look his very best before the five-member psychological panel.

Sweating, whether from stress, or maybe from downright fear, was not the impression he wanted to leave with the state board that held his life—and little Jared's—in his hands.

Trying not to make a big show of it, he pulled a carefully ironed handkerchief from the back pocket of his pants and swiped it surreptitiously across his damp brow and across his freshly shaved upper lip.

He quickly shoved the cloth back into his pocket when the dour-faced, gray-haired woman sitting at the end of the five-person panel—a woman Colin stopped just short of classifying as an old broad, out of kindness, not of truth—caught his attention and sent bolts of alarm through him.

Staring at him coldly, she tapped her pencil against the table in an erratic beat that hammered in a merciless, burning rhythm in Colin's brain that made him want to grab his head and run.

This from a man who didn't *get* headaches. But this was a special occasion, and the throbbing in his head matched the painful throbbing in his heart.

Ms. Dour Face stared at him without saying a word. He met her gaze straight on, letting her know in his own quiet way that he had nothing to hide.

She, on the other hand, was giving nothing away. If only someone on the panel would smile at him, give him some hope or encouragement that they were really considering his request, and not just paying lip service to it.

That he wasn't here on a lost cause.

His worst fear was that they'd made their judgment before he'd even had a chance to speak his case. They'd asked a few preliminary questions, but hadn't let him launch into the soliloquy he'd prepared on Jared's behalf, the one where he listed all the reasons he would make a good father.

With what he had going against him, it wasn't beyond the possibility that they'd sealed his fate without listening to a word he might have to say on his own behalf, or on behalf of little Jared.

He reminded himself that these were Holly's

friends and colleagues, but somehow, that only made him feel more alone. What he wouldn't give for Holly by his side right now. He, the king of independence, finally admitting it would be nice to have a woman's hand to hold.

No one had ever accused him of being good on his timing.

The board stirred, looking at their watches and then at each other, whispering guardedly behind file folders held up to block their faces from his view. Colin swallowed hard and resisted the urge to once again swipe at his beaded forehead.

"Mr. Brockman, can you tell the board how you originally came into contact with Jared Matthews?" A pretty young blonde on the panel asked that question.

Happy to have the opportunity to speak, Colin launched into the story of meeting Jared as part of the school project. The board clearly recognized and acknowledged Holly's name and role in this. Colin hoped she wouldn't mind that he'd mentioned her part.

At the board's insistence, he continued with how he'd returned to Marston House and befriended the boy, and then was there for him during various crises the boy had experienced.

"We have testimonials from Marston House on your behalf," the man in charge assured him.

Colin cleared his throat. "You do?"

"Yes, sir. It seems you have worked some miracles with Jared."

He grinned. "Yes, sir. Well, God's in the miracle-working business, but I'm always glad to help."

"Tell us truly," said the dour-faced woman, "why you would want to adopt a boy with autism."

He looked her straight in the face. He looked them all straight in the face. "Because I love him."

It was so quiet in the room, there wasn't a single paper rattling. "That's a good answer," said the pretty blond woman.

The board stopped and conferred with one another behind their files.

They were close to a decision.

Colin's heart was in his throat. When the leader of the board, Trey Adams, stood and nodded to him, he stood, as well—shoulders squared, feet planted and his head held high.

"Mr. Brockman," Trey began, then cleared his throat and looked for support to the four ladies that completed his panel.

Colin didn't like that pause, or the way Trey Adams pursed his lips.

"Let me start out by saying I've never met a man with your personal concern for a child not his own, particularly a young man with special needs.

"In my experience, most men don't take an active interest in social work, and certainly not to the point to which you've extended yourself by being here today. We are all very impressed, and you are to be highly commended."

Colin pinched his lips into a semblance of a grin and nodded his head. He could feel a *but* coming, and he knew before the words were spoken that it was going to be one big *nevertheless*.

"You must know that you more than qualify in most of the areas we were looking at today," Trey went on, a little less tentative than a moment before. He steepled his fingers and stroked the bottom of his thick black goatee. "We are concerned, however, that you lack one crucial quality, a characteristic that makes us more than a little hesitant to recommend you."

Colin stood rigidly, military stiff, and braced himself for the unwelcome news.

Trey paused a moment, cleared his throat and continued. "While your integrity and love for Jared are evident and highly commendable, and while you've shown yourself to be a good physical provider with a fine future ahead of you, it concerns us nevertheless that you are an unmarried man."

There it was, out on the table.

Colin fingered the collar of his dress whites. He'd wanted to create a presence with his uniform, but instead it felt confining, wrapping around him like a straitjacket and strangling him like a noose.

Finally, the matter had been voiced. It was out in the open for everyone to see. Now, if they'd only let him openly address the issue, he might be able to persuade them what a good parent he would be.

He had barely lifted his head to begin his first argument when he was stopped in his tracks by a voice from the back of the room, a rich, warm voice he knew as well as his own.

"Oh, but, Trey, you're mistaken," Holly announced, pausing to catch her breath as she entered the room. She'd obviously been running. Her face was prettily flushed and she was obviously struggling to pull in air, one hand propped on her hip, and the other bracing her knee, as if she'd run a marathon.

"What's this about, Holly?" Trey asked, sounding as baffled as Colin felt. "I think I speak for the rest of us here when I say I'm a little confused."

Holly pulled herself upright and marched to Colin's side, her sleek black attaché bouncing on her hip and her high-heeled shoes clicking with every step. She slid an arm through his as if it was the most natural thing in the world, and smiled up at him with a brand of encouragement that left Colin's heart racing and his head reeling.

She'd never looked better.

She turned to the panel with a confident, poised smile. "Trey. Panel members." She nodded to each one, addressing them as if she were the lawyer pleading his case. And indeed, that was what she seemed to be, especially when she spoke her next words.

"Colin and I have decided to step up our wedding plans the tiniest bit so we can take care of little Jared *together* at the earliest opportunity."

The word *together* reverberated through the room, echoing off the walls, bouncing from the window wells and ringing through Colin's ears.

Marriage? What marriage was she talking about? Last information he had, they weren't even on speaking terms, much less conjugal ones.

He slid her a look he hoped she'd read accurately. He wanted to know the truth now, before things got any deeper in the mud!

She refused to look at him straight on, instead choosing to address the panel once more. "Colin and I were going to get married eventually, so moving forward the date makes sense for all of us. Jared will have a real mother and father who love him and are completely committed to him from the first day he comes home to live with us."

She paused, making eye contact with every person in the room except Colin. "Colin and I agree that we want to give Jared a permanent, stable home. As you know, I'm a licensed psychologist, and Colin is currently in seminary to take orders to be a navy chaplain. I assure you that you won't find better parents than Colin and me for that little boy.

"What's more, Jared Matthews isn't just any little boy. We've both spent extra time with him, and we've both grown to love him very much. Each of us has faith in God that Jared can and should be a member of the home we are building."

She pulled tightly but surreptitiously on Colin's arm, nudging him closer to her. He noticed that she was gritting her teeth even as she was smiling, but he put on a good face for the panel, taking a kind of backward joy in the opportunity to wrap his arm around the woman he loved and planting a healthy, smacking kiss on her lips.

"My fiancée," he announced, smugly eyeing the panel of Holly's peers. "She'll make an excellent mother for Jared, don't you think?"

Trey made a surprised sound in the back of his throat and sat down. Again, papers and files surreptitiously covered faces as the panel whispered and deliberated amongst themselves.

Colin stared down at Holly, unable to find his voice through the emotion clouding his throat, but desperately wanting to know what was going on inside that pretty head of hers.

She still wouldn't look at him. Her fingers, gripping tightly around his waist, tapped an erratic rhythm, and Colin could only guess at her nervousness at being here.

His own gut was still tight with anxiety over the situation.

But now, for the first time, there was the real likelihood—the real *hope*—he might have a go at raising Jared.

Thanks to Holly.

Trey smiled as the panel grew quiet. "We want to offer our congratulations," he said, his gaze moving from Colin to Holly, and back again.

"Thanks, Trey," Holly said smoothly, covertly yanking on the back of Colin's uniform jacket to bring him up to speed. Colin couldn't think of what to do besides smile and nod, and let Holly do the talking. She was obviously good at it.

"We think you make a fantastic couple," Trey continued. "And we think you'll make equally fantastic parents to Jared Matthews."

Colin felt a rush of triumph at the words, but not for himself. For his future wife and son! He beamed down at Holly, his angel of mercy.

He offered a silent prayer thanking God for the privilege of being able to love a woman like Holly, and the opportunity to raise Jared Matthews. He knew he'd never be able to make it up to Holly for the sacrifice she'd made today, but one thing he knew for certain—he'd spend his whole life trying.

Colin was only glad Holly had finally come to recognize that she loved him, and that she was showing her commitment to him in a tangible way with her dedication to Jared. No one had to tell him that there weren't very many women in the world willing to make those kinds of sacrifices in the name of love.

Holly, though her face was bright with their

mutual success, refused to look him straight in the eye.

After a moment, she placed her knuckles against the table and grinned up at Trey and the board. "We do appreciate your confidence."

"We'll recommend your case be heard as soon as you sign the marriage license," Trey assured them both with a wide smile as he presented them with a variety of legal documents to sign. "Of course, this is only the first step, but we have confidence that you two are going to go the distance. Just let us know what your plans are, and we'll act accordingly."

He'd know, all right, Colin thought. The whole *world* would know when he made Holly his wife. They'd be able to hear him shouting a million miles away.

Nearly shaking with happiness and wondering how he'd ever lived without the emotions he was now experiencing, he took Holly by the elbow and escorted her briskly from the room. He wasn't about to give the panel any time to reconsider their assessment.

"Jared thanks you, and I thank you," he said, planting a juicy kiss on her cheek the moment they were outside.

He'd rushed her out the door, eager to take her in his arms, share the depth of his joy with her and properly kiss the woman who would soon become his wife.

But something in her eyes stopped him. Something was not quite right.

While she looked as radiant as he'd ever seen her, with her cheeks becomingly flushed and her sable hair glistening with red highlights in the winter sunshine, her eyes did not glow with the same intensity he expected of her.

With the same intensity he felt.

Her smile faltered and wavered, and then disappeared altogether. "There are some conditions," she said, her voice cool and collected. Too calm.

"I beg your pardon?" he asked coarsely, wondering how, in his happy delirium, he'd missed the part about the *conditions* of pursuing custody of Jared. Had it been part of the written paperwork they'd signed?

Was it something to do with their marriage? Did he need to purchase a home or jump through some hoop before they could really be a family?

Whatever it was, it would happen. He was determined to see to that.

"I agree to become a military wife," she began, finally looking him in the eye. She looked determined, but not particularly happy.

It wasn't what he expected at all, and definitely not what he wanted. He hadn't expected her to show up today. But when she had—well, he'd at least thought she'd be happy about it.

"I agree," she repeated. "But you, in turn, must let me take care of the children."

Colin felt like he'd been hit in the head with a sledgehammer. This wasn't about the panel, or even about adopting Jared.

He opened his mouth to ask what was really going on, but she held up a hand and cut him short.

"That's right, I said *children.* If we're going to be married, and apparently we are, it is going to be a real marriage, in every regard. A two-way street, with respect on both sides of the fence."

She paused, but he could tell she wasn't finished, so he didn't try to speak.

"I also want a real wedding. I refuse to run away and elope with you."

"Holly, I never said I wanted—"

"My parents won't settle for any less than the works. Dress. Flowers. Cake."

Visions of wedding works danced in Colin's head, and he swallowed hard. While he'd never actually considered eloping with her, he did have to admit the many details of planning an actual *wedding* had escaped him.

She swept in a breath and delivered her ultimatum with a grand gesture of her arm. "And I want children of our own someday."

Colin frowned, perplexed. Of course she wanted children of her own. She was going to make the world's best mother. There was no argument there. "Holly, I think you—"

Again, she cut him off. "I'm perfectly content with my decision, Colin," she assured him. But somehow that declaration only made him feel more ill at ease with the situation.

"You just caught me off guard, the first time. That's all."

Colin pressed his lips together and took a good look at the woman he was preparing to marry. Perhaps that was what was wrong—that he'd somehow botched the marriage proposal, dashing out to ask her to be his wife without first preparing her for the surprise.

But somehow, he thought it was more.

He *knew* it was more.

Maybe it had something to do with what she was trying to tell him that day in the stable. All that stuff about her past, her life before she became a Christian.

Whatever it was, he had to know.

He took her by the shoulders and locked his gaze with hers, not allowing her to turn away this time. He was a man determined to get answers. "Holly, I want you to take a deep breath."

She complied with an audible sigh.

"Okay, then. Now I want you to tell me what in the world you are talking about!"

Chapter Eighteen

Colin stopped fidgeting the moment he donned his white, navy dress uniform, but his heart was still wiggling around in his chest like a two-year-old on a hard church pew. With effort, he steeled his nerves and faced the mirror, attempting to make final adjustments to his tight collar.

"How do I look, buddy?" he asked Jared Matthews, who was sitting at a table in the corner of a room, assembling a puzzle.

Jared, adorable in a black tuxedo, looked up at Colin and strained to focus his gaze. "Colin...is... good," he pronounced slowly.

Colin laughed. "Wow, pal, I hope Holly thinks so, too. I can't believe how nervous I am."

"H-o-lll-eeeee," Jared agreed happily, before returning his attention to the puzzle.

Suddenly it sounded as if someone was trying to bulldoze the door down, and Colin whirled hastily, his clammy palm slipping against the door handle as he tried to turn the knob.

Ian McCade marched in, looking smart and intimidating in his Marine Corps dress uniform, his shoes spit-polished and his seams straight and even.

The sergeant didn't mince words. He strode to Colin and faced him down—or up, as the case happened to be, since Colin was four inches taller than his future father-in-law.

Colin was almost annoyed by the habitual way his own military training took over. Without a bit of conscious thought, he squared his shoulders, stood an inch taller and tipped his chin up, staring straight forward instead of directly into Sergeant McCade's eyes, which would have been a sign of disrespect.

"Are you ready to get married?" Ian barked into his face.

"What?" What else would he be here for, all decked out in his dress whites and getting ready within moments to proceed into the McCades' great room and stand at the end of an aisle, where wedding bells were ringing?

What was the man trying to insinuate?

In moments, he would gladly join his hand and his heart with Holly forever, giving her his name and his home in addition to his life.

"You hard of hearing, boy?" McCade shouted, stepping an inch closer than before, toe-to-toe and nose-to-nose with Colin. "Are you ready to get married? It's a simple question, young man."

"And I," Colin said through gritted teeth, frantically pulling for answers as to why he was getting such a grazing at this late hour, "have a simple answer. I *am* ready to marry your daughter, sir."

McCade seemed vaguely appeased and took a step backward. "Good answer. Now, I want you to tell me one more thing."

"What is the point of all this?" Colin demanded, slacking away from his military posture and putting some distance between himself and the crazy sergeant. If it weren't for his love for Holly, he would be thinking twice before marrying into a military family.

He jammed his fingers into his hair, and then realized what he'd done. With a frown, he picked up a brush from a nearby table and brushed his tousled hair back into place. "Why are you acting like the Inquisition when you know as well as I do that in less than fifteen minutes I'm going to walk out that door and meet Holly at the altar?"

"When was the last time you told my daughter you loved her?" Sergeant McCade asked, his voice soft, but retaining its usual gruff quality.

"I told I loved her when—well, I—I—" Colin stammered to a halt.

When *had* he said the words? His face flaming with guilt as he realized his oversight.

His *major* oversight.

"Oh, boy," he squeaked, jamming his fingers back through the tips of his hair again.

"Uh-huh," his future father-in-law agreed. "I'd say. It's just as I thought."

"Well, why didn't you say something earlier?" Colin snapped, then cleared his throat against the high-pitched sounds that kept coming from his mouth. His voice was taking on the tone of an adolescent boy.

"I've got to *fix* the problem."

But *how* was he going to fix the problem? His heart pounded against his chest. A cold sweat formed on his forehead.

"Don't think of it as a problem, son," Sergeant McCade advised, patting him awkwardly on the shoulder. "Instead, try to think of it as the building site of a future solution."

At first Colin stared blankly down at his future father-in-law. What was that line of philosophical prose, delivered with equal doses of drill sergeant gruffness and efficiency, supposed to mean?

Love.

Of course. Love was his problem—or rather, the fact that he hadn't actually mentioned the *word* love was the problem.

But love—the emotional candor he felt in his heart and had obviously not communicated to Holly and the world—was the...how did the sergeant put it?

The building site of a future solution.

"Where's Holly right now?" he asked, sounding every bit as gruff as Ian.

"That's my boy," the sergeant commended. "First hall to your right, two doors down."

"Can you watch Jared for a moment?"

Gramps, as Jared called him, was already sitting down at the puzzle, muttering quietly under his breath about how small they made puzzle pieces these days.

Colin took a moment to straighten his uniform and brush his hair. He'd already blown one proposal. He wasn't going to let a single detail go unnoticed this time around.

Never mind the big ones.

How must Holly be feeling? She was preparing to marry him with no assurance of his love. He couldn't even fathom why she would do such a thing.

She was a brave woman. Crazy, but brave.

He'd have to remember to tell her so.

Holly took a deep breath and sighed. Colin had taken her ultimatums about children and family surprisingly well for a man who claimed he didn't ever want to be saddled with either; but the happiness she expected to feel at winning that argument had somehow got lost in the translation.

The texture of the tea-length white satin wedding dress brushing against the sides of her calves wasn't quite what she expected. She'd imagined this moment a hundred times as a little girl. Now none of it seemed to be measuring up.

Not even looking in the mirror satisfied her, seeing in her reflection lace, ruffles, a bustle and a great big...*frown*.

Bittersweet longing pooled in her heart. Today she was getting married to the man she loved with all her heart and strength and soul.

This wasn't how it was supposed to be.

Her mother, crouched by her on the floor trying to mend a hem before the big moment, mumbled through the pins she held in her teeth, something about staying in one spot before the dress tore or Holly would end up with satin pinned to her ankle.

With effort and an inward sigh, Holly stopped her restless movement and forced herself to be calm and patient, at least on the outside.

Patience was a trait she'd no doubt have to develop, she thought wryly. She'd be needing a lot of strength and fortitude before this day was out.

And she was looking at a whole lifetime.

The odd thing was, she'd gotten beyond her doubts. Her mind and her heart were completely at ease. She was convinced she was doing the right thing.

She had no qualms about the time it would take to raise Jared. In many ways she was looking forward to becoming an instant mother.

It was instant *wife* that was bothering her at the moment.

"Holly, if you don't stand still, this hem is going to look like a roller-coaster ride."

"Sorry, Mom." She fidgeted unconsciously, and her mother sighed and rolled her eyes.

"Sorry," she said again. She set her jaw and focused all her energy on standing still.

After a few minutes, she'd finally managed to level out her breathing and stop her feet from shifting. She'd even been able to engage in a bit of casual, insubstantial small talk with her mother, who was busy sewing up the final hem.

"All finished," Gwen announced after what seemed like forever. "Why don't you spin around for me? When you were a little girl, that was always the first thing you used to do when you got a new dress—spin around in it to see if it floated."

Holly glanced down at her mother, sharing the moment of nostalgia. Her throat tightened and tears pricked at her eyes.

She remembered.

"Go ahead," her mother urged when she didn't move. "I'll just bet this dress floats like a cloud."

Holly laughed despite herself. Time had proven she was no fairy or a princess, but she didn't see any harm in reliving one whimsical moment. Her dreams of a knight in shining armor had turned into more of a white knightmare, but that didn't mean she couldn't have a little fun this one last time.

She lifted her arms, determined to give her best spin for her mother's sake.

Instead, she spun herself right into Colin's waiting arms. He hooted his appreciation for her effort.

"Colin Brockman, you get out of here this minute!" her mother admonished with a shriek. "You can't see your bride on her wedding day!"

"I need a minute, Mom," he said, grasping Holly around the waist and sweeping her around. "I promise I won't look."

He grinned down at Holly, his eyes sparkling. It was clear he'd already taken a peek, and his gaze told her he liked what he saw.

Well, she had that, anyway. There was nothing conventional about this wedding, anyway. What was one more break with tradition?

Her mother stood and pressed her hands to her hips, her stance belied by a big smile. "It's very unconventional, young man, but I suppose I can give you a minute."

Colin beamed.

"A *minute*," she warned. "No more."

As soon as her mother exited, Holly pried Colin's hands from her waist and held them in front of her, putting a little space between them. She couldn't think when he stood so near her, especially all decked out in his dress whites.

He was an attractive man in any attire, but he was so strikingly handsome in his navy uniform he took her breath away.

"What do you want?" she asked, hoping her voice didn't sound squeaky or hoarse.

He took a step back and brought her hands to his lips, pressing multiple small kisses onto her knuckles. "You look absolutely stunning."

She chuckled despite herself. "You aren't supposed to be looking, remember. And you haven't answered my question."

"Have I told you lately that I love you?"

Her heart bolted to life, though she hastily coaxed it back into its cave. Colin, she reminded herself, often said things off the cuff, things he didn't think about before he spoke.

He'd never intentionally try to hurt someone with his words, of course. He was too good a man for that.

But sometimes he did hurt someone, just the same. He had hurt someone. Hurt her. He'd scarred her heart with his words—or rather, his lack of words.

"You came in here to quote song lyrics to me?" she asked, hoping she sounded light and casual, and hoping she could find something else to think about on her wedding day other than the fact that her future husband didn't love her. This was going to be harder than she'd thought it would be.

He looked taken aback for a minute, and then he

grinned, as if suddenly getting the joke. "I'm a man on a mission."

"I hope so," Holly retorted, "or you're going to have my mother to contend with."

He held up his hands. "Don't scare me."

He paused for a moment, then caught in a breath and pulled her back into his arms before she could step away. His expression was as serious as she'd ever seen it, even more so than on the day of Jared's hearing. It made her nervous when he looked at her like that.

"Do you love me?" he rumbled from the back of his throat.

She nearly choked. "What kind of a question is that? I'm marrying you, aren't I?"

"That's not what I asked," he reminded her gently. "I asked you if you love me."

The dam burst, and all of Holly's pain and insecurity, feelings she'd been repressing and refused to deal with, rose to the surface, spilling over in her tears and in her voice.

"Colin Brockman, how dare you ask me such a thing. I've loved you since the first day I looked up into the top of the school auditorium and saw a thatch-haired thirty-year-old with mischief in his eyes causing trouble in my class."

"Yes. I'm a troublemaker. But do you love me? How do you love me?"

Holly laughed despite herself. "Let me count the ways."

He grinned, but his eyes were no less earnest than before. "Because…?" he prompted.

She shook her head and sighed dramatically. "Oh, all right. I love you for the way you are with Jared, so kind and supportive, always knowing what to say and do. I love that you make him laugh, and the way that you make *me* laugh.

"I love the way you smile at your cat. I love the way you walk. The way you talk. The way you brush your fingers through your hair so it stands on end."

She wiped her wet cheeks with the palm of her hand and chuckled throatily. "Yes…well. I love you. I think you get the picture. Is that what you were looking for? Or should I go on?"

Colin's smile was like sunshine. "I'll take the short version," he teased.

"But you better be ready for the long one," she threatened boldly, laying a hand on his chest, "because you're about to commit to a good, long lifetime of hearing it from me."

He reached up a hand and stroked her cheek, using first the back, and then the tips of his fingers. "I was hoping you'd say that," he said huskily, caressing her jaw with his palm. "Because I love you, Holly McCade-soon-to-be-Brockman, enough to want to marry you, have a dozen kids with you and watch us grow into a couple of old fogies together."

Holly closed her eyes, savoring the sweet words. She'd waited all her life for this moment. But there was still a lingering question.

"Why didn't you tell me you loved me before? Like when you asked me to marry you?" she asked huskily.

"Because I'm an idiot."

She chuckled. "I won't argue. But I think there's more to it than that."

"More to it, how? Holly, don't read a bunch of psychology into it where there isn't any. I just don't always know how to say what I'm feeling. I'm a guy. Cut me some slack."

That might be all there was to it. But even if he meant what he said—and he *was* pretty convincing—there was still something standing between them.

"There's still a lot that's left unsaid between us," she reminded him. "A lot we have never finished discussing."

"There's nothing you can say that will make me take back my words," he assured her. "Or my love."

"Nothing? Weren't you listening to me that day you proposed to me out in my parents' stable? I told you all about my past that day, remember? I was desperate for love, and I—"

Colin cut her off with a kiss.

When he raised his head, she tried again. "Colin,

I'm serious. You need to know about the things I did back then and how I—"

Again, he cut her off with a kiss.

"I don't need to know any more than you've already told me," he muttered, nibbling on her bottom lip and spreading kisses down her jaw. "What's in the past is between you and God. I'm sure you've made your peace with Him, and that's all that matters."

He deepened the kiss for a moment, then backed off again. "I'm not looking back. Only forward."

"Yes, but I—"

He laughed, his eyes shining as he bent his head in for another kiss. "If you don't stop talking, we're never going to make it down the aisle today."

She joined in his laughter and kissed his cheek, which was smooth and clean-shaven.

"I love you," he said again, cupping her cheek with his palm. "And I've obviously not said it enough. Believe me when I say I'm going to spend a lifetime making sure you hear it each and every day."

He kissed her again. "I love you."

All her fears and anxiety melted with those three little words. As shaky about herself and her life as she'd been a moment ago, that was as sure as she was now that Colin meant what he said.

It was funny how she only needed to hear the words aloud to know it was true. He'd been showing her all along, if only she'd bothered to listen to what he was telling her with his actions and his heart.

She turned her face into his hand and kissed his palm. "Until today," she reminded him, "you haven't said *it* at all, you big lug."

He grimaced. "I was afraid of that."

Holly chuckled. "I thought it was a rather large omission, myself."

"That's an understatement. I can't believe you never said anything. Or at least hit me over the head with your attaché. But you're a wonderful woman to let me off the hook so easily."

She arched a brow and smiled. "Who said I'm letting you off the hook, sailor?"

His eyebrows shot up. "Yeah? So what do you say to a big dope who doesn't have the sense to tell the amazing and wonderful woman he loves that she means the world to him?"

Holly slipped her arms around his waist and locked her fingers behind him. The intensity of his gaze matched the sharp intake of his breath. He wrapped his arms around her and held her close to his chest where she could hear the fierce rhythm of his heart.

This, she thought, was exactly where she wanted to be, and this is exactly where she wanted Colin— locked in her arms.

He leaned his face down into her hair and groaned. "What do you say to the idiot who forgot those three crucial little words—*I love you?*" he whispered raggedly.

She smiled, happier in this one moment than she'd ever been. "I do?"

* * * * *

Dear Reader,

Christmas is one of my favorite times of year, as we, God's children, reflect back on the precious birth of our Savior, and look forward to when He will come again in glory. In heaven, there will be no pain, no anxiety and no tears.

In the meantime, we live in a world where mistakes and misunderstandings happen all the time. As Colin did with Holly, sometimes we, or those we love, say and do the wrong things—or say nothing at all. I don't know how many times I've misread a loved one's signal, or jumped to a false conclusion. How wonderful that our God is a God of forgiveness, and He uses our mistakes and sins for our good and His glory. Hallelujah!

On another note—Kids Hope USA is a real, wonderful program through which individual churches and organizations can make a difference in their community schools by mentoring one child at a time. You can contact Kids Hope USA at 100 S. Pine St., Suite 280, Zeeland, MI 49464 or at http://www.kidshopeusa.org.

Do you have a comment or a prayer request? Write me at P.O. Box 28140 #16, Lakewood, CO 80228-3108.

Happy holidays!

Deb Kastner

Love Inspired
CLASSICS

#1 CBA Bestselling Author

DEE HENDERSON

brings you two heartwarming stories of love,
redemption and faith

The Marriage Wish

God's Gift

Available January 2012 wherever books are sold.

REQUEST YOUR FREE BOOKS!

2 FREE INSPIRATIONAL NOVELS
PLUS 2
FREE
MYSTERY GIFTS

Love Inspired HISTORICAL

Introducing a brand-new trilogy
from bestselling author

Linda Ford

www.LoveInspiredBooks.com

LIH82899